Buffalito Contingency

Lawrence M. Schoen

HADLEY
RILLE
BOOKS

BUFFALITO CONTINGENCY

Hardcover ISBN-13 978-0-9829467-8-7
Hardcover ISBN-10 0-9829467-8-3
Trade Paperback ISBN-13 978-0-9829467-7-0
Trade Paperback ISBN-10 0-9829467-7-5

Hadley Rille Books
ATTN: Eric T. Reynolds
PO Box 25466
Overland Park, KS 66225
USA
www.hadleyrillebooks.com
contact@hadleyrillebooks.com

For my Father,
whose easy storytelling,
made me long to tell stories of my own.

Acknowledgments

Writing a sequel is both easier and more difficult than writing that first novel. Fortunately for me, I've had a quite a lot of help. I'd be the lowest of the low if I didn't take time and space to name some of the people who have made this book possible. Let's take them in chronological order:

If you enjoy my writing, please join me in sending gratitude to Patrick J. Palmer, the CEO of the Wedge Medical Center (aka, my Day Job) who continues to provide me with an income and a flexible schedule, both of which are critical to being able to write novels. Next up are the members of NobleFusion (Tim Burke, Arthur "Buck" Dorrance, and Cathy Petrini) who have generously fed me endless insight during the early stages of this book. Continuing down the queue, Oz Drummond provided constant prodding to get me to apply to the celebrated Taos Toolbox where the brilliant talents of Walter Jon Williams and Nancy Kress handed me the keys to the kingdom that every writer needs, and where my cohorts at ten thousand feet (Ada Milenkovic Brown, Richard Baldwin, Lou J. Berger, Danielle LeFevre, Sean Craven, George Galuschak, Oz Drummond, Eric Kelley, Hallie Rulnick, Jason Musgrave, Amy Sundberg, Christian Walter, and Barbara Webb) gave me their feedback on the care and feeding of buffalitos. Also while at that altitude, Carrie Vaughn came by, and a conversation with her suddenly made clear in my mind where Conroy would be heading in the next book or so. After my descent to sea level, Casondra Brewster and Rohan Fenwick graciously read through drafts of the first act of this book, telling me things I needed to move everything along on the right track, and Paula Billig not only kept me hale with Pilates but also did yeoman's duty as a first reader of the finished manuscript and pointed out some omissions that I had in my head but hadn't remembered to put on the page. And then there's Eric T. Reynolds; thank you, sir, I could not ask for a better publisher nor a more patient friend.

To be fair, I should have started these acknowledgements with my wife Valerie, but I wanted her name to be the last one you see on this page. Day in and day out, I'm writing for her, because I love the look in her eyes when I tell her about what new adventures I've come up with. Thank you for being my muse, in addition to everything else.

Finally, as with the previous book, I want to thank you, the reader. Not just for returning to follow the Amazing Conroy—you didn't have a choice, subliminal hypnosis saw to that—but for your support of small press publishing. As the economy gets tighter and Big Publishing continues to consolidate and cut corners, it's the world of the small press that will keep the market filled with a wider range of authors and ideas. They won't have the budget for anything like the marketing or publicity of larger presses, and will need to rely on your good will and word of mouth to keep afloat. So, thanks for talking me up!

And remember to feed your buffalo dogs!

Contents

CHAPTER ONE

Adventures in Plumbing

"ON THE COUNT OF THREE you'll awaken from trance, refreshed and in good spirits, with no memory of anything that's happened since you came up on stage. No worries, your friends will tell you everything." I turned to the audience. "A show of appreciation, if you please, for these most excellent volunteers. One. Two. Three!"

Only a fifth of the audience stood and clapped their hands. The rest were Phloke, large beachball-like creatures with neither feet for standing nor hands for clapping. Instead, they bobbed in place, rustled their ribbons, and thrummed internally. The thrumming filled the performance hall of the Blue Citadel with thunder, even as the inaudible, infrasonic portion came close to knocking me off my feet. I took another bow. They'd never met a stage hypnotist, and for the past fifty minutes I'd altered the perceptions, philosophies, and memories of a handful of audience members to the stunned disbelief of the rest. Playing with people's subjective reality is my stock in trade. I'm the Amazing Conroy, and they couldn't get enough of me.

When the houselights came up for my final bow, there was an empty seat in the front row. I thought I'd seen a young Earthwoman there, a fellow traveler far from home. Had I been mistaken? I slipped behind the curtain and into the jangle of sound produced by a flurry of stage crew, wardrobe coordinators, agents, flacks, hangers-on, and assorted bystanders all seemingly intent on getting between me and the far end of the corridor that served as a communal dressing room for all the acts at the Blue Citadel. As I smiled and nudged my way through to my makeup table, I continued to wonder about the girl. Had she been Human? She'd been dressed in pico-fiber denim jeans and a black tee shirt imprinted with the smart logo of a NeoCoptic band from Omaha, incomprehensible lyrics scrolling slowly across her chest in color-changing Greek lettering. A Traken could pass for human and they often took up the fashion and trends from Earth. An alien Hresht was close enough as not to matter if you didn't mind odd-shaped pupils or an extra appendix. Even a Colian could pass for terrestrial, albeit only in poor light and with a modicum of clothing. The real deal just wasn't likely; as far as I knew, I was the only human being to ever set foot on Leftril, a recently terraformed world of the Phloke.

I'm a xenophile, and most days more than happy to be out here so far from home, but there's something about seeing a face that would recognize that same "home" that tugs at the soul. I just wanted to talk, to hear word of Earth, any bit of trivia, some cultural touchstone. I hadn't realized I was homesick before my glimpse of whoever had been in that front row seat, and now there was nothing for it.

An Arcturan singing troupe milled about me, preparing to go on next. The youngest of them smeared a fluorescent beige goo along his upper lip, a topical euphoric that eased stage fright in many species. To humans it smelled like rancid meat mixed with honeysuckle. I only had to cough twice before the singer bowed an apology and moved to the far end of the annex. The rest of the troupe engaged in some kind of vocal round-robin or warm-up exercise that wandered back and forth between a mournful longing for lost love and the sound cats might make if you swung them by their tails before slamming them into a barrel of water. I had two days left in my contract, and while I'm always eager to move on at the end of a gig, the inability of the Blue Citadel's management to appreciate the concept of private dressing rooms had me chomping at the proverbial bit.

"Excuse me, Mr. Conroy? I'm sorry to bother you, but I have a . . . proposition you might be interested in."

I turned toward the voice. The Arcturan singers paused in their ululations and did the same. It was the woman from the audience, and if I was the first human ever to come to Leftril, she was likely only the second. She was blonde, short, and plump, with a pleasant collection of curves, and smiling like there wasn't any place anywhere she'd rather be than backstage with me. Performers, even hypnotists, often have people showing up after a show, at the dressing room or stage door. Groupies. And yet, I wasn't getting that kind of feel from her.

I set aside my make-up towel and stood. "A proposition?" I gestured to an available chair near my own. "Would you like to have a seat and tell me about it?"

She stepped closer, taking in the curious stares of the singers who still had not resumed their practice. Her cute nose wrinkled and I realized that the younger Arcturan—whom I'd already labeled *Stinky* in my mind—had moved forward to join the rest. My visitor reached the chair but didn't sit. We'd been speaking in Traveler; she switched to English, acquiring a southern accent as she said, "My name is Svetlana Villanova. If you wouldn't mind, could we talk somewhere a little more private?"

More private? Maybe she was a groupie after all.

"I have a suite upstairs," I said, following her into English. "We could go there. It's less crowded, more comfortable. And you might enjoy meeting my buffalo dog, Reggie. He always likes seeing new people."

Her head began nodding before she answered, sending dozens of blonde curls bouncing. "That would be perfect."

I lingered to remove my stage make-up but didn't change out of my tux, then led her to the Leftril version of an elevator and we rode up to my floor. Along the way she regaled me with praise about that night's performance. I nodded, noticing the cute patterning of freckles over the bridge of her nose. Her hair smelled of a blend of patchouli and some flower I'd once encountered on Colson's World and knew by sight and scent but had never learned the name of; one that always made me think of summer picnics and lazy afternoons in tall grass and tree shade. I had a sudden urge to run my hands through that hair, and envisioned nuzzling it as we stretched out on a blanket, our lunch basket abandoned.

Except, it didn't fit. Something about the way she spoke, the words she chose, the cadence of her speech, put me more in mind of a professor lecturing than any groupie who'd wanted a bit of personal *trancing*. I attempted a few humorous remarks and she laughed in all the right places. She had a musical laugh that clearly got a lot of practice, not the nervous chuckle or artless giggle of a starstruck fan. Moreover, other than expressing an enthusiastic appreciation for my act, she showed neither the wide-eyed wonder of celebrity-induced infatuation nor the predatory clinginess of the habitual back-stager.

"So who's this 'Reggie' you mentioned?" She asked. "What's a buffalo dog?"

"Second question first. Imagine an American bison, with its rounded hump, curved horns, and shaggy coat, but enlarge the eyes to the point of cartoon cuteness. Shrink the whole thing down to about the size of a breadbox, and you've got your basic buffalito. They have all sorts of industrial uses, which is why you usually only find them in the possession of large corporations. Reggie's something of a special case." I smiled. Once upon a time, back in Human Space, I'd built a financial empire by breaking the buffalo dog monopoly held by the alien Arconi. Reggie was the sole reminder of those days.

"So . . . he's a pet?"

I paused outside the door to my suite, reaching into the pocket of my tuxedo jacket for my sponge key. "No, more like a companion animal. I think you'll like him; he's very friendly, playful really, with the sweetest disposition you could imagine."

Svetlana nodded as I spoke, her eyes never leaving mine.

Reggie must have heard the squish of the key in the lock, because before I had the door open he'd begun yowling. Svetlana and I entered the suite's parlor, but my buffalito was nowhere in sight. The wail came from beyond the bedroom. Something in that cry signaled more than minor discomfort. He wasn't sulking over a lumpy pillow or pouting because he'd eaten all of the treats I'd left out for him. I heard real distress. I forgot all about Svetlana and bolted across the parlor, through the bedroom, and into the sanitation complex beyond. That's when I found Reggie in the toilet.

Except it wasn't a toilet in the usual sense. Instead of a typical bathroom, the area opening off my bedroom consisted of an angled chamber scooped from a wall of polished, black stone. The floor was made up of thousands of marble and chrome shards forming a mosaic of gleaming swirls. A trio of colossal, half-melted, porcelain and bronze devices rose up in the center of the space. They glistened with curves and an excess of shiny protuberances and burnished fixtures, as if advertising the existence of a plumbers' heaven. You could gaze at them for an hour before realizing they were commodes.

When I'd first arrived and the beachball bell captain showed me the sanitation complex, the differences among the three devices had put me in mind of the kind of bathroom Goldilocks might have stumbled upon, assuming that her bears were actually the oversized saurian aliens that my suite had been intended for. Reggie was stuck in what I'd come to think of as the 'baby bear' throne; a toilet-like device with levers, foot pedals, and what looked suspiciously like a parking brake. It was the only one of the three apparati that came even close to accommodating a human-sized user.

The top of my buffalo dog's head stuck out above the immense porcelain rim. His normally springy ringlets of hair lay soaked and plastered flat, defining the shape of his skull. The instant Reggie's big, soulful eyes locked onto mine, he upgraded his yowl to a series of accusatory barks. Clearly, I was to blame for his current predicament.

The rim of the bowl caught me at waist level, roughly circular with a diameter of nearly a meter. I leaned across and peered down into the toilet to assess the situation. Most of Reggie's torso lay underwater, and his hind legs had disappeared into the narrow aperture at the bottom that curved out of sight like the tail end of a reverse suction cornucopia. His forelegs splashed just above the waterline, as his front hooves scrambled frantically for purchase on the bowl's nearly frictionless interior surface. More importantly, Reggie'd wedged himself in straight up, preventing him from reaching any part of the toilet with his mouth, which explained why he hadn't long since freed himself.

He looked exhausted and scared. I'd left to do my second show nearly two hours ago, and for all I knew he'd been trapped like this for most of that time. I needed to get him out, and I needed to do it now. I clambered up onto the device, balancing my knee on the rim for better access, and squeezed in past a pole that I'd swear was the twin of the gear shift on an antique roadster my great Aunt Fiona had once owned. I extended my free leg behind me as a counterbalance and reached for Reggie with both hands.

This turned out to be a mistake.

I hadn't touched any of the myriad controls, but some motion of mine must have triggered an internal sensor, and the apparatus immediately began its flushing sequence, one intended for the kind of industrial effluvia that comes out of alien dinosaurs. A hundred tiny, high-pressure jets began spraying in complex Fibonacci sequences, dueling with one another, singly and in groups, scouring the insides of the vast bowl. Reggie's barks cut off abruptly as the rapidly sluicing liquid caught him in the face. He squirmed and thrashed in an attempt to escape the streams even as I tried to get a grip on him. This went on for several moments without either of us having any success.

And then the toilet began to drain.

The same Coriolis force that makes water swirl back home on Earth also applied to *Daliesque* alien toilets on Leftril. Some hidden mechanism boosted the process with a vengeance, probably a useful feature when dealing with alien cling-ons, but less desirable where one's animal companion is involved. As the water picked up speed, Reggie began to spin with it, counter-clockwise. His yowl returned and rose in both volume and pitch.

"Your beast appears to be bathing in a Glamorkan training evacuator," said Svetlana, suddenly at my side, observing with a detachment I didn't feel.

"I don't think that's what it's for," I said as I hooked my knee around the facsimile gear shift, extended myself further over the bowl, and slid my arms into the water far enough to get a grip on Reggie's waist. Instead of trying to pull him out I followed a hunch and shoved him in deeper. Reggie yelped at the betrayal but by going with the flow instead of fighting it, I managed to stop his rotation. The water continued swirling, but for the moment Reggie had found the eye of the toilet's storm. He went silent and the look of gratitude and relief in his eyes was heartwarming. Encouraged, I tried to lift him free. As I did so, the suction force tripled and the toilet nearly snatched him from my hands. Reggie, true to form, yelped again, the higher pitched variety I've only heard him produce when his tail gets yanked. That tail, along with everything else below his hips, had vanished into the plumbing.

Sprawled out across the top of the device, I couldn't help notice when it began to vibrate. I could feel it in my back teeth, a low rumble like a faint earthquake. And beneath it, a malevolent grinding noise that didn't sound like it belonged.

"You can't just pull him out." Svetlana had moved closer so I could hear her over the noise of the toilet. Her hands rested on the lip of the bowl. She leaned in for a better look.

"I certainly can't just let him go. And pushing him in deeper didn't work."

"Of course not. It's a Glamorkan training evacuator." Her words had that professorial cadence again, the repetition spoken without any trace of urgency or regard for the situation.

"You said that before. What's it mean?"

"Um, think of it as an automated potty chair for toddler dinosaurs. I think you're in *tail cleaning mode* now."

"Reggie's tail is just fine," I said. "It doesn't need any more cleaning. How long until it figures that out and shuts off?"

She shrugged, her blonde curls bouncing. "It probably won't. I don't think its sensors are that sophisticated. It's probably mistaking your beast's back half for fligets."

"Fligets?"

"It's a Tramadgan word," she said, all calm obviousness.

"Tramadgan?"

"Tramadgan is a Glamorkan constructed language. Its roots go back centuries to the start of their space age, when they first expanded offworld and needed a common language to survive their diaspora. It's mostly used just among Glamorkan across the galaxy, much like you use Traveler with other races."

"So what's a filget?"

"Fliget," she corrected. "It's, well, it's tail poop."

"Tail poop?" I repeated, and realized after I'd spoken that my own repetition might produce another lecture.

"It's one of the seventeen polite terms in Tramadgan for a kind of waste produced by pre-adults. Most of the words are specific to a particular age, biological process, and in this case, a behavior pattern. Glamorkan toddlers go through a stage where, basically, they poop their pants for the pleasure of smearing their tails in it. The result is fligets."

I shoved down any thoughts on the things a saurian version of Freud would have to say about that. "And the toilet thinks Reggie is a fliget?"

She nodded. "That would be my guess. And a really big fliget at that, judging by the amount of suction."

"So, you know how to shut off the toilet, right?"

Curls of honey blonde hair swirled first one way and then the other as Svetlana shook her head. "I know enough to recognize the thing, but I've never used one."

"Something this complicated, a Glamorkan kid has to have gotten himself stuck in. One of these levers or pedals must be an emergency release."

"That doesn't necessarily follow. If a child were truly stuck, the evacuator's sensors would likely recognize the situation and cause it to respond accordingly. Your beast is less than half the size of even a newborn Glamorkan; he's being treated like an especially large and stubborn fliget."

I snarled, "Reggie is not dino shit, and he's not going to get flushed!" I kicked out with my free leg and smashed my heel into the plausible parking brake. Nothing happened. With my feet I started smacking at other levers and controls. Reggie's yowl began to climb the scale.

"Mr. Conroy, that won't help. Glamorkans are among the best builders in the galaxy, and they designed this evacuator for their children. You're not going to be able to break it."

"Then what do you suggest I do?" Before I'd even gotten the words out, I knew Svetlana was wrong. Something had happened. The suction on Reggie had started to increase again. I could feel him slipping ever so slowly, deeper into the plumbing.

"Let go," said Svetlana.

"That's crazy!" Give in to an alien toilet and let it flush my buffalo dog? Was she serious?

"If you let go, the evacuator will finish its cycle and shut down. And then you can call hotel maintenance and have them retrieve your beast."

"No, he'll end up in some Phloke sewer."

The argument was pointless. The suction had grown ever stronger and I couldn't hold on any longer. With one last plaintive yelp Reggie slipped from my cramped fingers and vanished under the water and down a coil of the drain. My buffalo dog was gone.

And just like that, the toilet fell silent. No swirling of water, no vibration, no grinding.

Svetlana was already across the alcove, one hand aiming for a wall. "I'll call maintenance. They'll have someone here in under a minute."

"Get the hotel's engineer," I said, trying to shimmy back off the rim. "Maybe they can isolate the outgoing pipeline and—"

I didn't get to finish the thought. The toilet erupted. Like Krakatoa spewing lava, the pride and joy of Glamorkan toddler–plumbing burst forth with fountains of pressurized water that exploded up and out of the winding passage of the evacuator's depths and struck me squarely in the chest. The force was so great it launched me into the air and bounced me off the ceiling. On the way down I collided bodily with Svetlana. We fell to the floor in a tangle of drenched limbs.

Water gushed everywhere. I could see Svetlana saying something but the ringing in my ears over-pealed her. From somewhere in the back of my head I would have sworn I heard barking. And then, like Aphrodite rising up out of the foam on her shell, Reggie geysered forth from the depths of the plumbing. Unlike me, he didn't hit the ceiling. Instead, he cleared the rim of the bowl and landed on all four hooves, skidding on the mosaic floor nearly all the way to the bedroom. Then he turned back toward the evacuator and the look on his perennially cute face spoke of outrage and revenge.

Free at last from the cruel device's clutches, Reggie went on the offensive. He circled his adversary once, twice, and then lunged. His tiny mouth opened wide and he bit the contraption. His jaw closed on a mouthful of gleaming porcelain and chomped right through. The geysers from the central opening lessened as water began to pour from the new, bite-sized hole. Reggie backed off, swallowed, and then advanced again. Another bite, and another, and again until he'd opened a hole large enough for the next unwary buffalo dog to escape through. Because that is what buffalo dogs do: they can eat through nearly anything. That, and they fart oxygen. Seriously.

By this time, I could see that the edges defining the individual pieces of the mosaic floor were actually cunningly hidden drainage slits which had been designed to open in response to the vengeance of an alien animal or the overflow from a stopped up toilet. As water gushed from the maw Reggie had ripped, it swiftly vanished into the pattern on the floor. No visiting Goldilocks would ever powder her nose here again, and come to think of it, I'd be finding myself forced to make use of one of the two larger devices when nature called.

Satisfied with his revenge, Reggie skittered over to me and began nuzzling my face where I still lay haphazardly entwined with Svetlana Villanova. Almost everything she'd said, and the way she'd said it, suggested she wasn't *that* kind of groupie—if she was a groupie at all—but there's something about lying tangled up on the floor with a pretty, young woman that makes even the best of us put evidence aside and entertain other possibilities. I pulled together what charm I possessed, and with my best stage smile turned to Svetlana and said, "Well, that's never happened before."

The object of my intentions sat up and slapped at her sopping clothing. The scrolling lyrics across her chest had gone dark while the shirt itself and her jeans stuck to her skin like paint. "I suppose the good news is that it's only water, right?"

Svetlana was speaking to me, but Reggie acted as if her remarks had been aimed at him. He planted his tiny hooves as firmly as the mosaic flooring would allow and immediately proceeded to shake himself dry, in the manner of most canines if not most bison. Svetlana caught the worst of it. She sputtered, bringing both arms up in front of her in a useless, thwarting gesture.

Reggie had shown this kind of behavior before. It wasn't that he minded sharing my attentions; he simply wanted his allotment first. Failing to rescue him from the clutches of an alien commode apparently hadn't qualified. I had to try and salvage something, a raincheck if nothing else.

"Look, I realize this hasn't worked out as planned it. How about a do-over tomorrow night? I promise, no exploding dinosaur toilets. Instead, we could enjoy the VIP table in the main restaurant; the chef prepares a fusion of several styles of Phloke cuisine that will dazzle your taste buds. And afterwards we can explore that proposition you wanted to make."

Svetlana tugged sagging curls of hair out of her eyes and shrugged. "Thanks, but I can't," she said, instantly composed and professional and, all things considered, very ungroupie-ish. "I have a seminar tomorrow at the academy in Zlempel until very late in the evening, and then I'm headed offworld. Let me just give you the pitch now, and you can sleep on it." She pulled an old style calling card from the back pocket of her jeans. It was surprisingly dry. "This has my code here on Leftril. If you're interested, pulse me any time within the next twenty hours. Otherwise you'll miss me, but I'll be back in thirty days and we can set up everything then."

I didn't take the card.

"Give me the pitch now? You mean, you weren't, that is, your proposition wasn't—"

"What? You thought I meant—no, oh, well, yes, I guess I see how that could have—look, no, I'm sorry, Mr. Conroy. Not that you're not attractive, and I admit some of the stories I've heard about you have me intrigued, but, well, I could never be interested in you in any kind of physical or romantic way. You're too human for me."

"Excuse me?" Surely I had water in my ears. "Too human?"

"The way I see it, I've had all the flings and fun I need with other Earthers. There's so much more to explore."

"Excuse me?" I repeated. Her professorial tone had returned, but gone off in an odd direction.

"It's like the galaxy is this vast candy store full of incredible confections, things you'd never imagine on your own, and, well, you're offering me a gumball."

"A gumball? I'm a gumball?"

"It's nothing personal," Svetlana insisted, and the way her lips came near to pouting made even the rejection look adorable.

And as quickly as that reality reasserted itself. Nothing remotely like my brief flight of fantasy was ever going to happen.

And yet, she'd come back with me for *something*. I got to my feet and found the touch point on the wall that opened to allow access to a stack of white, fluffy towels. I handed two to Svetlana, draped a third around my shoulders, and proceeded to wrap Reggie in a fourth.

"Then . . . what—"

"There's someone I'd like you to meet," she said while she did that trick that women do with their hair and a towel that I've never been able to duplicate. My towel turbans always come undone. "Well, actually, it wants to meet you."

"It? Your friend is an it?"

"Sorry, Traveler doesn't have the necessary pronouns. And technically, it's not my friend, more like my employer, though benefactor is probably a more accurate term. And actually it's met you before."

"We're talking about an alien then?" Somehow that made me feel better. I like most aliens better than most humans, though not in the way Svetlana apparently did. "Why didn't it just come talk to me after the show like you did?"

"It didn't attend your performance. It's still getting the knack of interpersonal communication, and really can't move among crowds yet. That, and it's not on Leftril. That's why I'm leaving tomorrow night. I'm catching a shuttle upwell to board an outsystem cruiseship so I can rendezvous with it. But don't worry; we'll change ships and make our way back. As I said, it's eager to meet you again, Mr. Conroy, though technically you haven't met it. My benefactor is a Celestial."

That must have been about the time I dropped Reggie, my towel, and probably my jaw. Reggie yelped more from surprise than pain and shot me a look of hurt at my second act of betrayal of the night. I barely noticed. I was having a hard time getting past the idea that a Celestial wanted to see me. A Celestial. And me. Again.

CHAPTER TWO

Agent of Change

CELESTIALS AREN'T LIKE any other sentient beings in the known galaxy. They're bigger, a lot bigger. The largest intelligent alien I ever met, an octopod fortune-teller from the hidden world of Lelk, stood five meters at the shoulder. To humans that may seem big, but it's all relative. A Celestial has a girth of between one and a half and three astronomical units. There's just a few orders of magnitude difference between five meters and four hundred fifty million kilometers.

Current theory describes them as 'imperceptible self-organizing patterns of interstellar hydrogen and meaningfully arrayed electromagnetic wavicles.' Which just means we don't have a clue what they are, and when you think about it, why should we? They experience reality at a level so vast, a time scale so relativistically slower, that we shouldn't even register to them. We're just too tiny and ephemeral. Imagine following the hourly epics performed by your own stomach bacteria, and that still doesn't come close. Celestials would need the equivalent of electron microscopy to detect us, and that wouldn't cause them to care. And yet they do care, ever so slightly. Across the span of recorded galactic history, on more than two thousand occasions they have noticed us. That's less than once every fifty thousand years, but what is time to such beings?

When I'd been in college, one of my professors pulled a string or two and found me a summer job working as the alter-shift crew on an automated interstellar freighter. The only other living thing onboard was a vat-grown husk who called itself Captain Coelacanth. It seemed to be some organic extension of the ship itself. Humans hadn't yet even heard about Celestials, and I didn't understand that the ship's intelligent system wasn't just a cunning piece of software. A Celestial had chosen the vessel's fourteen million cubic meters to house its awareness. Cramming a portion of its mind into such a tiny volume had scaled down its perceptions. At that size it could experience patterns of energy and combinations of matter that otherwise went unnoticed. It not only perceived the planets on our trade route, it could understand them as teeming biospheres that had given rise to countless tiny sparks of self-awareness.

All of which was fine for the Celestial, but little help to me when the ship exploded and marooned me on an alien world light years from home. In the way that one unforeseeable event begets another, being stranded had started me on my career as a hypnotist, prompted my fascination with other intelligent races, and begun my appreciation of gourmet cuisine.

Crossing paths with that Celestial had ended life as I'd known it, reshaped me, and created a future I couldn't possibly have envisioned. Now that same being had returned and wanted to meet me? Would the experience transform my life again? The youth I'd been would have scurried home and hidden under a rock, trembling and praying the giant alien entelechy didn't notice him. But the man I'd become saw possibility and opportunity, maybe even adventure. Fear too, sure, but only an idiot could be calm at the idea. Back then I'd had no say in the experience, hadn't even known I was in the presence of a Celestial. This time, I wanted a more active role. Was that what Svetlana was offering? What did it mean that the Celestial was her benefactor? I had a few things to think about, and far too many questions, but one thing was certain; I wasn't going to wait around for the Celestial to come back and meet me. Regardless of the cost, I intended to be on the same cruiser with Svetlana and meet her employer on my own terms.

Nobody likes feeling nonplussed, least of all hypnotists who make their living being described as 'Amazing.' I switched my attention to the wall comm and called housekeeping.

"Guest services. How may I help you, Mr. Conroy?"

"I know it's late, but do you have a plumber on duty? There's been an accident in the bathroom."

"I'll send someone right up. Will there be anything else?"

"You should probably ask for extra towels too," said Svetlana.

"And could you send some more bath towels?"

"Of course. Right away, Mr. Conroy."

I turned back intending to ask some of my questions, but Svetlana was gone. Likely she'd stepped out of the alcove for some privacy to wring out her clothing. I didn't pursue. I'm a gentleman, after all, and the lady had made it very clear she wasn't interested in me. It'd just be Reggie sharing my bed this evening, snuggled in at my feet like every other night. The important thing was that he was safe and sound. I had my rich fantasy life back in check.

"Svetlana? Are you decent?"

No reply. I waited a moment more, then rounded the corner. The bedroom was empty, as was the suite's anteroom. I moved to the door, hoping perhaps to catch her in the hallway. Instead I found a Phloke hovering at eye level.

"Housekeeping," said the smaller than average, beachball alien. Like all of the housekeeping staff I'd met here, she smelled of a blend of fresh linen and lavender. Her ribbons resting on the handle of a small cart behind her. Looking around the Phloke's curves, I saw no sign of Svetlana.

Reggie had followed me. He let out a bark and I immediately scooped him up. Something about the Phloke set him off since the day we arrived. Maybe it was their ribbony appendages, maybe something about the infrasonics they used. It might simply have been that he thought they were just big *play balls* hovering cruelly out of his reach. No Phloke had complained, and none ever would. Their culture didn't allow expressing negativity, and I'd worked the taboo into my act. Even so, I'd learned to keep a hand on my buffalito whenever Phloke came near.

"Thanks for coming so quickly." I stepped aside to make room for the housekeeper to enter. She didn't; nor did she look at me. She focused her attention on Reggie, who had begun to fart and squirm in my grasp. I held on tightly and tried again. "We've had a little bit of an accident with one of the uh, commodes. It's right this way." I headed to the trio of toilets. After a moment the Phloke followed with her cart.

"What you doing this room?" The Phloke spoke in choppy and heavily accented Traveler.

"Well, like I said, we had an accident, and—"

"No, no, not what you do, what you doing? Here? *This* room? This Glamorkan suite. It too big for you."

"Thank you. I've tried explaining that to three different clerks at the front desk since I arrived. I realize you're not used to humans here, but surely the resort was built to accommodate many different peoples."

Part of me didn't want to change rooms. The suite overflowed with more opulence than I'd seen since losing my corporate fortune. Every wall contained a programmable view of hundreds of vistas from dozens of worlds, including, much to my surprise, Earth! With a spoken command I could gaze with impunity at some of Throg's World's most brutal ice storms, tour Crenshelm's Grotto of Souls, or spy on people walking through New York's Time's Square. The bedroom featured a luxurious gravel bed filled with thousands of pea-sized nuggets of basalt, highly prized by the Saurians the room had been designed for, and paradoxically comfortable for humans as well. An idiot savant A.I. provided encyclopedic data retrieval, current news, and a vast selection of spoken literature in flawless Traveler in a selection of twenty voices. The outer room had a hidden door that opened onto a balcony with a sunning platform, a writing desk, a well stocked bar, and a holographic library interface that I still hadn't been able to completely figure out.

Sure, none of it fit my proportions, but I had a suspicion that these amenities didn't await human-sized guests. A Glamorkan had designed the resort, and she had saved the best for her own species. Never before had I gone off to do a show and been able to leave Reggie tucked in a blanket while the room whispered the epic of Gilgamesh to him in a seductive female voice. I really didn't want to give that up, and after several attempts to be moved to a more appropriately proportioned suite, I'd stopped trying.

"Yes, yes, you wait." The housekeeper drifted to the wall and replaced the decorative gleaming obsidian with the image of an elaborate control panel. Her ribbons stroked various touch switches and sliders. After a few moments she restored the wall's glassy dark appearance and turned back to me.

"No rooms."

"No rooms?"

"Conroy performing. Blue Citadel sold out. You no pay room."

"I'm Conroy, and yes, the room is part of the package. Quality accommodations and restaurant chits, all in my contract."

The Phloke gestured about her. "Quality. Best Glamorkan room. Only room left. You get quality." And with that she left the room, floating away at the legless version of a trot.

"Wait!" I scrambled around the towel cart and caught up as she activated the outer door. Reggie's flatulence had increased in frequency and sound. "What about the toilet?"

"We bill," She shut the door behind her.

"Like hell," I said. I took a moment to reposition Reggie into the crook of my arm, and set off in pursuit. The lift was just closing. I ran to it, slapped the call plate, and began rehearsing my arguments. I had no idea what it would cost to repair a Glamorkan training evacuator, but I didn't want to find out. There had been a paragraph in my contract about 'excessive damages' but it had been years since Reggie had destroyed a hotel room and I hadn't given it any thought when I'd signed.

The door opened onto a pod, empty except for a faint scent of linen and lavender still hovering in the air. I rode it down to the lobby. By the time I arrived, the housekeeping staffer was nowhere in sight, so I made my way to the front desk. A beachball with a managerial sticker affixed near the top of one of his ribbons looked up at me, and bobbed congenially speaking in a syrupy, unctuous tone before I could begin a word.

"Ah, Mr. Conroy. Thank you for coming down to see us. As I understand it, there's been a, how shall we say, unanticipated disturbance? Yes? In your suite?"

"The plumbing assaulted my buffalo dog. He could have been injured." Reggie yapped once at the manager, possibly in agreement, or maybe simply hoping I'd set him down now that there was another Phloke around.

"I see. How awful. But I'm so relieved to hear your implication that he's fine. He certainly looks the pinnacle of health. But too, this pet of yours shouldn't have been attempting to use the plumbing, yes?"

"It's a Glamorkan suite!"

"Yes, sir. This entire facility, indeed, nearly all the commercial and private structures on Leftril are of Glamorkan design and manufacture. I trust you don't have a bias against these beings, Mr. Conroy. The staff of the Blue Citadel would all, I'm sure, be greatly distressed to learn that a performer as talented as yourself possessed such unsavory and judgmental attributes."

"No, no, you misunderstand. The suite is designed for the *use* of Glamorkans."

The manager closed his eyelids and wobbled slightly, as if that tiny movement somehow indicated deeper cognition. After a moment he looked at me again and spoke. "Allow me to explain our position. Any damage resulting from improper functioning of our facilities is quite naturally our responsibility. But damage resulting from improper use of those facilities by our guests is theirs. That's fair, I'm sure you'll agree. All of this is stipulated in the appropriate sections of your contract. Naturally, as you're headlining for us, I can assure you we will only charge you the actual replacements costs, plus a discounted charge for the labor to replace any fixtures."

"Don't pay it," said a new voice, one with too much gravel to belong to any Phloke I'd met thus far. I turned around but saw no one.

"Down here," said the voice.

I lowered my gaze and stared into a pair of protruding eyes set wide apart on a dusky green head. That head lacked hair, a nose or even nostrils, and its lipless mouth sported a pair of upward projecting tusks that gleamed like an advertisement for a phosphorus-based dentifrice. The head attached to the body in the usual way, resulting in a six-limbed biped that stood just over a meter in height. He looked for all the world like some midget version of a Thark, out of a twentieth century Burroughs's novel. Clearly I was hallucinating. Reggie stared at him, stuck out his tiny blue tongue as if to taste the air, and yipped.

"Don't accept any of those charges," said my figment. He lacked shirt and shoes, reminding me of those signs back on Earth that would have prevented him receiving any service. His only clothing was a pair of wheat-colored overalls made from a waxy upholstery fabric and riddled with at least a dozen pockets and pouches.

"Sir, you are interfering in a transaction that is none of your affair," said the manager, ribbons rustling.

"Baby it is, and baby it isn't," said the newcomer. "But I heard it all, and you're out of line charging him when you've violated the inter-alien comfort clause of the consortium of hostels, hotels, and sleep facilities, to which this resort is a signatory."

"I did no such thing."

"You put a human in a suite intended for a species twice his size. Did you also include any protective gear? Any supplemental aids? Any instructive guides? Hah! I can see the answer by the color of your ribbons. In fact, you didn't just fail to see to the comforts of this guest, but you're guilty of potentially endangering him as well!"

The manager's ribbons fluttered and tangled. "He's . . . he's not actually a guest, he's an employee of the resort."

"Don't get cute and technical," said the little green man. "The consortium doesn't care if he's your doorman's incontinent grandmother, if he sleeps under your roof, he's a guest. End of discussion. Perhaps you don't realize it, but Conroy is a famous human. He came to your resort expecting you would keep him safe from injury—"

"What injury? I see no injury!" The manager's tone had lost its velvety professionalism and acquired a distinct shrill.

"Are you a licensed physician? Do you feel competent to diagnose the first human being that's ever stayed in your facility? Don't worry, I'll take care of that, and I'll be sending you the appropriate reimbursement paperwork too. Before that though, I suggest you void the bill you were about to scam this guy into paying, and hope he doesn't pursue your flagrant breach of guest services and shut down your entire facility."

"I . . . I . . ."

"And send a repair crew up there to fix things. You can't expect the Amazing Conroy to wait around while you blow in the breeze. Stop wasting his time."

"I . . . yes, of course. I'm terribly sorry, Mr. Conroy. I'll see to it at once."

The little green alien reached up with both of its right hands and tugged on my arm. "C'mon, we've got things to discuss. Let's do it over breakfast. We can beat that whole post-dawn rush."

I pulled free and glanced back at the manager. He looked only too relieved to see us go. "What just happened here?"

"I saved you from a hotel scam and put the fear into them so they won't try that crap on you again."

"Who are you?"

He drew something from a pouch with a middle hand and shoved it at me, a rectangle of stiff, linen paper. I hadn't seen a business card since I'd left Earth. Printed on one side with gold ink were seven words: IMPROBABLY MANAGEMENT: A PLAN FOR EVERY CONTINGENCY. I looked up from the card and into his protruding eyes.

"The name's Billi. I'm going to be your agent."

Billi flagged down the Leftril equivalent of a cab and instructed the driver to take us to an out-of-the-way eatery near the shipyard on the far edge of the port city. Few businesses on Leftril ever closed, but at this hour the place didn't have anyone else in it, and our waitron managed the trick of looking surly despite being a bright pink beachball. He sequestered us in a corner booth, then slapped his ribbons against the tabletop to bring up a menu in several scripts, none of them anything I could read. Other than the smart Formica, the place reminded me of the kind of greasy spoon that still existed along the highways of the American Middle West back on Earth. Everything was old and worn, from the dishes and flatware to the tables and light fixtures. Since the unnamed city was brand new, it meant that everything had been distressed to achieve the effect. If the Phloke had truckers, they would have fit in fine.

"Do you like groats?" asked Billi. The waitron had brought a booster seat for my buffalo dog. Reggie sat there, staring at Billi, who stared right back. "I'm confident your friend here would like the groats. You'll like them too." He pressed a finger against a line on the menu, causing it to flash. "Hey, garçon! Three of this!"

Our waitron fluttered his ribbons in our direction, which seemed to satisfy Billi. And then it hit me. *Groats*? *Garçon*? Neither word existed in Traveler. He'd spoken English.

"How do you know about groats?"

"I'm a Pelk." He fiddled with his pockets, transferring small objects from one to another.

"And?"

"You haven't seen one of us before, have ya? You're a long way from home, Conroy. And I'm just the touchstone you want. But it goes both ways, I've been waiting for you a long time too. You're the birthright I was promised years ago."

"What are you talking about?"

"When a young Pelk comes of age, there's this ritual, see? There's fasting and cleansing and the ingestion of some really foul herbs with psychogenic properties. It's all highly regulated today, but the specifics go back tens of thousands of years to the time we were crawling around on all sixes in the salad deserts of antiquity. But the point is, at the peak of the experience, as he passes into adulthood, each Pelk gets to ask the gods for a boon. Of course, there's a price for this boon so it's really barter, but it's considered blasphemous to talk about bartering with the gods, so we call it a boon."

"What does any of that have to do with groats?" As if by invocation the waitron floated over and set heaping bowls of steaming mush in front of us. Reggie immediately dove in, face down into the bowl. I reached for a utensil and sampled my bowl more slowly.

"I'm getting to that." Billi shoveled a mouthful past his lips without pausing or swallowing. "See, I come from a long line of taxidermists. It's delicate work and a real art form if you dedicate yourself to it, but I didn't. I don't like the smells. I wanted to be a pilot, even got the training and my provisional license, but that didn't work out. Long story . . . Any way, all three of buy parents hoped I'd continue in the family business, and the only way I could see getting out of it was to bake it a boon from the gods."

"You lost me. You bought your parents and the gods baked your boon?"

"Bake, not bake." He slapped his head. "I asked the gods to fill this cabeza with knowledge, specialized info that would help guarantee success in a career that didn't involve taxidermy. And all it cost was some words and a little confusion here and there."

"I understand the confusion part, because I still don't follow what you're saying. What do you mean about the words?"

"Words that start with certain sounds, just two sounds, I always say with another sound. It's a straight substitution, and you'll learn to understand it fine. Real fast. I promise." He sighed then, a wistful expression bloomed on his face, quite at odds with his fierce tusks. "I'll tell you, though, Bomb didn't take it well."

I jerked back from my groats; my spoon-knife tumbled from my fingers. "You have a bomb?"

"Bomb, not bomb. See? That's what I'm talking about. I've got a bomb and a dad and a fledge. I get that you human types don't grok about fledges, but you only have two biological sexes. Pelk have three."

"Bomb and dad . . . you're trying to say *mom*?"

"I am saying bomb, it's just the deal with the gods causes it come out as *bomb*. That's one of the sounds, and only at the start of words. I can say grandmom just fine. Right? You know, your bomb's bomb? Don't worry, you'll pick it up in beau time."

I looked at Billi without replying. Then I looked down at my bowl of groats and resumed eating, all the while trying to remember a tongue twister loaded with initial nasal consonants. The groats were really good, and after several moments of contemplative eating I felt up to giving the conversation another try.

"You're saying your gods took away your ability to say words starting with mmmm and nnnn sounds. Let's stipulate that all that's true, because it's just too bizarre for you to make it up and tell to total strangers. So, what did you get in exchange? What kind of anti-taxidermy knowledge?"

"I got everything about your home, Conroy. Earth stuff. Everything I could possibly ever bead to represent humans out here where so few humans have actually come. Language and history and several lifetimes' worth of experience. Like groats. You're enjoying your groats, right?"

I was. They weren't like eating bulgar back home. They had a richer, heartier flavor to them that was incredibly satisfying. Filling, without leaving one feeling stuffed. It might have been the best breakfast bowl I'd had in my life.

"Okay, the groats are good. But knowing where to go for breakfast in the middle of the night really isn't high on the list of job skills I look for in an agent."

"That's the beauty of it. You get that expertise without any extra cost to you. Trust me, Conroy, I'm going to be the best agent you could possibly have. And I've got lots of incentive. Your people aren't exactly popping out of the woodwork in this part of the galaxy, so I can't afford to let you down."

"I appreciate that, but the thing is, I don't need an agent here. I like to keep traveling, seeing new people and places—"

The Pelk slapped the tabletop with both its middle hands. "I'm the same way. See? We're going to be perfect together. I can get you a gig at a resort in the southern hemisphere in less time than it will take us to travel there."

"No, Billi, you don't understand. My contract at the Blue Citadel ends after tomorrow's show. I'd been toying with signing an extension, but something has come up. I'm headed offworld."

"Where?"

"Excuse me?"

"Where are you going? I've got connections on a hundred worlds, Conroy. I'll have a gig waiting for you."

I thought about that. Svetlana hadn't said where she was going.

"Some of the details aren't set yet. I'm still working out the specifics."

Billi shrugged. "If you say so. Fine. When do you leave?"

"When? Uh . . . the day after tomorrow."

"Got a ticket?"

"Excuse me? Look, it's not your concern—"

"You only just decided to go. So, you probably haven't booked passage. Don't worry, I can handle that for you. But last second tickets don't come cheap."

"Look, just stop. You're not my agent, and you're not handling my transportation. I haven't even figured out what vessel I'm going on."

"That would be the *Shpeshnoltoc*. It's the only passenger ship that will be at Leftril by tomorrow. It leaves orbit a day later."

"How could you possibly know that?"

Billi smiled, revealing sharpened teeth as blindingly white as his tusks. "All part of my job as your agent. Just hand over your financial codes and I'll bake all the arrangements for us both."

"You're joking, right?"

"How else do you think we're going to pay? I work for you, and I'll do good by you, but I can't pull cash out of thin air."

I sighed. "I appreciate you helping out back in the lobby, I really do. But I'm about to be in-between jobs, and booking passage on the *Shpeshnok*—"

"*Shpeshnoltoc*," he corrected me.

"Right, booking passage on the *Shpeshnoltoc*, just for Reggie and me, is going to use up most of my pay from my current gig. Even if I was looking to take on an agent—which I'm not—I'm in no position to buy an extra ticket. Okay?"

"I understand perfectly. Don't worry about a thing, Conroy. You're the talent. As your agent, I'll take care of all the financial stuff. I'm already working out a plan."

I stood up and though Reggie hadn't quite finished his bowl of groats I pulled him from his booster seat any way. He bleated his frustration, but I had enough of my own. "Billi, for the last time, you're not my agent. Got it? Thanks for breakfast."

I stormed out of the diner, ignoring the glare of the waitron. Reggie let loose with a particularly musical stream of farts. Yeah, it was definitely time to get out of town.

CHAPTER THREE

The Play's the Thing

I WAS HALFWAY DOWN the block, imagining what I'd say to the Celestial at our first meeting, when the back of my hand chirped. The annoying Pelk had planted a comm-patch on me. I tried to pluck it off but succeeded only in accepting the call.

"I already said no!"

"So you'll think about it. Right, you want to sleep on it. Digest those groats. We're going to bake a great team, you'll see."

I tugged, but the patch wouldn't budge. It was like trying to remove my own skin. "What kind of adhesive did you put on this? Comm-patches are supposed to peel right off."

"It's a custom job. That patch is a direct line. Call any time, light or dark. As your agent, I'll always be there for you. Any time—"

Custom job or not, the thing still had an off-switch.

I flagged down a passing cab. Local midnight had come and gone while I ate my groats, and I was in serious need of some sleep. On the drive back to the resort, Reggie curled up for a nap in my lap. I tucked his sleeping body under my arm as I headed for my room. Trellbello, the resort's entertainment manager was waiting for me outside my door. Her ribbons glistened with a metallic sheen, which indicated either profound agitation or thirst. Probably not thirst.

"I know why you're here," I began, hoping to establish my contrition and then take advantage of the legendary Phloke inability for negativity. "I want you to know I'm very sorry about the plumbing."

"Plumbing?" Trellbello rotated in place to gaze at me. "I am not here about plumbing." Her ribbons flittered beneath her as if battered by a strong wind. "I am here to formally acknowledge that you have voided your contract, Mr. Conroy."

"Excuse me? I haven't voided anything. What are you talking about?"

Trellbello spun around, effectively turning her back on me. She activated the door to my suite and floated inside. She slapped the wall controls in the anteroom and conjured up a display of a news zine that reported on all the latest fads and happenings on Leftril. Her ribbons flicked among the pages, stopping on a specific story detailing the entertainment reviews in another city:

Amazing Conroy Beyond Belief!

"So, what's the problem? I'm a hit. Your customers love me."

She drummed several ribbons against the wall. "Your contract with the Blue Citadel is exclusive."

Which was true enough. The Phloke tended to be proprietary in all things, and I'd taken advantage of that bit of psychology in my act. Howls of beachball laughter ensued every time a hypnotized Phloke began outlining plans for a creative commons approach to everything from artistry to manufacturing. My deal with the Blue Citadel restricted me from performing anywhere else; I couldn't do so much as a simple induction at a child's birthday party on my day off—and I hadn't.

I'd filled the main lounge to capacity, night after night. I was good for business. Trellbello knew it, just as she knew that twice now, Phloke from other resorts on Leftril had lingered after my shows and hinted at much sweeter contracts. I'd laughed and politely refused; I don't like people trying to buy me out from under a current gig. There's something to be said for loyalty, and too, Trellbello had treated me fairly throughout. So what had set her off now?

I stepped up to the wall and began reading the article under the header. And stopped.

"Trellbello, that's not me."

She glared down at me, bobbing energetically in place all the while, ribbons rising and falling with some emotion that might have gone beyond agitation to all-out rage. I had a handle on the basics of Phloke body language, such as it was, but a lot of the subtleties eluded me.

"Denial does not change the facts, Mr. Conroy. The review is quite clear. That is you."

"Did you read the article? Yes, I'm the Amazing Conroy, but that's not me they're talking about here. Someone is using my name as the name for a play." I rapped my knuckles against the wall to forward to the next page, skimming it quickly. "See? Here in this section, it says the play isn't even by humans or from Earth. It was a special, limited engagement, and is being performed by the Royal Traken Theatre Company. Traken are very similar to humans. We're very hard to tell apart, but this is all just some coincidence."

Trellbello bobbed faster. Her eyes bulged and quivered, and she seemed to be fighting to retain her composure. "There can be only one Conroy," she bit off each word with a violent throb. "You guaranteed. Your name. Your likeness. Exclusive!"

One of her ribbons slashed across the wall, driving the display to the next section. An image of seven men stared back at us. Seven men wearing black tuxedos identical to the one I wore for my shows and still had on. Seven men who all shared my build, hair and eye color, and enough of a resemblance that we could have been brothers, all of them in their late thirties. The caption read: *the Amazing Conroy, Traken style.*

I called up the next image. Seven beautiful women gazed back at me. Seven women who could have been sisters. And the caption: *Calinda, the Baroness Parmaq.*

My fingers slid from the wall. My arm hung lifelessly from my shoulder. Trellbello may have resumed speaking, but all I could hear was the rapid pounding of my heart. "Calinda," I whispered.

Reggie reacted to the name. He squirmed in my arms until he'd turned himself around and planted his front hooves against my chest. His tongue darted out, licking my chin. Seven years, and someone on her world had written a play about us and taken the show on the road. Trakus lay within the boundaries of Human Space; Leftril did not. How many productions were out there, on how many worlds? Had the play reached Earth? How many people had seen it?

Trellbello also heard my whisper, and it must have confirmed something in her mind. She floated to the exit and flung open the door. Her ribbons waved my way, banishing me with an irrefutable gesture. "There is nothing further to discuss, Mr. Conroy. Your tenure here at the Blue Citadel is complete. You are fired."

"This is a misunderstanding. I didn't authorize any of that, or performed anywhere else. I haven't violated the contract." She wouldn't even look at me. She just hovered by the door, waiting for me to leave.

I sighed. Things had been going so well. "Fine. The contract was almost up any way, and I'd already decided not to renew. If you don't want me to do my last show, that's your choice. Pay me what I'm owed and I'll clear out."

That got her attention. "I don't believe so, Mr. Conroy. Your departure leaves the Blue Citadel in an unfortunate position. I believe the term you use is *the lurch*. The embarrassment of refunding tomorrow's performance will cost us reputation and money. Your pay will help recover that sum."

"You're only in the lurch because you're firing me. I did my shows, you made money on me, so pay me."

"I disagree, sir. Your pay is forfeit."

"Not going to happen, my friend."

Her ribbons stopped fluttering. "I must ask you to leave *now*, Mr. Conroy. Your welcome at the Blue Citadel has come to an end. Take your belongings and depart, or I will summon security to assist you."

I frowned. It wasn't being fired that bothered me. I've been fired plenty of times, and the gig had all but ended any way. But interplanetary travel wasn't cheap, and if I didn't get paid I couldn't follow Svetlana and meet her Celestial on my own terms. I didn't care about salvaging my job, but I had to straighten things out enough to leave with money in my pocket.

I set Reggie down and tried to look stern. "Stay." Reggie shook himself and got his legs under him, but stood still. I walked over to the Phloke and took up a position in front of my now-former boss. "Do you remember the demonstration I gave you the day you hired me? Do you remember who my *volunteer* was?"

Her face blanched and her ribbons shifted to a cream beige, losing their metallic sheen. "You mu-must leave. At once. Now, Mr. C-Conroy, I will not ask you ag-gain!"

"Amun Guava," I said, and just like every other Phloke I'd hypnotized, at the mention of her trigger phrase she crashed back into trance.

"Trellbello, listen carefully. In a few moments, you're going to begin counting, from one to one thousand. When you finish, you'll wake up outside the door to this suite. This meeting, this conversation, will have never happened. You won't recall any of it. Instead, you'll remember receiving a message from me that I've gone off to talk with someone about the play that's upset you. Do you understand?"

All the earlier tension had left her body, and the color returned to her ribbons. "Contradictory human. When you return, you are fired."

"Ah, but I'm going to return by this time tomorrow, and I'll have proof that the play was put on without my approval. When I do, you're going to pay me what you owe me. It's the right thing to do."

"I'll give you until tomorrow. Be back with your proof, and on time, or you'll forfeit this kindness." Her whole body nodded, and she floated into the hall, taking up position outside my door.

I stepped into the bedroom, where I grabbed my bag from the corner of a closet. Reggie trotted after me, and bleated faintly as I reached down and scooped him up, securing him in the crook of my arm. I hadn't done much nesting, and other than a few snacks and beverages in a chiller set behind another wall panel, there was nothing that belonged to me here. I went back to the door and Trellbello, pausing only long enough to glance at the wall and memorize some details from the article displayed there. The theatre was on a different continent. I dragged a finger across the wall. A moment later, it spoke.

"Concierge's desk. How may I help you, Mr. Conroy?"

"I need a ticket and transportation to this show. Can you make that happen?"

There was a long pause as he concierge reviewed the particulars on my wall screen, followed by a faint sound that might have been ribbons slapping against a display.

"No problem, sir. There'll be a seat waiting for you. Just ask for Reyn, and say Jesther sent you."

"That's great. Can you, uh, bill that to my room?"

"Easily done. But if you're to make the opening curtain, I should summon a personal transport for you now, sir."

"Thank you, Jesther, that would be ideal. I'm on my way down."

I joined Trellbello in front of my room, closing the door behind me. "I'm leaving now. As soon as I'm gone you'll begin counting. Do you remember what will happen when you finish and wake up?"

The Phloke bobbled in affirmation. Reggie tried to squirm free to lunge at her, but I held him back.

"Yes of course. My memory is superb. I have a loci mnemonic based upon the resort itself. I waited for you, but you did not arrive. You sent a message, and you claimed you would return with evidence of your innocence. But I'm still firing you."

Reggie whuffled once, possibly sharing the Phloke's impatience with me or just frustrated at being so close to a big ball and not being able to play. Either way, it was time to leave. The elevator beckoned, and I let it take me away.

On the ground floor a youngish, fresh scrubbed beachball bounced up to greet me as I approached the concierge's desk; with a flourish of his ribbons he gestured me toward a waiting transport. Reggie writhed in my grasp, yipping at the Phloke.

"No time for that now, Reggie. We're going to the theatre."

Although the vast majority of Leftril had yet to be developed, its handful of completed cities had not been built in proximity to one another. Each had been given plenty of room to grow, positioned to experience different climates, and adjacent to varying geographical features. The Traken theatrical company was performing in Primalt, the planet's main spaceport and oldest city, nearly halfway around the world from the unnamed city of the Blue Citadel. Door to door the trip took the better part of eight hours. I spent the first half hour trying out different approaches I could take to get the play's director to explain things to Trellbello, with Reggie acting as stand-in. After a few of these he got bored and started yawning. I can take a cue as well as the next performer, and besides my subconscious could do a better job sorting out the best tact to take than fretting would. I sprawled out in the backseat for some overdue sleep and Reggie curled up on my chest to do the same.

The automated transport woke me moments before arrival, and deposited me at the end of a short line in front of the theatre's ticketing kiosk. Rather than wake him, I'd slipped Reggie into my carpetbag, where he curled up on my spare clothes. The line moved forward quickly.

A bored-looking Phloke floated in the kiosk. "Ticket?"

"I don't have one, but—"

"I'm sorry, sir, this is the last performance and we're entirely sold out." She looked past me. "Next!"

"Excuse me, we're not done. There's a ticket waiting for me. Jesther told me to ask for someone named Reyn..."

"Your name?"

"Conroy."

"No, sir, not the play, *your* name."

"That is my name. I know, quite a coincidence, isn't it?"

I was never to know if she agreed or not as a teenage Traken boy chose that moment to race up to me and gush. "You're here. You really came. This is incredible, incredible." He gasped for breath.

"Hi. I'm guessing you're Reyn?"

He bowed repeatedly, seemed to think better of it, and instead grasped my right hand and began pumping it like he was churning butter. An instant later he pulled back, blushing and muttering, "Sorry, I shouldn't presume... Oh, moons above, this has to be Reggie!"

I glanced down and discovered Reggie's head sticking through my bag's opening. Reyn leaned closer, bending at the waist to bring his face nearer my buffalito's. Reggie obliged him with a lick that started at the left edge of the youth's mouth and ran at an upward angle and didn't end until it reached past his right nostril.

Reyn staggered back, grinning like he'd just been kissed by the prom queen. "If you'll come with me, Mr. Conroy, I have a special box waiting for you."

"You don't have to go to that kind of trouble. I'd be happy to watch the show from backstage, any place where I wouldn't be in the way. And after, I really need to talk with the director—"

"The director's my father. And he insisted you have the box. Please, come with me, we haven't much time before curtain."

Reyn escorted me into the darkened theatre and led the way to a private orchestra box furnished with a well-padded loveseat of ambiguous design to accommodate a variety of body types and sizes.

I took a seat and then eased Reggie from the bag and settled him on my lap. When I glanced up, Reyn was still there, staring. He looked on the brink of tears. "Enjoy the show, sir." He swallowed several times. "It's an unexpected joy to have you here with us." He slipped away into the gloom.

When the lights came up and I found myself directly in front of the stage, with the best seat in the house. Reggie bleated softly, and the play began. Clusters of men and women swarmed onto a green lawn. In the Traken tradition, multiple actors perform together for every major role, each having responsibility for a different aspect of the character's emotional life. Smaller parts were handled by fewer actors, but on Trakus even a soliloquy requires two people. This explained the bunch of seven staggeringly handsome men in tuxedos who quickly revealed themselves to be the title character. They strolled across the stage, followed by a trio of Traken children crawling on all fours, dressed in bodysuits of shaggy, brown fur, with darker humps across their shoulders. Moments later they met the septet of women I'd seen on the wall of my former suite, the actresses playing Calinda, the Baroness Parmaq.

The Conroys and Calindas all carried croquet mallets, and a delightful afternoon began to unfold. Each hypnotist held hands with a baroness, and a couple of me boldly slipped an arm around a waist or shoulder. Spring was in the air and all was right with the world, until the sudden arrival of four men soured the mood. The newcomers all wore a cross between a corporate executive's power suit and a fairytale prince's best ballroom finery. These were Lord Nerkt, the bully and jilted lover who would be dead before the end of the first act. A confrontation began and grew to a brawl. The Nerkts, despite their fewer number, started beating the crap out of the Conroys, while the trio of Reggies bleated and stamped. I winced watching every blow, as my namesakes just stood there, taking the pounding, prevented from responding by the Nerkts' telepathic powers. The battle ended when several of the baronesses used their croquet mallets, conking the Nerkts into unconsciousness, which is pretty much how it had really happened, albeit with fewer people involved.

The play continued, depicting events from that time of my life, but I stopped paying attention. I couldn't tear my eyes from the women making up my sweet Baroness. They looked so much like Calinda, but not quite. This one had more of a sparkle to her eyes, like Calinda sometimes had when she laughed. Another had a slightly slimmer shape that somehow made me think of Calinda when she was being serious or somber. None of them were her, but they summed to become her.

Once upon a time I'd built a financial empire out of buffalo dogs. Along the way I'd traveled to a worldlet named Brunzibar, where I'd met Calinda and we'd fallen in love. The Traken nobility have a telepathic gift that causes everyone around them to respond to their unconscious desires. It's why I hadn't been able to strike back at Nerkt. And it's how my Baroness had unintentionally caused Nerkt's murder, shattered the mind of an innocent man, and disgraced her mentor. Her talent had manipulated the minds around her, moving them like game pieces to eliminate the people who disapproved of our relationship. It happened because she loved me, and without any awareness on her part.

The play captured all of it, including the final act with all the Conroys confronting all the Calindas. The Baronesses couldn't accept what they'd done, and the face of every Conroy showed his realization that it would happen again, because nothing could stand before the power of her love. One by one, the seven actors portraying me hypnotized their respective Calinda, left her in a deep sleep, and sacrificed his happiness to save the woman he loved from causing further harm. As one, the Conroys left the stage and the curtain fell.

The audience erupted with multiple species' applause. The noise expanded to fill the theatre but ended abruptly, as if they knew the precise duration acceptable for displaying their pleasure and took pride in not wasting a moment more. I hadn't applauded. I couldn't. I'd played that final moment over in my own mind countless times, asking myself if I'd made the right choice. This time, I knew I had. Seeing it from outside made the decision obvious, so simple, but still tragic. A shudder rippled through me, and I set down a burden I hadn't known I'd been carrying.

Reyn reappeared, but instead of leading me back the way we'd come he took me down a sloping corridor that opened out like a river's delta into the theatre's green room. The entire cast stood waiting for me. An additional Traken I had not seen on stage, but who nonetheless looked familiar, stepped forward to take my hand.

"This is an unexpected honor, sir." He pumped my hand with a vigor that identified him as Reyn's father, the director. "None of us ever dreamt to perform for you. And Reggie, of course. An actual buffalo dog. I never. . ." His arm moved to clasp my shoulder and turn me, walking me back to the actors. "My friends, it is my unforeseen pleasure to present to you, the original, Amazing Conroy!"

The roar they made couldn't have been louder than the applause the audience had given them, but the smallness of the space made it seem so. I leaned close to the director, whispering into his ear so he'd hear me over the din.

"I'm flattered, really, but I hope you can help me with a small problem. Your play has convinced my employer that I'm in breach of my contract. I need a disclaimer from you—"

He thumped me on the back as he interrupted. "The legendary Phloke exclusivity clause, eh? No worries, my friend. I've dealt with it before. I'll draft a letter clearing you of any wrongdoing and have it waiting in your employer's message queue before you return. But now, you must indulge us, I cannot hold the troupe back a moment more."

He shoved me into the throng of actors, and with a cheer they engulfed me. It was time to celebrate! As a veteran entertainer, I understood the need to release that euphoria that follows a successful show, particularly the last one in a run. It was time to party! I had a moment of concern for the chaos and carnage so many enthusiastic performers might unleash. I had the arrest record to prove my point. But Reyn's father had taken care of everything. The cast and their party flowed from the theatre to a neighboring restaurant and brewpub where we'd be free to be as giddy and demonstrative as mood and circumstance required.

The Phloke aren't much for intoxicants, but being generous hosts they're happy to accommodate the specialties and preferences of a plethora of offworld visitors, if not necessarily Humans or Traken. The venue we'd landed in featured a beverage favored by the Matan, a race of bipedal, chicken-like aliens who never overindulged in their blend of fermented, mashed grains—sort of a combination of malted barley and corn whiskey. The Matan are wise that way. A single shot produced a mild and pleasant buzz. The Traken had arranged for several kegs of the stuff and would not allow my cup to dip below half full. By my third round I'd have sworn my optic nerve had shorted out, and by the fourth I didn't care. Traken physiology is close enough to human that we were all happily in our cups in no time.

The owner of the restaurant had past experience with cast parties, and assigned us to a back room with soft lighting, an assortment of dark, stain-resistant sofa-like furniture, and walls upholstered in a pale cushiony fabric that partiers could bump into without damage to themselves or the walls. Stoic Phloke employees discretely sealed the doors, ensuring that our drunken revelry would not overflow the room and offend the delicate sensibilities of any other customers.

I hadn't attended a wrap party in far too long, and since given that I concluded my run at the Blue Citadel I decided to think of it as my party too and surrender to the spirit of things. It quickly became a blur of conversations with too many people who looked like people I knew and had loved or hated, befriended or fooled. I'd set Reggie down, allowing him to wander freely, basking in the attention and eating whatever assorted doodads the cast members offered. I mingled as well, wandering contentedly for hours in and out of a sea of conversations.

"No, I'm Nerkt the business man. You're confusing me with Nerkt the jilted lover. Don't worry about it, happens all the time."

"They're both named Reyn. Old Reyn is our director and business manager, and Young Reyn handles every odd job that comes up, like meeting you before the play."

"Actually, Chancellor Vishto retired soon after returning to Trakus. He spends most of his time at a country estate with his great-grandchildren."

"Would you hypnotize me, Mr. Conroy? It would help me understand my character so much more, I'm sure."

"An anonymous patron financed the whole production, even provided us with our own ship and crew. Nobody knows who he is. Old Reyn thinks he might not even be Traken."

"Did Novato really smoke those cigars? Ugh, what a disgusting habit."

"Personally, I think there should be more than three of us playing Chief Miles. There are depths to the man that have barely been hinted at."

"The Baroness doesn't remember any of it any more, Mr. Conroy. The playwright acquired the memories after she'd had them siphoned off."

Time stopped. A cup slipped from my hand, bounced, splashed, and I didn't notice. One of the Calindas was talking, had been for a while, as I nodded and smiled, until her words cut through my stupor. My hands closed upon her arm, harder than I'd intended. They scarcely seemed like my hands any more. Her eyes widened in surprise.

"What do you mean, she doesn't remember?"

"Mr. Conroy, you're hurting me!"

I let go and slumped back, shaking my head. "I'm sorry. Please. You said her memories had been . . . siphoned off?"

The actress stared at me. I'd frightened her, but she moved closer. "After you left, and after she returned to Trakus, she mourned you as if you had died. Her entire estate observed death rituals in your name."

"She acted like I was dead?"

"She was trying for closure, trying to get over you. But it didn't work. She despaired and wandered around listlessly for months. In desperation, her family brought in a siphoner from offworld, a Bluie who had talent and training. Chancellor Vishto objected. There was a great deal of gossip about it, but as you know he'd been disgraced and everyone ignored him. The siphoner worked on her for days, isolating the specific memories of you, and the related recollections and ideas they'd become associated with."

She'd taken my hands in hers, and the contact steadied me. "I've never heard of Bluies. A siphoner? I didn't know anything like that could be done."

She nodded. "It's a big galaxy. Search hard enough, you can find anything in it. When the siphoner was done, it was as if that period of the Baroness's life had never happened. They say she remembered boarding the yacht that took her and her retinue to Brunzibar, and then a few months later she was home again, with nothing in between."

"I don't understand. Where did the play come from, then?"

"Before meeting you, the Baroness had been the darling of the Traken court, and when she returned her despair fascinated many. Once word leaked that a siphoning was under way, a playwright contacted the Bluie in secret and offered to buy the memories. The Bluie asked permission of the

Baroness—whether in her mind any longer or not, they were still her memories. She . . . consented, and the siphoner put them into the playwright. They couldn't last long, his brain wouldn't map with hers, but long enough for him to experience it as she understood the events, and to write them down in a flurry of days without sleep."

"Did she . . . did Calinda ever see the play performed?"

The actress stared at me. She pulled one hand free and raised it to my cheek. "Do you remember my name?"

"I'm sorry." I waved in the general direction of one of the pitchers of Matan brew.

"I'm Carina. My mother and father work on the Baroness's estate; I grew up there. I saw her when she first came back. I'd never seen anyone so sad. And I wore the mourning veil, along with every other woman there, for all the days of your funeral service and the days after."

I gazed at the actress's face, so like the woman I'd loved, and wondered if Calinda were present, if she'd even recognize me. "And after that?"

"She continued to mourn, and still did not recover. I saw her the day the Bluie came, and saw the tears of hope in her eyes. Yes, she came to the play. She sat in the royal box with a few of her closest friends. She smiled at the warm parts of the story, and she cried at the sad parts, same as everyone else in the audience. It didn't matter that seven of us took the stage in her name. As far as she knew, the story wasn't about her, had never happened. It was all fiction."

"You're saying she doesn't even know I'm alive?"

"She knows there really is a hypnotist named Conroy, and that she met him once, thought he surely must be amazing, and maybe even loved him, but it's just a play she saw. It never really happened to her."

The room spun around me and one of the Nerkts put a hand on my shoulder. "You okay, Mr. Conroy?"

"He will be," said Carina. "I think he finally got some kind of closure. Orlio, be a sweetie and get him another drink?"

"Sure, no problem," said the Nerkt. He passed out of my field of vision and returned a few moments later. "Here you are." He pressed something into my hand.

My fingers closed around a cup and brought it to my mouth. I drank. The liquid burned as it went down.

"Hey, not so fast. You sure you're okay?"

I let him take the cup from me. I shook my head to clear it, not in answer, and a moment later said, "Yeah, thanks."

I rubbed at my eyes with both hands for a moment and when I stopped the actress was still there, studying me. I studied her right back. She had stopped looking so much like Calinda and more like her own person.

"You said your name was Carina?"

She smiled, and if I could remember a brighter smile it didn't matter when or where.

"I did."

The party continued around us, drunken Traken thespians renewing old arguments, running lines, performing scenes from past plays, drinking in pairs and trios and quartets throughout the room, whispering and grinning and joking to one another. None of it had anything to do with me any more.

"Would you like to tell me more about yourself?"

She took my hand and led me to a small sofa away from the general frivolity. I snagged a pitcher and two cups along the way. We sat together, and as I leaned to set the pitcher on the floor my body kept going and I collapsed onto my side, passing out but at least managing not to spill anything. Smooth.

CHAPTER FOUR

Armed and Flatulent

I SAT AT A ROUND BOOTH in some restaurant with a spoon in my hand and a bowl of groats on the table in front of me. At first I thought it was the place where Billi had taken me, but it didn't fit. For one thing, every spoon I'd seen on Leftril had a knife's edge as well; the one in my hand was just a spoon. For another, the rest of the place just sort of faded out of existence a few meters beyond my booth. No sharp edges, no other tables, just . . . nothing. But the biggest clue was the lettering in the restaurant's front window that spelled out CONROY'S DREAM in reverse letters. What my unconscious mind lacks in subtlety it tries to make up for in style.

I looked around for whatever symbols and metaphors my brain had chosen to populate the dream. I wasn't alone at my booth. Diners blocked me in on either side. The one on my left wore a rich suit of dark liquid that easily cost him more than purchasing the restaurant would have. A half-cape draped across his shoulders, pale gray and matching his shirt. A blood red cravat added a splash of color and guided the eye to his face, its strong jaw, the barest point of a beard, and on up to high cheekbones and hooded dark eyes beneath thick brows. He was a handsome man, the kind used to wielding power, though not necessarily well. I'd seen his likeness on stage recently. I remembered his name, Lord Nerkt, in the same moment that I remembered he was dead.

The fellow on my right had nothing in common with Nerkt or myself other than a humanoid silhouette and a similar bowl of groats. Naked, hairless, he had flesh of a mottled, greenish hue, and if you'd told me he'd spent the last year soaking in a vat of brine I'd have believed you. The only adornment he wore lay around his neck, a merchant ship's command and control medallion of burnished black metal on a simple chain. More than twenty years had passed since I'd seen him: Captain Coelacanth, the husk who had blown up the ship bearing the consciousness of a Celestial that had wanted that husk for its own. Just to be clear, Coelacanth was dead too.

"Life," said my former captain as it pulled an empty spoon free of its lipless mouth. "It's just one surprise, after another. You know what I mean?"

"Indeed I do," said Nerkt, his attention still focused on his bowl. "Take this mush, these . . . what did you call them again?"

"Groats," I said, shocked that I'd spoken at all.

"Yes, these groats. What a simple pleasure, and a complete surprise to me."

"Because you're dead?" I asked.

Lord Nerkt turned his gaze upon me for the first time. "No, of course not. Because they're so damn tasty."

"I agree completely," said the husk. "And I don't normally take in sustenance in this manner."

"Because you're dead?" I said again.

Captain Coelacanth pivoted its torso to look at me, its head being unable to turn independent of its shoulders. "No, Mr. Conroy, not because I'm dead, because my physiology doesn't require it. I typically ingest artificial, highly concentrated carbohydrates, which I store for later use, breaking them down via a photosynthetic process which, I assure you, is not an appropriate topic for conversation at table."

Nerkt's familiar sneer curled his lips. "Really, Conroy, your manners are atrocious. Did your great Aunt Fiona teach you nothing about politeness or etiquette?"

"Why bring Aunt Fiona into this?"

"Because she's dead," they said in unison, and then returned their attention to their respective bowls of groats. I looked down, dipped my spoon into the bowl before me, stirred and inhaled the warm, rich aroma.

"Yeah, life," said the captain. "You think you've got it all planned out, and then *wham!* Along comes one surprise after another."

"Too true," said Nerkt. "You'd think we'd have caught on to that fact a lot sooner."

"Oh, I don't know," I said, bringing my first spoonful of groats to my lips. They had a curious aroma somewhere between vanilla and honeysuckle. "Actually, I think that—"

WHAM!

The spoon fell from my hand and my arms flailed at my sides. I didn't strike either of my dining companions; they had vanished. So had our table, the booth, and any source of light.

"No more of that, if you please," said a pleasant voice.

My head felt like someone had wrapped it in thick towels, which muffled the throbbing I felt and that promised to leave sooner than the pain it masked. My mouth tasted wooly. Had Reggie shoved his hoof into it as I slept? I opened my eyes to locate him, and maybe also to identify the owner of the nice voice, and why she was in my room.

Only it wasn't my room. Reggie was nowhere in sight. Through a thinning mental fog I remembered losing both my suite and my job. This place was also of Glamorkan design, and the view I had from lying on my back began painting adjectives across my brain. Big, clean, efficient, with one wall of shiny vertical bars. It was probably one of the best cells I'd ever been in. I thanked my subconscious memory for its excellent job and tried to sit up. The throbbing increased and a moan slipped from me.

"Take your time, I'm not in any hurry."

A beachball hovered in front of me, her ribbons fluttered in their own breeze.

"W-where's my buffalito? And who . . . are you? What's . . . going on?"

"Good. Good. Questions are the beginning of advertency. In reverse order then. You started flailing about, and I worried you might hurt yourself," said the Phloke with the pleasant voice. "You're the first Terran I've had here, but I've found a good bounce to the head can awaken most humanoids."

I tried sitting up again, this time with more success, and discovered I'd been lying on a bench. I took quick stock of myself, and other than the worst hangover Leftril had ever seen, I didn't seem too worse for the wear.

"Next. I am Detective-Inspector Martny. Early this morning I received a call from a brewpub in the theatre district—that was some while ago; you've been asleep the entire day. The proprietors have filed complaints of destruction of property, theft of property, and desertion with intent to defraud."

"I don't understand." I rubbed the back of my head where I was storing the effects of an evening spent drinking undiluted Matan brew. "I remember the pub . . . The cast party. . ."

"As for your . . . buffalito? I'm sorry, I don't know anything about that. I actually saw the play the other night. Am I to understand that creature is real, and continues to travel with you?"

I nodded, and the gesture set off a new round of hammering in my skull. It provided a fine counterpoint to the sudden sick worry in my stomach. "He was with me last night. We attended the play together, and the party with the cast afterwards."

"There was no one and nothing else present when I was called in. Just you, sir. And this note."

The Phloke held out a paper between two ribbons, a scrap of a playbill.

CONROY—

WE TRIED TO WAKE YOU, BUT COULDN'T MANAGE IT. FOR REASONS KNOWN ONLY TO HIMSELF, OUR MYSTERIOUS PATRON HAS SENT WORD FOR US TO LEAVE IMMEDIATELY. I'M SURE YOU UNDERSTAND. A GREAT HONOR AND PLEASURE TO HAVE MET YOU, SIR.

YOUR SERVANT,

REYN THE OLDER, MANAGER

P.S. I TRANSMITTED YOUR MESSAGE TO YOUR EMPLOYER AT THE BLUE CITADEL. ALL IS FORGIVEN.

"They . . . left?"

"The cast has departed the planet, yes. Presumably en route to their next venue. Perhaps your creature went with them. I take it they didn't share any of their plans with you?"

"Not that I can recall, no."

"That's most unfortunate, and I'm sorry to be the one to surprise you with this, but as you were party to that, uh, party, and the only one remaining behind, our legal system has no other option than to hold you responsible for the accumulated actions of all the offenders. Mr. Conroy, you're under arrest."

I rubbed my head some more; it didn't help. "I'm sorry, I don't understand what you're talking about."

"I'll try to be clearer, sir. What little crime we have tends to involve traffic violations, overdue permits, and simple civil disputes. They're usually resolved with financial penalty, but as I understand your situation, you're no longer employed, and you lack sufficient funds to cover the debt."

"Well, yes and no. My contract has run out, but there should be a paycheck waiting for me at my last job."

The Phloke sighed. "I'm afraid not. I contacted your last employer, and I was informed that your arrest and the charges against you violate the morals clause in your contract, voiding any debts owed to you. I am told those funds will be used to distance the establishment from any negative association your crimes might bring. As a result, I didn't have any choice but to hold you here, until someone buys your ticket."

"My ticket?"

"It's only fair. To recoup what you owe them, the injured party has exercised their right to your indenture. There'll be an auction tomorrow morning, with the proceeds going to the people you've wronged. The winner of your ticket will take you away. Until then, I have to ask you to accept these accommodations."

"You don't understand, I'm on my way off-planet as well. I have an appointment, with a Celestial."

The look in the Phloke's eyes spoke of doubt and infinite patience. "That won't be happening. You won't be leaving Leftril any time soon."

"You can't just sell me into slavery! Don't I have any rights? Don't I get a trial?"

"Oh my, yes, of course, if you insist. Given the facts of the case though, that you were seen by many other patrons of the restaurant as attending the actors' gathering, that your name is featured in the title of their production, that you are of the same humanoid morphology as they are—"

"No, that's not true. We're similar yes, and I can understand why you might make that mistake, but I'm a human, from Earth, they're all Traken—"

Martny waved her ribbons at me, displaying shock that I'd interrupted her. "Ahem, as I was saying, given all these facts in evidence, I assumed you'd prefer to forgo the costs of a trial, as that would only add to the span of your indenture."

"How long a span are we talking?"

The Phloke's ribbons rose in that universal gesture of a shrug. "I'm not an expert on such things, but given the debt your friends incurred, unless you have some useful talents that are needed by your ticket holder, I'd imagine it would be between eight and twenty months. I'm sorry I can't be more precise. I'm confident the magistrate will provide a better estimate tomorrow, before your auction. In the meantime, I suggest you make yourself comfortable. I'll be back to check on you in the morning." Martny floated to the bars, running a pair of ribbons along the left side of the wall. Several bars withdrew into the ceiling, providing enough room for her to float out of the cell. They dropped back into place the instant after she passed.

This wasn't the first time I'd woken up in a jail cell after a party, though I'd never been threatened with a term of indentured servitude before. I was still dressed in my tuxedo, but someone had emptied my pockets. My shoes were still laced, but untied—as if someone had removed and then returned them to my feet. The Pelk's comm-patch had been removed from the back of my hand, leaving behind a red mark where the adhesive or its solvent had irritated my skin.

Inventory completed, I tied my shoes and then moved on to an assessment of my cell's accommodations and accoutrements. The floor and three walls were made of a porous ceramo. Someone had painted them a pale lemon yellow or that was just their natural color. I gave the back wall several solid thumps. Dense, or thick, or both. My head echoed the assessment.

The fourth wall held bars, shiny and very solid. The whole room was about three meters high and deep and six meters wide, and yet it held only the bench I'd awakened on. At both inside corners, bronze tubes dangled from the ceiling. I reached up and jumped to touch the nearer one. A torrent of water poured down, soaking and chilling me to the bone, before it disappeared into the floor. The flow stopped, but not before it had cured my hangover and replaced the throbbing in my head with the chattering of my teeth. I didn't know how or if the Phloke dealt with the traditional problems of bodily elimination, but I was pretty sure this was as close as I was going to get to plumbing in my cell. At least it wasn't a Glamorkan toilet.

That thought hit me like a slap across the face. Reggie! The last I remembered, a couple of the Nerkts had been playing with him, taking turns feeding him things and laughing as he consumed their miscellaneous bric-a-brac. Blame my inebriation, but I hadn't been concerned to note they'd been breaking off bits of furniture, decorative knobs, pieces of trim, and wainscoting. The damn actors had vandalized the room and fed the evidence to my buffalito.

But then what? Had they taken him away? Reggie's a pretty autonomous fellow, but we share a reciprocal loyalty. Just as I couldn't imagine going any great distance or span of time without taking the little guy along, I didn't for a moment believe he'd leave me behind either. So where was he? He'd probably curled up and gone to sleep under a table back at the party, but would have long since awakened all alone. He'd be confused, maybe even frightened. I had to get out of here and find him.

But, where was I? Martny hadn't bothered to mention the location of her police station. Was it a local constabulary, a block or two from last night's restaurant, or the only facility in Primalt, perhaps kilometers distant?

I stripped out of my tux and wrung it out, piece by piece, then used the drier bits to dry my hair. I spread my clothes on the floor in the faint hope that whatever mechanism in it that absorbed water might dry my tux too. Somewhere along the way my teeth had stopped chattering. Naked and damp, I sprawled out on the bench intending work through my possible futures only to fall asleep instead.

A sound awakened me. Something familiar. Faint and muffled through the wall of the cell, but something. Maybe a bark, or maybe just wishful thinking shaping my perception.

"Reggie? Reggie?" Had I dreamed it? How long had I been asleep? Minutes? Hours?

Two more faint somethings.

Then silence.

Then a noise I'd come to recognize: galumphing that stands out because it's unlike any other sound. The sound of a buffalito taking a bite out of a substance too hard and dense ever to be viewed as pet food.

I pressed an ear to the wall. The noise continued, an intermittent chomping. I followed it, mistakenly went past it, doubled back until I was over it. Reggie was taking regular bites out of the wall. I banged on the spot with the bottom of my fist.

"Reggie? Can you hear me, boy?"

The chomping sound stopped, replaced by a sound that this time was clearly a bark. The chomping resumed, punctuated I was sure, though I couldn't hear it, by the occasional burst of breaking wind.

This is how I'd made my fortune, renting and leasing buffalitos because of their two unique abilities. They can eat—and eat through—anything, and they fart oxygen. With a little imagination from my marketing department, and a little operant training from a team of psychology graduate students, we'd found hundreds of high-paying projects for the critters, from demolition to archaeological retrieval, terra-forming to waste removal. I'd never thought to have one eat me out of jail. Reggie had come up with the idea himself. Clearly, I'd been a bad influence.

I'd been awake all of five minutes but already a small spot on the wall had vanished as Reggie's blue tongue pushed its way into view. It took him only a few seconds to gnaw the edges, enlarging the hole until he could step through into the cell. He jumped at me, knocked me back onto the bench and licked my face with that same tongue that had eaten through my jail cell wall.

"I missed you too, Reggie. Where have you been, and how did you find me?"

He locked his eyes with mine in a serious and knowing gaze, then farted loudly out his other end. It was as good an answer as I was likely to receive. Despite having been on his own for most of a day, other than some clumps of reddish mud here and there on his fur, and a tangle of vines that had caught on his horns, he looked none the worse for wear. I scritched behind his ears, ran my hands through his thick fur, and cleaned him up as best as the circumstances allowed. There'd be time for a bath later.

I sat up and carried him back to the hole he'd made, noting that the pale yellow color of the wall on my side wasn't paint, but did indeed run all the way through, a good thirty centimeters or so. The wall did not border open space and the great outdoors. Peering through, I could see into another room. Under my direction, Reggie nibbled the edges of the hole and then climbed back in, expanding it enough for me to follow him.

It was a tight squeeze, but I pulled myself through into what was probably Martny's office. I caught a faint scent not unlike vanilla, but sweeter. In the dim light from the room's sole window on my right, I could make out the familiar cradle and slanted glass display panel favored by Phloke in lieu of the traditional desk a humanoid would find comfortable. The wall on my left held several stands of records cabinets. Opposite me was a looped video portrait of a pair of smiling Phloke, and next to it the door to my freedom. At the bottom of the door, I noted a ragged, buffalito-shaped hole. Reggie dashed through the opening; I opted to tap the wall plate and let the door open for me instead.

The hallway brightened in response to our presence. Reggie scampered down it and turned a corner. I followed. Around the bend, the corridor branched in several directions. Reggie continued along the leftmost route to an outer door he'd already eaten through.

I stepped outside, descending a ramp from the headquarters of the local constabulary. Night had fallen. I didn't recognize any of the buildings on the street. Reggie had already crossed and was halfway up a ramp into the opposite structure that occupied an entire block, a botanical garden of some sort judging by the leafy and blossoming sigils above the lintel. The rows of towering and flowering plants visible through the translucent panels were also a big clue. To the left of the threshold, a jagged hole in one wall told me he'd been there before. "Reggie! Hold up, boy." He stopped, turned to look back at me, and then sat to wait.

Reggie had never left a trail of destruction quite like this. Eating his way into my cell I could understand, but chomping through one building after another made no sense. Whatever route Martny had taken to transport me through the city wouldn't have included a detour through a greenhouse. Somehow Reggie had tracked me, but why hadn't he simply stampeded down the open street rather than eat his way through irrelevant buildings?

I cradled Reggie to my chest and entered the garden building, tracing his zigzag route of trampled, chewed, and missing vegetation to another gap at the far end. A nearby, intentional exit returned me to the evening air. Nothing on this side of the greenhouse looked familiar to me either.

A broad consortium of shops, high-end boutiques, artisan galleries, and the occasional bistro lined the avenue ahead of me. Not a one was open at this hour, but several official-looking transport pods had parked askew in front of a gallery. I came around the side of one of the pods. It was an ambulance, not a police vehicle. Reggie had made am impressive entrance eating right through the gallery's display wall and the abstract painting on the other side of it. The gallery's double doors had been flung open, and inside a pair of low-hovering Phloke flitted to and fro as they tended to several others sprawled upon the floor, their ribbons crumpled and dark, their beachball shapes partially deflated.

"Reggie, what have you done?" He stirred in my grasp, but I wasn't about to set him back down.

As I watched, the medical team revived one of the collapsed Phloke. It's ribbons twitched and lightened and the flattened lumpiness of its shape began to round out. It staggered into the air, and its eyes opened, blinked, and focused on Reggie and me.

"Eeek! It's back! The creature is back! Save yourselves. Hurry, that brave man can't possibly hold it back for long. Get away! Get out before it attacks you too."

Reggie's squirms increased geometrically. He began barking as if challenged.

"I'll just be leaving now," I said to no one in particular. I turned but a familiar-looking Phloke blocked my path. Her ribbons came together in a tight cluster to hold a small wedge of thin metal. 'Hold' might not be the right word; 'aim' would be a clearer description.

"Didn't I leave you in a cell, Mr. Conroy?"

"Detective-Inspector. Nice to see you again."

"I wish I could say the same. I don't know how you got out of the cell, but I am losing patience with you, sir. I already had to fetch you from the scene of your previous crime, and now I'm called in to deal with a second major incident—two in one day when I haven't had anything more daunting than a civil fine in years—and I find you on the scene. Would you care to explain?"

"It will have to wait," said one of the medics, floating through the doorway of the gallery. Reggie strained to get at him as he drew near. "The owner, her assistant, and a visiting artist have all been physically assaulted and two are in deep shock. I need you to authorize a Nembly protocol. That's why I called you to the scene."

Martny bobbed, the Phloke version of a curt nod. "So authorized. You and your associate are witnesses that I have invoked Nembly. You may proceed." The medics sighed and both dropped to floor level and applied a salve to the two insensate victims. The gunk smelled like fish guts, and made the deflated Phloke shrivel further still.

Detective-Inspector Martny floated closer, peering at the process. She gasped. "Is that Wu, the ceramicist? I'd heard he was bringing some of his work to the city. His red clay series is supposed to be exquisite. Will he be all right?"

"Physically, yes, but I can't say how long he'll be affected by the trauma from the attack. I've never seen anything like it. They don't train us for this kind of violence."

The constable moved in, hovering alongside the one she'd called Wu. "What are those markings all over body? Is that, clay?"

"Yes, officer."

As if blown by a hurricane, Martny rushed through the air until she floated at eye level in front of me. Reggie whined and strained to escape, desperate to leap out of my arms and reach the Phloke. "Some of those marks resemble hoof prints." Fearlessly, she tapped one of Reggie's legs with the metallic wedge still clutched in her ribbons. "And the creature in your arms has the same color clay on at least one of his hooves."

Clay, I thought. *Not mud, clay. Crap.*

"I'm sure it's just a coincidence. After all, I was in your cell when this happened."

"We won't know precisely when any of *this* happened until a forensic team gets here. And you've managed to leave that cell."

"I can explain that."

"I'm sure you can, but you'll do so to a magistrate, not to me. This goes far beyond simple debt or destruction of property. Three citizens have been physically assaulted. You couldn't live long enough to earn out the indenture for one of the victims, let alone all three. I don't know your role in all of this yet, but I have a feeling it's going to be ugly."

"Baby it will, and baby it won't!" said a new voice with a speech impediment that filled me with both surprise and relief.

"Billi? What are you doing here?"

"I'm looking out for a client." He sauntered up alongside me and tapped the constable's wedge with a talon from one of his upper hands. "Lady, how about pointing that at another target? Or are you planning on blowing a bigger hole in him than he has room to blow?"

Detective-Inspector Martny didn't lower her weapon or aim it away from Reggie. If anything, she showed great restraint not pointing it at the Pelk. "And who are you?"

"I'm our boy's agent. You can call be Billi." From one of the pockets of his overalls he withdrew a business card and offered it to the constable. She ignored it. Billi shrugged, and held up his palms in an all too human gesture that didn't quite work because he used four hands. "I really think you want to stay on our good side."

"How's that?"

Billi smiled, revealing multiple rows of shining teeth, each as brilliantly white as his tusks. "If his creature did this, and the evidence points that way, you should also acknowledge that he's able to contain the wild beast's yearnings to wreck still greater havoc. He's the only one who can. You shouldn't be arresting him, you should be giving him a citation for bravery and a hefty reward!"

Martny glared back in response to the smile. "You're not the first Pelk I've met. And while you spin a good story, I think we'll wait for the forensic team to give us the timing and sequence of events. Here, and back in his cell. Meantime, we'll hold off on any rewards, okay? And your client had better hope these people make a full recovery."

Something chose that moment to beep. Martny demonstrated that a beachball didn't need a mouth to manage a scowl. She freed up one of her ribbons long enough to stroke a spot on the side of her body, about where an ear might have been. "I'm getting reports of additional victims at several other sites." She paused, and her scowl transformed into a grimace. "Four more sites, all of them in a line between here and the restaurant where you and your Traken friends had your party last night. Six other Phloke assaulted. Other aliens were also present. They've attributed the attacks to an animal that fits this thing's description."

Martny's grimace turned angrier and her ribbons did something to the wedge. A violet ray of light streamed out spattering my chest and most of Reggie with purple flickers. She gestured with the wedge, the ray bending as she did. I took a seat on the floor, settling Reggie on my lap.

"I'm being told that despite the presence of multiple species at the other sites, your creature only went after Phloke. This is looking worse and worse for you, Mr. Conroy. Not simply violence, but hate-crime. This won't wait until morning, Magistrate Spigyromo is on his way here right now."

"Wonderful," said Billi, standing at eye level with me. "I can hardly wait to beat him."

CHAPTER FIVE

The Snark Defense

THE MAGISTRATE ARRIVED in the largest ground vehicle I'd seen on Leftril. Like every other Phloke, he resembled a beachball with painted-on eyes and a couple dozen silk ribbons tied to the bottom for good measure. But instead of having a diameter of a meter or so, Magistrate Spigyromo was twice that and more. He was a medicine ball of a Phloke, and he bounded out of his transport with the speed and purpose of a final point serve at a volleyball championship match. Several normal-sized Phloke followed more diffidently, dragging small carts loaded with recording gear. Spigyromo drifted into the gallery and hovered a moment over each of the victims before moving on to confer with the medical technicians. His associates set up their gear around the Detective Inspector who continued to keep her wedge trained on Reggie and me. The flickering purple light hadn't produced any effect on either of us and probably wouldn't as long as I stayed where I was and kept my buffalo dog still. Good plan.

The magistrate joined us. "Tell me, if you please," said Spigyromo, his voice several octaves lower than the Phloke norm, "which one of you is the rampaging, murderous alien creature that couldn't wait to be sentenced in my chambers at a civil hour?"

"Your impartiality is legendary, your honorableness," said Billi, shoving his way in front of me and extending his middle right hand to the magistrate. "Just to be clear, you should understand the real reason you're here is because some overanxious and overreacting—though surely well-intentioned—officer of the law dragged you from your home to see an innocent and adorable pet."

"What's this about pets? Martny! This is a Pelk. I was told I'd be meeting an Earthperson."

"That would be me, your honor." I stood slowly. Martny raised the wedge and the beam followed me up. Reggie stared at the massive Phloke in front of us and stopped squirming; he knew his limits. "I'm Conroy."

Spigyromo rotated his immense sphere until he had oriented on me. "Conroy? I saw you onstage."

I nodded, "Yes, your honor, I was performing at the Blue Citadel until yesterday."

"What? No, no, at the theatre a few blocks from here."

"That was a play based on him, your honorariness," said Billi, coming around me once again to confront Spigyromo. "This is the real deal here, don't confuse him for a fraction of a Traken character study. This is the Amazing Conroy his own self."

The magistrate performed the Phloke nodding bob, and turned to the Detective Inspector. "Martny, unless you're planning on firing that thing, turn it off. It's distracting and obscuring my view." The other Phloke said nothing, and a moment later the violet ray winked out. Spigyromo raised a pair of ribbons to gesture at my buffalito. "I take it this is Reggie? You at least bear a resemblance to the actors from the stage; he looks nothing like any of them."

"You have a keen eye, your honoration. The play used tiny humanoids, youths, to portray his pet. The genuine article is considerably less dangerous."

"Certainly he was portrayed as well behaved and of pleasant disposition," said Spigyromo. "You'll pardon me, but Phloke do not keep pets as such. The only animals on Leftril are in our zoological gardens."

"And doubtless all are bore dangerous than my client's buffalito."

"Excuse me? Am I boring you?" The magistrate's glare fixed on Billi, then turned back to me.

"Please accept my apologies, your honor, he has a speech impediment. It doesn't show up in his native tongue, but he has a bit of problem with certain phrases in Traveler."

"Fine then, let's get on with this." His expression shifted back to neutral and he lifted his ribbons as he continued, counting off each point. "My clerk accessed the immigration records on our way over. Your creature is the only one of its species currently on Leftril. Ever. Nor are there any animals of similar morphology in any of our zoos. My clerk is thorough and cross-checked with them any way; none are missing any of their charges. I am also in possession of multiple eye-witness reports that a creature matching the description of your pet physically assaulted no fewer than six citizens, in each instant without provocation. In the absence of any conflicting evidence, I conclude your pet is responsible for these acts of violence, and as you are the established owner of the animal, I find you culpable."

Billi eased off to the side until he was standing alongside Detective-Inspector Martny. "I was with you right up to the final part, your honorivisity."

I waved to shush the Pelk but one of the clerks laid a ribbon on my arm and wiggled its body like a human would shake his head.

The glare returned as the magistrate pivoted to face Billi. "Excuse me?"

The Pelk waved Spigyromo's remark away with his middle left hand. "That's okay, I can see how you'd come to that erroneous conclusion. But see, the real issue here is the heedlessness of the Detective-Inspector."

Martny's ribbons fluttered as she spun to face her accuser. "That's ridiculous, I've done nothing."

"That's kind of the point. Let's go back a bit further and look at all the facts. Your own immigration records will show that Mr. Conroy has been present on your fine planet for nearly forty days, and in all that time his pet hadn't assaulted anyone."

"So stipulated," said Spigyromo, waving some ribbons at Martny who looked about to object again. "Continue. Where are you going with this?"

"The reason is Conroy himself. He serves as a calming and controlling influence on the creature. At this very instant, he is performing that task, despite his great personal strain and distraction."

"I fail to see your point. The animal is his. Keeping the animal under control is likewise his responsibility. Failing that task, he is culpable for the consequences."

"But he didn't fail. He was prevented!"

"What?"

"Conroy here was in full possession and control of his creature, right up until the point where the Detective-Inspector took him away. That's when the trouble started. In fact, Conroy went to heroic lengths to reunite with his pet, in a concerted effort to prevent any further problems."

"What heroic lengths?"

"Billi, this isn't helping," I said.

"He broke out of custody," said Martny. "That's in addition to the other charges against him."

"Oh please," said Billi. "That charge is absurd. Classic Snark defense."

Spigyromo scowled. "I am not familiar with that legal precedent."

"It's from Earth. You can't charge him with escape because you've already stipulated to his alibi: he wasn't there."

One of the clerks' eyes crossed, while the other's ribbons hung limp. Martny sputtered. Spigyromo simply hovered for a long moment and then said, "That makes no sense whatsoever."

"Baby it does, and baby it doesn't. But that isn't important. The real point is this: charging Conroy doesn't resolve anything, it only diverts blame from the Detective-Inspector. Worse, it increases your problem. You've acknowledged that he's kept the creature tame, and you haven't any reason to believe there is any other person available who can accomplish the same thing. So what happens to your fair city if you sell him into servitude? That beast is going to run amok, that's what will happen."

"What do you propose instead?"

"Extradition," said Billi. "Once we're off Leftril, your problem is solved. Until then, if it pleases you, remand him into ol' Billi's custody, both him and his savage creature. I'll bear full responsibility if there's any further trouble before we leave."

"A very tidy solution," said Magistrate Spigyromo. "I find myself impressed, Pelk."

"Magistrate, you can't seriously be entertaining this idea," said Martny. "It's not just what his creature did to these poor people; he's also responsible for major damage to a restaurant, attempting to make off without paying his debt to them, and . . . and . . . he escaped custody!"

"Yeah, I wouldn't keep talking about that," said Billi. "It doesn't paint you in a good light."

The magistrate dismissed Billi's remarks with a wave of his ribbons. "All of what you say may be true, Martny, but the issues of damage and debt are minor compared to maintaining the public safety." He laid the ends of several ribbons on the Pelk's shoulder. "How soon can you, your client, and his creature be gone?"

"There's a transit shuttle at your local port. In two hours it runs its final delivery of supplies and passengers to a Cliveden vessel in orbit, your honor. And that ship will be on its way out of your solar system soon after. I imagine if your office contacted them, they'd find room for us. We can vanish that swiftly, and this whole kerfuffle with us."

"Magistrate! How could he possibly know that? This is all some elaborate ruse." Martny was aiming her wedge at us again.

"Oh, please. I'm a talent agent. Of course I know when our ride is leaving. It goes with the job."

Spigyromo waved to his clerks. "Send word to the port authority. Let them know the city will appreciate their assistance in this matter, and to find passage for these individuals."

It was all happening too fast. The clerks bobbed once. Ribbons stroked devices and events were put into motion. "Wait! I didn't say I was willing to leave."

"I don't recall asking you. More to the point, I don't care. I am remanding you into the custody of your agent. My ruling is this: transportation for life. We will not meet again, Mr. Conroy. You and your creature are banned from ever returning to Leftril. Detective-Inspector Martny, escort them all to the port. Stay with them until they are onboard their shuttle, and do not take your eyes off the vessel until you personally see it lift."

"But your honor—"

"You heard my ruling, Martny. I've had enough foolishness for one night. People who are plays, animals that eat through buildings, and Pelks! If it weren't for the citizens who've been injured, I'd be trying to convince myself this was all a bad dream. Now get these people out of my city and off the planet!" He spun, and darted back into his vehicle, followed at once by his clerks towing their gear. In less than a minute they had packed up and driven off, leaving the Detective-Inspector sputtering.

I watched them recede into the distance, standing perfectly still until Martny pressed a ribbon into my back and guided me toward her own transport pod. I petted Reggie as I walked. Billi skipped alongside me. I glanced down only to be greeted by his hideous grin.

"I told you I was going to be your agent."

CHAPTER SIX

No Home Like Space

THE *SHPESHNOLTOC* WAS a luxury cruiser owned and operated by Cliveden, an alien race that has never been seen in Human Space. They're all far too busy, being one of the handful of sapients in possession of the portal technology that controls who can and cannot travel instantly between solar systems. In the corner of the galaxy that includes humanity's borders, access to transit portals are available to everyone, for a fee. Not so in that part of space containing Leftril. With few exceptions, the Cliveden allow only their own ships to use their transit portals. Anything moving between stars, from passenger vessels traveling between worlds to the super-ships carrying cargo to nearly two hundred planets, belonged to and were crewed by the Cliveden families.

I'd traveled to Leftril aboard a registered Cliveden ship, but the experience provided no instruction. Reggie and I had caught a berth on a freighter loaded with containers for various planets in Cliveden space. It was an eight-day trip through two portals and we endured it traveling inside a passenger cube, a metal and ceramo crate about three meters per side. The amenities differed from traveling as freight by the inclusion of a tattered couch, boxed meals, and a fold-out commode. No entertainment console, no other passengers with whom to wile away the trip, nothing but eight days of boredom and a fidgety buffalo dog for company in my box.

Under the unhappy gaze of Detective-Inspector Martny, Billi, Reggie, and I boarded a shuttle to the *Shpeshnoltoc*, the interstellar equivalent of the kind of luxury ocean linear that a century ago on Earth would have frittered away far too much time traveling between exotic ports of call while its passengers gorged themselves in round-the-clock restaurants, as up-and-coming performers and past-their-prime celebrities provided a variety of distracting entertainments. The Cliveden themselves are a reptilian species with scaly epidermis that runs from shades of pale blue to lavender. They have coronal crests instead of hair, black eyes, bifurcated tongues, and no appreciation for what I tend to think of as life's pleasures. As aliens go, they're an efficient race, and it's just cruel irony that puts them in charge of a luxury vessel when they have no interest in fine dining or quality entertainment. On the other hand, their ships always depart on the dot, and arrive at their destinations with time to spare.

A deckhand dressed in black shorts, a sleeveless shirt, and gloves met our shuttle and without uttering a single word he escorted us through opulent corridors into the heart of the ship. His skin azure skin had a sheen to it, and he gave off a faintly spicy scent as we followed him through the ship. His crest stood barely a centimeter above his head, hinting at his youth. He deposited us in a large, tidy office. Before leaving us he handed me a printed card stating that the ship's purser would join us in short order. Billi used the time to wander the room, inspecting inscrutable objects upon the shelves, peering behind framed images on the walls, opening the drawers of the desk, and helping himself to long draughts from a bottle of unknown liquor he found in a cabinet. I went to stand in the corner farthest from the door, and maintained a grip on my buffalito. Reggie kept his eyes on Billi for a bit, lost interest, and began scanning the room for potentially tasty knickknacks.

The door opened revealing a light purple lizardman with an impressively tall crest. He wore the same garb as the deckhand who'd led us there and now stood at attention in the hallway. A sibilant gush of sound passed between the two of them, a language that no one would ever mistake for Traveler. The newcomer strode in and immediately took up a seat behind the desk. He opened the middle drawer, frowned, and set five objects in a neat row on the desktop. They looked like five different colored gumdrops. He gestured to seats in front of him, and Billi and I took them. The door whooshed closed behind us. He allowed us a moment or two to get comfortable, and then spoke.

"I am Thindar po Rens. You may call me Thindar. Rens is my family name, and by extension the name of nearly every member of the crew. I am informed that the legal authority on Leftril has petitioned my captain to take you on board, and she has assigned me the task of attending to you, and if possible, keeping you from being a burden during our voyage. Let me be clear, under the terms of the captain's agreement with the local government, we are obligated to provide you a berth for restorative needs, access to sanitary facilities, and a minimal portion of appropriate food and fluids. These things I have already set in motion. What more you receive to make your time onboard *Shpeshnoltoc* to your liking is what we are here to determine. Do you have any questions?"

My new agent swung himself out of his seat using two hands, set the bottle down with a third, and began rhythmically snapping the fingers of a fourth as he sauntered around to the Cliveden's side of the desk. "I think we're going to get along swimmingly, friend Thindar. I always enjoy good relations with Cliveden. You're direct and to the point. You don't do subtlety, or surprises. Pragmatic. Rational. I always say, when you're dealing with a Cliveden, it's clear what's what. So, let me introduce you to this lug over here."

He waved both his left hands at me, gesturing me to stand. I didn't. "This is the Amazing Conroy, and I have to tell you, he really ought to upgrade his title, because *amazing* doesn't begin to describe what he does. You might as well tell your current headliner to jump ship, because ol' Conroy will cause him to look like yesterday's cheese."

Thindar po Rens turned his black gaze on me. "You are an entertainer?"

"Is he an entertainer? Why, just look at him! I'll tell you—"

Thindar's index finger cocked back and then flicked forward, connecting with the side of a cherry red gumdrop. It darted straight to the Pelk's upper lip, flattening out on impact. In an instant it spread to cover his whole mouth, both tusks, and a good portion of his chin. "Let the entertainer speak for himself."

I glanced at Billi. He hadn't made a move to strip away the glop covering his mouth. He slumped back and sat on the floor. His eyes stared blankly ahead and his normally olive green face paled.

"Is he all right?" I asked. "Can he breathe like that?"

"An excellent question. Tell me of your skills as an entertainer, before we discover to our regret. Quickly now."

"Yes, I'm an entertainer, a hypnotist." The Traveler creole doesn't have a word for *hypnotist*. The closest equivalent was a compound that translated something like 'suggestionater and alterer of consciousness.'

"And how is that entertaining?"

"I can cause people to believe impossible things, for a brief duration. The combination of an impossibility with an individual's earnest belief creates a juxtaposition that many find amusing."

"Indeed. And you have worked in this capacity before?"

Billi still hadn't moved. His face had grown paler. "All of my adult life."

The purser smiled. Reptilian smiles are not intended to put humans at ease. "You'll forgive me, please, but I am not acquainted with your species. You could be ancient, or freshly moulted for all I can tell."

"Call it twenty years then," I said. "I typically perform on a stage with an audience of anywhere from a thirty to several hundred. I've worked on cruises many times." The Pelk's skin had turned a greenish gray. "Seriously, can you take that gunk off him?"

"Of course, Amazing Conroy." He flicked another of the gumdrops—a blue one this time—at Billi's face. It splattered much as the last one had, and everywhere it touched the red gunk both fizzled and dissolved. As the portion covering his mouth sublimated, Billi gasped deeply and his color immediately improved. But that was all; he didn't move.

"He's going to be okay, isn't he?"

Thindar smiled again; the effect was no better. "As I said, I am charged with attending to you and ensuring you are not a burden. I could hardly be said to be doing my job if I caused any permanent harm to you. The goo produces a lax paralysis in most warm-blooded species, and I have dealt with Pelks before. He will be fine in a few moments, and doubtless jabbering ceaselessly soon after. While we have a moment more of quiet, let us agree that I will try you out in *Shpeshnoltoc's* tertiary lounge tomorrow after the evening's second dinner service. In the meantime, as you claim to have experience, I will award you and your companions a provisional upgrade to three class nine staterooms, one for each of you."

I shook my head, and lifted Reggie up for his inspection. "This is not a sapient individual; he's my companion animal. He won't require his own room."

"But we'll take upgrades to two class eight rooms in exchange," said Billi, his words marred by a slur. "With additional upgrades to be forthcoming as you receive positive reviews."

"I'll agree to the former, and as for the latter, I think you'll find that Cliveden are great supporters of meritocracy."

Billi worked his jaw and ran his tongue over his the ridges of his mouth. "Really? I'd have thought bepotism."

"Despotism?"

"I think he meant *nepotism*," I said.

The purser laughed. Like his smile, it occupied the opposite end of the spectrum from pleasant. "Quite the contrary. Nepotism is impossible when you're related to everyone else onboard. Do your job well, entertain our passengers, and your performance will not go unnoticed. Do you have any other questions?"

"What about food?" said Billi. "Do we eat with the crew?"

All amusement left Thindar's face. "No, you will not. Cliveden take their meals only with other Cliveden. You are free to avail yourself of any of the thirty-seven restaurants aboard ship. You may keep to yourselves or fraternize with the passengers, so long as you do not offend or displease any of them. Menus, hours, and shipboard locations associated with each dining site can be obtained from the information panels in your rooms, or at any junction of two or more corridors. *Shpeshnoltoc* is a very active and popular ship; you will not want for company, but that company will not include Cliveden. More to the point, I am to be your sole contact among my kind. You will speak to none of the crew without my instruction, and I assure you, none will want to speak to you. Anything else?"

"So . . . we shouldn't expect an invitation to dine at the captain's table?"

The purser glared at Billi, glanced down at one of the remaining gumdrops on his desk. His finger twitched, but not enough to fire off another missile. Instead he opened the desk drawer and swept the remaining gumdrops within, then closed the drawer and folded his hands together on the desk.

"No, most assuredly, you will not."

"If this is a class eight room," I said, "I can't imagine what they're selling people as class nine."

After concluding our orientation with the purser, a Cliveden youth barely taller than Billi had silently led us to our cabins. While they may not have occupied the actual bowels of the ship, I could imagine a faint, intestinal gurgling not far away. Billi's upgrade had landed Reggie and me in a room smaller than the crate I'd traveled in to reach Leftril. At two and a third by three and half meters, my box of a stateroom came with a modest float mattress that could reshape itself into a half-sized picnic table, or raise up entirely into a recess in the ceiling. The middle section of the wall at the top of the room held a collection of storage drawers. A watertight ripple door pulled down from the ceiling to lock into place and turn the far third of the room into a variety of sanitary facilities. Every surface showed the same dishwater gray, and had the texture of cotton broadcloth. The entire place smelled of stale bread with a faint hint of lime.

Billi snorted. "Are you kidding, this is great!"

"Maybe for you. But I'm almost twice your height."

"Yeah, yeah, but I've got half again the limbs as you, so it balances it out."

"Not hardly. I guess claustrophobic passengers have to be able to afford a better class of room."

"If you don't like the walls, turn them off."

"What does that mean?"

"Hey, *room*! Give us a woodland scene, your choice of any island in an archipelago of the southern hemisphere of Kwist."

The room vanished. Thick, leafy groundcover lay spread out in all directions, punctuated by wiry indigo trees no thicker than my arm. A hint of something piney tickled my nostrils, replacing the limeish bread smell.

"It's a helluva lot cheaper to put smart walls in every room than to bake the rooms bigger," said Billi. "And it tends to keep the passengers out of the crew's hair twenty-three hours out of twenty-five. Just don't try going on any nature hikes or you're liable to smash your skull against the wall. Your bed's still around here somewhere, and if you can't find it just tell the room to *reset*."

Which it did, leaving us again in the drab cabin. "Is there a menu?"

"Yeah, you can read it while lying in bed if you like."

"Maybe later. I need to prepare for my debut performance tomorrow."

"So? What's to prepare? You already know your stuff, don't you?"

"I've never been on a Cliveden ship before, except as freight. I have no idea who else might be onboard. I need to do a little research. The best way to accomplish that is for me to mingle."

"Bingle? How you going to bingle?"

"By checking out one of the ship's thirty-seven restaurants." Reggie knows the word *restaurant* and he yipped in approval at the suggestion.

"That's a great idea, but you can't go out in your present state. You look like you've slept in those clothes."

"I did—"

"And as for the stink, trust me, we're both lucky that Cliveden can't smell for beans. You go ahead and hose yourself off."

"And what am I supposed to wear in the meantime?"

"Put on your arrival duds."

"Excuse me?"

"It's a common custom in the Cliveden cruise trade. Arriving travelers wear a complimentary outfit in the ship's colors. With passengers coming onboard at every port of call, it draws attention to you and gives everyone else a chance to welcome you."

He tapped on one of the room's storage drawers and pointed inside at several grey and white lumps about the size of my head. "After you've defunked, take one of those and smash it against your chest. Be sure and jump up before it finishes dressing you, or your shoes won't have soles. Now strip, so I can take your tux and get it cleaned and back to you before your show tomorrow."

Much as I didn't want to admit it, Billi was right. I'd slept in my tux twice since my last performance two days ago, and I didn't want to think how I must have smelled. The Pelk was going to take some getting used to, and we'd have to get a few things straight about who worked for whom, but he knew his stuff. And I was already thinking of ways he might help when I caught up with the Celestial.

"Make sure they don't use too much starch." I took off my jacket and tossed it at him.

Billi left with my clothes while I experienced my first Cliveden shower. It was thorough and effective, in much the same way a sponge bath with hot sandpaper might be. After the water drained away and the ripple door rose back up into the ceiling, I took up one of the blobs of travel clothes and whacked my chest with it. Billi needn't have warned about the shoes; the fabric expanded and grabbed at me so quickly I nearly leaped out of my skin. And just like that I was suited up in a loose-fitting, gray and white onesie that screamed *newbie* to everyone onboard. Good thing I wasn't looking for anonymity.

I couldn't figure out where the information panel in my room was, so with Reggie under my arm I set off down the corridor and paused at the first intersection where a mounted display was evident. I tapped the surface and it brightened from a slate black to a glossy version of the wall's matte café au lait.

"I'd like directions to the nearest restaurant, please."

A map appeared, bright yellow lines marked along the sides with tiny red ellipses that I understood to represent hallways and doors. A blinking star showed my position on the map, and a rippling wave flowed from that spot down the passage to my left, past two more intersections, before flowing to the right and crashing at a flashing purple rectangle. I put Reggie down and we set off; moments later we arrived. Sort of.

Our route had taken us to a passenger lounge, not a restaurant. The room had sufficient tables and seating to accommodate a hundred people, though only a couple dozen were spread out among them now. Nearly all were at some stage of a meal. I didn't see a greeter or maitre 'd, any waitstaff, or even a door that might lead to a kitchen. I sat at a small booth that offered a good view of most of the occupied tables. Reggie curled up against the booth's edge. He rested his head upon his hooves and settled down for a nap. The table was a fat ellipse of black glass with two silver, dinner plate-sized circles inlaid at the position of the ellipse's loci. I placed a hand upon the tabletop and whispered, "I'd like to see a menu. Something to eat."

Colorful icons bloomed under the glass surface representing different styles of cuisine. I recognized a few. I tapped one of those at random and the rest faded away. A menu appeared, complete with glyphs from Traveler, but I couldn't understand the names of most of the dishes—if they even were dishes. I touched the table again and said, "whatever the chef recommends," and in the next instant everything blanked out and it was just a table again. Had I ordered?

"It takes some getting used to," said a familiar voice. I looked up into the sea green eyes of Svetlana. She winked at me and slid onto the opposite bench.

"What are you doing here, Mr. Conroy? Is this why you never pulsed me?"

"Not exactly." I stopped short of adding a clever remark that would have made her smile. There was just something adorable about her that kept making me forget she was also some kind of gatekeeper or flack for the Celestial that had transformed my life. "Some random circumstances kept me from following up."

"The Cliveden don't believe in coincidence or random chance. The very idea is offensive to them."

"And yet here I am. So, uh, where's that Celestial friend of yours?"

"My *patron* isn't on this ship yet. It will rendezvous with us at an upcoming stop. It will be very pleased to find you onboard."

"I'm looking forward to it. How is it you just happened to drop in here? More coincidence?"

She laughed. It was like music, damn it. "No, not at all. I received a message that another human was onboard, so I started looking around to see who it was. You really stand out in those clothes."

"It's not like they're neon pink."

She held up a monocle on a short chain. "Take a look through here. It adjusts for the Cliveden visual spectrum."

I brought the glass to my left eye and looked down at my sleeve. Along with the grey and white cloth I saw glowing bands of purple and yellow and red, all of them writhing in slow motion. "Oh. I see." I returned the monocle.

"Yeah. Any way, when I saw it was you, I had to come right over and confirm your buffalo dog wasn't any the worse from his experience in the Glamorkan training unit."

Her concern for Reggie trumped my infatuation and helped me to think straight. "Buffalitos are much tougher than they appear. And Reggie's always been a trooper. I think he's put the incident behind him. He's fine, but thanks for asking."

"I'm really glad to hear that." She leaned across the table to peer at my buffalo dog. "Hello, Reggie. Nice to see you under drier circumstances."

Reggie opened his eyes, yawned, stretched, and popped his front legs up on the table, pulling his head up for a look around. She reached out and scritched him behind his ears with both hands. Reggie pushed off from the bench, clattered unto the table, and skittered across to her for more thorough attention. Svetlana wrapped her arms around him and pulled him onto her lap. She alternated petting him and providing vigorous belly rubs.

"You said you've been on these cruise ships before. Can you explain why this place seems more like a cafeteria than a fancy restaurant?"

"There's a nuance there that doesn't come through in Traveler, but it makes perfect sense once you get to know a thing or two about the Cliveden."

"Such as?"

"As a species, they're very xenophobic."

"They're in the transit portal business, responsible for maintaining the traffic across several dozen star systems. How can they be xenophobic?"

"Fifty-two, actually. This ship, and the others in the luxury cruising fleet, covers a circuit that includes eighty-one planets across fifty-two star systems. That's not counting inhabited moons and artificial stations where some of them make calls. And yeah, it's crazy, but the only people they like are other Cliveden. So they don't actually have any restaurants onboard."

"The ship's purser told me there were thirty-seven restaurants."

"Like I said, nuance. It kind of depends on what you think of as the salient features of a restaurant. In actuality, there are thirty-seven different kitchens. Each of these is staffed by some really incredible chefs, all of them Cliveden. You won't ever see any of them though. They keep to the crew sections of the ship, where you and I and any other non-Cliveden are forbidden from entering."

"If this isn't a restaurant, why do all the people around us have food?"

"If you define a restaurant as a place people go to have a meal, then it's a restaurant. Absolutely. If you define the word to mean a place where you pay someone else to cook for you, where someone else serves you, then no, sorry, the ship doesn't have any of those."

A spot in the middle of my forehead started to throb. "Then where did they get their food?"

Svetlana reached a hand out to one of the silver plates set flush with the tabletop. "Tah da!" At her touch the circle irised open and an actual dinner plate rose up from below, steaming with what I could only assume was the chef's choice.

"How long has that been there?"

"It's all in the timing," she said, still smiling. "Seriously, it only just arrived. The table vibrates for a moment when the order arrives. This was made at one of those thirty-seven kitchens and shuttled here via some elaborate delivery system that is probably an engineering nightmare, but so much better from the Cliveden point of view than having to interact with any icky aliens."

I frowned. "How did you know it would be under that locus?"

"You're not seated in the center of your side." She pointed to the plate. "Your slightly closer to that one, and the table can tell, so it accommodates you by putting your food within easier reach. Once you get past the fact that they can't stand to be with us, the Cliveden are very gracious hosts."

"How do you know all of this?"

Svetlana ignored the question, her smile changing to a slight frown as she bit her lower lip. "Are you going to eat that?"

"Is there a reason I shouldn't?"

"It looks . . . disgusting. Like scrapple, if scrapple was a mottled cherry color, and had tentacles."

"It's farvtesh, an Arcturan delicacy, and the parts you're mistaking for tentacles are actually a root vegetable that only grows in the polar regions of their homeworld. Arcturans won't eat animal flesh of any species; it's a spiritual thing. Eating scrapple would probably constitute a state of moral crisis."

"How do *you* know all of that?"

"I asked you first."

"I'm a philologist. I love languages, the more bizarre the better. This ship is like a lifetime of Christmas presents for me, so many different alien languages to delve into. And you can't really understand a language without delving into the culture that produced it. They might as well be wrapped up together in pretty paper topped with ribbons and bows."

I nodded. "Which explains that bit about *nuance*, I suppose."

She returned the nod, and her smile was back. "And you, and the not-scrapple?"

"I'm a foodie. Whether back home or out here beyond Human Space, I always look to see what there is to eat. And unlike our Cliveden friends, I really like meeting aliens, which helps a lot."

"Well, see, we have that in common. That's part of why the Celestial wants to see you. I'm so glad you're onboard. It's hinted about having big plans for you."

Alarm bells sounded in my head, but I kept them from showing on my face. "I'm eager to meet up with it too. And to hear about its plans."

Arcturan cuisine is always eaten without utensils, and as I broke off a piece and popped it into my mouth an aroma like cheddar cheese rose from my plate. I wondered whether Svetlana knew that or thought I had the table manners of a lout. More importantly, why did I care?

She leaned back in the booth. She stopped playing with Reggie and passed him back to me across the table. "How would you feel about a trade of information? I can fill you in on some of the linguistic and cultural aspects of the many different species traveling with us?"

I settled Reggie next to me, breaking off a root from my plate and allowing him to eat it from my hand, while mentally reviewing past disasters resulting from performing for unfamiliar aliens. "That's a compelling suggestion. You could probably give me some great insight into the audience here. What are you looking for in return?"

She gestured at the table. "I can read the menus, but that doesn't necessarily help me to order. Going back to the ocean liners on Earth, the best thing about being on a cruise is the food. I feel like I'm missing an incredible opportunity because I'm afraid to order most of it. Will you teach me a bit about alien cuisine?"

"I think we have a deal."

* * *

Svetlana made a quick list, and we then spent the next several hours crossing off the species I had already encountered while performing in Human Space, and going over cultural taboos and eccentricities of some of the others. Most of the points she had to share couldn't be incorporated into my act, but they'd keep me from making innocent glitches that could get me put off the ship at the next port—if not sooner. The aliens were more or less humanoid, favored bilateral physiognomy, and possessed a similar sensorium to humans. There were variations, everything from epidermal pigment to extra or specialized limbs to differing ranges of perception, but at a practical level most of us could use the same furniture, breathe the same air, and interact with our shared environment in comparable ways.

Their faculties and relative suggestibilities were a complete unknown. I wouldn't be sure whether or not I could hypnotize any of them until I tried. And if a particular alien didn't go under the first time, I still wouldn't be sure if it was an individual problem or indicative of the entire species. I like to bring several different people up on stage. It's a group effect kind of thing, and lessens the odds that none slip into trance. Even one not going under can seriously undermine the audience's perception of my abilities, and in the hypnosis game perception quickly flows into reality. I had to find out which of the types of aliens I hadn't met yet would make for good subjects, and I had to find out before my show.

Svetlana and I parted company, and I wandered the ship for the rest of the afternoon, poking my nose into shops and theatres, galleries and spas, gambling dens and sensory diversions. As the dinner hour approached, I tucked Reggie in the crook of my arm and together we sought out one of the larger dining areas. The tables ranged from charming meal-for-two spots to large rounds designed for somewhere between eight and fourteen to long cafeteria-style benches that could accommodate fifty or more.

I focused my attention on the benches and easily found one that met both of my criteria: it had a sampling of four or more alien species I'd never met, as well as openings for additional passengers eager to chow down.

"Hello. May I join you?"

A lemon-colored behemoth with cartoon-like porcine features and a six-pack of what I assumed to be breasts visible beneath her translucent shift patted the seat. "Make yourself comfortable, sweetling." The spindly, grayish fellow on the other side of the empty spot merely grunted.

"Thank you." I sat, tapped the table to bring up some options, and tapped a few more times to place my order. I was clearly getting the hang of the system. I settled Reggie in my lap while waiting for my meal to arrive and regarded my tablemates. The friendly, yellowy person on my left was a Wolly. Svetlana had warned me about discussing family with this species as portions of their culture practiced ritual abandonment upon reaching the age of maturity. I didn't understand it, but mentioning a Wolly's sister or father would close off any further conversation—let alone hypnotic induction.

Based on my lessons, the stick figure on my right was either a Fmoot or a Buzli; the two races had a common ancestor but had diverged several million years earlier when the Fmoot developed the technology to leave their shared homeworld and never looked back. Biologically they were the same but behaviorally the resemblance vanished. Fmoot, as a species, were your classic Type A personalities, an entire civilization of overachievers. Whereas, no Buzli ever found a task that couldn't be put off for another day. Whatever it was, it had focused its full attention on a very tall mug, sipping and slurping from it with obvious pleasure.

Across the table from me were a pair of Ersommerey, a furred species that to human perceptions resembled upright bear cubs. The two appeared to represent two different genders, and as Svetlana hadn't told me to expect anything different, I assumed them to be male and female. Sitting between them and looking uncomfortable was a Ninst, its gender unknown even to itself prior to entering into season when its papery white skin would take on one of six vivid hues, depending on which sex manifested. What made the trio particularly odd was that according to Svetlana all Ersommerey were prone to happily exaggerate anything they said, and by contrast an unmated Ninst was the very personification of sadness, it's dour response to any suggestion, opinion, or directive was *no*, and only went more negative from there.

"Did you just board, sweetling?" said the Wolly. "I don't think I've seen you here before. And I know I've only seen one of your kind ever. By the way, my name's Theodarast."

"I've met many of his kind," said one of the Ersommerey. "One time, I was stuck in a lift room with five of them. They were very standoffish, but that could have just been because of the situation. No one likes being stranded in a box that could fall and kill you just for stepping out to get a quick tipple or snack."

"I was buried alive with nine of them while on a desert excursion," said the other Ersommerey. "They didn't care for sand at all. Do you? Oh, I'm sorry, I'm Mil and this is my husband Kel. We're on our way to Sekestri."

"No you're not," said the Ninst. "This vessel doesn't go to Sekestri. Where are you going, newcomer?"

With a nod to the Wolly I said, "My name is Conroy and I boarded earlier today. I'm not sure what my final destination is to be. Mostly I just needed to leave Leftril. I'm working my passage as an entertainer. My first show is this evening. I hope you'll all attend."

"What kind of entertainment?" asked Mil. "The last time we were on a cruise, they had a fellow who was his own father, and set some of the guests on fire, and then ate them."

"Never happened," said the Ninst. "Kel, can't you make her stop?"

"Rara is right, dear. That never happened. That fellow was his own *grand*father, and he didn't actually eat the guests, he just promised they'd be on the menu the next day."

"I was with you both on your last cruise," insisted the Ninst. "That never happened."

"You were asleep," said Kel.

"Fast asleep," said Mil. "Snored so loud everyone on our corridor thought the ship had been hulled by stray debris."

"Don't mind them," said Theodarast, patting my arm with a hand that was nearly as large a small pony. "They're like this every meal. I find it anchors me to listen to them, and prepares me for whatever wonders and miracles may await. But do tell us what sorts of entertainment we can expect from you. And when and where."

"He's in the tertiary lounge," said the Fmoot or Buzli, breaking its silence. "The ship's briefing had a line about it. Something called a *suggestionater*, whatever that is."

"I don't see how that would be entertaining," said the Ninst. "In fact, it sounds stupid."

"Not everyone is open to my suggestions," I said, modulating my voice, and attempting to catch the eye of each of them in turn. "I've never attempted it with any of your peoples, but I'd be curious to try."

When you make your living hypnotizing aliens, there are things you learn to look for. We all have patterns of unconscious behavior in response to particular directions of conversation. Take control of the conversation and you can learn how someone is wired. Similarly, observing their gaze and patterns of intonation can reveal whether someone will make a good subject. Over the course of a wonderful meal of Ploger omelet—the eggs are usually only available on worlds occupied by Clarkesons; they're each about the size of a human thumb, cooking up to produce a creamy texture with a tart flavor—and fresh baked Sisal bread—rather like a cross between whole wheat and a chocolate soufflé, and especially popular among Taurians—slathered in something very much like butter, and a pitcher of some kind of fruit juice—I satisfied myself that all five of them had the potential I needed. I'd know better come show time. They all agreed to attend. The Ersommerey were confident that I could easily suggestionate the entire audience that they were all newborn fish. The Ninst expressed equal certainty I would fail but gain the moral backing of the passengers for the effort.

I left them with the idea that even though it would prove difficult to do so, they should each endeavor to arrive early and hand me a piece of flatware, and that as the day wore on, the longer they held onto their particular utensil, the more open to my suggestions they'd be. They all nodded and laughed at the notion, but I was pleased to discover several utensils had vanished from the table before I finished eating.

CHAPTER SEVEN

Better Than Steerage

THE TERTIARY LOUNGE onboard the *Shpeshnoltoc* reminded me of a proving ground. It was the cellar, the practice room, the place where seasoned performers went to break in new material, and rookies attempted to break into show business. It was the worst of all possible venues, a large room with bad acoustics occupied by people who had as much interest chatting among themselves as listening to whatever unfortunate soul perched upon the stage. The stage itself was a bare, rectangular platform at one end of the room, about a meter higher than the rest of the place and scarcely four meters wide and two deep. The floor of it bore the stains of whatever gunk had been thrown at performers by unhappy audiences past. That didn't bode well. Worse still, all the acts had the same duration, just over five minutes. That's enough time for a comedian to tell a few jokes, a musician to sing a song, a juggler to toss assorted objects around. It is not enough time for a decent hypnotic induction, let alone manage to do anything interesting once it's done.

The custom here was for all the acts to come on stage at the beginning for a quick introduction. This gave the audience members some forewarning of what was to come and the option to stay or flee. After the intro and before the first entertainment began, the rest of us stepped down and found seats along the room's back wall to wait for our respective turns. The performers had been ordered randomly and I was lucky number thirteen of eighteen acts appearing in the lounge that night. It could have been worse; the impressionist who preceded me had to go on immediately after two other impressionists, and none of them was very good. My other predecessors included two alien variations on torch singers, a regurgitater, a very amusing Wolly lecturer who gave new meaning to the term *shaggy dog story*, a puppeteer, an Arcturan dance troupe, eight-limbed flame jugglers, and two comedians of different species (neither of whom was funny).

Somewhere between the dancers and the unfunny jokesters each of my five dinner partners found me among the other waiting performers and came to wish me luck. As they shook my hand, patted my arm or back, or gave me a warm smile, each also slipped me a piece of flatware. The pessimistic Ninst handed me a soup spoon even as it assured me that no matter how bad I was the audience didn't have any expectations and it would all end well.

"You don't really believe that, do you?" I asked it. The Ninst paused, gave me a carving knife and a ladle, and shook its head. Then it blinked once, and left, jangling slightly as it did so. My trepidation vanished; I wasn't going to need to do an induction after all.

The third impressionist bombed worse than the two before, and was rewarded for his efforts with catcalls, the sounds of fists pounding on tables, and a pelting of vegetable pudding that smelled like week old fish mixed with shoe polish. That was my cue to go on. The emcee for the lounge introduced me by promising the audience a special treat, playing up my exotic status as a human being as much as my talents as a hypnotist, and mispronouncing my name as the *Ambulatory Conway*. Not the best of starts.

The audience had grown surly during the last act, and those that weren't grumbling amongst themselves had gone on to other conversations with their tablemates. The tertiary lounge was the very definition of a *tough room*. As I bounded onto the stage I caught a glimpse of Billi sitting on the lap of a very attractive female Glamorkan. We caught each other's eye and he gave me a thumbs-up. A smattering of polite applause greeted me.

"Gentle beings, I am the Amazing Conroy, and for those of you who may not have heard of me, I am a hypnotist. In the space of just a few minutes I am going to take a volunteer from among you and alter reality before your very eyes. Right now, as the sound of my voice carries throughout this room, my powers are focusing on a specific member of the this audience, changing that individual's very being. I am causing joy and delight and optimism to flood that person's heart like never before, a feeling of such well-being that is building, burbling, about to explode. Let it out! You know who you are, you can feel the transformation happening! Don't try to keep it inside any longer. Share it with the rest of us right now!"

On cue, the Ninst leaped from its seat, forks and spoons flying from the sleeves of its clothing. "I've never felt so happy," it exclaimed, as tears ran down its face. "Everything is so wonderful, bright and good."

"Of course it is. Gentle beings, please, some applause for this happy-go-lucky Ninst in our midst, surely something none of us has ever seen before. Let's give it some encouragement to join me here on stage and discover what other wonders await us."

The audience burst into applause. Svetlana had been right; an upbeat Ninst was an oxymoron that resonated for the rest of the audience. I'd won them over in my first minute on stage, and by the end of the remaining four I had them eating out of my hand as enthusiastically as Reggie did.

I returned to my cabin after my triumphant opening performance. I'd left the place looking like a tropical island beach when I'd stopped in to get my tux. Now I found Reggie sleeping under the shade of some palm trees. Gentle waves lapped nearby. I loosened my bow tie, kicked off my socks and shoes, and wriggled my toes in some pink sand. I was feeling pretty good.

Someone knocked. The sound came from midair. Reggie woke and barked, scrambling around in search of the noise. I put the beach on hold and opened the door. A short Cliveden stood there, likely the same youth who had earlier walked Billi and me to our cabins. He bowed his head to me and kept his gaze down, as if inspecting the frozen wave.

"Mr. Conroy, the Captain has sent me to you. She requests your presence, and bids you permit me to take you to an audience chamber where she may discuss with you such topics as occupy her thoughts. Now, if you please."

"The captain wants to see me? Are you sure you have that right? Thindar po Rens was quite adamant that he was the only Cliveden we would meet on the ship. You're not going to get into trouble for speaking to me, are you?"

"No, sir. Under normal circumstances, what the purser told you would be the rule. But . . . the Captain is free to make up or change rules as she sees fit. Won't you come with me please?"

I was pretty sure that lizard people couldn't sweat, but the youngster in front of me was making a valiant effort all the same. It probably had something to do with getting me to the captain as quickly as possible and here I was asking pointless questions as the seconds ticked by. I waved for Reggie to follow me and we departed the tropical stateroom.

A short ways down the corridor my guide slipped through a narrow door that I hadn't even noticed. It opened onto a parallel corridor meant exclusively for Cliveden. The instant we stepped through I felt an itch. The sensation didn't go away, but it didn't grow any worse either, only wandered here and there over my skin, a distracting tingle that had no noticeable cause other than our location in crewspace. If Reggie felt it, he gave no sign. He trotted along beside me, head turning side to side to take everything in. Reddish light reflected off a faint bas relief on the walls and ceiling, intricate swirls in fractal patterns that pulled at the eye, challenging in the dimness. The floor absorbed nearly all sound. Its vermillion gravel crunching faintly beneath my feet; every step created tiny plumes of fine dust that wafted a sweet, citrus odor into the air. There were no ninety-degree angles. The sand curved to meet the walls, curling up in rippling scallops on either side. Above my head, at the junction where walls should have met ceiling, corrugated pipes or tubes flowed along both sides, one large and two smaller, looking a mottled black and green in the dim red light. The air here was hot and dry, reminding me of the Arizona desert back on Earth. I cataloged all the details against the unlikely day that I might perform before an audience of Cliveden; a part of my brain already planning suggestions that involved soggy swamps and wintery slush.

The Cliveden didn't speak, didn't look at me. He just kept walking ahead of me, setting the pace, his feet dragging silently through the gravel. The back of my neck tingled, like someone was following me. After a good half kilometer without passing a single doorway or branching corridor, he stopped. Reggie and I did the same.

"Now what?" I said.

"Press the entry call," said the Cliveden. "I cannot leave until you pass inside."

"Entry call? Pass inside where?"

The alien nodded and raised a hand toward me. Reflex made me step back, but I needn't have; he wasn't going for me. His fingers came down upon a portion of the wall on my left, tracing a section of the design.

"Sorry. They said you might not be able to see it, but I didn't believe them. The mark must be beyond your spectrum."

A section of the wall lost some of its opacity, and from its outline light flooded the corridor. A voice followed.

"Do come in, Mr. Conroy. We have much to discuss."

Reggie glanced up at me, dancing from foot to foot, eager to move forward but reluctant to do so before I led the way. I leaned in, easing head-first into what still looked like a solid—albeit translucent—wall. As I broke the plane of it, the itching stopped. The air was cooler on this side, the light brighter and less actinic. My feet arrived on a solid floor, free from shifting gravel. Reggie scampered in a moment later. I was in a parlor of sorts, lacquered wood, dark velvet curtains, and stylish wallpaper. It could have been taken from an illustration of a book on nineteenth century homes of Boston's Back Bay, and it probably had been, as I recalled Billi's remarks about the ship's smart walls. A pair of vintage chairs, all scrolled wood and embroidered cushions, faced one another across a low table. The nearer chair sat empty. A well-muscled Cliveden occupied the other. She wore the same black shorts, sleeveless shirt, and gloves I'd seen on my guide and the purser, but hers had been shot through here and there with metallic blue beads. Her scales were a complex pattern of dark violet fading into black. A coronal crest rose above her head like a proud flag. Her black eyes had the barest scattering of gold flecks.

"Make yourself comfortable." Her Traveler lacked the faint sibilant background I'd heard from other Cliveden. "May I offer you a beverage? Wine? Tea? Sarsaparilla?"

"Whatever you're having." I settled into the open chair. Reggie leaped into my lap, turned in place, and sat facing our host, giving her his full attention. I did the same; she was only the third Cliveden to speak to me—two more than I'd been led to expect. I'd been too worried about Billi suffocating to study Thindar po Rens when we'd met, and the youngling who'd led me here had said as little as possible and wouldn't make eye contact. The captain had no such problem; she studied me intently and I returned the favor, much as I had with the Ninst and Ersommerey the day before. I might never actually have the opportunity to hypnotize a Cliveden, but I wanted to learn whatever I could all the same.

One gloved hand tapped the table twice, and at each spot she touched there rose a frothing glass containing what was probably the closest thing to Uncle Waldo's raspberry root beer that I was likely to see this side of Human Space. I reached for mine, nodded to her as I raised it to my lips, and drank. It went beyond bitter, just this side of vile. Either my host had gotten the recipe wrong, or I held in my hands the reason the American Old West had died out.

"Thank you for joining me, Mr. Conroy. I am Captain Telfano sa Rens. My mother was captain of *Shpeshnoltoc* before me, and her mother before that, and so on, going back to the ship's maiden voyage some seventeen generations ago. I have had a long and satisfying life as captain, and I near the end of my span. Within a six-year we will dock at the same port as *The Opulent Fog*, where my daughter currently serves as under-captain. She will be promoted to this ship, and the reins will pass from my hands. My people are long-lived by your standards, and in all the years of that life, I have met fewer than twelve twelves of beings who were not Cliveden, fewer than one a year. And so you may well be asking yourself, why I sent for you." She reached out for her glass, watching me over the rim as she drank half of it down.

"I confess, I've been thinking of nothing else since receiving your summons."

"Please, invitation."

"I beg your pardon, ma'am. Invitation."

Captain Telfano gestured with her sarsaparilla, taking in our surroundings. "As you can see, despite my genetic predisposition to avoid contact with aliens beings, I am nonetheless a student of the galaxy. Few in this part of space have visited your homeworld, and fewer still of your species have ventured out this far. And yet my resources are such that I can provide you with the familiar comforts of your home. I do so, happily, because I see a rare opportunity, one of mutual benefit."

"I'm just a simple entertainer, Captain. I doubt I have anything that would interest someone like yourself, unless you seek the diversion of a performance. Or did you want me to explain the principles underlying my work?"

"You are being too modest, and not completely honest. I confess, I do not know if your family name is a common one among humans, but my studies have taught me that some time in the past twelve-year a human named Conroy acquired a specialized type of creature from the Arconi. A buffalo dog. That worthy then went on to break their monopoly and build a small empire for himself, which has since crumbled. Now here in my parlor I sit with a human bearing the name Conroy and he possesses a buffalo dog. Is this coincidence?"

"No, Captain, I am that Conroy," I said.

"I do not know the particulars that brought us together, sir, nor does it matter to me. I know little of the Arconi—their worlds lie further away than your own, and I understand them to be somewhat parochial and not fond of travel—nothing of their culture, their arts, their language has found its way to me. But I have heard of this creature that you have brought with you. And I wonder if you will indulge my curiosity, and test a hypothesis that has become a distraction to me."

She rose fluidly despite her century and more of age, and glided to a spot on the wall behind her. Her fingertips danced, pressing places that all looked the same to me, but may have had some hidden markings or symbols in a frequency of light I couldn't see. She followed this by placing her palm against the wall. A seam appeared and a wooden cube popped out, less than five centimeters on a side. She handed the object to me before returning to her chair. "Open it."

I rolled the box around in my hands. It changed weight as it tumbled. The box's faces were unmarked, fine-grained and smooth, cool to my touch. As I handled it I triggered some mechanism and one side flipped open. A faint blue light shone from within.

"Pour it out onto your palm. It's perfectly safe."

I tilted the box and a tiny glop of liquid blue metal flowed into my cupped hand. It gleamed like mercury, if you could add a sky blue tint to mercury. And it was heavy, heavier than anything this size had a right to be.

"I've never seen anything like this." Reggie craned his head nearly all the way around to look and sniff.

"It is the product of a singular species in this part of the galaxy. The Veng. They call it *drift juice*, though it is more typically known by the slang, *liquid gravity*. Liters of it form a critical component in the drive mechanism of Cliveden transit craft, such as this very ship. Fractional drops can be put to use in myriad devices. And, much like your Arconi did with their buffalo dogs, the Veng maintain a strict monopoly. The similarity does not end there. While your creatures were fabulously expensive, drift juice would make them appear cheap. For the quantity you hold in your hand, less than a cubic centimeter, I could buy a thousand Arconi buffalo dogs!"

The comparison so startled me I nearly spilled the glop. By rights I should have, but it clung to my hand. Or no, more accurately, my hand clung to the glop. It was a peculiar sensation. Holding the box in my other hand, I scrapped the blue gunk along one open edge, coaxing it back inside. As if alive, it cooperated and slipped inside. I returned the cube to the Captain.

"What does this have to do with me or my buffalito, ma'am?"

"My studies tell me that your creature is impenetrable to conventional scanning technologies. Is that true?"

I nodded. "So far as I know, yes."

"Quite the opposite is the case for drift juice. It can be detected in any medium down to a concentration of one part per trillion. But back to your creature: whatever he eats, he converts into oxygen, is that also correct?"

I nodded again.

"Very good. One last question: have you ever found him to devour something, but not eat it?"

"I don't understand what you mean, Captain."

"Mmm, a limit perhaps of the language we are using. Can he . . . put something in his mouth, without consuming it?"

I was about to answer in the negative, but stopped. There'd been a time back on Earth when I'd been attacked and knocked out by a tranq-dart. In defending me, Reggie had bitten off my assailant's fingers and held them in his mouth for hours until I'd regained consciousness. "There's precedent for it, but it's uncommon."

"Excellent. Would you be open to exploring this further? I'd like you to see if your creature can ingest drift juice without performing his miraculous conversion to oxygen. It's a highly complex molecule. The Veng boast that the process of its creation occupies years, and that once formed it can never be reduced. They would have us believe it is the most precious substance in all creation, and the inability of any other race to so much as break it down into constituent parts suggests they may not be exaggerating. I wish to see if in fact it is too complex for your creature to digest."

"Toward what end, Captain?"

"As you have never had dealings with Cliveden before, understand that we lack subtlety. We do not waste time in haggling or dissembling. It is not our nature. Accordingly, I will be blunt. For now, I wish to satisfy my curiosity as to whether the thing can be done. Depending on that outcome, I may want to engage your services in an illegal enterprise."

"You have the wrong man. I'm just a hypnotist."

"Don't insult me, sir. More accurately we both know that is just one face you wear. You possess another. Onboard my ship I may find the talents of Conroy the hypnotist a useful diversion for my passengers, but I have a more pressing need for Conroy the smuggler. I am aware how you broke the Arconi monopoly. You walked right into their midst and simply took a buffalo dog, brazen as you please. You are two creatures at once, one inside the other. The smuggler may be hiding inside the hypnotist, but he is there. I might wish to let him out for a time."

I shrugged. No point in denying what she already knew to be true. "You want to create drift juice on your own and break the Veng monopoly."

"If only it were that simple. Unfortunately, drift juice doesn't reproduce like your creature there. But if I am right, he could be used as the perfect smuggling tool. A mouthful of drift juice would make the entire venture pay for itself many times over. And, if successful, it could be repeated again and again."

"You'd still need access to the stuff though."

"When detection is so easy, protection becomes very lax. The Veng store their treasure in vast tanks, dribbling it out as needed to ships that call at port. Acquiring it onworld would be simplicity, requiring only a reason for you to be there, and I can provide you with that reason. Passing it through the sensors at customs is where the impossibility lies. Unless it were to be hidden inside your creature."

"Why would I be on a Veng world?"

"Easily answered, Mr. Conroy. I'm moving you out of the tertiary lounge. You're going to perform for some of my most prestigious passengers, a private show. Among them will be a Veng known as the Elder Glarp. You have only to dazzle him with your talents. His own nature will do the rest."

Someone was knocking on my door again, waking me up from a sound sleep. Could the captain be summoning me back again? If I didn't answer, would whoever was out there go away?

"Open up, Conroy. I have booze!" Billi paused for a reply. I gave none, and the knocking resumed. For a little guy, he really knew how to pound a door.

"All right, I'm coming. Room, open the door."

A portion of the horizon dissolved, allowing a rectangle of light into an otherwise dark sky as seen from a grassy meadow on one of the moons orbiting the Taurian homeworld. Billi's six-limbed silhouette waved at me, backlit by the ship's corridor. His feet made no sound as he stepped into the tall grass.

"You killed 'em last bite."

"Thanks. But the rest of the entertainment didn't set a very high bar. If you can get me more time, I can do a much better show."

"Spoken like a real pro. I like that about you, and that's why I've been haggling with our friend Thindar. He's a sharp tack, but I'm sharper. I threw that bearitocracy stuff back at him."

"Bear wha—" I stopped myself, and did the mental switch of sounds. Images of an ursine royal court slipped from my brain as swiftly as they'd appeared. "How so?"

"You've been bumped up. Tonight you perform for a select group of first class passengers on the primary stage. And the purser also upgraded your accommodations to a two-room apartment in that section of the ship. Ask any wall panel and it will guide you right to it. What did I tell ya? You're on your way, pal."

Reggie had awakened at Billi's entrance and jumped off the bed. During the Pelk's announcements he had made a frustrated attempt to graze on the illusionary grass beneath us. He barked once and butted his forehead against my knee, a clear signal that if I didn't get him something to eat, he'd find something himself. I didn't care how smart the walls here were, they wouldn't be able to get out of the way of a hungry buffalito.

"Oh, I almost forgot. I have a present for you." Billi took a box out of one of his many pockets and handed it to me. It looked like an antique, leather wallet.

"What is it?"

"Collapsible luggage. We got off Leftril in a rush, with only the clothes on your back. I get that you like to travel light, but you're not a Pelk; you can't get by with just pockets. Go on, just give it a thump with your thumb."

I did so and the thing unfolded and expanded into a reasonable facsimile of my old carpetbag.

"I don't know what to say, Billi. Thanks."

"Just get yourself some stuff. We have a generous line of credit with the ship as of today. Buy whatever you want."

"I don't have a use for much *stuff*," I said. "All I need is a set of traveling clothes, a pair of comfortable shoes, a pair of dress shoes, my tuxedo, and my kit. And Reggie needs even less. You never know when you're going to have to leave in a hurry."

"Conroy, Conroy, Conroy. I was so sure you'd say that, I didn't bother to get you a bigger bag. But you have to stop thinking that way. That was before. You don't have to worry about any bisunderstandings with the law from here on out. I'm watching out for you, ensuring you play classy joints, quality places. And part of your job is to look the part. When you're out and about on the ship, bumping elbows with them first class passengers, you can't be looking like a schmo. Don't worry, I've been browsing through the shops here—did you know they got something like eighteen full-service stores? I'll find something to suit you and have it sent to your new room. And if I don't, I'll put one of the ship's tailors to work on a custom job. I've got your sizes, don't worry."

"What do you mean you have my sizes?"

"What kind of agent would I be if I didn't? Go off and bingle with the passengers. Start working up your act for tonight. You've arrived, Conroy, this is the big time."

I queried a wall station and found my way to a suite of rooms more lavish than anything I'd experienced. The bathroom was larger than my original cabin. In addition to a massive bedroom and sitting room, there was a child's room off to one side complete with a play wall of brightly colored, geometrically-shaped protuberances that were in reality activation switches which caused the room to fill with an assortment of alarming honks and beeps and buzzes coupled with patterns of flashing color. Reggie needed only a minute to learn to butt his head against them to achieve new combinations of stimulation. The effects changed with each use.

I worried he might get over-stimulated, but stopped when he took a bite out of cherry-red dodecahedron that had just blasted him in the face with a gust of minty air. The knobs weren't holographic effects from a smart wall, and like the Glamorkan toilet he'd destroyed earlier, I didn't want to think how much it would cost to repair them. As Reggie swallowed his mouthful the rest of the thing fell from the wall. A tiny red bud marked where it had been. The bud buzzed and expanded into a perfect duplicate of the earlier shape. Reggie gave the replacement doodad a quizzical look and I relaxed. The state-of-the-art kids' room was kid-proof.

Not that I *needed* a separate room for my buffalito. He'd done just fine hanging out in our class eight room. Then I noticed a familiar wooden cube in one corner of the playroom and it made sense. A separate room with all these bells and whistles—literally—could also mask an array of other sensors, and keep track of the fortune in drift juice in that box if or when the goods mysteriously vanished from detection.

I'd been going over ways that Reggie might manage the trick. This was the room where he'd learn to do it. Later though; I still had to prep for tonight's show. An information panel in the sitting room gave me directions to a nearby salon—which in Traveler translated as the *intercoursarium*—where I could expect to meet and mingle with various first-class passengers, my potential *volunteers* for the evening's show.

None of the passengers in the intercoursarium would have been down in the tertiary lounge the night before. That show had gone well, but I needed to make a bigger splash with the next one, and wanted a bit of the old meet and greet over the course of some hors d'oeuvres and a delightful beverage. I had Reggie tucked under my arm, and even if he wasn't devouring things or farting oxygen, he had enough innate cuteness to break any ice and start a conversation. That would create an opportunity to size up volunteers and begin planting suggestions.

The entrance to the salon rippled into view as I rounded a final curve. It was a water door, and although mammalian races found it a bit odd, to the sapient amphibians of the galaxy it was the best thing since sliced bread. I didn't need to, but I took a deeper breath before stepping into it. Reggie bleated as we pierced the surface and soaked ourselves leaving the corridor and crossing the threshold. The effect was something like falling into a kiddie pool and coming out the other end, except on the vertical plane and completely dry after the dousing. Glancing around inside the intercoursarium I noticed applications for drift juice where it fell into the hands of the idle rich. Localized gravity generators throughout the room created shafts and tunnels and complex caverns of crystal blue water, pockets and columns which, like the door, stood utterly self-contained. One could walk through the air filled portions of the room without a need to encounter any of the water, or step, dive, or burst into a fluid structure at will. Scattered throughout both areas of density an assortment of the galaxy's beautiful people sat in floating divans and chatted with one another while they sipped nonalcoholic beverages from siphon bundles. Billi had warned me that the Cliveden had a profoundly toxic reaction to alcohol, and anyone found with so much as a jigger of whiskey or a glass of wine was assumed to be an assassin and immediately prosecuted as such. The ship's captain acted as judge and jury.

I set Reggie down on the carpeted floor. The place was pretty quiet. A five-person Sasnakian sex wrestling team—one of the other acts on this evening's ticket—was the only source of noise. They had pushed together several tables and were using them as a practice stage. I surveyed the rest of the place, finding it nearly empty of other occupants. I spotted a trio of splashing Taurians, a pair of Wolly pressing foreheads and whispering in a heated debate, a couple other tables with handfuls of aliens of species I didn't recognize, and . . . Svetlana? She noticed me at the same moment—perhaps my entering splash had caught her attention.

"Reggie!" Her squeal of his name sent my buffalo dog stampeding her way, straight through a shimmering column of water and out the other side. He sprang onto the lower edge of her lounge chair and scrambled up her legs to her outstretched arms. I followed more slowly, taking my time and the drier route. I slid into a free chair I snagged along the way. With a few flicks of the controls on its side I locked myself into a fashionably slow conversational orbit around Svetlana's seat and watched her as she scratched Reggie's beard and murmured to him in baby talk.

"I didn't expect to find you here in this bar. Are you a first class passenger?"

My chair hovered slightly higher, and had come around to directly face hers. She stopped playing with Reggie and looked up at me, freezing me with a disapproving lift of one pale eyebrow and the gleam of green eyes. I found myself distracted for a moment by her freckles.

"It's not a bar," she said, correcting me in that tone I'd already dubbed her *lecture* voice. "It's a intercoursarium."

"There's no such word. And if there were, it would refer to having sex in a fishbowl."

"Conversation, not sex."

"Sex can be conversational, especially if you use the right verbs and know how to really conjugate." I didn't say this in a smarmy or lecherous kind of way. I did it with an ironic lilt in my voice and a wry lift of one eyebrow. I don't know why I bothered.

Svetlana shook her head in disagreement and the myriad tight curls of her hair rippled in support of her. Yeah, adorable.

"Conjugation can be sexy, but not in all languages. English barely uses conjugations. Russian conjugations are interesting, but I wouldn't call them sexy."

English was my native language, and I'd picked up a bit of Russian in years past. I'd long since learned to consider it gauche to use Earth languages in space; we had both been speaking Traveler.

"And to answer your earlier question, no, I'm not traveling first class, or rather, I wasn't. Someone came by this morning to inform me that I'd been upgraded. Something to do with the ship's sensors. Do you know anything about that?"

I shrugged. "I was upgraded. My agent told me that the ship would recognize me and allow me access to wherever I needed to go at this level. Maybe it doesn't have enough data to distinguish between humans; I wouldn't be surprised if we're the first two to travel on the *Shpeshnoltoc*. Maybe it was just easier to upgrade you as well."

"In that case, thank you very much. I guess I have to forgive you for calling this place a bar. The Cliveden don't even have a word for such a thing in any of their languages."

"What do you know about the languages of the Cliveden? What about their conjugations?"

Those green eyes twinkled. "Have you ever heard anyone speak a Cliveden language?"

"Only the Cliveden on the ship."

"Then you haven't. It's considered a moral outrage for them to use any of their native languages unless they're by themselves. Entire family lines have been condemned because a single member was overheard by an alien that had gone unnoticed at first."

"But I've *heard* them talking."

"I'm sure you did. Probably in Shpoto or Hrel."

"What was that? Shoo podo? Hell?"

Svetlana cleared her throat and manipulated her divan's controls to create a tidal lock with mine, leaving us face to face, then she set us on a new, joint orbit through the intercoursarium. "Shpoto and Hrel," she repeated. "They're creoles, trade languages like Traveler, that developed to facilitate communication where different alien species gathered."

What were the odds that of the handful of humans that had probably ventured out to this part of the galaxy, the one that I'd meet up with would be a xenophilic polyglot? Her lecture continued.

"The Cliveden have never ventured anywhere near Human Space, but they have considerable contact with the Sasnak and the Flenk. The Sasnak use Traveler, but they also often use Shpoto. The Flenk have never been to Human Space and don't interact much with anyone who does. I've never met one who knew anyone who spoke Traveler, other than me leastways. When they're out and about in the galaxy they tend to speak Hrel, and since the Flenk provide maintenance services for Cliveden transit craft, the Cliveden also speak Hrel, at least when dealing with the Flenk."

It hadn't occurred to me before, but I never imagined that there were other common tongues. The galaxy's a big place, and for an Earthborn human I'd seen a surprisingly large portion of it. I just assumed that everyone would be able to speak Traveler. That had worked fine in Human Space and the immediate ripples beyond. I'd left all of that far behind. "You're telling me there are places where different species come together and none of them speak Traveler?"

Maybe there was a delayed effect to the wry eyebrow raise and ironic tone because she actually smiled at my question. When I didn't return the smile her expression grew pained.

"You're serious? Of course there are. Traveler accounts for less than eight percent of the trade languages spoken in the galaxy."

"How do you know that? How could anyone know that?" Reggie squirmed in Svetlana's lap and turned to look at me. Either he agreed with Svetlana's sudden reassessment of my intelligence, or was just reacting to the upset in my voice. He yipped once, and then again.

"I asked my patron." As if that explained it all.

I might as well have stepped into one of the room's static columns of water. "The Celestial. The one you want me to meet . . . That's my point. If Elroy is going to talk to me, it must speak Traveler. If a sentient being of that magnitude speaks Traveler, wouldn't it make sense that—"

"Elroy? Don't call it that." Svetlana's jaw dropped. She had perfect teeth, even the molars way in back. "It doesn't have a name. It's too vast a being to have a name. And the reason it would speak Traveler to you is because that's a language you know. It could pull it out of your brain. It can speak whatever it needs to speak, to increase the likelihood that we'll be able to understand it."

"How do you know that?"

Svetlana shrugged. "That's how it learned to talk to me."

Before I could ask her to elaborate, one of the Sasnakian sex wrestlers slipped his opponent's erotic hold, and vaulted free like a bar of soap in a squeezing fist. One hundred kilos of sweaty, bluish-violet alien plunged into and through an adjacent column of water and rained down upon us. Svetlana barely saw him in time to lift Reggie up over her head and out of harm's way before the fellow's bald head landed in her lap. His right knee landed squarely in my gut, knocking the breath out of me. The alien's right knee was followed in quick order by his left knee as he rolled over onto his back and gazed up at her like a lover lounging at a picnic.

"Excuse me, but you know you have the most beautiful eyes," said the Sasnakian. "In the jungles of my island home, we have a flower that blooms but once every hundred years and only for a day. Birds that drink of its nectar are believed to become immortal. Its fragrance is said to make strangers fall instantly in love."

Svetlana smiled down at the alien. "Why are you telling me this, o thou wrestler from the islands of the middle west?"

"Your eyes. They are the exact same color as the petals of the flower. And though I have only seen that rare bloom in images and never directly, I have gazed upon your eyes, and I know that were I a bird, a kiss from you would leave me immortal."

I groaned. They ignored me. The guy was obvious, but give him credit, he was smooth too.

"But you're not a bird." Svetlana's smile widened.

"No, I am not a bird. I am but a stranger. And gazing up into your eyes and breathing in your scent I have lost myself to you. Please, tell me you feel it too. Tell me you feel love."

"Oh please," I said, and shoved the wrestler's legs off of me, dumping his lower half onto the floor. "He's an erotic wrestler. His sexual organs are all internal bands of muscle. The way he's built, your classic Greco-Roman clutching and squeezing is the equivalent of advanced foreplay. He pretty much just arrived fresh from a public orgy."

"That doesn't mean my eyes aren't making him fall in love with me." Svetlana's voice had turned into a coo.

The alien nodded sincerely and placed one hand upon his shiny solar plexus. "It's true, I swear. Here, give me your hand, press here and you will see the truth of it."

Svetlana's hands had remained above her head during the entire exchange. She lowered them now, drawing the wrestler's attention to Reggie. "I'm sorry, truly I am, but my hands are full at the moment." She pouted and gave the squirming buffalo dog a shake not far from the alien's face.

"Then promise me you'll come and see me perform tonight. I will dedicate the match to you, and knowing you are there watching me, I will wrestle with the strength and stamina of ten. All for you."

"I do like stamina." She encouraged the lout with a wink. "I suppose I could come by and watch you perform. I'm sure it'll be very stimulating."

"Until tonight then, my flower. I will hold you in my heart." He jumped then, doing a back flip in midair, and bounding over to the rest of his team. Svetlana watched him the whole way there.

Reggie barked softly and she shook her head. "I'm sorry. What were we talking about?" She gave the buffalito's beard another scritch and handed him back to me.

"Nothing important. I actually came here hoping to check out some of the people that might come to my show tonight, test their suggestibility, maybe prime a few. But it looks like I picked the wrong time for that."

"Not by much," she said. "You're just a little early. If this intercoursarium is anything like the one I visited on my last ship it will be packed in less than an hour. A lot of these races don't like to engage in serious conversation over breakfast. It's a digestive belief sort of thing."

"So once the main breakfast service ends—"

She nodded. "Yep, this place will be stuffed with thirty or forty different alien races. I'll probably spend my whole day here, just soaking it all in." She paused, cocked her head a bit and then said, "what do you want to talk about until the throng starts to arrive?"

I smiled, looking into her eyes and wondering if the wrestler had made up that bit about the flower, or if it had been true.

"Tell me more about Shpoto and Hrel," I said, and might even have actually been interested.

CHAPTER EIGHT

Friend or Faux Pas

As Svetlana predicted, the intercoursarium soon flooded with people of all description. Some I'd encountered years ago, like Clarkesons and Phloke and Taurians. Others I'd only recently met onboard ship like Wollys and Ersommerey. But there were plenty I'd never seen yet. Many followed the general humanoid shape that accounted for better than ninety percent of known sapients, walking around with a variety of skin tones, feathers, scales, and fur. Other shapes and sizes were represented too, the only limitation seeming to be the ability to breathe the common atmosphere on the ship.

The galaxy has more than two hundred billion stars. Human beings have met aliens who have met aliens who have met aliens who come from around a million of those. We live in a big place. Experiencing even an infinitesimal fraction, say by sharing a salon with a couple hundred alien beings, still overwhelms me. As eager as I was to meet, chat, and size up many of them, they were even more eager to get to know me! Svetlana and I were like conquering heroes returning to a small town. More than celebrities, we were exotic mysteries. Everyone else here had encountered, socialized, fought, or done business with every other race present. Humans were newcomers to these parts, making us the stars of the intercoursarium.

Svetlana dazzled them with her natural charm, and followed it up with her quick ear and quicker study of language. She had them laughing in ones and twos with obscure multilingual puns that left everyone else in the group confused. Then she'd turn to the next handful and tell one that they could understand, leaving the first group as baffled. I watched and listened more than I talked. A good hypnotist has to be able to catalog communication, both verbal and nonverbal responses, particularly unconscious ones. An ordinary conversation breaks down into parts: Pitch and rhythm of speech, word choice and pacing, facial expressions and eye movements, kinesics and proxemics, micro-gestures, all that sort of thing. In hypnosis any of these can offer insights into how a person thinks. Knowing how someone thinks in turn provides the key to manipulating them into greater suggestibility. With aliens it comes down to figuring out what's important and what's utterly irrelevant.

I'd have been more than content to just sit back and observe, gathering more data points and building up ever better models of how all the various aliens communicated and noting patterns of behavior I could spin for the amusement of an audience. That opportunity vanished when Svetlana mentioned I would be performing that very night. In an instant everyone wanted to know what kind of entertainment I'd be providing, how it worked, what they might expect, how long my show would last, would there be more than a single performance, was it going to be interactive or passive, could they volunteer, would it hurt, would they like it, how had I come to be involved in such an unusual profession, and on and on and on. When they weren't pinging with questions about me, they wanted to know everything about Reggie! Where had he come from, how had I gotten him, did he really eat anything, wasn't that dangerous, how much could he eat, how exactly did he convert it all into oxygen, was *that* dangerous, did he know any tricks, was he for sale, where could they get a buffalo dog, how long did they live, were they good with children, how smart was he, and more.

Forced out of my data-collecting I smiled and moved on to stage two. This involved subtly testing the limited models and patterns I'd been able to construct, fine-tuning my understanding where I had something wrong, pushing the limits to see how far I had something right. It requires a kind of mental detachment, to focus sufficient attention to be analyzing another being's communicative stylings while modifying and tweaking your own to measure the resulting effect, all the while still managing a conversation sufficiently engaging to let you do the first bit. Like anything else, it requires practice. I've never met anyone who could just jump on a unicycle and start riding it the first time out, let alone while juggling an assortment of mixed fruit. You start out small, breaking it down into simple pieces, master each piece, and one by one combine them, until there you are. Like I told Thindar po Rens, I'd been at this for twenty years. I knew my profession, and I was good at it.

It was exhilarating. Maybe it was having Svetlana there as an audience, maybe it was the natural rush of being the center of attention, or maybe it was simply that I hadn't had an opportunity to exercise this particular skill set, at this level, in a long while. I spent four hours in that chaotic press of alien races reveling in the diversity of the galaxy while I built my act. The Amazing Conroy was back!

Eventually, people drifted away. Everyone promised to attend the show. Exhaustion swept over me; I'd never gotten a chance for a meal. I made plans with Svetlana to meet her the next morning and begin her instruction into the wonders of alien cuisine, then took Reggie back to our suite. Along the way I tapped an information panel and ordered something from room service to meet me there.

I took Reggie into the kiddy room, snatched up the box of drift juice and sat in the middle of the floor in a lazy man's lotus position. Reggie obligingly sat on my legs and gazed up at me as if to ask what was up. I opened the box and with a little shaking and jiggling succeeded in coaxing the drift juice to flow onto my palm. Reggie stared at it, and who wouldn't? It cast its own ripples on my hand, the metallic blue changing hue ever so slightly as it moved.

"Give it a try, boy. See if you like it."

Reggie pushed his nose into the tiny puddle and the drift juice scattered! It broke into a hundred miniscule beads of blue metal and flew in all directions, like buckshot from a cartoon shotgun. An instant later all the beads just stopped. They hung in the air, forming individual miniature teardrops, but not oriented towards the floor. Rather they turned, the pendulous belly of each tear yearning back toward all the others, the attenuated points of them all radiating outward.

With a loud yip, Reggie leaped for the nearest of these, jaws gaping. His mouth engulfed the teardrop, and closed around it as he dropped to all fours on the floor. He gave a bark of victory, letting me know what a great hunter he was. And all the remaining drops reoriented, as if sighting on my buffalo dog. Reggie ignored them. He began chewing and chewing, the effect you get by feeding peanut butter to a more traditional pet. I'd never seen Reggie do that. The chew toys I occasionally gave him were more euphemistic than literal. He enjoyed the hardness of them, but he'd had to learn not to devour them in a heartbeat. On the few occasions when a simple chomp and gulp hadn't sufficed, Reggie never worked his jaw more than a couple of times before swallowing. This was different. He kept chewing. From the perplexed expression on his furry face, he found the experience strange indeed.

"How's that taste, boy? You like it? Any problems?"

I waved him over. He trotted to me, and the remaining drops reoriented accordingly. I pulled him onto my lap, stroking his wooly hide and tickling him under his beard. Then I pried open his jaws with my fingertips, tilted his head back, and peered inside. I'm not sure what I expected, maybe that the bead of drift juice he'd eaten would come flying out. It didn't. There was nothing in his mouth. He'd swallowed it; it was gone.

The moment I let go Reggie jumped away, running around the room like a rambunctious puppy. He circled me at top speed, once, twice, three times. Then he lunged into the air, and devoured two bits of drift juice. The remaining tiny tears again oriented on him, a clear case of buffalito tropism. I stood up. The drift juice beads didn't appear to care. Neither did Reggie. He'd gone back to racing around in circles, stalking the rest of his prey or maybe trying to lull it into a false sense of safety. He only did two revolutions of the room this time before leaping and snagging another couple pieces.

I stepped into the parlor and found the receiving portal that yielded up lunch at a touch. While I ate, Reggie continued his new game, barking occasionally after a particularly impressive leap or snatch and then settling in for some serious chewing before moving on to the next morsel. Time passed, and we finished our respective meals about the same time. I offered Reggie the option of licking my plate—or even eating it. He padded over to sit in my lap, but showed no interest in the plate.

"Everything okay, boy? Is it sitting well?"

Reggie wagged his tail, stretched, and yawned. Then he jumped off of me and sauntered out. I followed him into the master bedroom, where he'd already curled up in my bed. A nap sounded like a good idea to me; my head was stuffed full from the intercoursarium, and a little sleep would give my unconscious an opportunity to do a bit of processing for me. I kicked off my shoes and joined my buffalito on the bed. Elsewhere in the ship I assumed the Captain's sensors were reporting on the disappearance of a small fortune of drift juice.

My show that night was a huge success. I was the third and final performer with the better part of an hour for my act, plenty of time to pull a few volunteers from the audience, perform a traditional induction, and run my new hypnotic subjects through a variety of atypical behaviors for their respective races. The audience ate it up, and begged for more. I obliged with two encores—the first involving an Ersommerey giving an incredibly dull recitation of a day in his life as the galaxy's most boring accountant, and the second had a Taurian explaining that he was the ambassador of a new cross-species, part Cliveden part Phloke, that would soon be accepting investors in a fleet of transit craft. My audience rewarded me with heartfelt applause. It was good to be back.

As I started toward my dressing room Billi galloped down the hallway toward me on all sixes. He jerked to a halt and reared up, repositioning his spine so that he was standing on his bottom pair of hands. The simple motion transformed him from looking like a miniaturized Barsoomian draft animal to a sentient biped no different from you or me, except for color, height, and an extra pair of limbs.

"Conroy, I've got something exciting to tell you!"

One of the day's topics of conversation at the intercoursarium had involved Pelks, on the assumption that some of the representatives of so many alien races had to know a thing or two about my agent's species. I'd learned a lot, including that any of their six limbs worked equally as well as arms or legs. I'd studied comparative alien religions back in my college days, but that hadn't prepared me for the range of spiritual beliefs and interactive divinities popular among the major Pelk cultures. I'd heard plenty of examples of bizarre god-bargains and sacrifices involving newly matured Pelk that made Billi's problem with initial nasal consonants a bargain by comparison. And since my name isn't Moore or Nicholson, I didn't think it would be too much of a problem.

"Hey, Billi. Can your news wait until I get out of my tux? This bowtie is killing me."

"Keep the tie on. We're headed to the bar."

"Why do I need my tie?"

"Because there's someone you have to beat."

I winced. "Did you pick another fight?" Another thing I'd learned about my new agent: he had little tolerance for hecklers. Word in the intercoursarium was that a Pelk had sucker punched an intoxicated Flenk for making insulting remarks during my previous show. Billi certainly seemed scrappy enough, but any Flenk had to be twice his size; fortunately the loudmouth had a glass jaw or Billi might have been squashed or forced to punch out the jerk's kneecaps. But that was back in the tertiary lounge amidst weak impressionists and bad comedians. I'd just come off the main stage of the first class passengers entertainment locus. Had he been in the audience to catch my debut there, or starting a brawl that he'd come to me to help him finish?

"Beat, bot beat," he said, but I just shook my head at him. He responded by punching my calf with his left middle fist.

"Who's at the bar?" I stepped back out of his range, at least for a moment. "And why do you want me to beat him?"

"The Elder Glarp, you buffoon!"

"Glarp?"

Billi skitted around behind me. He put all four of his middle and upper hands on my buttocks and started pushing. "The biggest business guy on Bisto's world. Half of the three largest islands there are either owned or controlled by him. He saw your act tonight. He liked it. A lot. So, you will keep your tie where it is and let him buy you a glass of fruit juice or fizzy water at the bar. You got that?"

"He wants to 'meet' me!"

"That's what I'm saying. Let's go!"

Using my backside as a bridle, Billi guided me to a different salon than I'd visited earlier. This one featured a massive bar, alcohol-free of course.

"Here he is," said Billi from behind me after stopping us at a corner booth near the back. "Forgive us the delay, Elder Glarp, but Conroy is shy."

This was news to me, but Billi had gone into high sycophantic mode and I didn't want to contradict him. Instead I channeled the spirit of my old college roommate, a Kansas farm boy who could do the *aw, shucks* routine at the slightest word of praise. I shuffled my feet and lowered my eyes, but not before taking a long look at the Elder Glarp.

I'd met forty or fifty different aliens that morning, including a couple of Veng. This one didn't look any different from those two, which is to say he was just over a meter and a half tall, with scaly, orange skin, and triangular flaps that lay flat against his head where humans keep their ears. The Elder Glarp was dressed better though. The others had worn simple, beige togas of a coarse weave. This fellow also wore a toga, but his was black silk and glittered with ornate, metallic embroidery depicting constellations which I later learned could be seen in the southern hemisphere of Bisto's world. He sat at one end of a circular booth designed to accommodate a party of six or seven Veng, or perhaps as many as five human-sized patrons.

"Gentlemen, please, make yourselves comfortable," said the Elder Glarp. He rubbed the tabletop calling up a menu I'd never seen before, an elite list of items that not even the first class passengers had access to. "Would you like a drink? Something to eat, perhaps? I'm sure performing must be taxing, Entertainer Conroy, please order anything you like. You as well, Agent Pelk. But, your pardon please, I am just finishing up here."

I didn't need the butt-nudge from Billi to slip into the booth's open end and slide over to make room for the Pelk. When I did, I realized that the Elder Glarp had company. The tiny figure seated next to him was a Veng, but scaled down to half the height of the others I'd seen, smaller even than Billi. It couldn't be a child. I'd learned Veng were oviparous and made use of a process for concatenating multiple fertilized eggs, resulting in newborns emerging fully-grown. They had young adults, but no kids. With a flip of mental gymnastics I leaped the other way. I was looking at a very, very old Veng. Maybe they collapsed in upon themselves with age and this fellow was the Veng version of Methuselah. Even in the lounge's dim lighting I could see that its skin was a darker shade of orange, its scales shinier, almost gleaming. I couldn't see its face; it sat slumped over, nearly hidden by the relative height of the table, holding its head in its hands.

If I was staring, Billi's protruding eyes were even more obvious. "Is your, uh, guest all right?" he asked and glanced a question at me. I returned a confused shrug.

"Kenkle is fine," said the Elder Glarp, focusing on us once more. "He is just concentrating on his task. I'll need to give him my full attention in just a moment or so, after which we will have our chat. Have you seen this before, Entertainer Conroy?"

Billi used one of his middle hands to flash me a code signal which could have meant anything from *agree to anything he says* to *don't be a smartass and don't say anything stupid.*

"I'm not sure what I'm seeing, Elder Glarp."

"Few Veng have, and fewer Tallers. We call it *the skimming.* Only the most powerful can afford the process, and it is part of what makes them powerful, something of a self-perpetuating phenomena."

Before I could ask what was being skimmed Kenkle jerked upright and threw back its head. Except for their earflaps and lack of hair, a Veng's head has everything you'd expect to find: a normal face with two eyes, a nose, and a mouth. Kenkle sat rigidly, its jaw hanging open and its tongue lolling to one side. A tiny bubble of snot hung from one nostril. All of that registered in a moment but none of it mattered. Where it should have had eyes, the tiny face held only empty sockets that demanded all of my attention.

Delicate wisps of glowing green gas began to curl up and out of those twin black holes, coalescing in the air above Kenkle's head.

Billi clenched my arm with two of his hands. He hissed something in a language that wasn't Traveler and sounded like he'd said "*Shustapukooof!*" I couldn't have expressed it any better. I just stared.

The vapors rose. Several bits broke off to form chartreuse rings that drifted wider and wider. A hysterical giggle started building in my throat. Maybe the little Veng had somehow swallowed a pipe and was simply blowing smoke rings of some exotic alien tobacco, never mind that he was blowing them out of a pair of gaping eye sockets. My giggle died away as more gas emerged, absorbed the smoke rings, and formed a melon-sized cloud that floated over and hung above the Elder Glarp. Within seconds the cloud thickened, its shape grew more defined. It took on the appearance of a smallish upside-down head; smallish by human standards, but as the likeness of earflaps became defined on either side it was just the right size to be a Veng head.

The Elder Glarp had expected the ongoing sepulchral manifestation. "This is the skimming, Entertainer Conroy. I employ the most talented essence shaper on all of Bisto's World. And my own talents are such that Kenkle can skim off enough essence for a fresh rendering every few days."

As he spoke, the upside-down head had sprouted an upside-down neck, which in turn began producing an upside-down torso. Billi still clutched my arm, the grey points of his nail thorns cutting through my tuxedo coat, my dress shirt, and into my flesh. I didn't know what he found so disturbing until I realized that the green head had taken on sufficient detail and its lips moved in time with the Elder Glarp's. It mouthed his words perfectly, even as tendrils of green gas continued to rise from the essence shaper, adding to the growing body.

I attempted to disengage Billi's hands from my arm while continuing to make polite conversation. "Every few days, you say? Really? That's, uh, certainly remarkable. But, uh, what does one do with such a, uh, rendering?"

"Do? I do whatever I choose to do, Entertainer. I simply do it in two places at once."

The apparition had sprouted arms and legs, and these in turn acquired their requisite hands and feet, fingers and toes. These grew more defined, solid seeming.

"Why does it have a toga and slippers?" said Billi, his voice sounding almost normal. Funny the things you don't notice. What's odder after all, that one's dinner companion conjures up a ghostly version of himself, or that when he does the thing is fully clothed?

"Not just a toga and slippers," I said, as my eye caught the emerging detail on the toga. "That's the same toga the Elder Glarp himself is wearing."

"Of course it's wearing my toga. It's my rendering. It's me, just as I am right this moment. What good would it be, if it wasn't me?"

Before either Billi or I could venture any reply, Kenkle gasped softly and slumped over, sprawling on the bench seat of our booth. Its eye sockets had stopped leaking their ectoplasmic vapor.

"Gentlemen, excuse me now," said the Elder Glarp. "I need a moment of concentration."

As we watched, the Veng reached up with both hands, even as his glowing green doppelganger reached down. They clasped hands, and in a situation of too much strangeness already, the evening went a bit more bizarre. The Elder Glarp began crushing his double. He squeezed the thing's hands in his, smashing them into what looked to be a soupier substance in his palms. Then he used his fingers to pull the duplicate's arms down, bit-by-bit, squeezing and wrenching and mauling them as well. As the thing's arms vanished and the Elder Glarp started in on its shoulders, I realized he was mashing and compacting the thing, destroying the shape it had so recently grown into. It didn't resist, but crumpled like a burning marshmallow.

He continued, working the mass smaller and smaller even after he had crushed any semblance of shape from Kenkle's creation. In the end he was left with a double handful of green ooze, which he half coaxed, half poured into a glass vile he wore on a neckthong beneath his toga.

"I won't need this until tomorrow, at the earliest," said the Elder Glarp as he capped the vial with its stopper and began retying the thong around it. "But best to perform the skimming as soon as one is capable, so the next one comes that much sooner."

"So, the rendering, it keeps?" I said.

"Keeps?"

"Stays fresh? It doesn't spoil or, um, go bad?"

The Elder Glarp laughed, long and loud. Aliens at several nearby tables stared our way, but only briefly. After just a moment Billi joined in, adding his nervous giggles.

"Oh, Entertainer, please, you must remember not to perform when you are not onstage. You devalue your craft when you entertain too generously." The Veng wiped at his eyes with a napkin.

"Sorry. I didn't realize I was being funny."

"Oh? Your question was genuine? But of course, you do not have essence shapers among your own kind."

I nodded at this. "No, I can safely say I know of no one where I come from who does what Kenkle just did."

"My apologies. I meant no offense to your profession."

"None taken, Elder Glarp."

"To answer you then, no, the rendering does not spoil. Quite the contrary, it matures and learns even as I do. It is my essence, a part of my mind, my spirit."

"It learns?"

The Veng nodded, repeating "As I do. It will remember our present conversation as clearly as I will. Otherwise, it could not act in my place when I have need of it."

"I . . . see." I wondered what I would do if I had a bottled version of myself that I could set free to help out as circumstances dictated. "How long does it last, once you, uh, decant it?"

"Not long," said the Veng. "Most of a day, and then it is drawn to reunite with me, except in the most dire situations."

"Dire?" said Billi. He had composed himself and seemed eager to become a part of the conversation again.

"I am the leader of my rist," said the Elder Glarp. "But, no, you do not have rist any more than you have renderings. Let me try again. I mentioned power before; I am . . . you might call me the Patriarch of my rist, my family on Bisto's World, one of just over two hundred such. Such a position brings with it both responsibility and danger. There are those, my opposites in a few other rist who might attempt to assassinate me. If one were to succeed, my rendering would avenge me."

"But if you were dead, how could it act?" said Billi.

"How could it even know who your killer was?" I asked.

"It would know," said the Elder Glarp. "It would know everything I knew, up until the moment of my death. And because it was no longer bound to return to me, it would continue to exist until it completed its purpose of vengeance."

"That would be horrible," said Billi.

"Oh yes," said the Elder Glarp. "A rendering does not tire, does not sleep. It has no physical body that can be injured or destroyed. It is an implacable instrument of vengeance. But the practice of skimming is not commonplace. Few Veng actually face assassination, and fewer of them possess renderings. As I said, I am most fortunate to have Kenkle at hand to serve me and a few of the closest members of my rist. But enough of such talk. Let us speak instead of your performance tonight, Entertainer. I was most intrigued, most delighted, by what I witnessed. I have a proposition for you, if you care to hear it?"

I'd already had one proposition this trip. This one was going through proper channels, and was clearly why Billi had brought me here. He perked up and took over. "He'd love to, sir, he would love to."

The Elder Glarp grunted, and looked to me for confirmation. I nodded, and that seemed to be enough to let the Veng know how Billi and I liked things. I did the hypnosis and he handled the negotiations. That too was part of the plan.

"Well then, Agent Billi, let us discuss while your client diverts himself with food and drink."

Orange fingers pressed on the tabletop, and pushed the image of the menu across to me. The available options made the first-class passengers' fare look like swill. Heaven. I studied the menu, tuning out the discussion at the table and letting Billi work.

A surprise greeted me when I returned to my suite. Reggie sat on the far wall of my bedroom. Not *by* the wall, or *near* the wall. He had his furry butt positioned firmly on the wall at about eye level, front feet planted in front of him just as I'd found him comfortably seated on the ground any number of times. Except he was on the wall, proud as you please. He yipped as I came into the room, and ran around in circles on the wall until I rushed over and plucked him off, as easily as I might have lifted him from the floor. Squirming, he pushed his tiny hooves against my chest. It felt like he'd jumped on me. I almost let go in surprise, but it wouldn't have mattered. He was now standing on my chest, having found his own definition of gravity.

"I'm guessing this is a side effect of the gunk you ate, boy. Are you still feeling okay?"

He walked up a little higher, knelt on his forelegs and licked my face. Other than a small problem with what 'down' now meant, he seemed perfectly fine. Except . . . I couldn't recall him farting since before he'd eaten the drift juice. If there's one thing I'd learned when I'd run Buffalogic, Inc., it was that buffalitos didn't go very long without breaking wind. It was the flip side of their coin: chomping down on anything they pleased at one end, and producing a steady supply of oxygen out of the other.

The mysteries of the buffalito alimentary canal had not been solved by the Arconi, and my first assumption had been that they just lacked the curiosity to pursue the question to its end. I'd let Elizabeth Penrose throw a few hundred million bucks at it, building a team of physicists and a shiny new lab for their use. Two years into the project they'd produced several scholarly papers that described some of the numbers of the process, but had edged no closer to an explanation. Stuff went in one end, and regardless of the nature, mass, or atomic structure of that stuff, what came out was oxygen. Something inside a buffalo dog ripped molecules apart, stripped off protons left and right from anything that had more than eight of them, or jammed in extra if they had fewer, repacking all of it with an octal bias. The physicists couldn't explain the mechanism for the process, only that it had to be releasing insane amounts of energy. Except it didn't. None of the buffalo dogs that I'd leased had ever exploded like an old style atom bomb. When I'd pointed this out to my team of physicists, they'd just shrugged, shoved their hands deep into the pockets of their lab coats, stared at their shoes, and muttered "well, it has to be going somewhere."

I'd fired the lot of them and returned to the simpler definition I'd gotten from the Arconi: Buffalo dogs can eat anything, and they fart oxygen. Period. A few hours ago mine had eaten a fortune in drift juice, and he hadn't farted since. I didn't need a physicist to tell me something was wrong.

I pulled Reggie off my chest and tucked him under one arm. It was a bit like moving a gyroscope. I took him back into the kiddy room. I was convinced that Captain Telfano had sensors in play, and I didn't want her to think I was trying to make off with her goods. I set Reggie down on the floor near the wall of blinking, flashing, brightly-colored shapes, and then I stepped closer, raised my foot, and brought it down on a particularly obnoxious, purple, tetrahedral protrusion. It did me the courtesy of snapping right off and bouncing across the floor. Reggie immediately ran after it. He caught it on its second bounce and pinned it to the floor with his left front hoof. He looked back to me as if seeking approval.

"Go ahead, eat it."

He didn't wait for further coaxing. He bit down and an instant later a large piece was missing from the thing and Reggie was swallowing. In under a minute the thing was gone. Reggie dashed back over to me, prancing, and probably wondering if this was a new game and if I was going to break off another snack for him.

And then he burped.

Reggie never burps. Ever.

I'd never seen *any* buffalo dog burp, they're just not built for it. And from the look of surprise on his face, Reggie knew it too. He plopped down on his belly, limbs splayed in all direction, and lowered his head to the floor. He burped again, letting his jaw hang open in a long sustained belch. I knelt down in front of him. What if I'd hurt him by feeding him the drift juice? He started panting. His tongue hung over the side of his mouth. He didn't seem to be in any pain. If anything, he had a goofy, almost drunken expression.

He belched, and followed that with a cough. Then he threw his head straight back, until his nose was pointing over his hump. He puked straight up, a thin stream of glistening blue liquid that hung in the air like a metallic fountain. It held that shape for almost a full second, and then collapsed in on itself into a collection of tiny globules hovering above Reggie's head. Of the chewed up pieces of purple tetrahedron he'd just eaten there was no sign.

Once he'd finished his projectile vomiting, Reggie appeared fine. He stood up and began trotting around the room, eventually heading over for another polyhedral on the wall. As he built up speed, he jumped and took a bite out of a particularly appealing yellow pyramid, already swallowing the piece by the time he hit the floor. In addition to the sound of his clattering hooves, I caught the distinct sound of him breaking wind.

"Well, there you have it, good as new."

Any further celebration was put on hold by a knock on the entrance to the suite. A voice followed it.

"Mr. Conroy? This is the Captain. Would you mind if I joined you?"

The door opened before I could answer, admitting Captain Telfano. She walked through the parlor and right into the kiddy room. Her gaze flicked over Reggie by the toy wall where he was biting off another piece that had grown back, then to me standing in the center of the room, and finally stopped upon the floating bits of drift juice less than an arm's distance from me. She showed no surprise at any of it. If anything, her expression might have been one of avarice, but with aliens it can be hard to tell.

"I am well pleased, Mr. Conroy, you've wasted no time. Better still, you've been quite successful. According to every detector onboard the *Shpeshnoltoc*, a certain amount of drift juice suddenly vanished from this room some hours earlier, only to reappear moments ago. How did such a thing happen?" She reached out a finger as she spoke, pressing it into the middle of one of the larger beads and dragged it into a collision course with some of the others. It absorbed them, and the whole grew greater. She did this several times, as she waited for my response.

What was I supposed to say? There was something different in her manner than when we'd met before, as if she were playing for an audience. Her sudden arrival confirmed my suspicions that she had the room monitored; perhaps everything in here was being recorded as well. She'd given me the drift juice, pointedly told me to coax my buffalito into ingesting it, and now wanted to act coy? Perhaps she wanted an *official record* giving her some kind of plausible deniability about the smuggling. Fine by me; the more I played along, the more insight I'd gain into another aspect of how her mind worked.

I shrugged. "It's part of my act. I hypnotized him into believing it was actually chocolate pudding. The same way I might hypnotize one of your crewmen and convince him he was an Arcon with a plan for the enlightenment of all Cliveden. Assuming I ever had such a chance."

She'd taken out a small box, identical to the one elsewhere in the room. Her head turned and she treated me to a hard stare from those black eyes. Then she laughed.

"Very good, Mr. Conroy. Most amusing." She opened her box, and with a deft gesture captured all of the drift juice within it. "You'll be pleased to know that my sensors report the return of virtually all of the drift juice."

I frowned. "What do you mean *virtually?*"

"No system is one hundred percent efficient, Mr. Conroy, not your creature, nor even as complex a substance as drift juice. But believe me when I tell you, you would not notice it. The equipment aboard the *Shpeshnoltoc* is incredibly sophisticated, and I had it specifically attuned for this event. Less than three millionths of one percent of the sample I loaned to you has been left behind. Such a minute loss is acceptable to me, and judging by your creature's behavior, it is within his comfort zone as well."

She closed the box and tossed it from hand to hand. "I understand that your agent has succeeded in booking you an extensive engagement at the Pyramidal, the premiere entertainment venue in the Elder Veng's home city."

"It's a resort."

"A very large and prestigious resort. Preparations are already underway to grant you the necessary rist to perform there, and that same rist will make it unthinkable that you would wander where you are not welcome, such as into an area where drift juice is being stored."

"I thought rist referred to Veng families."

"That and more. Rist is part of the social structure of the Veng. Something of a combination of tribe and caste. Two hundred and four combinations, to be precise. Every Veng is born into one of them. They maintain this system on each of their many worlds. Those worlds are not closed to other races, but they are heavily restricted. Visitors are assigned membership in one of several fairly benign rists, each with its own perks and limitations. I will provide you with some helpful learning modules before you depart. The point is, at the proper moment, you will be able to access an unprotected quantity of drift juice, cause your creature to ingest it, and then take transport to a shuttle station where you will put in a call to my ship, and I will dispatch one of my officers to lend whatever support you might need to deliver your shipment through customs where your creature will foil all scans."

"You've obviously given this a lot of thought." I was getting a glimpse at yet another way her mind worked. I didn't like it.

"Smuggling should not be a task which one undertakes lightly. Particularly for an individual of my station."

I nodded. "Right. Well, no offense, but you never actually asked me if I wanted to do this for you."

"I saw no need, Mr. Conroy."

"Excuse me?"

"When the possibility presented itself, I considered only two things. First, what you might *want* to do would not necessarily have any impact on what you *would* do. Many races in the galaxy engage in behaviors that they have no desire to perform, and I have been assured that your own is among these.

"And the second thing?"

"I knew you would do it because you've done it before. Again, my research into your people shows that you are capable of extraordinary originality, but also are quick to lapse into previous patterns. You've been a smuggler before, Mr. Conroy, and you built a financial empire upon that audacity. I'm putting you in the position to do it again. Your very nature assures that you will repeat the act."

"And if you're wrong?"

She shrugged, and at the same moment the tip of her tongue slipped out and licked her lips. "In that event, then I will have wasted some of my time, and you will find yourself unable to secure transport off Bisto's World for many years."

"You're saying I'll do what you want because, by my very nature I don't have a choice, but just in case you're wrong, you're ensuring I really don't have a choice. You'd don't think that's pretty cold-blooded?"

"Ah, but that is *my* nature."

After Captain Telfano left I sat with Reggie in my lap and pondered the situation. On the one hand, after spending several years doing the whole wealthy CEO thing, I'd finally realized my true happiness was traveling from planet to planet, meeting new and exotic people, and doing my hypnosis act. My life was back on track, even allowing for a slight detour to learn why a Celestial had an interest in me. I'd be foolhardy to put all of that in jeopardy by taking up a side career as a smuggler. On the other hand, there was the extenuating factor of transportational extortion. No matter how much the Elder Glarp or any other Veng loved my work, I didn't want to be stuck in the same place waiting for a Cliveden captain to decide—if she ever did—to let me leave. Then again, I didn't have any emotional or moral investment in allowing the Veng to keep their monopoly going. I'd just be doing a job, moving goods from one place to the other. Was it fair of the Veng to squeeze the Cliveden and stifle their productivity by limiting the amount of drift juice they could have? But then too, I didn't like the idea of using Reggie as a vehicle for theft. I was juggling too many factors to make a decision. After mulling it over in my head the one thing I felt certain of was that I needed to get the perspective and input from someone else, someone I could trust.

Lucky for me, that wouldn't be a problem.

I closed my eyes and relaxed, breathing in through my nose and out through my mouth. I eased myself into a meditative, almost trance-like, awareness. I didn't want to overdo it, but each time I attempted this it got a bit simpler. I slipped into a kind of detached mental state and remembered how it had felt the first time I'd reached out to that aspect of my long-dead, Great Aunt Fiona's consciousness that still existed. An alien telepath had taught me the trick of it years ago. I didn't understand if it was a spiritual thing, or just some physics of personality and memory. I only knew that when it happened, I'd be talking to my aunt, one of the very first people to leave Earth behind and set off into the galaxy to meet aliens. The sensation was a little like falling asleep, a little like poking your tongue into that gap where you'd just lost a tooth, and a little like knowing you're about to sneeze except that the fact that you know is making it impossible to actually sneeze.

And then she was there. At some level of my consciousness, she sat right next to me, a tall woman with bushy white hair and a wrinkled face that showed both her years and how much she'd liked to laugh. She wore the comfortable, plaid, pico-fiber shirt that I remembered as her favorite, the sleeves rolled up just above her elbow, and a pair of pseudo jeans that looked like the classics from Earth but which could only be bought from Clarkeson merchants out of hastily unfolded tables in unreputable marketplaces. Steel-toed boots that had stood upon dozens of worlds and walked thousands of miles protected her feet, even though she wouldn't be walking anywhere ever again. She looked at me and smiled.

"That was quite a show you did tonight. Very clever. Very good. I'm so happy you've found your path again, boy."

"If you know about that without my telling you, then I guess you also know about the new twist in that path."

"I do, and I understand your dilemma, but I think you're looking at the questions in the wrong way, and that's where you're going astray."

"You've lost me."

"It's not about whether or not you're being forced to choose one thing or another. When you frame it that way, you've already given up all your power and become a victim. Other people are making your decisions and deciding not just your fate, but who you are. I thought you'd given that up."

"No, you're right, I want to be in control of my own destiny."

"Then control it. Who do you want to be? And when you answer that, you'll know what to do."

I was about to say something more, but I stopped myself. Aunt Fiona smiled at me, bringing a hand to her mouth and miming putting a key to her lips, locking them tight, and tossing the key away. She wouldn't give me any further advice, nor tell me what she thought I should do. I didn't need her to. She'd already reminded me of what I had known all along. The only way other people had control over my life was when I let them.

So what kind of person did I want to be? "I'm a hypnotist," I said aloud. Fiona nodded. "And a traveler. A gourmand, when I can be. And arguably even something of an adventurer. I'm sometimes a bit of a rogue, but I'm not a thief. And that's the role the captain wants me to play. Or worse, a puppet thief. That's not me."

"So what are you going to do about it?"

And just like that, I knew. The same thing I knew every time I stepped on stage and put some innocent volunteer under. I was going to change the rules, alter perception, and take back control. Captain Telfano thought she could manipulate my actions to achieve her ends, and maybe her experience as a captain had given her some skill at that. But I was the Amazing Conroy. People did what I wanted, and believed it was their own idea. This was my stock in trade. I didn't know how I would manage it, but like Billi, I knew I'd come up with a plan as the contingencies unfolded and opportunities presented themselves. In that instant, all my worries vanished.

"You're going to be fine, boy. That lizard captain doesn't have a chance. . ." Aunt Fiona faded out of existence.

She'd left behind a simple truth. When it came to a question of who could out-manipulate whom, I had nothing to fear. It didn't matter whether or not I was on stage, or if my opponent was someone I'd ever hypnotized. The mindset was the same. I knew I'd win. It was my nature.

CHAPTER NINE

Dinner and A Show

OVER THE NEXT several weeks I did one show a night, rotating through the seven lounges and stages enjoyed by the *Shpeshnoltoc*'s first through fifth class passengers. I refined the act to reflect the aliens onboard. There were never any Cliveden among my audiences, but that didn't stop me from convincing the occasional volunteer to believe himself to be one of our xenophobic hosts. I also dabbled with the Wolly penchant for monochromatic art, the tendency for Fmoot to travel in odd numbers, and the Veng system of rist. This last was more an extension of the learning modules that the Captain had been leaving for me, a preparation for the gig to come once we reached Bisto. I'd already learned that the Veng were a gregarious race. They didn't tend to venture out among other species, but every planet under their influence had an open immigration policy. Veng like to be among other races, they just want the other races to come to them.

The Captain made several more surprise visits, always bringing larger portions of drift juice. She kept them brief, but I used every opportunity to ease a word or two past her conscious mind. It wasn't hypnosis per se, but bit-by-bit I was making her more susceptible to my influence. I still didn't have an actual plan, but I was getting ready for when I did.

After each of her visits I'd coax Reggie to consume the fluidic fortune, and to refrain from eating anything else for a half a day or more. While the drift juice itself was impervious to the processes going on inside my buffalo dog, it didn't tolerate any company inside him. The slightest other morsel would disrupt the balance and result in projectile *decanting*. When that happened, Captain Telfano would silently appear, recover the goods, mark the volume, and depart. Reggie seemed none the worse for these experiences, and soon maxed out the quantity of drift juice on hand for experiments, about twenty cc's of the stuff. Whether he could handle more—and if so, how much—remained an open question.

The good ship *Shpeshnoltoc* stopped at three other planets during my tenure, with anywhere from a day to four days parked in high orbit. Shuttles came and went, ferrying passengers and crew. Svetlana made a point to drop down and walk around on every planet we visited. Whether she did so to pick up new language or new aliens I didn't care to know. I kept watch to see if she'd return with the Celestial, but she never did. We'd gotten in the habit of taking meals together at least once a day for people watching or menu exploration, depending on whose turn it was. In another five days the ship was scheduled to arrive at Bisto, where both the Captain and the Elder Glarp expected me to disembark. Svetlana had just come upworld from Havre and wanted to meet for dinner. I already had plans to eat with Billi, so Reggie and I met up with both of them in the intercoursarium and I introduced them to a series of salad-like appetizers unique to a peninsula on the second oldest of the Taurian worlds. While they chewed over a combination of sweet grasses and tangy, braised root vegetables I traded discretion for impatience.

"You told me you'd be meeting up with your Celestial on this cruise."

"Hmm?" She paused in mid-chew, resumed, and swallowed. "I did. I am. I will. In about a week."

"Are you still going on about that?" said Billi. "You don't want to get bixed up with one of those."

Reggie farted, looked up as if to ask if anyone had noticed, and then lowered his face back into his bowl of Taurian cuisine. I glared at my agent and turned back to Svetlana. "So, it's not waiting for you at Bisto then?"

"No, Gelarkva. Why did you think Bisto?" She shoved her fork into the next appetizer and dug in.

"I was hoping. I have to leave the ship there."

She stopped chewing, brought her napkin to her face and more or less discretely spat her mouthful into it. "You told me you wanted to meet the Celestial. Wasn't that your whole reason for being here?"

"We've got a gig on Bisto," said Billi. "Big plans. Our boy's going to turn the Veng entertainment industry on its ear flap."

"But that's the next stop. And you already have a job here on the ship. Why leave it for another when you can stay onboard and in just another week finally realize your goal?"

"There are . . . complications. I—"

Billi waved me to silence with three hands. "Conroy's a professional. We're signed up for Bisto, so that's where we're going."

"But what about the Celestial? It wants to see you."

"On Leftril you said you would be coming back, specifically to bring the Celestial to meet with me. Maybe you can bring it to Bisto instead? It's closer."

She looked back down at her grass and tubers, spearing another bite. "I don't know. Part of the reason for Leftril had to do with the Phloke. The Celestial is at ease with them. It's had encounters with them before. I don't think it's ever met any Veng."

"Has it ever met a Pelk?" I asked.

"Actually, yes. It told me it had. Why?"

"Just because I have to disembark at Bisto doesn't mean Billi here does too? What if he stays onboard until you arrive at Gelarkva."

"What? Why? What would I do on Gelarkva?"

"Be my agent," I said. "Talk to the Celestial, and convince it to come back to Bisto."

"Conroy, I want you to be get everything you want, but that's outside my job description. Besides, you bead me at your side to keep the Elder Glarp happy."

"All he needs to be happy is for me to show up and do my act. I don't need you for that. I do need you to get the Celestial to come back to Bisto."

Svetlana frowned. "People don't *get* a Celestial to do things."

"Baby they do, and baby they don't, but I don't like being told that I can't do a thing."

"Don't call me baby."

Reggie broke wind again.

"Great. Then it's decided."

Previous shuttle flights from the *Shpeshnoltoc* had terminated at ports on the planetary surface. Not so on Bisto. Its cities lay deep underground, sealed away from nonstop electrical storms, hundred kilometer winds, and an atmosphere that was more methane than oxygen. The shuttle docked at a domed island floating leisurely above the equator. Flying taxi-like pods carried passengers and cargo from there, hurtling through weather to gain access to the web of tunnels that linked Bisto's cities. The island was part immigration, part customs center, and part warehouse; it even had its own hospital.

With the exception of the knowledgeable captain of the *Shpeshnoltoc*, most people out this way weren't familiar with buffalo dogs, and I worried about potential problems clearing customs. I needn't have. A work permit signed by the Elder Glarp eased me through every question and past every inspection agent. Every line was short and efficient. Every corridor well-lit and sweet smelling. Everyone was extremely friendly and helpful. They showed only a polite interest in Reggie, and only a moment's consternation that none of their scanning equipment could penetrate his wooly hide.

As I neared the departure platform and began searching for a taxi to take me to the Elder Glarp's city, a pretty woman waved at me. She carried a projection sign that flashed my name and the news of my upcoming engagement at the Pyramidal, cycling through a variety of colors, writing systems, and languages. She'd have stood out from the crowd even without the sign. Though not tall by human standards, she towered above the Veng. She had milky skin and flowing black hair that reached to her waist. The traditional Veng tunic, skimpy on her slender frame, was turquoise with a dark orange sash across it from left shoulder to right hip. She wore nothing else, not even shoes. Her eyes, which I couldn't actually make out, marked her as a Bluie. Sometimes I could see the outline of one orb or the other, but never both. A thick, cobalt blue fog flowed from those eyes, obscuring them and then dissipating to nothing a few centimeters later. I'd never met a Bluie before, but a dining companion back on the ship had told an amusing story involving a Clarkeson, a Bluie, and a mutating retrovirus, and the bit about the ocular fog had stuck with me.

"Mr. Amazing Conroy? said the Bluie. "Over here! Hello, sir, my name is Relliope. Welcome to Bitso. I'm from the Pyramidal. They've assigned me as your guide to get you settled in. If you'll follow me, sir, I have a pod waiting for you. Right this way."

Reggie leaped from me and was bounding across the causeway toward the Bluie, barking with excitement. Somewhere, there's probably a psychology student writing a dissertation examining the responses of people when small alien animals come hurtling their way at great speed. It correlates and describes personality types based on reactions. Relliope would have scored well. She squatted in place and swept Reggie into her arms, spinning and rising as she pulled him in to her chest in a great hug. A full three hundred and sixty degrees later she was upright, stroking Reggie's fur, and cooing baby noises at him while he writhed in mutual adoration. My buffalo dog is a great judge of character, and as I stepped forward to introduce myself I knew I was going to like her.

I wish I could say I was headlining at the Pyramidal, but the Elder Glarp had only told the manager there to hire me, not to treat me like a star. Prior to his report no one on Bisto's World had ever heard of stage hypnotism, let alone the Amazing Conroy. The name sparkling throughout the city's travel tubes in eight-meter tall polyglyphs belonged to a Veng prima donna, a vocalist named Tintalerra. Her sixteen-night engagement at the Pyramidal was her only stop on Bisto, part of a six planet, twenty-two-city tour. A recording of her blared through our pod, and vibrated up through the seats with an intensity designed to boil the marrow in my bones. I didn't care for her voice and I didn't understand the language of her lyrics, but Relliope assured me the Veng here surrendered up a standing ovation and much painful whistling at every show. Part of that may be because the Veng have six sexes, and five of them are variants of male; I attributed a good portion of her popularity to that ratio.

I shared second billing—meter-tall static glyphs visible here and there throughout a much smaller portion of the transit tubes—with an Arcturan pyrotic ballet troupe that arrived days earlier on a different ship. The dancers moved with the kind of beauty and grace you'd expect from Arcturans. The only time I'd ever seen anything more exquisitely fluid happened at a candy factory and involved the mixing, shaping, and pouring of several metric tons of liquefied milk chocolate. According to Relliope, the Veng didn't much care for the ballet troupe. Maybe Veng don't do a lot of dancing—that five to one sex thing again. The dancers were already on their way out, impressive pyrotechnics not withstanding. That's the way it is performing for aliens, you never know what will win over an audience until you try it, and either succeed, crash and burn, or offend some moral precept that unites them in common cause to seek your death.

I wasn't worried. The Elder Glarp had brought me in and he knew what other Veng would like. When we arrived at the hotel it was late morning local time and Relliope whisked me into the main lounge where I'd be performing that night. Plenty of people were there, mostly Veng, all dressed in turquoise togas with dark orange sashes. One of them came forward as we entered. Speckles of black triangles decorated his orange sash

"That's the manager," Relliope whispered into my ear. "You might want to have me hold on to Reggie for a bit; the Veng don't like pets."

"No?"

She shook her head, causing blue vapor to swirl around her. "I haven't seen one since I've been on Bisto. I was told only crazy people have them."

"Wonderful first impression." I handed Reggie over. Then I put on my best smile, and turned to meet my new boss.

"Entertainer Conroy, I am Selstrin. It is my pleasure to welcome you to the Pyramidal. Assembled here to join in your welcoming are the members of the staff who work in the lounge, waitrons and tenders and chefs and assorted others who see to the comforts of the audience that are coming to be entertained by you."

The Veng do not shake hands, nor do they engage in bows. Such rituals are only practiced between members of the same rist. Instead, as a sign of respect or regard, they tend to maintain gaze, typically for longer than humans find comfortable. Selstrin locked eyes with me like he expected us to go ten rounds in a staring contest. Looking away was not an option.

"Thank you very much." I didn't dare to even blink. "I am excited to be here. This is my first visit to a Veng world, and I hope you will find my work to your liking."

"No doubt," said Selstrin. "And toward that end, we have a small tradition here when new talent arrives. I trust you will not mind favoring us with a small sample."

"A sample?"

"Of your act. Here. Now. For the staff. Please, allow me to escort you to the stage."

Selstrin closed his eyes and kept them closed for a beat, then turned and began walking through the assemblage of workers to the stage and followed him up a ramp.

Usually when I'm up on stage, I'm either caught in the flood of a spotlight or the other lighting does an equally good job blinding me to everything else in the room. But this wasn't an actual performance. The house lights were on and I could see across the sea of tables going all the way to the bar at the back. I like to think most stages—even among aliens—are made of wood out of respect for the earliest, pre-technology traditions of the entertainment. Maybe the Veng didn't have that history; this stage was dark gray ceramo with a series of concentric rings of dark metal spaced a half meter apart radiating from the center all the way to the edge. Selstrin stepped between them, altering his stride as if deliberately avoiding the rings. I put a foot down on one and stopped. It wasn't exactly sticky, but my foot lingered there and a trickle of electricity darted up my leg for just an instant. I touched another ring as I followed Selstrin. The stickiness was the same, but the tingle felt different. If they were all like that, with some practice I could probably tell exactly where I stood on the stage by the feel from the rings.

"Your pardon, Entertainer, but I am not familiar with your style of performance. If you require any props or some kind of instrumentation to perform, I am unaware of such facts."

I shook my head. "No, nothing like that. But I do need a few volunteers. Three or four would do. And a like number of chairs."

"I offer myself." Selstrin turned to face his staff. "Who else would care to join me?"

Several Veng started toward the stage. I waved back all but the closest three. A couple others pulled chairs from some nearby tables and lined them up on the stage facing the audience.

I began with a bit of patter that I'd worked up while on the ship to calm any jangled nerves for audiences that had never met a human being before, let alone a hypnotist. I followed that with some polite and friendly questions of each volunteer, taking the measure of their responses and planning accordingly. From there I eased into a simple induction and as I'd found onboard the *Shpeshnoltoc*, Veng are excellent hypnotic subjects. They go down easy and they go down hard.

The staff watching gasped as I pushed their boss into a chair, and one by one had the others slump down next to him. I moved into an abbreviated version of my last show, going for splash rather than subtlety. It captivated them. The staff hung breathless on every bit of the routine. I froze their coworkers. I made them imitate the Veng equivalent of barnyard animals. I convinced several volunteers they could smell cold and hear heat. I caused people to believe they were other people with other lives. I made them forget basic things like numbers and kinship terms. The usual stuff that you might see at any hypnotist's show. The mainly Veng audience watched transfixed, as if I were transmuting lead into gold or water into raspberry root beer.

That kind of reaction exhilarates a performer. While it lasts there's nothing you can't do. But it empties you out too, and most times when the curtain falls and the spotlight goes dark, all I want to do is head back to my room and fall into bed. I finished my little command performance, delaying only a moment to leave a whispered trigger phrase in Selstrin that would cause him to slip back into trance. I left my volunteers with the suggestion that they'd awaken refreshed and with delighted memories of their experience on stage. Despite this my new boss only muttered a vague approval of my work and sent me on my way. I didn't care; I was past ready to see what kind of accommodations I'd be enjoying by heading there at once and taking a nap. Alas, it was not to be.

Now that I was actually on Bisto with the possibility of a long-term contract I needed to learn a lot more about the Veng concept of rist than Captain Telfano's learning modules had provided. Relliope had given me a datastick entitled *Compliance*, compiled by the Bisto Visitor's Bureau, specifically to introduce non-Veng to the many social taboos to be found here. So instead of pursuing that much needed nap, after finding my room I plugged the datastick into the information system and let it play.

It began with something I already knew, that every Veng was born into one of two hundred four possible rist. Rist wasn't just about what job you could take or what school you could attend. At some dim point in Veng history, most rist had declared eternal and irrevocable blood feud with at least one other. Limitations on vocation and education restricted members of feuding factions from meeting frequently, or if they did, kept such encounters to neutral zones where all historic animosities were largely set aside. Other rules of the system kept interactions at the level of dirty looks and the occasional shove or biting remark. Actual violence was limited to individuals, one Veng against another, and only at the higher ranks within a rist could it become lethal. Precise biological and social requirements had to be met—though the datastick didn't specify what those might be—but under the right circumstances a Veng could issue a challenge and then simply kill his opposite number in a feuding rist.

There was more information, quite a bit about Veng creation myths and their impact on social interactions, and something about a legal system of checks and balances that actually encouraged renewing the insults that had begun the ancient feuds. It went on and on, and somewhere between an explanation of sash colors and the judicious use of intoxicants as a way toward spiritual enlightenment, I found myself flat out on a round mattress that was too short for me. Soon after I was asleep.

Call me old fashioned but I normally wear a tuxedo when I perform. Selstrin wouldn't hear of it. He insisted that I had to be clothed in garb of traditional Veng cut. That meant a toga. Only tourists wore anything else. Even non-Veng who settled on Bisto adapted. It wasn't like they had much choice. Veng society has no concept of fashion; even the fabrics and colors they wear are dictated by their rist.

I gave up my pants and jacket, but Selstrin did allow some compromise. By feel, it was a classic Veng toga, but instead of being a solid color, I'd had it dyed to look like a buttoned tuxedo coat, white ruffled shirt, and loosened bow tie. The sash was a smoke-colored gauze that turned transparent under the stage lights and left me looking like an old world diplomatic ambassador at other times. On my feet I wore black slippers, polished like dress shoes. I missed having pants, but the tux-toga made me feel more myself when I stepped on stage for my first night at the Pyramidal.

The audience was packed, but they hadn't come for me. I was opening for Tintalerra. They all wanted to hear her. Hundreds of short, scaly, orange aliens greeted me with uncertain applause, as if to acknowledge they had to sit through whatever nonsense I had planned before they could get to the good stuff. Half of them looked disinterested, and the other half restless. Selstrin stood off in the wings anxiously drumming his fingers on the curtain. I wasn't worried. The Veng had no history of hypnosis, and the sheer novelty of my act blew them away. Within hours of that first show word of the wonders that I could elicit had begun to spread. The next night I faced another packed house, but nearly as many had shown up to see me, as had come for Tintalerra and her stylistic screechings.

The crowds kept coming, even after Tintalerra's tour moved on to another city. Selstrin assured me I was drawing a lot of repeat business. You couldn't prove it by me; despite my sincere attempt at discrimination, except by the color of their toga or sash I still couldn't tell one Veng from another. I had to believe that the manager could though, and just to be safe I cycled new bits into my act.

I'd been performing for ten days when Selstrin summoned me to his office. It overlooked the stage, a wide room with a curved back wall of one-way glass that from the other side just seemed to be part of the back of the club. It was the first time he'd called me in, though it was my second time there. Not a day had passed without him manufacturing some fault, offering up a disparaging comparison to a past performer, or whining that some change I'd made in my patter lacked proper diction. I'd worked for his kind before; most had been human, some not, but what they all had in common was an inability to be content or happy with the acts they hired. It didn't matter how large the crowds were, how big the night's receipts. They could always find something to complain about, always talk down any performer's success. The trick to dealing with the curmudgeons of the galaxy was to smile and nod, agree with them whether they were right or wrong, and then go ahead and do what struck me as the best course. Since there was no pleasing Selstrin, best to please myself instead.

Part of that had included dropping by his office for a surprise visit to test the trigger phrase I'd slipped into his unconscious memory during my demo performance. It worked, and he'd dropped into an immediate trance. I'd added a couple suggestions for post-hypnotic effects with simple triggers. I'd wiped his memory of the visit and left him to count to himself for a few moments while I let myself out.

On this second occasion in his office he was more out of sorts than usual. He had the lights low; a patch of illumination fell on Selstrin where he sat in an overstuffed chair behind a low slab of a desk. Another pool of light spotted a simpler chair in front of him. Couches and shelves faded along the side walls into darkness. The floor was a spongy carpet that absorbed my footfalls. I came into the room, stared at him in acknowledgment, and sank into the free chair. The air held a faint scent not unlike a mix of fried clams and violets that was oddly calming. I'd left my buffalito behind in my dressing room. Over the past few nights, Selstrin had made several grumbling remarks about Reggie, and I saw no point in fueling the club manager's ire any more than I had to.

The Veng didn't speak. He studied me. His shoulders and neck were tense. Some emotion had written itself across his face, the tightness of his lips, the set of his jaw. I couldn't get a good read on him; he seemed happy and annoyed and frightened all at once. We sat in silence for several minutes, him stewing and me becoming more bored than anxious. When he spoke, his voice was half its usual volume.

"Entertainer Conroy, I've received a message on your behalf. This is rarely acceptable. The relationship of my rist to yours should prevent my ever acting in anything resembling a secretarial position for you."

Who could be sending me messages? Billi wouldn't go through a middleman, least of all my boss, and supposedly he was on some Cliveden ship bringing the Celestial back with Svetlana. The only other people who knew me and knew I was on Bisto were either on the *Shpeshnoltoc* and had no reason to contact me, or were also on Bisto and could drop by to see me directly.

"My apologies. It was never my intention to put you in such a position. I will inform whoever sent the message not to do it again."

"You will do no such thing. You will pass along nothing of our conversation here today. Rather, you will dress in your finest attire and present yourself at the Hidden Wind tonight, at midnight."

"The Hidden Wind?"

"It is the finest restaurant in the city. Provide your name when you arrive, and you will be escorted to the Elder Glarp's private table. He has requested that you dine with him."

"Requested?"

"Don't be naive, Entertainer. Men such as the Elder Glarp have the rist and rank to receive anything they wish. You are performing here at the Pyramidal because he suggested that you should. As it turned out, you are a good fit for us, but even were you a lunkhead doing inept hand shadows on the back wall you would still appear on our stage if it pleased him. As for this dinner, you will go. You will be polite. You will not upset your patron. Am I clear?"

"Perfectly. Is there anything else?"

The Veng slumped in his chair and the warring emotions on his face resolved their battle. Annoyance had won out.

"Yes. Be sure to bring your creature with you. The Elder Glarp specifically requested that you do so."

I took a pod out to the edge of the city, where the travel tubes ran in simpler patterns. The proprietors of the Hidden Wind had located their restaurant at the intersection of several lines of naturally occurring magnetic force. I didn't understand the geology or meteorology involved, but storms built and exhausted themselves above the restaurant's transparent ceiling, built flush with the surface.

The decor was stark and angular, and very black; Selstrin's office would have been considered well lit by comparison. Flickering candles at the center of each table provided the only steady illumination, and little competition for the violent displays of the luminous storms overhead. Imagine using lightning for mood lighting, and then magnify the effect. When the storms hit a visual crescendo, it was as if dozens of lightning bolts struck, flashing not just in blinding white, but with strokes of red and yellow and blue that burned their shapes upon the retina causing after images to swim through the restaurant after every burst. A whiff of ozone in the air added further flair.

A waitron in a blue-black toga and a light blue servitor sash met me at the entrance. I'm not sure whether it was seeing me or seeing Reggie, but he took me by the hand, and guided me through a darkened maze of diners to an intimate three-sided table far away from anyone else. He placed a booster seat on the chair between us and gestured for me to set Reggie there. Then he left.

"Ah, Entertainer Conroy, you have come. I'm sorry, but I've been detained elsewhere, a matter of business which I hope to set to rights shortly. I expect to join you soon, but in the meantime please make yourself comfortable."

I don't startle easily, but disembodied voices in dark rooms punctuated by alien lightning can make me jump. Nor did my pulse slow when I turned toward the voice. A glowing, green apparition came toward me, the ghost of a Veng. It hovered low enough to the floor to give the impression that it actually stood there, though its slippered feet didn't quite touch. Other than its translucent appearance, this Veng looked to me just like every other one, but I recognized the voice.

"Elder Glarp?"

The waitron reappeared, pulling out my chair for me. I sat, and he vanished into the gloom again. The ghost of the Elder Glarp floated into its chair, and pretended to sit. Reggie was on his best behavior, sitting comfortably and waiting patiently. The storm display had cowed him a bit, but he seemed genuinely interested in the spectre at our table.

"Meaning no disrespect, but I don't know the proper protocols when speaking to a . . . rendering."

"None taken, Entertainer. I am the Elder Glarp, with his full memory and faculties, as he had them earlier in the day. We diverged the moment we parted company and I began having different experiences, perceptions, and cognitions. My unique memories and impressions will be integrated back into the original when he arrives and reabsorbs my essence. Or, I should say, his essence."

"So, in effect, there are two of you right now?"

"To an extent, though a rendering has minimal physicality. I won't actually be able to dine with you, though my form does have sufficient mass to let me use furniture, and to resonate the air to allow me speech. But I did not invite you to dinner here to speak of skimmings and renderings. I want to discuss some aspects of your act."

I chose my next words carefully. I don't let anyone tell me what I can and can't do on stage, but the Elder Glarp represented a rist that was responsible for running large portions of several cities on this and other planets in the system with a manner reminiscent of a crime syndicate. He personally owned most of this city. "I hope there's nothing in my act you found offensive."

"No, no, nothing like that." Before he could say more our waitron reappeared at our table with a bundle. He unwrapped the cloth out over the table, revealing a ring of colorful, bite-sized pastries. Then, with a flourish worthy of a magician pulling a tablecloth out from under a fully set banquet table, he fell back out of the candlelight, vanishing, cloth and all.

I blinked, and then looked more closely. The brilliant pastries glowed like faceted jewels, and hovered a millimeter or so above the table, surrounding our single candle.

"Try the blue ones, Entertainer. I believe you'll find them especially tasty."

Obligingly, I reached out, careful not to touch the surface of the table. I delicately pinched an azure hors d'oeuvre between finger and thumb and brought it to my lips. It was more dumpling than pastry, crispy and warm. It smelled of cinnamon and onions. I took a bite and tasted the most succulent crab ever, with a texture and consistency of semi-soft cheese.

"This is wonderful." The apparition of the Elder Glarp smiled.

"Feel free to give some to your pet, Entertainer. I confess I'm curious to see if a creature that I am told eats stone and steel will have a liking for crelteckle."

"Crelteckle? Hmm, I'd never imagine something with that kind of name would taste like this." I picked up a second crelteckle. "I try not to let Reggie eat a lot of dense stuff, except as treats. How is it you know of buffalo dogs? I didn't think the Arconi trade syndicate reached this far."

"They do not. Nor do the Arconi maintain any diplomatic relations with the Veng. Their worldview causes them to be all the same, egalitarian and indistinct. I believe it is linked to their utter lack of prevarication. To the last of them they misunderstand rist, and we cannot tolerate such disrespect. But I have heard of their creatures, and it is a rare pleasure to be in the presence of one. Is there anything it can't consume?"

I shrugged, and kept from my face any thoughts of the experiments back onboard the *Shpeshnoltoc*. Nothing in any of my research had hinted that the Veng possessed the slightest bit of telepathy. But they hadn't talked about the ectoplasm thing either. If the rendering in front of me could see my thoughts dinner was about to take an ugly turn.

"I haven't done exhaustive tests, and this far out from my homeworld I'm constantly finding new substances that I hadn't ever imagined," and I gestured at the tabletop, guessing some variant kept the pastries afloat.

"Ah, you've touched on the source of much of my people's wealth. Drift juice. I don't imagine you'll get the chance to find out if it agrees with him. Even so little as the faint film bonded to this table would cost you more than you'd earn working at the Pyramidal for a century.

I looked around the room, trying to recall how many tables I'd seen. The Hidden Wind wasn't small. There had to be at least twenty tables, maybe more. Did they all have a coating of drift juice? I waved a hand to take in the restaurant. "That seems pretty extravagant and wasteful for a restaurant. What's the point of it all?"

"Pure display." The Veng's doppelganger rose from his seat and turned to stare, and as if summoned by his gaze another Veng emerged from the dark. Lightning struck, and I wondered if the Elder Glarp had timed his entrance to take advantage of the effect.

"From what I've learned of humans," said the original Elder Glarp. "I expected you to appreciate this, Entertainer Conroy. It is a manifestation of rist."

"I understand that rist functions similarly to castes and clans among some historic human cultures. It's like a class system, only much more complex. That's what you meant about the Arconi, everyone in their society is equal."

The Elder Glarp snorted and took the vacated chair while his ghost responded. "And yet, as preposterous and unnatural as that is, they nonetheless have a successful, space faring society. It is a puzzlement I cannot fathom, and I have been privileged to be schooled by our finest scholars."

"And that's the point of this restaurant. Privilege."

"Of course. Privilege is but one corner of the triangle of rist," said the flesh and blood Veng.

"And the other two?"

"Prerogative," said the apparition, "and Power." It bowed to me and then pressed a palm to either side of the Elder Glarp's head, just above his earflaps. As I watched, the ghostly figure grew more translucent until, after only a few seconds, no trace of it remained.

The Elder Glarp had closed his eyes while this happened. He opened them now, took a deep breath, and let it out slowly. "Now then, back on track if you don't mind. I asked you here to talk about your work in my club. No, nothing in your act offended me. Quite the opposite, Entertainer Conroy, quite the opposite. Reports of your performances inspired me to learn more about this hypnosis of yours."

I needed only a moment to realize he was following up on the conversation his doppelganger had begun. Weird. "I'll be happy to answer anything I can."

"Excellent. So, tell me, do my people make good *subjects* for this hypnosis?"

"There's always variation within a race, but I'd say yes, the Veng psychological profile lends itself nicely to suggestion. Most of hypnosis involves bringing an individual to a state of consciousness where he is especially amenable to suggestion.

"Yes, yes, I saw how you altered and manipulated the beliefs of your participants back on the *Shpeshnoltoc.* And these changes, they are only temporary? They last only so long as the hypnosis itself?"

I nodded, fed Reggie another snack, and helped myself to one as well. Lavender, slightly sour and peppery at the same time, with a tantalizingly gritty texture. Utterly delicious. "Generally that's true. Some suggestions can be caused to linger after the subject has left the trance state, but even those are short lived without some kind of reinforcement."

The Veng looked delighted and swept several of the pastry-dumplings up in his hands, nearly juggling them. "Excellent, sir, most excellent. Now, I'm told you made one fellow believe he was of a different rist. You took a common Administrator, and convinced him he had been born a Legislator. You changed his rist!"

I laughed, "No, distinguished Elder, I did not. It was just a bit of entertainment. There was nothing real there."

"Yes, yes, of course, I did not mean it literally. No one witnessing the act believed the fellow was anything but an Administrator still, but subjectively—"

"Oh, well, subjective experience is different. While it happened, the change was real for him, he believed it, knew it had always been that way. Like a dream."

"I understand the concept, but what you don't appreciate, Entertainer, is that the Veng do not dream."

"Excuse me?"

"We sleep, as you do, but we do not dream. The body rests, the mind recoups, but there is no nightly, internal, phantasmagorical show for my kind, as I understand other beings experience. We go to sleep, and later we awaken refreshed, and remember nothing of the span between."

"I didn't know that."

"So, you will appreciate then that while one of my people might indulge in some slight piece of fantasy, a minor musing of imagination that he is other than the rist of his birth, there is never any weight to it, never any belief." He ate the pastries he'd been holding, then added, "Until you put it there."

"Elder Glarp, please, I meant no offense. I—"

"Be at ease. But I am intrigued. To think, for the duration of your performance, a person might be other than his birth had made him, free of his rist's responsibilities and obligations and bound by a completely different set. Truly amazing."

"That's what they call me." I followed it with a sheepish grin. The Elder Glarp smiled in response and with a wave summoned the waitron.

"Next course," he told him then returned his attention to me. "Entertainer, I hope you will indulge me. You are the first human I have had the desire to share a meal with. The demands of my position make it unlikely that we will meet again, but I would consider it a privilege to gather your impressions of some of our local cuisine."

I practically beamed, and made a mental note to thank my agent; I had no doubt that Billi had suggested the idea to the Veng back when he was working out my contract. "The pleasure is mine, I assure you. And anything you can tell me about the different stages of our meal would be most welcome."

"Excellent! And your creature must sample it all too. The novelty of it intrigues me."

The waitron appeared, and with one hand swept the remaining portion of our appetizers off our table. They took on the properties of an edible landslide as they skittered across, granted temporary group identity by the drift juice. The waitron had certainly practiced this before, as all of it flew unerringly into an open sack he held with his other hand. Reggie watched them vanish with as forlorn an expression as I have ever seen, and the Elder Glarp watched him watching.

"All of those were made from crelteckle. It dates back thousands of years to the Veng homeworld, where it was intended to represent the full range of possibilities of a meal, so that no matter one's expectations for what might be served, you could never be disappointed."

More food came. The Elder Glarp narrated its history and meaning, all of it variations of finger food that could be plucked up from where it floated above our table. We went through seven courses, each exquisite and each with its own rich history. I'd never had a patron who appreciated fine dining before. And this was the man Captain Telfano wanted to steal from. Dinner strengthened my resolve to turn the Cliveden's game back on her, and to find a way to do so without harming my host, a decent enough guy, despite being a short, orange crime boss. He hadn't asked a thing of me. And then—

"Now that we've shared a fine meal and conversation, I feel I know you much better, Entertainer. Well enough, in fact, to ask a small favor of you."

I swallowed my disappointment. The Elder Glarp was a businessman before all else. "I can't begin to imagine how I could be of assistance to you."

"I have a grandson. He is the only child of my youngest daughter. I know you've studied up on us, you're surely aware of how rare a female child is among my people. Most families have none, and I have been blessed with two. Perhaps in balance for that, my daughter's son has been born without ambition and a paucity of intellect. A good looking boy, he is like a pretty stone, content to sit and watch the world go by, to occasionally be noticed and regarded by passersby, but unmoved even by such attention."

I ventured a sympathetic nod. "This must cause your daughter sorrow."

"Quite the contrary, she encourages him in his ways. He is everything our rist is not. Worse, she named this useless boy after me, and while he will not replace me when I have died, it is likely my successor will raise him to a position of power and authority, as a gesture to honor my name. Can you imagine the chaos that will ensue? The ruin that will come to my rist?"

I spread my hands open before him. "What can I do?"

"I would have him shadow you, Entertainer. I believe he could learn much, perhaps even become inspired. Here you are, a lowly performer, yet in your way you can transform and juggle the rist of the Veng who fall under your spell. You travel the galaxy. You honor the customs of your hosts. You sit comfortably at table with your betters and converse with intelligence. If my grandson could be stirred to appreciate even one of these things by associating with you, you would have my undying gratitude."

"I don't know what to say."

"There is nothing to say. I will send him to the Pyramidal to meet you. It will not delight the manager there, but he understands his rist and will accept the situation. It is all but done. Aid me in this, Entertainer. Even a man of distant Earth can understand the value of having my appreciation."

CHAPTER TEN

Like Shooting Pickles In A Barrel

SELSTRIN SHOWED UP in my dressing room the next night, a few minutes after my second show of the day. He didn't knock—no one in Veng history ever invented knocking. Or whistling outside a doorway. Or even a polite "I'm here, and I'm coming in now" before entering a private room. If your rist allows, you to go in; if it doesn't, you wait to catch the person somewhere else. My rist was such that I had to be grateful I had privacy in the bathroom.

"I don't know what you said or did at your dinner last night, but the Elder Glarp has informed me he is sending his grandson to intern with us, starting tomorrow. With you, specifically."

"You sound happy about it."

"And why shouldn't I be? My work here at the Pyramidal has been noticed and deemed more than satisfactory for the Younger Glarp to visit and learn from. You will *not* ruin this for me, Entertainer. I expect nothing but your best while we host the Elder Glarp's grandson. Your very best!"

"Any idea how long this hosting will run for?"

"That's not for me to say, or either of us to know. It will end when it ends. And then we will see where we are."

"Anything else, Mr. Loompa?"

"Excelsior!" Selstrin clapped his hands together twice, turned smartly on his left heel, and departed. If there'd been a witness, I had a ready explanation about testing the effectiveness of post-hypnotic triggers on the Veng mind. More simply, I'd tired of Selstrin's management style, and a harmless trigger or two was my way of staying happy in my work place.

My dressing room was one of several sharing a corridor that accessed the stage at one end and an elevator down to employee housing at the other. On any given day most of the other dressing rooms were vacant. Selstrin preferred to have his acts double and triple up rather than afford each performer his own space. It was just one more irritating thing about the man, particularly considering that my dressing room's space was smaller than my living quarters. It was one simple room with only a few chairs, a makeup table, and a small partition wall with a bathroom around one side and a shower alcove around the other. The walls were bare, off-white ceramo, and only the door to the corridor marred any of them in any way. The only adornment to the room was a scattering of rugs.

Reggie had come down to the dressing room with me before the show, curled up on a fluffy towel beneath my makeup table and gone to sleep. He'd slept through my performance, and through Selstrin's surprise visit. I roused him now so we could go out and catch a late night snack before heading back to our room.

A knock on my door startled me and Reggie yipped. I opened the door to find Svetlana. She wore a toga of white linen with a dark blue sash, and the same utility belt she'd worn every time I'd seen her. Her eyes lit up and she smiled.

"I caught most of your show. I especially liked the part where you made that commodities broker believe he was a female lounge singer. I'd never have expected a Veng to behave like such a diva."

"You haven't seen the real thing. Believe me, he wasn't exaggerating. But you didn't drop in to review my show. Are you back already? Is Billi with you? Did you bring the Celestial?"

"I'm obviously back. Billi too. We arrived early this morning and parted ways through customs. He said something about meetings and setting up additional bookings and that he'd get to the Pyramidal within a day or so."

"And the Celestial?"

"Well, after you left the ship, I stayed on until we reached Throg's World. That's where my patron was in, uh, storage. Billi and I disembarked and met with it. It expressed frustration that you had left before reaching it, but Billi made arrangements and very quickly he found us passage on another Cliveden ship doing the counter-route just a few days later."

"Where is it? Did you get a room here in the hotel?"

"I did, but it's not there. In fact, it's not actually on Bisto."

"You said you took a ship back from Throg's World—"

"We did. And we got off here. There's just a small problem."

"Which is?"

"The Veng wouldn't let the Celestial come down to the surface. They're keeping it on their stupid floating island, in quarantine."

"You told me it's walking around in a vat-grown husk. Its body is a closed system that's immune to disease. Why is it in quarantine?"

"It's not a health issue, it's more . . . political. The Celestial didn't fit any of their specifications when it came through the immigration scan."

I grunted an acknowledgment. Visitations from Celestials were rare enough that its husk might not conform to any of the known biological profiles for traveling sentients. "They released you though? How did you escape quarantine?"

"I scanned clean." She smirked, and the change in her expression made my stomach flip flop. "I'm only the second Terran to come through their system, but they had a profile on file. I don't know if or when they'll let the Celestial out."

"How am I supposed to meet your patron when Elroy's in quarantine?"

"I wish you wouldn't call it that. And it's not like it's offworld, just off the surface."

"You can get past a quarantine order?"

"Never doubt it. The surgeon general has branded me the Celestial's *mintaro*."

"I beg your pardon?"

"Sorry, there's no Traveler equivalent. It's a pre-Industrial Veng term. A *mintaro* is a coincidental, unrelated individual, typically of a different rist who, due to circumstances of time and place, is burdened with legal responsibility for another. It's also something of a derogatory term as it devalues the bearer's rist."

I frowned. All non-Veng visitors, depending on their stated reasons for visiting, were assigned to one of the rist that had no blood feuds. This went a long way to preventing alien ambassadors from being assassinated by feuding Veng, and indeed, apart from the rist sanctioned murder associated with blood feud, the Veng engaged in no violent crime whatsoever.

I retrieved my passport from my toga's internal pocket and opened it to the page impregnated with my rist chemo-glyph by the immigration service of Bisto's World. Wisps of fragrance rose from the document.

"I am of the emerald eastern snowfall," I recited, inhaling the crisp, snowy odor with its hint of pine. "An entertainer, generally limited to the city sectors but welcome in the homes of all who seek diversion from the day."

Svetlana smiled. "Emerald eastern snowfall, right. That's not an accurate translation, but it works well enough." She unrolled her own passport from a spot on her utility belt and flashed her glyph too quickly for me to catch its scent. "Precious stone, ordinal direction, weather effect, blah blah blah. I'm glossed as a natural philosopher, or I will be once I lose the stigma of being mintaro. Either way though, I'm harmless."

I nodded but it didn't help my frown. That covered two of the eleven feud-free rist to which non-Veng could be assigned. The others accounted for merchants, the insane, artists, menial laborers, two classifications of diplomats, and three kinds of bureaucrats. "If you're mintaro to the Celestial, you can't be of the same rist. What rist did they assign to it?"

"That's part of the problem they're having with it. The Celestial is defying their classification system."

"It's not cooperating?"

"Oh no, it's quite cooperative. The system is the trouble. Not only does the Celestial not fit neatly into one of the available rist for non-Veng, it doesn't fit into any of the rist at all. The Celestial's responses to the battery of questions they asked resulted in an answer that doesn't parse into the existing array. Immigration is in a tizzy. All the more reason for them to invoke mintaro. Which, since the Celestial isn't comfortable with crowds and moving among humanoids, works out fine. I'm free to visit any time I like, and bring along whomsoever I choose."

"You said the Celestial's attempt at classification produced a response that didn't fit any existing rist. What was it?"

"Deity," she said. "So, you ready to go?"

The pod ride to the floating island took an hour, most of it spent transferring to the hospital itself. Virtually all of the traffic flowed out, not in. Like salmon eager for a hot date, we forged against the current until we reached the level of shared jurisdiction between the hospital proper and the end of Immigration.

The hospital décor resembled nothing I'd ever seen before, and was god-awful. Except for the occasional matte black conduit or pipe, everything had been constructed using a pale, translucent yellow material. Picture building an entire hospital out of amber, but instead of a warm glow, shift along the spectrum a bit to a sickly, lemony hue. Maybe being orange-skinned the Veng find a jaundiced view mildly refreshing. I didn't.

The walls, floors, and ceilings all hurt my eyes as we wound our way through corridor after corridor. Svetlana had no problem, but I found myself flinching at people walking by on the level overhead, and stumbling to avoid stepping on people actually a level or more below us. Looking straight ahead didn't help. The corridors all curved, which meant constantly looking through walls into patients' rooms.

"Are we almost there?" My stomach had been gurgling since we'd left the reassuring opaque shaft of the elevator pad. Reggie had spent the past five minutes craning his head around with worried looks.

"Nearly. Quarantine is all the way in. I imagine it's a precaution in case anyone ever tries to break out."

Around the next arc we nearly bumped into two Veng wearing loose-fitting togas the same shade as the walls. They stood to one side with their heads bent together, conferring in whispers and sharp, staccato gestures. I couldn't understand a single word. Svetlana smirked as we passed, and glanced back over her shoulder.

"Did I miss something?"

"Interns." She raised a hand to her mouth, stifling the louder part of a delightful laugh. "You just caught a glimpse of the Veng version of rock, paper, scissors."

"Oh?"

"A ship's come in that may have been contaminated with some viral agent. Everyone onboard has to endure a two-day isolation, and one of the passengers was a female Veng. The interns were playing to see who gets to treat her."

"You picked up all that in a few seconds?"

She shrugged, and her nose crinkled as she said, "Bistprof has a lot of redundancy built in to it. I just extrapolated from the little bit I heard."

"Bistprof?"

"That's not their name for it of course."

"Whose name for what?"

"The Veng language used by the professional rists here on Bisto. You've really been relying on Traveler too much, you know?"

I started counting on my fingers. "Just how many languages do you speak?"

"I don't speak Bistprof."

"But you just—"

"I understand it, but I don't speak it. No one here would speak it back to me. I'm the wrong rist. Not to mention being mintaro at the moment. Oh, look, we've arrived."

And we had. Our curving corridor opened onto a large cul-de-sac lined with entrances to many smaller chambers. I could see into every one. A few were dark and empty. Most contained two or three of the rounded mounds the Veng favored in lieu of mattresses. A pair of Veng armed with stun batons flanked one doorway. That room lacked the sleeping mound and instead contained a nearly vertical slab. A human-sized figure lay propped against it. Through layers of pale yellow wall I couldn't determine its coloring, only that it was darker than the scowling Veng standing next to it. It looked neckless, lightly muscled and apparently sexless.

"That's your Celestial?" I asked and pointed.

"Yep. That's it. And from the expression of the quarantine physician, I'm guessing it's not actually here."

"I'm looking right at it."

"Just because the meat is cooked, doesn't mean it's been eaten."

"What?"

"Sorry, ancient Akkadian expression. I've been trying forever to find a modern application; I guess that wasn't it. Any way, the body's here, but that doesn't guarantee the Celestial is actually inside. It hasn't yet gotten used to being our size, and claims the husk still chafes a bit, though what it has to chafe is beyond me. Any way, sometimes it skips out. C'mon."

What could I say? I'd never broken in an artificial body before. I followed Svetlana past the pair of security guards in black togas, through the door, and into the presence of the Celestial.

The Veng physician glanced up as we stepped in and motioned for me to close the translucent door behind me. I did and then turned to get my first good look at the Celestial. I gasped. It was Captain Coelecanth!

But it wasn't; it couldn't be. The vat-grown husk from that long distant summer job had perished with the ship it had sabotaged. The mottled green figure laying in front of me only looked the same. It made sense. Someone, somewhere, grew the husks using a form of organic manufacturing that had never been seen on Earth. Why shouldn't one product off of its assembly line look like any other?

"What was that?" said Svetlana, glaring in response to my reaction.

"Nothing. For a moment it reminded me of someone I used to know."

"Very funny. Have you been watching Picklemen of Kandahar?"

"Picklemen of Where?"

"Kandahar. It's a city in Iraq, back on Earth."

"I know that. Just as I know they don't have Picklemen."

"Oh, so you know who does have Picklemen then?"

"What the hell are Picklemen? What are you talking about?"

"Nothing. I made it up. What are *you* talking about? You said it reminded you of someone. There's nothing that looks like a Celestial."

"Except maybe another Celestial. Or the husk it's waiting to fill. Remember, I've met one before."

Svetlana's eyes widened and she opened her mouth to say something, but the physician interrupted her.

"Ah, the other Earther." The Veng looked me over. "I suppose that either makes sense or is the most improbable, if not both at once."

I looked at Svetlana over my shoulder for an explanation but she merely shrugged.

"Are you expecting it to wake up any time soon?" I asked.

"It's not asleep," said the doctor. "Only living things can sleep. This is a synthetic device."

"Since when?" Svetlana marched up to confront the doctor, breaching his personal space that by Veng custom went far beyond getting into his face. "We were both fully cognizant life forms when we disembarked this morning, and you quarantined it."

I edged closer to the husk on the slab and pressed my fingertips against its arm, much as I'd once touched Captain Coelecanth, and felt a room-temperature rubberiness. "And you attempted to assign it rist?"

"Our diagnostic instruments were . . . malfunctioning earlier, creating the illusion that this thing possessed true life." The Veng blushed brown across his cheeks and forehead, but quickly recovered. He glared at Svetlana. "There are those on my staff who believe we have been the victims of an elaborate ruse, and the prothonotary has twice inquired if perhaps the use of illegal, self-aware technology was employed during your disembarkation. He has offered the forms for filing a suspicion of criminal intent."

Svetlana looked like a woman who liked an argument for its own sake. Before she could engage the doctor in one I pressed on. "So, you're saying it's not a living being, right?"

The doctor snorted, a sound that I've found most aliens make, and for the same reasons, throughout the galaxy. "It is nothing more than a cleverly shaped gourd."

"Then I suspect there's no reason for it to remain under quarantine any longer."

Svetlana caught the direction of my thinking, switched her own mental gears, and chimed in with a convincing "Maybe I ought to talk to your prothonotary about the forms for incompetent diagnoses and malicious delay."

The Veng stood up straighter. Despite his shorter height his posture gave every indication of staring down his nose at Svetlana. "I will not be spoken to in such tones by a mintaro."

"She's not mintaro," I said.

"I'm not?" Svetlana blinked with confusion.

"Of course she is," said the doctor. "I was present when the surgeon general himself devalued her rist and bound her to this . . . thing."

"This thing you've described as a *cleverly shaped gourd*? Tell me, doctor, can a gourd have rist?"

"Of course not. Don't be obscene."

I shrugged. "As I've had the term explained to me, one can only be named mintaro to an individual of another rist. Since a gourd can't have rist, she can't be its mintaro."

The doctor's earlier blush was nothing compared to the deep umber that now colored his entire head as he realized the enormity of the insult he'd made. He dropped his gaze at once, ducked his head, and hurried past us, opening the door and slamming it behind. Through the pale yellow walls I watched as he barked some instruction to the guards. Svetlana aimed a smile my way that almost made me forget her bias against humans. Almost.

"That was wonderful," she said.

The two guards stepped inside. "We've been instructed to help you carry your luggage," said one of them. The doctor himself had gone.

"Luggage?"

I moved away from the slab and nudged Svetlana with an elbow. "The husk."

"Oh, right. Well, if you each take an end, I'm sure you can manage it with no trouble. Is there a waiting area nearby?"

"There are several throughout the hospital," said guard number two. "Would you like us to lead you to one?"

"Yes, please. The one farthest out."

They nodded. Each took an end of the Celestial's husk and hoisted him into the air. They carried him out of the room.

"A waiting area?" I said to Svetlana as we followed.

"Where better to wait for the Celestial to return? It will climb back into its shell sooner or later, and when it does, we'll be well placed to walk out of here."

Ten minutes later we were comfortably ensconced in what Svetlana assured me was the avian lingery, which sounded to my ear like the way I always think 'lingerie' should be pronounced. It was the waiting space for family members of any winged aliens undergoing medical treatment. The weather of Bisto guaranteed few flying tourists and the location saw little use. The pair of guards deposited the Celestial's husk upon a low bench upholstered with a design like an explosion in a mustard factory. They closed the door behind them as they left. That door, like the walls, floor, and ceiling of the lingery, was refreshingly opaque.

"How long are we going to have to wait?" I set Reggie on the floor and he scampered around the room. The design reminded me of a birdcage. The floor plan was an equilateral octagon. The walls rose up the height of three floors through the rest of the hospital. An open stair wound around the inside of the room, with landings and perches at several points.

Svetlana knelt alongside the husk, one hand resting upon its chest. "I don't know. It depends on how long it's been away. When I left to attend your performance, the Celestial still inhabited its body."

I completed my circuit of the room and started another one. "And in all this time, Gordo's never told you why it wants to see me?"

"Gordo?" She raised her head, her eyebrows lifting higher.

I shrugged. "You didn't like the name Elroy. I have to call it something. You're the one who said Traveler lacked pronouns for it."

Svetlana rose and advanced on me, her face transformed with anger. "This is a being whose natural state occupies a volume greater than a planet. Its consciousness has existed longer than our species has. How about a little respect?"

"When I meet your Celestial I'll be respectful. All I've met so far has been a patronizing doctor, a pair of security guards, and a Pickleman from Western Canada."

"Kandahar." She scooped Reggie up into her arms and snuggled him.

I smirked. "I thought you made them up. If they're imaginary, can't they be from Canada as well? The climate likely produces a better brine. Keeps them crunchy."

Svetlana's anger crumpled away. "You're not making any more sense than I was."

<<What is the advantage to being crunchy?>> The voice was flat, almost affectless. I'd heard more lively machine voices, but I turned toward its source all the same. On the bench, the eyelids of the Celestial's husk snapped open, followed by the slower lifting of a pale green nictitating membrane, to reveal glistening white eyes that lacked any apparent pupil. It turned to lock its gaze on me, causing it to swivel its torso and partially rise up from the bench. <<And what is brine?>>

Svetlana whirled and all but genuflected, dropping to her knees alongside the bench. "I have brought the hypnotist as you instructed." She switched from Traveler to English, speaking it with some variety of twang from the American South.

The Celestial's eyelids half closed as it regarded me, a gesture I decided was the equivalent of a nod when your face and head flow directly into your chest. It raised its left arm, folding back the fingers as it did so, like some ancient vegetable hitchhiker. With the other arm it pushed itself up until it was in a sitting position.

Svetlana hissed at me. "Kneel."

I frowned. "I don't think that's going to happen."

<<It is not obeisance I require.>> The Celestial still sounded like a bad translation machine. <<I ask only that you bring your forehead within my reach.>>

"Oh. Sure." I stepped closer and bowed. The Celestial reached for me. It grazed its thumb up the arc of one eyebrow and down the other. I had a flash of disequilibrium, and then its thumb was sliding down the side of my face and then back and over my ear, and then it stopped.

<<Remarkable,>> said the Celestial still in English. <<And you two are of the same race? Remarkable.>> It lowered its hand to its lap and regarded me with large liquid eyes, waiting.

Something clicked for me.

"Your voice has changed. You have inflection and contour, color and timbre. Presence." The difference was unnerving; what was happening?

<<Do I?>> It turned its torso toward Svetlana. <<Am I understanding him as I believe I understand him?>> This time it spoke with a different diction and pitch. And a twang. It spoke with the same dialect that Svetlana had used.

"Yes, though I've never seen the effect so clearly before."

The Celestial turned back to me as it continued, switching back to the voice it had used a moment before, rounded tones that projected and filled the lingery. <<I believe that is because of Mr. Conroy's profession. It inhabits his use of language.>>

Everything fell into place. The Celestial had spoken to Svetlana in her own accent, her own style of speaking, and it was doing the same to me, using its own version of my stage voice. It mimicked me perfectly. And it had started after touching my head.

"Why did you do that?" I said, holding up a thumb.

<<I needed your language.>>

"No, you didn't. You already had English from Svetlana, and if you spoke to the Immigration officials earlier or to the doctors, then you already have a command of Traveler. You didn't need to get either from me."

<<I did not say I needed English, I said I needed your language. Not the language you speak, the language as you speak it.>>

"Why?"

<<To anchor me. There are so many of you here, orders of magnitude more in this space that feels infinitely compressed to me. Anchoring helps me to find my way back to this form.>> It crossed its index fingers over the thumb of each hand in a gesture I'd never seen before and pointed them at its own chest.

"Why me? Why not one of the many Veng around here? Why'd you want me for an anchor?"

<<For the same reason I chose Ms. Villanova.>>

"What, because we're Earthers?"

<<Earthers? No, that wouldn't make any sense.>>

"Sense to you and sense to me are not exactly a matching set."

"You're talking to a Celestial, Mr. Conroy, a Celestial!" said Svetlana. "You can't talk to it that way."

"No, apparently I'm supposed to talk to it just this way, because this is my way of speaking, and it likes it so much it copied it for itself."

The Celestial interrupted before Svetlana could rebuke me further or before I could descend to even snarkier comments. <<I chose you both because of the shape of your fields. I discovered it when you served under Captain Coelacanth. It was the first time I could discern an individual amidst so many others. The configuration is rare, though by no means unique to Earthers. I believe it is what causes you to move among others not of your kind.>>

That made no sense to me and my face must have shown it.

"It means our brains," said Svetlana. "It believes that's what makes us ultra-xenophiles."

"So I like people. And I admit I have a very loose definition of the word. So what?"

<<That preference facilitates my own communication at this level.>>

"What, you couldn't funnel down to our size and talk to just anyone?"

<<Funnel? Ah, yes, further evidence that you are the proper choice. But, no, because talking is the least part of it. Humanoid speech required mastery of symbol systems and acoustic encodings, but offered no real challenge.>>

"Yeah, a child could do it." Svetlana frowned at me. "So, if it's not communication, what's the problem?"

<<Reducing the scale of perception to the correct range, but no further. Attending to the proper variety of stimuli, and filtering out the rest, lest they distract or influence my experiences at this level. Anchoring.>>

Finally something that made sense. Every living organism, sentient or otherwise, needs to be able to pick and choose what is and isn't important in its surroundings. Half of hypnotism is knowing how to manipulate another person's attentional filters, dictating what they focus on, and what they ignore."

"We provide the Celestial with the reference points it needs," said Svetlana. Her voice rang with a mix of awe and adoration that I'd heard before. Svetlana Villanova *was* a groupie after all; she just wasn't mine.

"Okay, I get that. But, and this is the part no one seems to appreciate, I didn't ask to be a reference point or an anchor, and I don't recall anyone asking me, either."

"Are you an imbecile?" asked Svetlana. Any hint of awe or adoration that had been in her voice a moment before had vanished. "You're being of assistance to a Celestial! Half the races in the galaxy feature them into their eschatologies! It's an honor and a privilege that one even notices your existence."

She was right. I knew she was right, and any other day I'd have probably agreed. But I've met a lot of aliens, and if I've learned anything, it's that it never pays to let them push you around.

"Maybe, but not if Elroy here is going to be rude about it. Or are we excusing clouds of super-intelligent dust from the need for simple courtesy?"

<<I ask for no special treatment. Nor do I wish your acquaintance with me to be a burden. I would welcome the opportunity to converse with you again, at times of your convenience. And I would also like to observe you at your work altering the perceptions and memories of others.>>

"Why?"

The Celestial's mouth opened slightly and held there, like it'd been frozen in the midst of eating soup. It took me several beats to realize this was the closest a husk could come to a smile. I glanced at Svetlana for confirmation, and caught her own nervous half smile.

<<I'm curious as to the technique. I know how I would attempt such a thing, through direct manipulation of the cortical fields of my target. But I do not detect the ability to do this in you. My interest is the same motivation that inspired me to walk among you in this body. I am curious.>>

"I'm all for curiosity. That's something I can relate to. So, yeah, you're welcome to catch my show, any time. I'm sure Svetlana can get you the schedule. And if there's time after, we can talk for a bit. Because I have questions for you too."

Svetlana handed me my buffalito, frowning all the while.

The Celestial didn't appear to notice. <<I will answer anything I am able, Mr. Conroy.>>

That turned out to be the end of my audience. Svetlana ushered me out of the lingery, all the while explaining that she'd catch up with me later but for now had to make special arrangements to summon an industrial pod—one with a commercial length cargo bed. While the Celestial's husk had ripened enough for its habitation it had achieved full maturity. The immobility imposed by its quarantine had stiffened its muscle articulation leaving it as bendable as a girder. The Veng pods were roomy enough once you were inside, but entering them did require at least minimal ability to bend at the waist. Long story short, I wouldn't be sharing any cab rides with the vegetable embodiment of any alien mythology any time soon.

I just shook my head and made my way back out to the spot where Relliope had met me when I'd first arrived, and caught a cab back to the Pyramidal. I never did get my late night snack. By the time Reggie and I got back I wanted sleep more than food.

CHAPTER ELEVEN

Nepotism and Death

MY ROOM at the Pyramidal didn't have smart walls like my cabin back aboard the *Shpeshnoltoc,* but its basic amenities were of high quality. The ceiling was a tad lower than I'd have preferred, but given the height of the Veng it made sense. A gorgeous, hand-woven rug occupied a spot on the floor alongside the bed, making it the first thing my bare feet touched when I woke up. Housekeeping swapped it out every night while I slept. The size stayed about the same, but the design, weave, and texture changed. Every morning I stepped down onto something different, sometimes springy, sometimes scratchy, sometimes soft and warm. It says something about the Veng psyche that they want their hotel guests to start each day with a new and uncertain tactile sensation, but I'm not sure exactly what. It was an odd custom, but I liked it.

I'd planned to sleep in until noon, then rise for a special performance. A quasi-community group had formed, made up of Veng who worked at the time of my evening shows. They'd filed a complaint with the government, which in turn had required the Pyramidal to accommodate the grievance with an occasional matinee. I'd never heard of performance by legislation before, but there's a reason why they call it an *alien* world after all. It was my luck that the matinee would be the morning after my late night with the Celestial. There's a reason there are alarm clocks too, but mine never got the chance to go off.

"When does the *amazing* begin? Or does that only apply to your stage work? Or is it just a name and semantically irrelevant?" The unfamiliar voice came from a Veng in the short hallway formed by my room's far wall and the space used by the closet and bathroom. I stared at the ceiling clock. I'd learned enough of the prevailing script on Bisto to read the time displayed there. Not even close to noon. My buffalito awoke in an even grumpier mood and before I could start swearing at the intruder Reggie launched himself from his sleeping spot at the foot of the bed and began barking at him.

"Entertainer, contain your creetlebaum!" The mocking tone acquired a hint of fear. "If you don't, I'll tell my grandfather."

Oh, I thought, followed promptly by *shit*. I sat up in bed, rubbing sleep from my eyes with one hand and covering my yawn with the other. Both arms went up over my head in a stretch and I rolled my head from side to side.

"Reggie, heel!" Wonder of wonders, he did.

"That was smart of you. My grandfather would not have been pleased."

"Is that really how you want to start this relationship? With threats of your grampa? We'll get along better if you leave the posturing behind and avoid the whining."

"I will not be spoken to in that manner by an employee!"

Reggie growled, and backed up to the bed, ostensibly to protect me.

"I'm not your employee. I work for the Pyramidal. And before you start in about how you can wiggle a finger and get my manager in trouble as a means of getting back at me, keep in mind that the Elder Glarp asked me to do him a favor. If you're going to act like a brat then maybe I'll have to talk to him about *you*. Got it?"

Amidst an understandable degree of stammering and fuming the Veng nodded.

"Great. Now, I could apologize for embarrassing you just now, and in theory you could apologize for coming in here and acting like a jerk, but why don't we start off fresh?" I wrapped the bedsheet around me, toga-fashion, and stood up, offering my hand to the Younger Glarp. "Call me Conroy. We'll leave the *Amazing* part for the paying customers. So, what do I call you?"

"I am the Younger Glarp—"

"No, not your title, what's your name?"

"I—my friends call me Lew."

"Not to be presumptuous, but if it's a choice between being a friend and an underling, I think I'll go with friend. Now why don't you head down to cafe off the lobby and I'll join you after I've had a moment to clean up, okay?"

I don't make a habit of taking Reggie into the bathroom with me, but it seemed the wiser course. I knotted up some bath towels for him to chew on, and stepped into what passed for a shower at the Pyramidal. One day I'm going to publish a treatise correlating alien civilizations with their achievements in bathing and sanitary plumbing; I'll probably be awarded doctoral degrees from multiple universities back on Earth for it. But that would have to keep for another day. Today I had to figure out what to do with Lew.

The Pyramidal is home to several restaurants, including a rather nice breakfast café with the bizarre name of *The Frustrum*. I'd been taking my meals there most mornings since my arrival, and I still hadn't worked my way through the menu. The staff knew me, a few had even been present at Selstrin's command performance and others had caught my show. They always kept a table for me in an especially sunny spot despite the entire complex being hundreds of meters beneath the surface—something to do with mirrors and shafts.

As we stepped up this morning the hostess took one look at the Younger Glarp and ushered us past my usual table to a back courtyard I'd never seen before. The space held only three tables, but had room for a dozen more. A low fountain burbled to itself, dominating the courtyard. Here and there slow-moving kinetic sculptures turned according to the directions of their inner workings, releasing bursts of fragrance similar to honeysuckle and lilacs. The decor was more opulent, the tables and chairs more ornate, the art on the floor more vivid. A musical trio softly playing stringed instruments, half-hidden by some fronds. The hostess herself took our orders. My companion either didn't notice, or found none of this unusual. Rist had its privileges.

Lew said nothing as we waited for our meal to arrive. I'd requested a huge bowl of vegetable chowder for Reggie, and he lowered his face into it the moment the hostess set it in front of him. Lew stared but remained quiet. As I cut into a local variation on steak and eggs—the eggs and steak were both from a domesticated amphibian something like a cross between an iguana and a cat, though Veng dietary custom required they not be from the same family line—that changed. My newfound best friend pushed aside his breakfast and began to whine.

"Grandfather believes that by spending time with you I will gain insight into being Veng. This makes no sense. You are Human. What could you possibly teach me about being Veng?"

From his expression, he really expected an answer. I took a bite of steak. I chewed pensively. I swallowed, took a sip of fruit juice, and set my utensils down. Celestial entelechies might be out of my league, but I could handle the occasional idiot grandson.

"You're taking him too literally. Obviously I can't teach you to be a Veng. Your grandfather believes I have certain traits worth emulating. He's hoping some of them will rub off on you."

Lew made a face that normally requires the use of a lemon and a considerable amount of sucking. "What, like a skin disorder?"

"Again, not literally. Look, you've probably had a life of privilege, surrounded by people telling you what they thought you'd want to hear, or at least what they imagined would be best for them to tell you. I'm not going to do that. We're just going to spend some time together, talk about this and that, share a few meals. You'll watch me work, and if you have any questions about anything, I'll do my best to answer them. Sound good?"

"Entertainer, it sounds stupid."

"Right. Glad to see you're going to be open-minded. And call me Conroy; remember, we're going to be friends."

"This is a waste of time. I should be working, not sitting around with a low rist alien."

"You have a job? Now see, that's something your grandfather hadn't mentioned. What kind of work do you do?"

"I'm a Presence."

"Excuse me? What does that mean?"

"Do you know nothing? I abide. It is a demanding position."

"You'll pardon my ignorance, but why and where and for whom do you abide?"

The Younger Glarp had picked up a spoonish implement and begun mixing and mashing the separate items on his plate like a five-year old. He sighed, dropped the utensil, and looked upon me with the kind of pity usually reserved for small children, the elderly, and the mentally infirm.

"For the past half year I have been the senior Presence for the Tvost refinery on the northern edge of the city. I linger by turns in the business offices, the laboratories, even the warehouses on occasion. This raises the market value of their merchandise."

"Just by you standing around?"

"Yes. It's critical to their profits. A temporary absence won't cause a significant impact, but if my grandfather insists I stay with you for more than a couple days it will wreck havoc with their stock price. I need to let them know I won't be coming in today; unless, do you suppose my grandfather already told them?"

I shrugged. "I suppose it's possible. It probably wouldn't hurt to call or drop by. Maybe you'll give me a tour?"

"Why would you possibly care to see such a thing?"

"I never know what's going to be useful to work into my act, or what Reggie might enjoy. What kinds of things do they refine there?"

"I told you, industrial things. Fuel for the floating island, drift juice for visiting ships, low friction gels for use in the city's travel tubes. Stuff like that."

I paused in mid-chew. Other than the ostentatious display at the Elder Glarp's restaurant I hadn't encountered yet encountered any drift juice. "Really? Then we should definitely tour. I'm more curious than ever, to see both the facility and how you do your job."

"There's nothing really to see in either instance. The refinery produces assorted gunks, and like I told you, I abide there and their value benefits accordingly."

"Does that only happen when you're on the job? If you're hanging out with me, you'll also be attending my performances. What happens then?"

"I would expect the Pyramidal to raise their prices. Even when not on duty, I can't help but influence the popularity enjoyed by the things I touch."

Reggie pulled his head out of his bowl and gave me a look that meant he wanted to eat the bowl too. That had upset the Frustrum's staff before, and while the presence of the Younger Glarp probably meant I could get away with it today, it was still a bad idea. Instead I picked him up and settled him on my lap so he could eat what was on my plate. I'd been almost done any way.

"Good to know. Why don't we finish up here, then you can watch my matinee. We'll have our field trip after that!"

It's always a pleasure to perform for an enthusiastic audience. The Veng attending the matinee so hungered to be there that they'd filed a lawsuit. Stage performers draw on the energy from a good audience. I basked in it that afternoon, and any leftover sleepiness vanished like piñata candy at a children's party. I strode onto the stage and found my mark using the tingling metal rings embedded in the floor. I wrapped myself in the excitement of my audience, and began what looked to be my best performance on Bisto.

Near the end of the show I had three volunteers up on stage with me, all entranced and accepting whatever I told them as irrefutable fact. They had the audience laughing so hard that dozens of Veng were shooting alcoholic citrus juice through the nostril slits of their flat faces. My participants had all been Veng when they volunteered. I'd convinced two of them that they were Glamorkan architects from rival firms, vying for the privilege to build a series of aerial prisons for the third volunteer. She believed herself to be a character out of Bisto folklore, a methane-breathing demon with a fondness for tormenting children.

The two architects took turns pitching bizarre structures for the incarceration of young Veng, each speaking with the exaggerated precision and painful slowness of the oldest of Glamorks. The demon put them through their paces, suggesting more and more horrid means for instilling anguish in school children as a method of softening them up prior to roasting them for dinner.

In the midst of a particularly ludicrous description of ventilation shafts made of toxic gases and rancid meat, as the audience members lay gasping with laughter and thumping their tables in delight, I glimpsed something that sounded alarm bells in my head. One Veng wasn't laughing.

The lounge at the Pyramidal consists of some fifty round tables; each one accommodates between two and six Veng. At the table nearest the stage, a somber alien fidgeted and cast dirty looks at an oblivious Veng at another table. None of the other audience members noticed, but I had. I also saw Selstrin. He stood in the wings off stage, watching the show with a smile on his face. I dropped one hand behind my back where the audience couldn't see as I waved to get his attention. I was too late. The unlaughing Veng shoved back his chair, leaped onto his table, and proclaimed, "Keleph Jobono, Third Seat of the Octagonal Gem, I am for you!" Then he drew a squiggly knife from within his toga and threw himself into the air. He came down in the middle of the adjacent table, and plunged the blade into the chest of a startled Veng, presumably a fellow named Keleph Jobono.

I froze. My volunteers didn't stop. The instructions I'd given left them oblivious to the rest of the world. But the audience didn't react either. Even those sitting at the murderer's and victim's tables barely noticed. They moved their chairs slightly as the corpse slumped forward, but kept laughing at the antics of my hypnotized players. Only the handful of non-Veng in the audience, scattered throughout, in ones and twos, blanched or gasped or, in one case, became ill at the addition of a homicide to the afternoon's entertainment. But the Veng didn't care.

Nor did any of them so much as lift a finger to detain the murderer. He struggled for several moments, trying to wrench the knife free of his victim's chest, failed, and finally gave up. Leaving the murder weapon stuck there, he rolled off the table and returned to his own seat at the next table, presumably with every intention of sitting back and finally getting to enjoy my show.

That's when the ghost appeared.

It rose from the neck of the dead Veng's toga, a slight wisp of greenish vapor. It grew in density and volume, a solid column of ectoplasm that congealed into the form of a Veng, the same Veng that lay dead beneath it. And then it spoke.

"In life I was Keleph, husband of Jelayna, father of Seward and Chelt. I served the Thane of the Octagonal Gem with loyalty for forty-three years. As a token of his grace he bestowed upon me the means of my revenge. Petara of the Vitreous Lozenge has slain me and taken me from my family. I shall not rest until I have returned the gift." The ghost of Keleph floated in the direction of his murderer. Judging expressions on alien faces is tricky at best, but from my vantage on the stage I would have sworn that the emotion the killer displayed was not fear, but surprise. He ran for the exit. The ghost followed, flowing through audience members with the effortless motion of every cartoon apparition I'd ever seen. On the stage my volunteers continued their respective parts, while the Veng watching them laughed and laughed.

Somehow, I finished the show. It wasn't the murder that had unnerved me, audience members have killed one another during my act on three previous occasions back in Human Space. But in each case the decedents had shown proper courtesy; once they died they stayed dead. None had ever been so rude as to manifest a ghost. I didn't believe in vengeful spirits, or at least I hadn't before Seward and Chelt's freshly departed daddy rose up and took off in pursuit of his murderer. That kind of thing goes a long way to reforming the thickest of skeptics.

What had chilled me was the lack of reaction. I let my two architects babble on a while longer, until one of them finally offered to use his own saurian children as part of a construction demo for the demon, which really brought the house down and had the Veng in the audience on their feet and applauding wildly.

Leaving on a high note is a standard trope of the entertainment biz, and the image of the ghost was still fresh in my mind. I put my three volunteers back to sleep on stage. The audience hung on my words as I wiped the trio's memories of everything they'd done. I added a few suggestions for feelings of well-being and satisfaction, wishing all the while that someone could do the same for me. Then with a staccato command and the snap of my fingers I brought them to full wakefulness. They stood, sheepish and confused; the audience cheered them. As they stepped down to rejoin their respective tables I thanked them, thanked the audience, reminded them of my name, and tapped the remote I had strapped to my wrist. The stage lights winked out instantly. The audience gasped and I slipped back behind a curtain. An instant later the houselights came up on a bare stage. My tux-toga felt clammy against my skin where the sweat of the stage lights and my own anxiety had dried. I wanted a drink to calm my nerves, but first I needed to make sure Reggie was alright. There's not much in the natural world that can harm a buffalo dog, but the supernatural might be another story. As I made my way through the backstage corridor to my dressing room Selstrin came charging at me.

"Conroy! I demand you control your creetlebaum."

"Are you talking about Reggie? What's to control? When I'm on stage he sleeps in my dressing room."

"You mean destroys your dressing room. I did not want to say this in front of the Younger Glarp, out of concern for your standing with him, but this cannot continue. Your creetlebaum has on three separate occasions eaten large portions of your rugs."

"Rugs? The area rugs around my makeup table? Those rugs? I thought your staff was swapping them out."

"Indeed they are, as they should be. The exchanging of rugs is an ancient tradition among Veng. This facility proudly boasts more than ten thousand distinct rugs, and they move throughout our every sleeping room and office. Three of these are now out of circulation until they can be restored. It is chaos!"

"I had no idea Reggie was eating rugs. I'll take them out of his reach."

"It is not just the rugs. Two days ago he devoured the cleaning automaton as it attempted to vacuum your dressing room. And yesterday he ate through the conduits that pipe water to staff housing."

"I'm sorry about that. I'm working on it with him. He had a traumatic plumbing experience recently."

"I do not want to hear excuses. Resolve the problem, or I will. Find a Bluie veterinarian if you have to, but get it done. Even with the automated sensors he has flooded several rooms before they could shut off the flow."

"I'll look into hiring a sitter for him while I'm on stage. Will that satisfy you?"

"You don't appear to comprehend the seriousness of this, Entertainer. Do you appreciate the damage this has caused? Or the labor I've had to divert to clean and repair? I am deducting the costs from your salary."

I pushed past him. The corridor curved and the door to my dressing room was in sight. Selstrin dogged my steps, muttering about replacement charges.

"Whatever. I don't want to hear it just now. In case you didn't notice, a man was killed this afternoon, in the middle of my show."

"What? Don't be a dunderling spoke, of course I noticed. Not a thing happens in this hotel that I don't know of the instant it occurs."

"You're not concerned the murderer escaped, or that the victim's ghost pursued him?"

"I'm relieved that Keleph's *rendering* chased the killer out of the club. One less body for my staff to have to deal with it. But that's the extent of it, Conroy. The victim wasn't of my rist, and he certainly wasn't of yours. The Pyramidal is a popular site. We get two or three feud deaths a season. That's more than anywhere else on Bisto. I know people who would kill to be killed here. What are you getting squeamish about? You never seen a corpse before?"

"I've never seen an audience unmoved by a corpse in their midst."

"Get over yourself, Entertainer. Your only worry should be keeping the audience happy." He scowled. "I admit, you manage that pretty well. Just keep that beast of yours under control, and you might have a future here."

I shook my head. "Not if people keep getting murdered in my audience."

"Bite your tongue. Just be glad that Keleph wasn't one of your volunteers."

CHAPTER TWELVE

Sweat Shop

THE YOUNGER GLARP sat on a rug on the floor of my dressing room playing with Reggie. He held one end of a second rug with his right hand. My buffalo dog gripped the other end in his mouth. They were deep in the throes of a fierce game of tug-of-war doomed to result in two smaller rugs. Neither would care. Ignored by them both, a long, shallow puddle paralleled one wall. Someone had shoved a laundry cart's worth of towels along the line where the wall met the floor, sopping up the worst of it and leaving behind a prodigious, soggy mess. As I closed the door behind me, the Glarp sat up, pulling Reggie into his lap.

"Are you ready to visit the refinery now?"

"Lew, a man was just killed. In the middle of my show. One guy just stood up, called this other guy out, and shoved a knife into him."

The Veng nodded, unwinding the towel from his hand. "Selstrin mentioned it a few moments ago. The Octagonal Gem. I suppose it's all my fault."

"Your fault? Why?"

"These things come in waves. This is only the second feud killing in the city in over a year. There's always a cascade effect. Tempers get short and offenses that might have been settled less lethally instead elicit more extreme repercussions. I expect at least one more before things calm down again"

"But why is that your fault?"

"Ten days ago I cut off the head of a nephew of the youngest, great grandson of the thane of the Vermillion Beam. You didn't hear about it? Under other circumstance it would have been a tremendous violation of rist for someone of my status to kill someone so far below me, but there'd been a huge insult in front of many witnesses. Grandfather says I should have let it go, but he's so old he's forgotten how defend his own honor."

"What was the insult?"

"He sloshed a glass of slinko on me and my fiancé-to-be. Looking back, it was probably just an accident; if it had just been me, I'd have ignored it, but you can't just go soaking the toga of a high-ranking woman and not expect repercussions. Grandfather has forbade me from carrying anything that might be used as a weapon."

"And now other Veng are going to be running around killing one another?"

"No, of course not. We're not barbarians. Other than the killings associated with the sanctioned days commemorating the anniversaries of feuds, assassinations only occur between specific rists, and when justified. Over the next few days we'll probably learn that someone in the rist of the Vitreous Lozenge—"

"The what?"

"That was Petara's, the killer's, rist. Probably a member of that rist recently was, or was about to be, disgraced in a way which would have brought dishonor on the entire rist. Today's killing, and the soon-to-come vengeance of the victim's rendering, will go a long way to distract from that humiliation."

"You're saying the murderer knew this Keleph had a rendering on a dead man's switch?"

"If he didn't, the elders of his rist who suggested the killing surely did. Why else would anyone bother? The cycles of blood feud are well established. Today was not one of the sanctioned days for these two rist to engage with one another. It's a very loose secret who has the means for renderings. I know you've seen my grandfather's. I have three uncles with renderings as well. I received mine when I was promoted to Presence. It adds to the position, making my work that much more desirable."

"You're a better lingerer because you have a rendering?"

"Not better, just more valuable. Here." He stood and handed Reggie to me. "There's something odd with your pet. He's much lighter than he looks. But then, sometimes, he's not."

I snatched him away, which Reggie took for a new game. He bleated and attempted to lick my face. "It's just a trick. Something I've been teaching him for use in the act." I pressed my palm against one of Reggie's hooves, and without him moving a muscle I felt the slightest bit of something pushing back.

"You're very strange, Conroy. As if it were possible to teach a creetlebaum tricks. Delusional! I still think spending time with you is a waste, but you're not as boring as I imagined you would be. Come now, get out of your work clothes. I've already summoned a pod to take us to the refinery."

"It won't take me long. I'll even show you a trick that I taught my *creetlebaum*. Watch." I sat down in front of my makeup mirror and put Reggie on the table. He sat back on his haunches and regarded me with serious concentration. I leaned forward, and braced myself.

"Reggie, makeup away!"

The buffalito lunged, jaw dropping wide as he went for my face. He slobbered all over me for a moment. I had an instant's tingling, and then he was licking my face like before. The difference was that all of my stage makeup had vanished.

"Hah! Now *that* was amazing!" The Younger Glarp was laughing and staring at the same time.

I transferred Reggie to the floor, and wiped my face with a hand towel. "Give me a minute to grab a shower and change, and we'll be on our way." I pushed back from the table and stepped around the corner to the alcove housing the shower stall. The shower didn't use water. I didn't know what it used, sonics or ionized air or phlogiston. To make it work I stepped into the stall, clothes and all, waved my hand over an activation sensor, and then slowly turned in place two or three times. Moments later I and my tux-toga were grime and odor free. I pulled my work clothes off and shrugged into an ordinary toga for my assigned rist, snow-white with a lush green sash. Back in the dressing room the Younger Glarp had Reggie in his arms again. Or rather, in his hands. He'd brought them together, palms up. Reggie balanced on them, his four tiny hooves gathered under him in a point. He looked a bit like a child's top, and despite the precariousness of his footing, appeared quite comfortable. I frowned, and took him up in my arms before Lew could comment.

"Come on, you said you had a pod waiting. Let's go see where you do your abiding."

The entry point of the Tvost refinery was scarcely the size of my dressing room. It opened unto the pod pad but was otherwise an open box with a small desk in one back corner. A receptionist glared from behind that desk as I stepped across the threshold, defined only by a change in the color of the floor from dark gray to light. He had enough attitude to spare some for my buffalito too. He slid off his stool and stood, as if blocking my access to the back wall.

"You're lost, friend. This is not a public facility. And even if it were, livestock wouldn't be permitted." His toga had an ugly pattern of diagonal pale blue and green stripes. The bouncers at the Pyramidal wore the same design. I did my best to look nonthreatening.

He came closer, and despite my greater height I had the feeling he was looking down at me. "Do you have a pod waiting, or do you need me to call one for you."

"He's with me, Kranf," said Lew coming in behind me.

Those few words transformed the receptionist like an incantation. He went from a polite but firm security guard to an obsequious doorman.

"Oh, your pardon, I didn't see you there, sir." Kranf replaced his bluster with equal parts grovel and simper. "You're not on the list today. Supervisor Geofp called an agency for a temp. I was told you might be away for several days."

"There's a Presence temp agency?" I asked.

"Of course. You can't expect them to operate without a Presence? Can you imagine how it would affect the value and reputation of Tvost?" Lew rolled his eyes at me. Kranf studied me like I was some kind of economic-anarchist.

"Sorry. We, uh, do things a bit differently where I come from."

"No harm done, Entertainer. After all, I shouldn't expect someone in your position to have anything more than the skimpiest knowledge of corporate structure or high finance."

I bit back a retort about having been CEO of an interplanetary company that probably rivaled the refinery that *employed* him. But nothing would be gained by matching the Younger Glarp for petulance. He wouldn't have believed me any way. My rist defined my role and actions as surely as physical laws and insisted it couldn't be true. Besides, I'd left the company in ruins, and I didn't want to mention that part.

Lew gestured for me to follow, then walked through the back wall as if it wasn't there.

"Oh." I followed him. The illusory wall blocked both light and heat. Passing through it felt like stepping into a vast oven. Reggie likes it warmer, and the change in temperature elicited a contented yawn from him. He shifted his position, snuggling into the space between my arm and side for a nap.

A diffused light came from overhead, dimmer than the anteroom. We stood in what had to be a warehouse or manufacturing facility. I'd been expecting a robotic assembly line or some intricate collection of centrifuges and chemical assay devices or an alchemical laboratory with endless alembics and retorts and coils of glass tubing. Instead the place reminded me of an enormous elementary school cafeteria. Eighteen rows of industrial-style picnic tables receded into the distance. Mounds of pasty goo filled each table and uncounted Veng sat on those benches, their hands buried in the mass before them. From the movement of the goo I suspected they were kneading it from within, working their fingers through it.

"What are they doing?"

Lew gave me another impatient look. "They're making drift juice."

"Out of that mess? It looks like bread dough."

"The *weltenscal*? No, of course not. That's merely the temporary substrate that facilitates the process."

"You lost me, Lew. What process?"

"The creation of drift juice, Conroy. Don't you know anything?"

I shook my head. "I know that gunk isn't drift juice."

"Of course not. This is the near end of the process. The people at these closest tables are working on no more than the first hundred or so chemical reactions. When they finish those, they pass their work on to the next table, who perform the next suite of sequences, and so on all the way down the line. A couple hundred thousand reactions later, at the last tables in each row, you get drift juice, the most desirable substance in the galaxy. At least that's what my grandfather believes. To me it's just expensive sweat."

"Drift juice is made out of sweat?"

"Veng sweat. That's the first stage of it, any way. Each person here sweats, works it into the weltenscal, and then recycles it back into their bodies. That process kicks off a chemical reaction which results in a different kind of sweat. The cycle continues up the line, growing more and more complex."

"Your people have that kind of control over the chemistry of your own bodies!"

"Some do. It's a trait that can be nurtured. There are only a few rist that possess it, and among those that do there are special schools for training. Some never get past the first few tables. Some master the entire spectrum of reactions. Most specialize in certain stages."

"So there are Veng who can do it all? Start off by working up a healthy sweat and work it all the way to drift juice by themselves?"

Lew sighed at me like I was a dim witted relative at a family reunion. "Of course."

"What's to prevent them from bypassing the whole refinery corporation and selling a bit of their own on the side."

He laughed. Not a small chuckle but a deep belly laugh like I'd never yet seen from a Veng. His arms went around his waist in a great self-hug and he doubled over. His entire body shook with the raucous noise of it. Veng sitting at all the nearer tables turned to stare. Eventually, he managed to quell his mirth and straighten up.

"Ever the entertainer, eh? What you describe can't happen. You might as well ask, what is to prevent you from performing brain surgery on poor Kranf out there? Or teaching the young how to swim? Or preparing crelteckle for my grandfather. It's rist, Conroy. We are who we were born to be. Only in the make believe world of your stage show could it be otherwise. That's a fantasy. This is the real world here."

Before I could reply another Veng came striding down one of the aisles between the picnic tables. His toga had a zigzag pattern of pale blues and greens. He was shouting as he neared us. "What's gong on here? What is the meaning of this? Do you have any idea the kind of disruption you could be causing? We have a schedule to maintain, and if your misbehavior has resulted in the slightest delay I will personally ensure that you never, ever again, so much as—"

Lew turned his back on me to see who was yelling, which had the salutary effect of cutting it off in mid-shout. He spoke into the sudden quiet.

"Hello, Geofp. Allow me to introduce my companion and temporary mentor, the Entertainer Conroy. Entertainer, this is Supervisor Geofp. My grandfather groomed him for this position himself. He's been in charge of this refinery for twenty-three years. And you know what? He's never missed quota. A credit to his rist, is our Geofp."

"Thank you, sir. Please forgive me, I didn't know it was you. You're, um, not supposed to be here today. We secured a temporary replacement from an agency. He's making his rounds now, over in section sixteen, I believe, if you wanted to look in." Running and shouting had left him winded. He studied me out of the corner of his eye as he caught his breath and finally turned to acknowledge me. "Hello, Entertainer." His face screwed up as he faced the Younger Glarp again and asked, "Temporary mentor?"

"It's the Elder Glarp's idea. My grandfather believes that I can learn something of value by spending time with him. If there's any truth to that, it makes sense to bring him here. Unlikely I know, but consider what an enhancement to my work as a Presence would mean for Tvost? He's one of the few humans to ever come to Bisto. Grandfather personally booked him to perform at the Pyramidal. You should catch his show. I can have a table saved for you, if you like."

"Table? Oh, yes, thank you. Most generous of you, sir. If you'll excuse me, I, uh, need to check on something. Quota, you understand."

"Absolutely. We're almost done here. I just want to show him the other end of things. We'll catch a pod from out back by the loading dock and be no trouble. Come along, Conroy."

Lew sauntered off down the aisle formed by two rows of industrial picnic tables. I nodded to Geofp, muttered something like "nice meeting you, hope you'll come to the show," and followed. Between his casual pace and my longer legs I caught up with my protégé almost at once, but waited until we were out of the supervisor's earshot.

"I see that rist also conveys all the benefit of pecking order."

"Pecking? What are you going on about now?"

Instead of replying I stared at the Veng we passed. None of them looked up at us. Judging from Geofp's reaction, the place didn't receive many visitors. Where was the interest from the rank and file? Instead of a curious glance our way or comment to a neighboring coworker, they all stayed focused on their work, gazing blankly at the place where their wriggling fingers were buried wrist deep in sweaty dough.

We were causing an effect though. As I looked out at the continuing rows of tables and benches, I detected a ripple. All around us every Veng sat up a little straighter. It was like watching dominoes tumbling around me, the entire cascade set in motion by our being there. But it wasn't me, it was all Lew. Just as I was physiologically incapable of sweating drift juice, I lacked the proper Veng trait to recognize, consciously or otherwise, a Presence. Pride underlay that ripple. The hundreds of Veng we passed might be little more than cogs in a vast machine of the refinery, condemned by their rist to a life of literal sweat, but they were Tvost employees. A living symbol of all that meant walked among them. They perked up, without diverting from their work. Lew didn't just raise the stock value, he also raised morale.

We kept walking. The sameness of it started to wear on me. The stupefying heat of the place, the endless tables of innumerable orange Veng all in identical beige togas kneading and sweating, sweating and kneading. The logistics of how any of them ever took a bathroom break gnawed at me. Nor was there any end in sight. My height gave me an unobstructed view ahead, but other than the leading edge of our ripple all I saw beyond were more tables and more Veng.

"It's not much further," the Younger Glarp said to me over his shoulder. "Trust me, it will be worth it."

I looked down at the back of his head and almost missed the trick. The ripple had stopped moving forward. That same unending prospect in front of us vanished in an instant. The heat, the noise, the tables, the Veng, just ceased to exist. Reggie stirred, yawned soundlessly and opened his eyes. I spun around and there was a wall behind me, flat and unadorned. I knocked on it. Solid.

"Did you drop something? Do you need to go back?" Lew's eyebrows waggled the question.

"What just happened?"

"What do you mean?"

"We were there, and now we're here."

"Yeah? So?"

"How?"

"How . . . what?"

"How did we get here from there?"

That patient, patronizing expression returned to Lew's face. "We walked. You and I. We started at the far end of the production room, and now we're here."

"Which is where?"

"The next room over. What, did the heat get to you? I really like crossing the wall myself. The temperature change is refreshing."

Wall. Like the other, keeping in light and sound. And if one side could be made to look like a blank wall, apparently the other could be outfitted with a projection of workers. I thought of parakeets with tiny mirrors in their cages.

"Sorry. I . . . didn't realize the walls only went one way."

"Well they don't, of course. That's just how this one is usually set. If we need to go back in I can have Geofp change the coding. Are you sure you're okay? You're acting a little odd."

"I was a bit disoriented, but I'm okay now." The room we occupied had about the same dimensions as the reception room, far narrower than the factory we'd just crossed. "If we'd walked down a different aisle, what would have happened when we reached the wall?"

Lew took this as another opportunity to roll his eyes, further evidence—

if he needed it—that the idea I had anything to teach him was ludicrous. "We'd be standing in one of the adjacent storage rooms. Now snap out of it, this is what I brought you here to see."

Our current location, this *storage* room, was a closed cube, painfully bright and white, featureless and empty except for us and a rectangular white pedestal in the center. Lew rapped his knuckles on it and the top opened to reveal nearly a square meter of shimmering blue of drift juice.

"Is this a clean room?" I asked.

"Of course it's clean. Janitorial automata come through on a regular basis."

"No, I mean clean as in free of all dust and bacteria, for manufacturing purposes."

"What? No, I told you, this is storage. This room is for the culmination of effort of the two rows we walked between. Go ahead, take a look. That's drift juice, Entertainer. It's why everyone else in the galaxy wishes they were Veng. There's enough there to barter a planet with."

It looked like the stuff Captain Telfano had shown me, but in vastly greater quantity. "Can I touch it?"

"Certainly, but don't press too far beneath the surface. This batch has already cured. It's stable in that container, but even so with that kind of quantity if you pushed your whole hand in the gravimetric fluctuations could rip it from your arm."

I advanced to the pedestal and leaned over the surface, gingerly grazing it with a fingernail. I caused a ripple, and I felt *something* move through the air, a tiny wave of force pushed me backward and simultaneously pulled me in closer. I dipped forward, positioning my body to block Lew's view of my buffalo dog as Reggie leaned in, awake and curious. He skimmed his tongue across the surface of the drift juice, lapping up several deep slurps before I could stop him, many times the amount he'd practiced with back onboard the Cliveden ship. I jerked away, stumbling back from the pedestal. Lew looked amused. Reggie looked perplexed, his mouth firmly closed as he chewed, just as he had back onboard the *Shpeshnoltoc.*

"What did you mean by *cured*?"

"After the workers complete the final chemical transformations, their secretions aren't yet drift juice. Living tissue can't sustain the real stuff. No, the last stage doesn't involve Veng biochemistry. The raw fluids are pooled, and then super-cooled. Then it's allowed to return to room temperature. Only then, after another week or so of internal stabilizations does it begin to exhibit all the properties of drift juice. At that point it's considered cured."

"So this batch is ready to go?"

"Yeah, pretty much. Storage rooms like this one are used for temporary holding, after final curing but prior to distribution. Say, is your creetlebaum all right? He's looking strange. I mean, even for a creetlebaum."

I cradled Reggie in both hands and brought him up so we were eye to eye. He was still chewing.

"You going to swallow that, boy?" I whispered to him. "Swallow it, or spit it up, one or the other."

I don't know if he understood me, or had simply reached some critical count, but he swallowed and opened his mouth to show me his tongue.

"I think we just got too close to the drift juice. Maybe we should head back to the Pyramidal."

"My thought as well." Lew stepped to the blank wall opposite the one we'd come through and knocked. An instant later the wall vanished revealing an open platform, empty except for a small desk along the wall to the right, and a very hostile-looking Veng standing right in front of us. He hadn't made a move in our direction, but his hands were in motion pulling a pair of stun batons from the folds of his toga, a garment with the same pale blue and green pattern as Kranf had been wearing. The batons changed direction and were swiftly put away as he recognized the Young Glarp, and the anger melted away even faster.

"My apologies, sir. I'd been informed that you were present, but not that you'd be exiting here. Did you need my help with anything?" And the way he said the last word, it was clear that it meant both Reggie and myself, as well as whatever form of discomfort Lew might like applied to us.

"Stuvo, how nice to see you. Please give my regards to your father. He is well, yes?"

"Oh, yes, sir. Annoyed that he was taken off the line after the accident, but adjusting well enough. I'll be sure and let him know you asked after him. Very kind of you, sir."

"Not at all. He's a good man. Oh, where are my manners? Stuvo, this is the Entertainer Conroy and his creetlebaum. My grandfather wanted me to spend some time with him, so I've taken him on a tour. Would you mind summoning a pod for us? It's time we returned."

The reference to the Elder Glarp worked faster than one of my posthypnotic triggers. Stuvo recalibrated himself before our eyes, and Reggie and I went from potential threats to blessed guests. There was more head nodding and a few more *yes, sir's*, and in short order a travel pod arrived and we were on our way back to the Pyramidal. We were nearly all the way back before I remembered that a man had been killed on my stage. The Younger Glarp had provided a nice diversion. I needed to find myself another one.

CHAPTER THIRTEEN

Cerates and Unguents

AS WE ENTERED the grand rotunda of the Pyramidal, Lew went right and I went left. He had errands to run but promised to catch up with me the next day before my show. He hinted he would have a big surprise then hurried off before I could discourage him. I don't like surprises, big or otherwise. As a professional strategy for keeping my head attached to my neck, I find it best to avoid surprises from the spoiled relatives of overly powerful aliens. Somewhere where along the course of my mentoring program I'd neglected to explain this to Lew.

Reggie made an odd gurgling noise and gave me that same quizzical look he'd first shown back onboard the *Shpeshnoltoc*. I'd kept a firm grip on him in the pod during trip back to keep him from snagging a bite of anything. I didn't want to trigger a regurgitation. Back on the ship he'd kept the stuff down longer, but maybe the greater volume would make a difference. My new plan involved getting to my room with all deliberate speed and feeding Reggie. If he was going to puke, I wanted it on my terms.

My brilliant plan was dashed by my agent, who rounded the same corner of the lobby as Reggie and me, but in the opposite direction. We didn't knock one another over, but only because Billi grappled three arms around my leg and torso to keep himself from tumbling.

"Conroy! Just the ban I'm looking for. The Veng love you. The Elder Glarp wants to extend your contract and have you perform at one of his other properties in another city. And with a twelve percent bump in your fee."

Billi talked as he extricated himself from the embrace of our collision. He paused to give Reggie's chin a scritch just behind the tufts of his beard. Reggie forgot his discomfort for a moment and preened, stretching toward the Pelk's fingers. Billi smiled, reached with a middle hand into one of many pockets custom-sewn into his toga and withdrew a small hunk of plastic for my pet.

Reggie lunged for it and had swallowed it whole before I could react. Crap.

"Hold open one of your pockets, Billi. Don't ask questions, just do it!" And then Reggie burped.

I held my buffalito behind his front legs, allowing me to position his torso as I liked. I aimed his face at the side of Billi's toga.

"I don't understand. What are you doing?"

"Just keep the mouth of the pocket as wide as you can. Any moment now. . ."

Reggie left off a string of four more burps, coughed, and then spewed. My aim was good, and the resulting stream of liquid blue metal landed in the waiting pocket. Better still, the angle and position of our bodies had hidden the details from any Veng passing by. They might see me clutching my buffalo dog, and they'd probably see Billi fooling with his toga, but the rest was blocked from view.

Reggie felt better instantly; he craned his head around as far as he could, attempting to lick my hands. Billi looked less pleased as he staggered to keep his footing. He managed to look both frightened and angry at the same time.

"Conroy, are you insane? Why do you have that? Barely any Veng are supposed to have that. That's worth a billion times what you could bake in a lifetime here. Are you trying to get us killed?"

"I'll explain it all to you later. For now though we need to get that put away somewhere safe."

"You *will* explain this, Conroy. But stay here. You're the one everyone is watching. I'll take care of this. Go have a drink at the bar. I'll join you there after I've changed togas. This one needs to be put in a hamper."

"The Veng don't use hampers."

His eyes bulged more than usual as he glared. "Go. Keep out of trouble for a little while. You can start working on your explanation. I'll be right back."

He pressed a middle hand over the pocket and dropped so that his other limbs were all legs. He sprinted towards the elevators and out of site. He was right, I did need to work out what to tell him. A little disinhibition might help, and the Pyramidal had nine bars. The closest, and the one I chose was the one intended for guests who had just checked in and were waiting for their rooms, were checking out but wanted to linger and enjoy the facilities just a moment longer, or anyone who wanted a quick break before getting on with their lives. It'd been decorated with an oceanic theme, the source for which didn't exist on Bisto and seemed to make the bar's patrons wistful for shorelines of other worlds. The furnishings and fixtures recreated a sandy cove with stone niches carved by absent waves. A salty tang of nonexistent seawater hung in the air. A few pre-dinner drinkers were scattered among a flotsam of tables but I continued past them and grabbed a seat at one end of a long driftwood-styled bar. I settled Reggie down on the counter and pushed a bowl of dried poki, a citrus-like berry that was the Bisto equivalent of bar peanuts, under his muzzle. They smelled a bit like tangerines and a bit like cherries, and in dried form, they quickly turned his mouth and tongue purple.

The bartender hurried over for my order. She was much taller than a Veng, with pale skin and eyes that leaked blue vapor. It was Relliope, the woman who'd met me when I first arrived on Bisto, and escorted me to the Pyramidal. Reggie had been distracted by the poki, or would probably have stampeded across the bar counter to reach her. As she arrived he launched himself into the air forcing the woman to catch him. He rewarded her by eagerly licking her face, painting purple streaks across her pale skin.

"Hello, Mr. Conroy." She gently set the squirming buffalo dog back onto the bar. "What can I get for you? And for your little friend?"

I pulled Reggie back and offered him the bowl again. He whuffled but settled down with it. "He's fine with the snack mix. As for me . . . I don't suppose you have any raspberry rootbeer?"

She shook her head, vapor expanding outward to either side. "Sorry, I don't know those terms. My Traveler isn't very good, I'm afraid. Can you break that down for me? I understand berries, but what makes them *rasp*? And I can serve you any of several varieties of beer, but I don't understand what you mean by their *root*."

I smiled. "My own fault. I was being parochial. What do most of your Veng customers drink?"

"They tend to ask for one of the varieties of *slinko*. I think it's vile, but maybe it's an acquired taste."

"What's in slinko?"

She shrugged. It sent a delightful ripple through her toga. "Straight slinko is just fermented poki fruit. Dark slinko is like regular slinko, but it's been aged in vats of rancid poki peels for at least a year. That's what gives it that dark purply color. Hot slinko is actually not hot at all, they just call it that. It's dark slinko that's been distilled. And once in a while someone will ask for dead slinko, which isn't really slinko at all; it's a distillation of the juices you get when you press the rancid poki peels used in making dark slinko. You have to drink it pretty fast; it smells awful."

"When in Rome," I said, still thinking about her toga. "Why don't you start me with a glass of the straight stuff."

"Coming right up!" She flashed me a smiled and scooted down the bar, the blue mist from her eyes painting a trail in the air. I watched as she pulled a cylindrical glass from under the counter and deftly parked it beneath the business end of a multi-tipped nozzle and squeezed the trigger. Slinko was apparently on tap, which made sense given its popularity. Seconds later she placed a glass filled with a foamy pink brew in front of me.

"Let me know what you think of it. If you don't like it, I'll be happy to get you something else." And then she was off again, back down the bar seeing to a patron waiting to settle up.

I sipped my slinko. It was . . . different. Mildly alcoholic, with a tart, citrusy aroma and flavor, but managing to be sour at the same time. Kind of like drinking a boozy, pickled pink grapefruit juice. Reggie had paused in his grazing of the poki mix, looking at my glass with raw curiosity. I spilled some slinko onto the bartop. He gave it a couple of licks, made a faint yipping sound, and returned to the dried fruit. Definitely an acquired taste.

Down the bar a Veng had paid and was receiving change from the Relliope, an assortment of triangular chits that the Veng used as hard currency. I watched him take one of the chits and place it back on the counter, presumably a tip; he gathered the rest into the palm of his hand which then moved inside his tunic. Relliope placed a hand over the chit and slid it back toward her, vanishing it from the bartop. She gave the man a smile and the blue fog receded for a moment. The Veng paused, reached a hand back into his toga, and placed another chit in front of her. She repeated the palming move and the smile. The blue vapor had returned to its normal depth. Again, as the customer turned to go, it receded, and again he paused, turned around, and left another chit on the bar. The man shook his head, as if in a fog of his own, and wandered toward the exit and the lobby beyond.

"What just happened?" I said when Relliope came over to check on me.

She frowned and as I looked at her for a moment I could almost see her eyes; the fog had faded again. Her eyes glowed faintly, a solid azure blue without any white. Before I could remark on them I was facedown on the counter as an imaginary white hot poker skewered the back of my head. My bartender had doubled over as well, her head resting opposite mine. Bits of blue vapor drifted into my mouth. I tried to remember how to breathe. We both lay gasping like fish out of water. No one came around to help us. It probably only lasted an instant, but the subjective experience was of a good ten minutes before I could even blink. Relliope recovered faster, raising her head and vanishing from my limited field of vision.

"Are you okay? I'm so sorry . . . I didn't mean . . . that's never happened before—"

"What exactly happened? Or didn't?" The words fell out of my mouth like lumps of porridge that had been living there for a few days. My lips and tongue felt numb.

"I tried to make you forget what you saw. I didn't mean to hurt you. You should have just lost a few seconds."

"You tried to what?" Something pressed against my cheek. I heard whuffling. Reggie was trying to help me. Proprioception told me my hands had found the bartop and I pushed against it, raising my head up. Relliope hovered in front of me, wringing a bar towel between her hands, tears rolling down her cheeks from the blue fog around her eyes.

"I'm a Bluie. It's what we do. Wipe away memory."

"Why would you want to wipe my memory?" I levered myself up. Dizziness still spun in my head, but the pain had faded away.

"I didn't. I mean, not all of it. I can't do that any way. Most of us can't. Just tiny bits. I'm not very good at even that. Usually just the last thought or so. I was trying to make you forget what you'd seen me do. Please, I don't want to get in trouble. That's all. I don't actually cause anyone any harm. I've done it hundreds of times."

"What, you wipe the memory of a customer tipping you so he tips you again? You don't see that as any kind of harm?"

She started sobbing. "You don't understand. I'm trying to save up enough for passage out of this place. I want to go home. But the Cliveden, they don't like Bluies. Travel costs are much higher for us. It's discrimination, pure and simple, but nobody stops them out of fear of being blacklisted and marooned themselves. And I didn't know that about them or I never would have traveled on one of their ships. And now I'm stuck. Nobody else takes passengers from here. I was dumped here months ago by a spiteful crew member, and I've been here ever since."

Whatever she'd done—or attempted to do—to my head, the effects had faded. "That's a tough situation, but it's not going to win anyone over. It doesn't justify psychic assault, not by a long shot. Believe me, you're not the first person I've had poke at my head."

She sniffled and nodded. "I know. I sclajjed it as soon as I tried to make you forget. That's why it didn't work and caused the backlash. Otherwise, we wouldn't be having this conversation."

"*Sclajjed*?"

More sniffling. She wiped at her eyes, briefly batting the blue fog away and rubbing the tears from her cheeks. "I'm sorry, I don't know the word in Traveler. It's . . . the perception of, um, I guess you'd call it like a marker in the mind. You know how you can return to a room and you have the feeling that someone has been there while you were away? Sort of like that, but, no, not really. But a little. I don't know how it works."

This was all new to me. "You're saying, when you make someone forget, you leave behind a mark that you've been there?"

"I guess. But when you sclaj someone, you can't tell who was there before, not usually. Not like in your case."

"What's that supposed to mean?"

Her jaw dropped, and more amazingly the blue vapor from her eyes completely stopped and I saw her face fully for the first time. "You don't know? You've been marked by a Higher Being of the Cosmos."

"Excuse me?"

"How can you not know? It's so strong, almost blinding or deafening, now that I'm sclajjing you. Your encounter had to have happened recently."

Oh. That. I rolled the title over in my head. I'd have to remember to mention it to Svetlana.

"Yeah. I recently met up with a Celestial." My fingers moved to trace the arc along my face where its thumb had grazed. "He might even be coming to see my show one of these nights. I'll introduce you if you like."

"You would do that? For me? But . . . I'm no one. I'm less than no one. And I meant to wipe your memory. And I hurt you. And you'd do that?"

I'd started second guessing Reggie's liking of this woman about the time I was pulling my head up off her bar after her accidental psychic attack. But just as quickly I'd changed my mind again. Maybe it was her attitude toward the Celestial, or maybe it was my own. Or maybe her story about the Cliveden was getting to me after all. Or maybe it was the sudden sight of my agent trundling across the lobby toward the bar with a look of grim determination that I'd set in motion. After all, I couldn't really claim any kind of moral high ground with Relliope. She was using her talents to skim some extra tips to get ahead of the demands of the Cliveden; I was using mine to smuggle goods worth planets. Maybe Reggie's character assessment had been right all along.

"Conroy! There you are. We bead to talk. Bow!" Billi stormed my way and didn't stop until he'd passed into my personal space and practically climbed up onto my barstool.

Reggie barked once, and put his head back down on the counter.

"Billi, allow me to introduce Relliope. She tends bar here at the Pyramidal, and occasionally greets new arrivals to Bisto. I'm sure she can hook you up with a refreshing beverage. Relliope, this is Billi, my agent."

He shifted gears, put on a big smile that showed his tusks to good advantage, bowed with a flourish involving his upper and middle arms. "A pleasure to beat you, I'm sure. As for that drink, baby later."

"Um," said Relliope.

"Bow, Conroy." He tugged me toward a private booth..

I managed to snag Reggie as I was carried off, and waved farewell to the Bluie behind the bar. "Sorry, duty calls. We'll talk more."

Billi dragged me to the booth, shoved me onto one bench and scrambled over the tabletop to stand on the opposite side. I set my buffalito next to me. Reggie gave me an irksome look; he'd had a full day already. Me too, but Billi was about to add to it. Escape was not an option. He pressed both middle hands palms down upon the table and locked his eyes on me.

"I am only going to ask you this once. Try to give the right answer."

I swallowed and nodded. "Go ahead."

"Do you have a death wish?"

I wished I had another slinko at hand. "That would be too easy. Take a seat and I'll explain. Remember how excited you were onboard the *Shpeshnoltoc* when we had that meeting with the Elder Glarp? It was a set up. . ." I explained about Captain Telfano sa Rens, her plans to use Reggie to steal drift juice, and her threat to leave me stranded on Bisto. By the end of my story Billi was literally hopping mad, bouncing in place on his bench.

"I hate stereotypes."

"What do you mean?"

"She's a lizard, so she's cold-blooded. I hate that. Why can't the lizards be all warm and cuddly, and the bammals occasionally be the heartless, calculating ones?"

"That's what upsets you about this? Not that I'm being manipulated to steal from the people who have hired me, or that if I don't do as she says we'll be stuck here? How about reorganizing your priorities?"

"Buy priorities are in the right place. If you wanted sympathy for your problems you should have shared them before, and not waited until your buffalito threw up in buy pocket. Would you have bothered to reveal any of this if he hadn't? Don't answer that. I don't want to hear what you'd say. Look, Conroy, ours is a young relationship, and I get that. But if it's to have a chance, if I'm going to be any use to you, you have to trust and confide in bee. Has anything else happened that you haven't bothered to share?"

I glanced over at the bar. With the blue fog around her eyes I couldn't tell if Relliope was watching me, but she was certainly oriented towards us. Was she still sclajjing me, or had the perception only happened when she tried to wipe away the memory of her extracting extra tips.

"One other thing."

"Oh?"

"A small thing. Barely worth mentioning."

Billi leaned forward, palms flat upon the table again. "And what's this small thing?"

"The Celestial I asked you to bring back? I met it before, when I was just a college kid. It's indirectly responsible for my becoming a hypnotist. I think it's been looking for me all this time since, and has plans for me.

"A Celestial? A being larger than this planet has been following your career for its own reasons, and you didn't think to say word one about this before?"

"Sorry." And then because I couldn't think what else to say, I added, "I call it Elroy."

Billi shook his head and grinned, showing his tusks. "Elroy. You call it Elroy. You sit there and just casually remark that you're involved with an entity older than either of our races, and you've come up with a cheery sobriquet for it? Thanks, I needed that. That's at least as cold-blooded as anything that Cliveden captain has done."

"It's really not that bad."

"Not that bad? Great googly boogly, Conroy, you've got me wishing I'd gone into taxidermy."

Reggie chose that moment to let loose with a stream of oxygen flatulence. I politely looked the other way.

Billi escorted me to one of the gift shops that lined the Pyramidal's promenade. We bypassed the smaller cheaper stores and arcades carrying the more traditional tourist gewgaws, travel necessities, and souvenir togas. My agent moved with determination directly into a posh space of mirrored walls and glittering display tables all piled high with gleaming bottles and polished wood boxes of all sizes. He dragged me through a riot of fragrant soaps, aromatic body rubs, and flowery toilet waters. In the middle of the shop a clerk stood poised as if to lecture rather than sell. Billi ignored him and headed straight to the back where the pricier items lived. Despite, or perhaps because of the imbalance of males to females among the Veng, the store had an impressive selection of perfumes. He picked one of the cheaper, domestic brands, interested more in volume than quality. The bottle held over a liter of something pink and oily.

"Will there be anything else?" asked the clerk from behind the sales podium. Another ubiquitous Veng, this one in a toga of lemon yellow with diagonally ascending pinstripes of pale violet. "Perhaps you'd like to see some lovely bath soaps or fertility creams in a complimentary scent? Or something for your creetlebaum?"

"Byah. This bottle of stink water suits us fine. You do recognize my companion, don't you?"

"Of course, sir. Everyone at the Pyramidal is acquainted with the Amazing Conroy. His shows are sold out for the next cycle."

Billi smiled and slipped the perfume into one of the pockets of his toga. "Great. Then you can just charge the cost of this to his account."

The clerk nodded. He ran orange fingers over what to me looked like a piece of polished stone mounted at a oblique angle to his podium. "Entertainer, if you would affirm this purchase we'll be done."

Billi double-elbowed me in the ribs. "Do it."

"I so affirm."

"Very good, gentlemen. Thank you for your patronage. If you find you need anything else, it would be my pleasure to be of service to you. We never close."

"Thanks bunches. We've got to be going though. The Entertainer has to get ready for his performance." Billi hustled me back onto the promenade. We walked at a leisurely pace with the rest of the window-shoppers and tourists. I set Reggie down to trot along beside me.

"What was all that about? Why do I need cheap perfume?"

"You don't. But you do bead a cheap perfume bottle." He patted the pocket with the purchase as the flow of pedestrian traffic carried us along. "I'm going to go back to my room. I'll dump this out and refill it with the . . . stuff you acquired. Then you can stash it in your dressing room amidst the other ointments and cerates and unguents you use at your bakeup table."

Traveler has a word for ointment that pretty much covers all liquids and creams that might be applied to the body. I stopped walking. Reggie stopped and sat down, looking up at me to see what was going on. "Cerates?" I said. "Unguents?" I doubted either word had ever been spoken off Earth.

Identical Veng in a myriad of different colored togas moved around us like a school of fish, diverging and reconverging on the other side. Billi rolled his bulging eyes. "You should be happy. Think of it as proof that, despite you dragging me down disreputable paths, I won't be taking up the family business. Now get to your dressing room; you have a show coming up. And try to keep your pet out of trouble; Selstrin keeps talking about billing you for repairs to walls." Another punch to my thigh set me moving again.

"Are you coming to the show tonight?"

More eye rolling. This time he managed to move one clockwise and the other counterclockwise. "Why? Anything different this time?"

"Maybe. The Younger Glarp wants me to hypnotize him."

This time he stopped. "You're trying to kill me, is that it?"

"No, I'm trying to keep Lew from being a complete pain. On the way back today he expressed a desire to experience trance. From his exalted position, he thinks he's doing me a favor. He actually said that by lending his *presence* to my show, you might be able to negotiate for an even higher amount on the next contract renewal."

He punched me in the thigh again and walked away. I watched him go, and then with my longer stride quickly caught up. Reggie trotted after.

"Just promise you won't embarrass him."

"It'll be fine. I haven't had a dissatisfied Veng yet. So does this mean you'll be at the show?"

"Like I have a choice?"

I had hours before my show, but didn't much feel like spending them back in my room. Billi went off to make the switch, promising to return with the perfume bottle. I remembered my last conversation with Selstrin and headed back to the bar.

"Hi, Relliope. How about we give that dark slinko a try?" I set Reggie on the bar and perched on a stool.

The bartender smiled, and a moment later set a tall glass of what looked like purple tomato juice in front of me. Reggie sniffed it once and quickly backed away. I sipped. Once. Forget what I said about tomato juice. Instead, imagine sauerkraut juice mixed with gin, lemon juice, and rancid meat, and then add more rancid meat. My mouth felt like it was at war with my tongue, and both desperately wanted to find somewhere else to live.

Relliope pushed another glass toward me, the contents black and thick. "Here you go. This will clear the taste out of your mouth."

I grabbed it with both hands and drank. Every taste bud that had been filling out paperwork for a transfer tore up the forms and began singing. Caffeine and ginseng and guarana and alcohol combined, exploding in my mouth and taking no prisoners. It was the Veng version of iced coffee.

"Better?"

"Much. Thank you."

"If you didn't care for dark slinko, you should really not even try the hot or dead varieties."

I nodded gravely. "You've done me a great service. I wonder if I can impose on you for another?"

She took the glass of dark slinko and vanished it behind the counter. The blue vapor from her eyes thickened as she regarded me.

"Maybe. What do you need, Mr. Conroy?"

I reached out and placed a hand on Reggie's hump, burying my fingers in the thick ringlets of his fur. "Selstrin doesn't want me leaving Reggie unattended in my dressing room while I'm on stage. If you're off shift at that time, would you consider sitting with him? I'd pay you for your time, of course, and he'll be no trouble. And he really likes you."

"I like him too. It's no trouble at all. And honestly, I can use the extra money. When would you like me to start?"

"Is tonight too soon?"

"Not at all. I'll come by your dressing room a bit before your show. Is there anything special I should know?"

"Keep him away from the rugs."

Reggie pushed open the dressing room door and I followed him inside. A cheer arose. "Ah, our host is here at last! Behold, the Amazing One!"

The speaker lay sprawled upon the floor, humanoid, male, hairless. His violet skin gleamed with deep blue highlights. Instead of the mandatory toga he wore a white sleeveless leotard with a brush-painted glyph in scarlet emblazoned across his abdomen, so sheer and tight that he might almost have been naked. A Sasnakian sex wrestler. Three more of them, another male and two females, all attired in leotards, leaned against the far wall or sat upon the one of the room's octagonal rugs. None sat in chairs. They were not the same troupe as had been aboard the Cliveden ship.

"About time you got here," said a familiar voice. "I've missed Reggie." Svetlana occupied the chair in front of my makeup table. A fifth Sasnak sat at her feet, holding them in his hands as he applied the business end of a pigment stick to her toenails. He'd already painted several a brilliant turquoise.

At the sound of her voice Reggie galloped to her. He clambered over the wrestler, and leaped the final distance to land in Svetlana's lap. She wrapped both arms around him in an eager embrace and cuddled my buffalito while the fellow at her feet watched with obvious envy.

"When did you get here? And who are your friends?"

"I have no idea," said Svetlana, pausing in the delivery of dozens of cutesy smooches all over Reggie's face. "They were here when I arrived ten minutes ago."

"We mean no offense," said the wrestler who had led the cheer. "My name is Oswalt, and I am the leader of our troupe." He pointed at the symbol crossing his waist. "The generous Selstrin instructed us to make ourselves comfortable here. He indicated we should consider this our *dressing room.* I attempted to explain that we had no need for such a facility, but he was most insistent."

Note to self: when it comes to Veng psychology, passive-aggressive behavior is definitely part of their repertoire.

"You're performing at the Pyramidal?"

"It is our great pleasure to open for you, Amazing One. We will dazzle the assembled audience with displays of our physical prowess." He laughed then, the kind of deep booming laugh you'd associate with lumberjacks and war heroes. "Not that it presents much of a challenge. These Veng are small and puny. We often invite challengers from the audience to pit themselves against us, but I do not believe we will do so here. I would fear snapping their tiny orange bodies in half, and our troupe has learned it is bad form to seriously injure the guests."

"You'd be surprised. The guests here are quite capable of injuring one another without any help from the performers."

"That really happened then?" said Svetlana. "I've read up on their feud behavior and the rules that govern it, but it still seems . . . tacky, to murder someone in the middle of a show."

The wrestler at her feet found his voice. "That is not very compassionate," he said.

"Cyrano, it's not a question of compassion. Ritual killings between feuding rists is part of their culture. I'm not judging it, I just felt bad for Conroy. It must have been very disconcerting."

"Speaking of different cultures, where's Elroy?"

<<I am here.>> The Celestial emerged from the shower stall around the corner and stood behind Svetlana. Its pickled husk gleamed in the light from the makeup table.

"It's developed a fondness for the shower systems here at the Pyramidal."

<<It is perhaps foolish, but the sensation is oddly pleasant to this form. Possibly addictively so.>>

"Worse vices exist," said Oswalt. "You will excuse us now, I hope. As we are sharing this space, I did not wish to depart before meeting you. Alas, we are now tardy for an appointment. We are touring a confectionary facility. Are you acquainted with *taffy*?"

"Taffy?"

"I am led to understand it is a chewy confection crafted by stretching and applying torque to a flavored mixture of sugar and glycerin. The process sounded intriguing and a pod is waiting to take us to the facility. Would you care to join us?"

"No thanks."

"Conroy doesn't like candy," said Svetlana as she stood, running a hand over the shoulder and smooth head of the wrestler who had finished with her toenails. "But I have a sweet tooth, and I'm becoming very fond of Cyrano here. I'm going to tag along."

The troupe leader smiled, gave a nod of his head toward Cyrano, and offered me an exaggerated wink. "Of course. Everyone is welcome."

<<If Mr. Conroy will allow me to remain, I'd like to stay and speak with him. I have many questions.>>

"Sure, not a problem."

"Then it is decided," said Oswalt. "My troupe will escort the lovely Svetlana, and as we witness the excruciations exacted upon this taffy, we shall vie with Cyrano for her attention. But rest assured, Amazing One, we will return in time to warm the audience for you."

He executed a quick arm gesture and the other Sasnaks leaped to their feet like coiled springs letting go. One by one they filed past, bowed their heads with respect, and exited. Oswalt completed the line. Svetlana carried Reggie over and placed him in my arms. He whined as she let him go, and then pressed his head against my chest, tilting up and back to gaze at me.

"He really is a sweetheart. But then, so are you. See you later."

Svetlana closed the door on her way out, leaving me with the Celestial. Part of me wanted to go after her. A wiser part knew it would be pointless, and only destroy whatever weird relationship we had. Even in the role of *well-meaning big brother*, I had no business getting in the way of whom she chose to bestow her favors upon. There's envy, and then there's stupidity. I had a plateful of the former, I didn't need to go asking for a serving of the latter.

Which meant I could finally spend time with good ol' Elroy. It also gave me something to think about other than what Svetlana and her new wrestler friend might be up to. I didn't think it would end at taffy.

CHAPTER FOURTEEN

Worse Things Than Hecklers

NOBEL LAUREATES back on Earth would have killed to be in my shoes, poised for a private one-on-one, conversation with an alien entelechy older than our species. But good ol' Elroy didn't want to talk to any of them; just me. Its anchor, or one of them. And maybe, just maybe, I'd get a glimmer of what it really wanted with me.

We settled into a pair of chairs and talked. Hour after hour. Interviewing one another. Our discussion topics could have filled a university's catalog of classes, but the Celestial always brought us back to the theme of Human perception. It couldn't get enough of the many ways perception could be molded and altered, particularly the distinction I made between the cognitive process that produced it versus the more direct experience of sensation. I spent half of the time explaining and reciting everything I knew about visual illusions, mirages, and other tricks of the eye, and from there we moved on to other senses: hearing, smell, taste, touch, heat, pain.

Elroy reached out with one mottled green hand and gently stroked the tip of a finger across my forehead. <<Is it like this?>> Pain flooded my being. Excruciating sensations ratcheted up and down my spinal cord. Imagine a hundred thousand fire ants eating you alive, their pinchers electrified with arcing voltage, sizzling with dripping acid, as they chomp chomp chomped endlessly. Now crank that up by a few orders of magnitude. The last thing I saw as I convulsed into sweet oblivion was the expression of disapproval and disappointment on the Celestial's artificial face. Who could blame it? It had come to me for help in understanding mortal sensation and here I went and passed out just because of neural overload. Oh yes, thank whatever deities exist throughout the galaxy, I passed out. At the end of round one, the score was clueless solar entelechy one, stupid as dirt hypnotist nothing. If I'd been conscious I'd have feared for a trend.

I awoke to a wet sandpapery rasp scouring my face and the sight of Reggie licking me. Twice in one day; not a good sign. His big, soulful eyes gazed at me with concern. I reached to pet him. Then I remembered the pain and spent the next small while wincing and sucking in air. I'd thrown out my back once and been hit with crippling pain out of the blue. One moment I'd been sitting comfortably in a restaurant, chatting merrily, enjoying good company and better food, living life without a care in the world. Then I'd reached for my dessert fork and something about the way I moved my wrist or left middle finger—or both!—had triggered something in my spine. A moment later and I was lying in a crumpled mockery of good posture under my chair, surrounded by broken crockery and a stained tablecloth. My dinner companions were all on their feet gasping and pointing and trying to be solicitous and helpful, while I strove not to scream in agony through clenched teeth. It had been like that, only more so. That the Celestial had put that kind of torment in my head made me long to go out and buy a pair of titanium-toed Texas boots and alternate kicking one and then the other, over and over, into its testicles in an attempt to partially recreate something of the sensation. That wasn't going to happen though. For one thing, the odds of finding any shop on Bisto carrying anything from Texas approximated zero. For another, the vat grown husk that Elroy wore didn't have testicles. Reluctantly, I moved on.

Reggie perched on my chest, his tiny polished hooves prancing back and forth as he worked his tongue over my face. A terrestrial dog his size would probably have weighed in at about ten kilograms. Buffalitos are composed of denser stuff. He massed closer to fifteen, and I had to dislodge him from my chest before I could sit up. Which is about when I realized I'd been lying on the floor. The Celestial still sat in its chair gazing down at me.

<<Did I get it right?>>

Thoughts of boots and kicking stirred again in my brain but I pushed them aside. I struggled to my feet, climbing up my chair to do so. The ghost memories of napalm replacing my spinal fluid lingered still. "Where did that come from?" My voice cracked.

<<Before we left the floating island, I toured the hospital's critical care ward medical ward. The nursing staff had never met an animated husk before and were quite generous with their time. I scanned their knowledge of their patients, and then all of their patients as well.>>

"Scanned them? How?"

<<Their patterns. As I told you, the physical brains of all sapient minds exhibit a magnetic field of wonderfully complex arrays of minute patterns generated by electrochemical signals at the cellular level. It's astonishing how much you accomplish at such a delicate scale.>>

"And you can read that?"

<<I was as surprised as you. Not the analysis of magnetic flux patterns, my kind have always been able to do that. No, the density of information astonished me. It's all around me, a cacophony of signals that I never noticed with my larger avatars.>>

Which made sense. That's what the husk was for, a quasi-organic shell that could contain a contracted version of its awareness and walk among flesh and blood creatures instead of conversing with the planet they inhabited. And I was its lucky interpreter in the kingdom of the flesh born.

"You're saying you can read the memories of everyone around you? Human, Veng, or whatever?"

<<Only in theory. There's too much too keep straight. I had to content myself with the little bit I sampled.>>

"There's someone in the hospital with that kind of pain?"

An expression of pleasure spread on its face, reminding me of a cracking watermelon. <<No, I synthesized the magnetic patterns that yielded that experience.>>

"What were you going for?"

<<Agony. Beings such as yourself experience sensation in interesting ways. Regardless of the intensity of the stimulus, you appear able to habituate to it. Realizing that, to achieve the concept of agony, my synthesis fluctuates the level of the pain, as well as alternating among a series of different types of sensations in a pseudo random fashion. I was trying to lessen the habituation so the agony could be experienced more fully.>>

I pulled myself up onto my chair. "Why don't we talk about finding you a new hobby?"

<<Certainly, but please, tell me, did I get it right?>>

"Yeah, I think you've mastered that one. Let's not try it again, okay?"

<<Are you distressed? Have I impaired your ability to perform tonight?>>

"I'll be fine. And, you know, the show must go on."

<<Must it? Why?>>

I shrugged. "You know, they never explain that part."

* * *

Elroy left the dressing room and went off to do whatever stellar entelechies tend to do when they're not experimentally torturing their anchors. I changed into the second of my tux-togas and sat at the table to apply the bit of makeup that allows the audience to make out my facial expressions even from the cheap seats in the house. While I was about it Reggie jerked up from the rug he'd been sleeping on and howled. As if in response to his noise, the door opened and a Cliveden let himself in with the same discomforting prerogative as any Veng of high rist.

He wore a black toga cut from shiny, synthetic cloth with a sash of black metal links like chainmail. There was something so bizarre about garbing a Cliveden in a Veng toga that I had to turn from my mirror and stare at him more fully, coronal crest to thorny toe, to realize I knew him. Thindar po Rens, the *Shpeshnoltoc's* purser, had arrived on Bisto.

"Mr. Conroy, do me the courtesy of assuring that you know who I am." He spoke to me but his attention fixed on my buffalo dog. Reggie stopped howling but glared back. I got to my feet and picked him up.

"I never expected to see you in my dressing room, but I know who you are." I watched his face, his eyes in particular. After his boss's many visits bringing Reggie practice drift juice back on the ship, I knew I could hypnotize her given the opportunity. Studying another Cliveden could make it easier. And if Thindar had come, I might need to try it that much sooner.

He bowed slightly from the waist. "I do as my captain instructs. In this instance, she has bid me to visit this place and impart the message that she awaits the pleasure of your company tomorrow morning at breakfast, local time, aboard the *Shpeshnoltoc*. The captain's personal yacht will be waiting at this facility's dock shortly after dawn to take you to the ship, with only a brief delay to clear customs at the floating island. I will be piloting it myself."

"Her yacht?"

Thindar smiled, revealing gleaming rows of teeth on both his upper and lower jaws. "The Veng well understand the perks of rank, and the occasional reminder serves our needs. You will disembark from the yacht, go through a cursory scan, and be back onboard with only a minor delay. No lines to wait in, no forms to fill out. It is a fine way to travel."

"I'm sure it is. Please tell her I look forward to breakfast."

"Of course. And one more thing. I have been instructed to stress that the Captain's invitation includes your creature. Captain Telfano has confided to me an unusual interest in the thing."

"Perhaps she's considering acquiring one as a ship's mascot?"

The smile vanished. A membrane slid across his eyes and back again. "Let us hope not. I will see you in the morning then. Please be punctual."

"Did you intend to stay for tonight's show? I can arrange for a good table for you, if you'd like."

He'd already turned to let himself out but paused. His expression suggested he wasn't certain if I was being courteous or mocking him, and he needed a moment to decide before replying.

"You are aware that the families of my kind do not enjoy the company of other sapients?"

I nodded. "Probably the first thing I learned after boarding the *Shpeshnoltoc*."

"Yes. And while my own tolerance is considerably better than most—a necessary trait given my position—I would find myself hard pressed to endure a packed house of hundreds of inebriated Veng, to say nothing of the smattering of additional aliens that comprise your audience."

"Your choice. I didn't want you to feel unwelcome."

"The closest I might come to feeling welcome on this planet would be in the private lounge the Cliveden maintain on Bisto's floating island. But I thank you for your hospitality." His eyes went to Reggie again.

"Just doing my part. Building a friendlier galaxy through hypnosis."

He frowned at that but did not reply. The door closed behind him with a faint click.

The sex wrestlers put on a good show. They grappled in pairs, in a constantly changing trio that involved tagging in and out, and finally in a massive five-person configuration of grasping and grinding and rolling about on the stage. Sasnakians have sex organs consisting of internal bands of muscle. The same Heimlich maneuver that might save a human being from choking provides an intimate experience for one of them. Sex wrestlers take this to new heights. They train like monks—well, maybe not exactly like monks—and develop the ability to achieve a meditative state. Wrestling then becomes more like an interactive kind of yoga; as they work through the forms they slip into that altered state, which then activates some kind of empathic projector in their brains, and everyone around them shares in their feelings, as the scent of the wrestlers' musky sweat wafts over them.

I wasn't sure how the Veng would respond. I'd seen very few female Veng, far fewer than their distribution among the population suggested. Part of the culture probably included closeting them away. And just as I still couldn't tell most Veng apart, I had no clue how to distinguish among the five male variations they possessed. Veng sexuality was a taboo topic, one that I'd decided to avoid in my act. I'd learned that a female and three different kinds of male were needed for reproduction, but it wasn't always the same three flavors. And I'd picked up some hints that recreational activity occurred, at least for males, both across and within the variations, one on one, as well as in combinations that rose into double digits. Maybe that was part of the appeal of the Sasnakian sex wrestlers. For all I knew, they not only inspired, they provided some intriguing ideas to aspire to for the Veng.

I watched the wrestlers from one wing of the stage as they neared the climax of their performance. And I watched the audience. None moved. The Veng sat upright and rigid in their seats, their drinks and desserts forgotten. The few non-Veng present appeared equally captivated as waves of arousal flowed over them from the stage. I glimpsed Svetlana at a private table right up front, slumped in her chair, head lolling to one side, arms hanging limp against her sides. Her beautiful smile looked broader than ever. She had her eyes locked on Cyrano, who at that moment was forming a living pyramid with the other members of his troupe, writhing as pairs of male and female Sasnaks took turns elbowing him in the stomach in a rising crescendo.

They finished to silence. The audience didn't applaud. For several seconds there was no sound at all. Then, almost as one, they sighed. The wrestlers had warmed them up alright. I didn't know if I could follow an act like that, but I didn't have any choice. I'd already begun rehearsing what I was going to say to Selstrin when I finished.

The stage went black. Somewhere a fan began to whirr, lessening the heady musk of alien sex from the room. The wrestlers tumbled from their pyramid and scampered off, their feet padding softly as they ran into the other wing. I straightened my bowtie and strode out, counting off the stage floor's metal rings in the dark until I reached my mark. I reviewed my mental outline for tonight's show, and pushed down the butterfly or two that still fluttered in my stomach at the start of a performance, even after all these years. I rubbed the palms of my hands against my thighs, and smoothed my toga. I'd started revising my introductory patter when the first ripples of the Sasnaks' arousal flowed over me. I needed to lay it on pretty thick to capture the audience after that. A spotlight blazed into existence, blinding me to the audience and making me the only thing they could see.

"Citizens of Bisto," I said with all the resonance at my command. "Visitors, guests, and friends. I am the Amazing Conroy, and I am here tonight to introduce you to impossible possibilities, to expose you to wonders of the mind, and to amuse with absurdities so profound that tales of this evening will trickle down your rist for generations. Your descendants will whisper your name in hushed tones because you were here this night. And for a handful among you, three or four who are brave and curious and spirited enough to step forward, these peers and cohorts I will transform. Before your eyes I will shatter things you know as true as weight and heat and color!

"But enough talk." On cue, the stage lights came up halfway and overhead spots illuminated stools behind me. "Who among you will step up and experience what few on Bisto have even been privileged to witness?"

A Veng in the front row stood up and a murmur raced through the audience. "I will." The spotlight blinded me from seeing the face, not that I'd likely have recognized it any way, but I knew the voice. It was Lew.

"I'm honored. Please join me on the stage. Who else?" I scanned the first few rows, unable to see anything more than silhouettes but looking for all the world like I was making eye contact and said, "what about you, sir?" Half a dozen Veng were convinced I was speaking directly to them. Four demurred, but two stood up. That would do.

I got them settled onto their stools and began my induction, all the while running through my patter and keeping the audience engaged. Veng drop into trance very easily, and these three proved no exception. I had them under in moments, then set up each of them with a whispered, individual trigger phase. It's rarely necessary, but when needed, a backdoor into someone's unconscious mind is a great thing to have. It pays to be thorough.

With my volunteers happily staring off into infinity I turned my attention to the audience. "Prepare yourselves. The men before you are in a state of hypnotic trance. They can hear and see only me. I am their entire world. What you're about to witness is impossible. Before your very eyes, I will change their rist, and with that transformation, everything about them will be altered! But before they become someone else, let's learn who they are now." I started at the end where I'd put Lew. "We'll go down the line. Please identify yourself for our audience. State your name, your rist, and your vocation."

"I am Glarp Lewilocus, known far and wide as the Younger Glarp. I am of the Pentahedral Diamond. I am employed as a Presence by the Tvost refinery."

"I'm Feleso Kester of Rectilinear Pearl. I'm a bookkeeper."

"Jolosol Vebs. The Iridescent Polygon is my rist. I run an auction house."

"That is reality," I said to the audience. "Or rather, the reality that held sway when you all arrived tonight. But on this stage, reality is mutable." I half turned, facing my volunteers but giving the audience my profile. "Each of you, hold out your right hand, palm up. Now make a fist."

Without any hesitation, they all complied.

"Think of your rist, something so familiar to you, something you've carried with you your entire life. And because you've carried it, realize now, for the first time ever, that your rist is a physical thing. It's always been that way, but you never noticed because it's the same for everyone, like having earflaps or knees. Your rist manifests as something small and round, like a marble. It is there in your fist now. Feel it there, held tightly. It is yours. That rist defines who you are. Now . . . open your hand and look upon your rist. Nod if you see it there."

Staring at empty palms, they all nodded. The audience gasped.

"As everyone knows, a Veng is defined by his rist. If he were not of the Pentahedral Diamond, the Younger Glarp here surely could not be a Presence. Jolosol could not run his auction house were he not of the Iridescent Polygon, and it is only because of the Rectilinear Pearl that Feleso can be a bookkeeper. What happens then if I take their respective rists from them, and swap them?" I walked in front of each volunteer and mimed snatching up the imaginary marbles of rist each held in front of him. Again the audience gasped. One by one my volunteers slumped on their stools. Their outstretched hands dropped to their sides. Their faces become lax and vacant as their identities vanished.

"Look at them," I instructed the audience. "They have no lives now. They are no longer truly Veng, for how can one be Veng without rist? It is inconceivable, and yet it is here before you." Several people in the audience began murmuring. I was bordering on heresy here, and I knew it. Time to pull back before things got ugly.

"It is an abomination," I assured them, "and one that we cannot allow to continue. Shall I give them back rist?"

With one voice the audience shouted their affirmation. I nodded solemnly. "Yes, of course, a Veng must have a rist. But they need not have the one they came here with." I spoke to Jolosol Vebs, "you are now, and have always been of the Pentahedral Diamond." I took his hand, opened it, and pressed my thumb against his palm as if returning the marble. Instantly his affect returned. And more. He sat taller, held his chin higher. "Tell us, who you are and what do you do?"

He gazed out across the rows of Veng before him, dusky shapes lost in the darkness and obscured by the overhead spotlights. "I am Kelbo Fagonst, the chairman of Pyramidal Consolidated. I have full authority over every aspect of thirty-seven resort properties throughout Bisto."

I nodded, winking at the audience. "Indeed you do. And speaking as one of your employees, let me just say I find the accommodations here quite nice." I moved down the line and took Feleso Kester's hand in mine, and returned a marble. "You were born into the Iridescent Polygon. You remember that now. Introduce yourself, please."

He sat up, and smiled broadly. "It is my good fortune to be Lelko Vin, second senior Acquirer. I travel the world reviewing estates of the newly deceased, bargaining with their surviving kin for items which may better serve the family through the proceeds an auction can bring. I hope to rise to first soon."

"I'm sure you will." I continued on to Lew. As with the others, I took his hand in mine. "And you, who imagined he had the stature of one called the Younger Glarp, in fact you have always been of the Rectilinear Pearl. When you are not daydreaming impossible fantasies, what is your role in life?"

Lew sat a moment and then yawned. "I'm Bathatar Konolo, and I do actuarial forecasting." He smiled shyly at me. "Are you familiar with the field? I work out the likelihoods of a wide variety of events and outcomes to aid in determining insurance rates. What's the probability you'll live to a ripe old age given that your parents and grandparents did? What are the odds your first child will be female? What is the likelihood you'll be slain as part of a rist feud? Things like that."

A figure in the audience stood and shouted, "That is an absolute certainty!" He rushed unto the stage, changing from silhouette to purposeful assassin. He gripped something in his right hand that might have been a knife, but the blade buzzed and blurred with motion. "Glarp Lewilocus of the Pentahedral Diamond, I am for you!"

Lew saw and heard none of it. His perceptions were locked to my voice and actions. It all happened too fast. The vibrating blade plunged into Lew's torso and his assailant whipped it around it, carving a broad circle in his chest. Blood erupted, soaking his toga and splashing onto the stage. Lew fell backwards off his stool. I shoved at the attacker, and my greater size was force him back. The weapon fell from his hand. He staggered ..us, lost his footing, and tumbled from the stage and into the first row of tables.

"I am Bathatar Konolo," said Lew's voice behind me. My heart soared at the realization that he hadn't been killed, until I turned and saw the wavering green figure of his rendering rising up from his bloody corpse.

"I am Bathatar Konolo, and I don't understand what is happening or why I am here."

CHAPTER FIFTEEN

A Pelk, A Husk And A Ghost Walk Into A Bar. . .

I KNELT AND LIFTED Lew's corpse in my arms. He weighed less than a child. Were all Veng so light, or had death emptied him somehow?

An olive drab blur bounded out of the audience and onto the stage. It stopped short of crashing into me, and slapped at the remote on my wrist. Darkness engulfed the stage, relieved only by the glow of the Younger Glarp's rendering.

"Get out of here, this instant!" Billi hissed, his tusks pressing against the side of my head.

"Billi? Wha—"

He stepped away, his figure just visible as he parted the curtain and gestured me backstage with every available limb. "Do it!"

I rose. "Bathatar, come on. Now. This way."

The ghost looked at the dead Veng in my arms and followed.

Selstrin waited in the wings. He ignored the corpse and waved his arms at the apparition. "What are you playing at? You can't take a rendering backstage. Send it after its assassin."

"Would you care to tell me how to do that?"

"Go after him? It wouldn't make any sense for me to do that. I'm of Rectilinear Pearl. The man who killed me was from Scintillating Oblong Veracity. That's one of the few things I *do* remember. Our rists haven't crossed in millennia, and have never known feud. I can't seek vengeance on him; my death must have been an accident."

"This was no accident," said Selstrin. "He called you by name, a bit informal but within the stricture of the law. You have to avenge your murder."

"You're mistaken. I'm Bathatar Konolo. But . . . I'm just an actuarial forecaster. I couldn't afford to have a rendering for vengeance."

that's good then," I said. "No vengeance means no need to go ..ı pursuit. You stay with me and I'll work it all out for you."

Billi was pushing at me again. "Yeah, he's got a good point, Bathatar. Our boy Conroy here will explain it all to you later. But we're busy worrying about bigger things."

"What could be more important than resolving a blood killing?" Selstrin positioned himself in my way, his stance suggesting that he really thought he could block me. Billi scurried around me and kicked the Veng in the shin sending him hopping sideways in pain.

"Listen you fool, when this is all said and done the Elder Glarp isn't going to care if the proper forms were followed and everyone's rist is satisfied. Planets and species don't factor into something like this. You don't get where he's got playing by society's rules. The only thing he's going to see here is that his idiot grandson was killed. In your club. During Conroy's show. You wanna talk revenge? He's not gonna settle for just killing the killer. Start thinking how your head will look on a pike."

"That's absurd. The Entertainer's shows sell out nightly. I've raised beverage prices ten percent without the least dip in sales. The Elder Glarp would not jeopardize such a venture, not once custom has been satisfied."

"Don't believe it. Blood's thicker than cash, you follow? Forget how great your house receipts have been lately, that won't buy back family. I'm invoking article seventy-six, section twelve of the Entertainment Guild constitution. You've got a criminally unsafe workplace. Our contract's canceled, with extreme prejudice. We're outta here, and if you're half as smart as you like to think you are, you'll alter your worklog to show you left on vacation after breakfast." He waggled a foot as if to kick again, and Selstrin darted out of the way.

"Now what?" I said as we raced along the corridor. The ghost floated after us.

"Don't worry. I had a plan in case this happened."

"You had a plan for the Younger Glarp being assassinated in the middle of my show?"

"I plan for every contingency. This falls under the *Conroy's royally pissed off a rich and powerful and eminently connected employer and has to get the hell outta Dodge* contingency. Step one: get you out of sight while I work on step two."

"Which is?"

"Getting you offworld and out of the Elder Glarp's reach."

"How are you going to manage that?"

"Guys like the Elder Glarp are touchy. Things can go sour with them without any warning. Soon as I got to Bisto I set up for a quick exit. It won't be cheap, but if we can get up to the floating island I have a guy who can get us into the Cliveden private lounge. It's like an embassy, sovereign ground and all that. Once we're there, the Veng can't touch us. Thing is, we can't just grab a cab; the Elder Glarp could get wind of the kid's death before we arrive and don't think for a second he couldn't get it turned back around. It could take upwards of a day for me to scrounge up safe transportation, which takes us back to step one and stashing you somewhere."

"I'll never doubt you again, Billi. But before I go to ground we need to stop at my dressing room first and pick up Reggie."

"I figured you'd say that. It's already worked into the plan."

Relliope and Reggie tussled over a chewtoy on the rug by my makeup table. The buffalito had the better grip, but the vapor from the Bluie's eyes confused him, or maybe she was just making him forget he'd grabbed it and it kept slipping free. He lost all interest in the game as we entered the dressing room and leapt into my already occupied arms. He landed on the Younger Glarp's chest and licked my face.

"Reggie. Down, boy."

Lew's rendering floated into the room behind me. "You have a creetlebaum." It leaned in, peering at the buffalo dog. Reggie flinched, yelped, and flung himself into the air. He landed on the wall and stayed there, hooves planted firmly, body oriented ninety degrees to the direction the rest of us thought of as *down*. He began barking at the ghost.

Relliope stared at the body in my arms. "Zoibles! That's the Younger Glarp! Oh, Mr. Conroy, what have you done?"

Billi pulled the door closed behind him. "He didn't do anything. Some Veng from a rival rist gets the credit. Conroy's just picking up the pieces." He glared at Reggie on the wall. "Fresh trick?"

"Perfume," I said, setting Lew's body down and pulling my buffalito from the wall. "Shhh. It's okay. Stop barking. He's a friend." Relliope took him from me and the barking stopped. Some of the blue vapor had receded from around her eyes. Right. I moved to my makeup table, snatched up the bottle of drift juice and tossed it to Billi. He slipped it into one of his pockets. I glanced around the room for anything else I needed, and settled for my carpetbag and Reggie's chewtoy. The ghost stayed hovering by the door.

I your friend? I don't remember. I can't recall knowing you prior ou on the stage. I can't recall anything before that."

"Yeah. We're going to fix that, Bathatar."

Relliope frowned at the ghost, cradling Reggie and turning her body so he didn't have a clear view of the ghost. "If that's the Younger Glarp's rendering, why are you calling him Bathatar?"

"Not important," said Billi. "Pretend it's a game. Better yet, pretend you didn't see any of us. We weren't here. C'mon, Conroy I've got to get you stashed away."

<<Stashed away? What a colorful expression,>> said a new voice, and this time it was my agent who startled and tried to climb up the wall. The Celestial stepped out of the shower alcove, its gnarled green flesh gleaming. <<What has Reggie been barking at?>>

I pointed to Lew's corpse and then to the rendering. "His ghost."

<<Where?>> The Celestial walked toward Bathatar and stared down at Billi who stood by the door beyond the ghost. <<I met this Pelk when he arrived with Svetlana. He identified himself as Billi. How could a living Pelk be the spirit of a deceased Veng?>>

"What is that?" Bathatar cringed.

I stepped in front of the Celestial before it walked its husk right through the rendering. "You don't see him?" I framed Bathatar with my hands.

<<I perceive neither anything solid, nor the fields of a thinking creature. There are a few loops of energy, but nothing of cognition. Is this typical of ghosts?>>

Billi scowled and began shoving me again. "We don't have time for a lesson on sensory dynamics or occult interpretations of ectoplasmic renderings. We need to get you and Reggie and the body and its rendering out of sight. So come on!"

<<I wish to follow along.>>

"Bot a chance. We're conspicuous enough as it is. Conroy, tell your pickle-friend to stay behind."

"Elroy, we're going to be moving quickly, and you're not exactly built for speed. We can't afford to wait for you."

<<I did not ask you to wait. Recall, you are my anchor. I can follow you at my own pace. I will not interfere, only observe you. Perhaps I can even be of assistance.>> It turned and lifted the corpse of the Younger Glarp into its arms, elbows locked so that the body lay across them as it might upon a

forklift. <<Unencumbered, you can move that much more swiftly. I will follow with the decedent.>>

Billi grabbed my right hand in both of his. "Good plan. But you should probably wrap the body in a rug or something, so it ain't so obviously a dead Veng, right?"

The Celestial dropped the body onto one of the room's rugs. The rug was small, but so was the Veng. It vanished as the Celestial rolled up the rug. <<Go. I will follow.>>

"Mr. Conroy, I don't understand what's going on. Are you going to be okay?" Relliope handed Reggie back to me. I tried to settle him in the carpetbag but he began barking at the rendering again.

Billi kicked me in the shin. "You've got to either shut him up, or decide which you want with you, the pup or rendering."

Relliope took the carpetbag from me and scritched behind Reggie's ears. He stopped barking. "I can carry him and keep him quiet."

"Hello? What did I just say about being conspicuous? Two aliens that don't resemble each other or any of the orange people here is bad enough. A rendering following after is worse. A third, different alien with a trail of blue fog and we're waving illuminated banners saying *Remember Us*."

<<Are you being deliberately ironic?>>

I looked from Elroy to Relliope and back again. "Huh?"

"Your Celestial has been explaining how my people do what we do. No one ever did that for me before," said Relliope.

Elroy lifted its arms and waggled fingers on either side of its head. <<She generates and can direct a chaos field. I can see how she does it, but I cannot perform the act myself.>>

"That's all very interesting but—"

"You go ahead. I can hold on to Reggie and follow after with your Celestial and the body."

When did Elroy become *my* Celestial?

<<Perfectly acceptable.>>

Billi was already dragging me toward the door. "You heard the barmaid and the pickle!"

Bathatar floated after us, sparing a glance at the rolled-up rug with his body. Reggie craned his head to see me leave, noticed the ghost staring at the floor, and started barking again.

* * *

Billi led me down deeper into the backstage hallways than I'd ever had cause to go. A series of turns through side passages and down dimly lit ramps led us into a lower level filled with stage equipment, props, and tools. Despite the frantic pace we were keeping, in its way, this was the closest thing to calm I'd felt since Lew's murder.

"Billi, there's something I need to tell you. I'd forgotten about it until just now."

"I don't like the sound of it already, but go ahead and spill it."

"Thindar came to see me right before my show tonight."

"Thindar? The purser from the *Shpeshnoltoc*, that Thindar?"

"The one and only. His ship's in orbit above Bisto and Captain Telfano wants her drift juice. She's sending her personal yacht for me in the morning so Reggie and I can join her for breakfast topside."

"Yeah? Good to beau. I'll see if I can't reschedule you for brunch."

"Billi, I'm serious."

"So am I! The Glarp's going to be turning this place upside down looking for you. You think you're gonna be able to just stroll across the lobby and through the red carpeted entrance of a Cliveden transit captain's personal yacht without anyone seeing? Use your head. Once the fan's been hit, your private ride won't be getting anywhere close to here. But it does change things a bit, and for the better. Instead of you trying to hide from the Veng and asking for sanctuary when we get you up to the Cliveden lounge, you can just call over to the *Shpeshnoltoc* and ask them to send some reinforcements. A Cliveden security squad will balance things for our side. Perfect!"

"I'm having second thoughts about going up to the floating island, Billi."

"Stick with the first ones, pal. Or leave the thinking to ol' Billi. I told ya, I've got a plan." He didn't slow down, or even turn his head to be certain I hadn't.

"No, seriously. We've left the scene of the crime. Even if you're right about the Elder Glarp not following Veng custom, I shouldn't have taken the body. There are probably rites or rituals to be observed, we're making things worse. As soon as the Celestial starts after us with the corpse, those possibilities vanish."

Billi whirled on me, stopping me with three outstretched hands. "I'm counting on that, and you should be too. You want to leave the body behind, but what about the rendering? Your buddy Bathatar here doesn't remember who it was in life because you invented it. You want to leave it behind too?"

"You invented me? What does he mean? Why are all you aliens running things any way?" The ghost hovered closer, shoving its face between mine and Billi's.

"Of course I wouldn't leave it behind. I've got to figure out how to fix things. But Lew's body is a different story."

"They were linked in life, flesh to ectoplasm. Are you sure that link doesn't continue even with the flesh dead? Leave the body and keep the rendering, and suppose the Elder Glarp can follow the link right to us? If you're wrong, we're screwed. If I'm wrong, swell, and you can say I-told-you-so when we're safely offworld."

He dropped to all sixes then and kicked a blank piece of the wall. It crackled and flickered revealing a low arch. "Cheap holographic cover. Lets the cleaning bots slip in and out without showing the access holes for the janitorial shafts. They're all over the property, linking up all the hallways. I found them my first day exploring. Welcome to your hiding place. What it lacks in height and width it compensates for with lots of length. The Veng don't use 'em, just the automata. If you run into one, just rap twice on it and it will go away. Get your ass in there, and your spook's ass too while you're at it."

"It's not a spook, it's an apparition."

"I don't care if it's the Ghost of Christmas Past, just get it in the shaft and out of view."

"What are you going to be doing?"

"A couple things. First, I'll head back to your dressing room. If the Celestial and the barmaid are still there, I'll send them your way. Then I'll wait for Selstrin or some other Veng to figure out they ought to come find you. I'll tell them that as your agent I've hid you for your own safety, and then I will reluctantly lead them on a wild goose chase, ditch them, and get on with arranging safe transportation for us to the floating island. Same plan if the Veng are already waiting in your dressing room when I get there. When the Celestial and the barmaid show up with the body and the pup, let 'em in here too, and keep everyone quiet. I'll come back for you as soon as I can."

Billi kicked and punched me in the shin and thigh. I dropped to my knees and crawled in. A vibration coursed through me as I entered, and I had to clamp a hand over my mouth as bursts of nausea beat upon me like waves upon a shore.

Billi called after me. "Don't worry about the vermin barrier. The effect is only around the exits. You'll be fine once you go a little deeper."

The need to keep my gorge down prevented me from cursing as I scuttled further down the tunnel. The amnestic rendering of the Younger Glarp floated in behind. The nausea ended, leaving a literal bad taste in my mouth. There was a faint crackle as Billi restored the holographic cover, and his rapid footfalls faded off into silence.

Janitorial automata don't necessarily use visible light. Under normal circumstances the shaft we occupied would have been black as the heart of a nightclub promoter. But I'd left normal behind a long time ago. Lew's ghost's glow had dimmed slightly but still provided more than adequate light. It folded itself into a sitting position and regarded me.

"I think you owe me some answers now."

Unlike the Veng, I was too tall to sit up in the shaft. I lay on my side, knees tucked in and one elbow resting on the floor so I could prop my head on my hand. "I'll try, but it's not going to make much sense. Why don't you tell me what you know about yourself?"

The ghost nodded. "I'm Bathatar. I'm a forecaster for the actuarial house of Konolo. My specialty is probability management."

"What else?"

"What do you mean?"

"What else can you tell me? Anything about your family? The names of your parents? Do you have siblings? Their names? How you spent your day today? What you had for lunch? Where you live? How you get to work each day? Anything like that?"

Since it had emerged from the vial on Lew's body, the rendering had spoken with his voice. Not quite his inflection of arrogance and self-importance, but nonetheless the same sound. It didn't sound like him any more. It just sounded afraid.

"There's nothing there. There's my name, my rist, my job, and nothing else. How is that possible?"

"Because none of that is real. Your name was Glarp Lewilocus. I'm an entertainer, what you would call a suggestionater. You were onstage and I made you forget who you really were, and started you confabulating a new identity. That's as far as you got before Lew was killed."

"Then, I'm not really even Bathatar. I'm not . . . anyone."

"Look, I'm no expert, but from what I understand of this, Lew's memories and personal identity have to be in you still. I just have to dehypnotize you."

"Is such a thing possible?"

"I have no idea." I fished around in my carpetbag and took out the chewtoy I'd gotten for Reggie, a mangled, strontium dunsel that resembled nothing so much as a melted pipe wrench. I held it by one end and let it dangle between my thumb and forefinger. It swayed back and forth. "Let's find out."

Over the next thirty minutes I tried every trick I knew, every induction, every technique. I started with the backdoor trigger that I make up for every person I put under. It should have worked, but it didn't. Nothing did. Lew's rendering focused on everything I said and did. It yearned to slip away into trance, but never did. Whether the cause lay in its ectoplasm or my abilities as a hypnotist, I couldn't hypnotize the ghost. Worse still, the ghost had forgotten things. It no longer recalled the flight to my dressing room or having met anyone there. From its perspective, it had gone from the stage to the tunnel we now occupied.

"I'm sorry, I don't know what else to try."

"I'm not hypnotized?"

"No. Not even a little bit."

Lew's rendering stopped talking. It sat in the shallow service tunnel, glowing and glowering, too short-lived to endure the kind of existential crisis my honesty had forced on it. Whatever I might have said to console it never emerged from my lips; something out in the corridor kicked the hologram-generating frame that hid our maintenance shaft.

"Incoming," hissed a familiar voice, and a moment Svetlana was crawling into the shaft. She gasped and her delightful smile transformed to a tight white line as she passed grappled with a sudden burst of nausea. She was followed a moment later by a violet man, naked except for an immodest thong; a Sasnakian sex wrestler. The vermin field appeared to have no effect on him.

"You did not lie, my darling," said the wrestler. "It is indeed the Amazing One. But who is his ethereal companion?"

The rendering floated further down the shaft. "Entertainer? You said we were in hiding? Have we been discovered already? Who are these aliens?"

"It's alright," I said, scooching along as well to make room. "These are friends. The woman is in the service of the husk you don't remember meeting from back in my dressing room. And her companion is, well, her companion. Cyrano, right?"

"You honor me, Amazing One."

"Yeah, uh, right. Svetlana, what are you doing here? How did you even find us?"

"The Celestial sent me. It called me to it, and then guided me here. What are you doing in here, and is that a Veng rendering? Are you going to introduce us?"

"Bathatar, meet Svetlana, a human like myself. And Cyrano there is another kind of entertainer, part of a troupe that performed before I went on stage, but that was before you existed as you are now." I gestured to the ghost. "And this is Bathatar, the rendering of the Younger Glarp, who I'd hypnotized moments before his death."

"I am third among my troupe, known far and wide as the Squozen," said Cyrano. "It is a great pleasure to meet you, avenging spirit."

"I never even dreamed of talking to aliens," said the rendering. "But I'm not an avenger. This is all a misunderstanding."

"Conroy, what did you do?" Svetlana looked like she wanted to spit.

"The better question is what am I going to do. Bathatar can't be hypnotized and I'm out of ideas."

"Perhaps a meditative state would help?" said the wrestler.

I shook my head. "Renderings don't seem able to alter their state of consciousness. Bathatar doesn't get tired, or dreamy, or suggestible. He can't seem to lay down new memories either. His emotions change, but little else."

Svetlana bit her lower lip. She glanced back over her shoulder at Cyrano and then forward again to me. "Then what are you doing here? And what happens if you can't undo this?"

"Billi's working to get me out of the reach of the Elder Glarp so we never find out, and in the meantime, I'm trying to think of some way to talk to the dead." Then it hit me. "You've given me an idea. Sit tight for a bit while I try something."

I closed my eyes, let my chin slump to my chest, and cleared everything from my mind but a single name: Fiona Katherine St. Vincent Wyndmoor. Bit-by-bit she took form in my imagination, her face, the sound of her voice, and the ease of her personality. An instant later she went from a construction of my will to a substance all her own. She stood on the stage of my mind, garbed in a dark, long-sleeved dress, her hair blowing in a breeze I couldn't feel.

"Entertainer, who is this now? Another human?"

I opened my eyes and found the rendering staring at the space in front of me where I'd imagined my Aunt Fiona to be.

"You see her?"

"Yes. Shouldn't I?"

"He does, boy," said Aunt Fiona. "And just as wondrous, I can see him as well. The others here I'm aware of, second hand through your eyes, but this person I see directly. Other than yourself he's the first thing I've really seen since I died. What a delightful surprise."

"You're dead? Did the Entertainer steal away your memories too?"

"Conroy, who are you both talking to?" said Svetlana.

"He communes with spirits! Truly he is Amazing."

I was about to do another round of introductions when the hologram crackled again and one of Selstrin's precious rugs slid into the maintenance shaft, all rolled up with the bald top of a Veng's head visible at its center. Relliope followed the rug, squeezing in over and past it, leaving her jammed alongside the Sasnakian. She held Reggie to her chest as she squirmed her way in, wincing with a brief bout of nausea. For his part, Reggie didn't appear to notice the vermin field. He yipped at me, but then caught sight of Lew's rendering behind me and began barking. We all moved further down the shaft, and then further still as the husk of the Celestial entered it, wriggling across the floor, its arms held tightly at its sides. It struggled to strike the reset switch with the mottled toes of one foot, but couldn't hit it properly.

"Allow me," said Cyrano, bending himself double against Relliope and stretching past the Celestial to reactivate the opening's hologram.

<<Ah, good. I was uncertain you would arrive here before me, Svetlana. I didn't expect you to bring your sex partner.>>

"Sex partner?" said Relliope, as the wrestler reversed position, all but writhing against her to do so. Reggie continued to bark.

"I didn't know we'd be ending up here, whatever this place is."

"Entertainer, is that my body? What is happening?"

"Nephew, you do me proud. Such an interesting assortment of people you meet."

<<Mr. Conroy, I am perceiving the loops you indicated were the remaining energies of the Younger Glarp, but there is another pattern of fields directly in front of you that resembles the forms of other humans, but is almost entirely recursive and is not bound to any matter. Who and what is that?>>

"You can see my aunt too?"

"Can he? Curious. I can't see him. Just you and your ghost friend."

<<Should I not?>>

"Uh, no, not really. She's not really here. She's the memory and maybe the spirit of my deceased great aunt. She only just arrived. I thought she might offer a fresh perspective on our problem."

"If she has her memory, why don't I have mine? That hardly seems fair."

The cobalt blue fog that surrounded Relliope's head had completely dissipated, and the solid azure of her eyes locked on my own. "I don't see her, but I can almost feel her. She's like the embodiment of every sclajing every Bluie has experienced. You perform miracles."

Cyrano muttered "Amazing One" to himself.

<<And has she? Provided a fresh perspective?>>

"I wish I could help you, boy. I'd have imagined that the assortment of talents and skills you've gathered around you could get it done if it were possible. I can see the situation from your memories of the last few hours, but short of resurrecting this young man, I don't see how you can undo your hypnotic suggestion."

"But I'm not real," said the ghost, capturing Lew's petulance perfectly. "I'm supposed to have a purpose."

The wrestler nodded. "We all must possess purpose."

"I think I've found mine," said Relliope. "It explains why I was stranded on this world, why I've endured everything I have known. To bring me here, to this place and time." She reached out a hand toward Aunt Fiona. Her eyes gave off a brighter glow than the rendering. I heard my aunt gasp, and everything went black.

<<He is regaining consciousness.>>

The Celestial's voice sounded far away. I opened my eyes and saw my buffalo dog looking down at me, surrounded by a miasma of blue fog. He licked my face, and as the fog dispersed I saw hands holding Reggie's sides, restraining him from the more energetic tongue bath he wanted to give me. My gaze followed the hands up their arms to Relliope's torso. Her face, what I could see of it behind the tendrils of vapor coming from her eyes, looked both distraught and relieved.

"Mr. Conroy, I'm so sorry. Please forgive me."

She let go of the buffalito and her hands clasped mine as she pulled me up to a sitting position alongside her. Reggie tumbled into my lap. I'd been lying on a couch; specifically, the couch from my dressing room. That made sense, because as I looked around, I realized that's where I was.

"How did I get here? It isn't safe."

<<It wasn't safe. Your agent now estimates the peril as negligible.>> Elroy leaned against the door, stiff as a board of picklewood. Svetlana occupied a chair to his left, and Cyrano sat on the floor massaging her feet.

"Why? What's changed."

<<Time.>>

"You've been unconscious for hours." Svetlana lifted her left foot from the wrestler's grip and offered him the right one. "It's morning."

Relliope let go of my hands. "I thought I'd killed you. But your Celestial insisted you had only been stunned and would wake up without any after effects. And now, you're awake. You're okay, right?"

I nodded to Relliope. "But what happened?"

<<The coherent fields of memory that defined your aunt are not compatible with the chaotic influence inherent in this person's touch.>>

"Which means?"

"I blew her up!" The Bluie cringed, bringing her hands to her mouth and all but biting her fingers.

<<Your aunt was unharmed. The patterns of her fields dissipated normally after you lost consciousness. But as the physical conduit that had maintained those fields, you suffered a kind of feedback shock.>>

"But how did we get here? And what about Lew's ghost?"

As one they all turned their gaze to the dressing room's shower alcove.

"You put him in the shower?"

<<No. I placed the corpse there when we returned. The rendering followed on its own. It no longer recalls any of us now, and has chosen to stay with its body.>>

Reggie poked at me with a hoof for attention. I looked down into his wooly face and he bleated at me. He was hungry. My stomach rumbled in reply. "I don't suppose anyone stopped for food on the way back here?"

"The little green man promised to bring back breakfast," said Relliope, "but he's been gone a very long time."

Billi's voice came from another corner of the room. "You try getting food for half a dozen different species, carrying it back without tossing your cookies half a dozen times in these damn tunnels, and all the while avoid a security team out for your blood." With a crackle he shut off the hologram hiding a janitorial shaft I didn't know was in my dressing room and emerged, dragging several shopping bags after him.

"You brought cookies?" said Cyrano.

Billi ignored him. "Conroy, I got good booze and bad booze for you. The good is that I was able to get some face time with the Elder Glarp himself and explain what exactly happened at your show. He was really understanding, and even apologized for having his goons chasing me all over the place."

Svetlana pulled her foot free and stood up. She took the bags from Billi and began passing out sealed plates to everyone. I took one and pulled back the lid. The warm scent of an omelet with meat and cheese made my stomach rumble again, never mind what kind of eggs or cheese or meat had gone into the dish. It smelled great, from the slight char of the crispy bits of the meat to the peppery fragrance that seasoned the eggs. Reggie tried to shove his face into it, but I pushed him back and gave him the lid to eat instead; it had a lot of the same smells and probably more fiber besides. All around me the others were digging into their respective breakfasts, with the exception of the Celestial who remained leaning against the door.

"So you're off the hook. What about me? Does he still blame me?"

"That's the bad booze. It's gone way beyond blame. He wants you dead. He's declared blood feud against you!"

CHAPTER SIXTEEN

Wrestling With A Disguise

SVETLANA DROPPED HER spork and leapt to her feet. "That's impossible! The Elder Glarp's rist is Pentahedral Diamond. Conroy's is Emerald Eastern Snowfall. There isn't a relationship between them. That's the whole point of the eleven rist that outsiders are assigned to; they don't have any ties or history to any of the other one hundred ninety-three rist that define the rest of Veng society and obligation."

Billi recovered her utensil and waved it like a baton, emphasizing his words. "That was then, this is bow. As the top of Pentahedral Diamond, the Elder Glarp has taken it upon himself to change all of that."

I set down my plate, barely noticing as Reggie stuck a hoof into the middle of it, pulled it his way, and began devouring both meal and vessel. "Change how?"

"He amended your contract, tripling your pay."

I rescued the little bit of my breakfast that Reggie hadn't consumed. "How is that a bad thing? It sounds more like an apology."

Svetlana nodded even as Billi shook his head. "He appealed to the planetary governing council, citing the impact of your shows and the pay rate, pointing out that it's greater than anyone in Emerald Eastern Snowfall has ever received, and that is ample precedent. Whether they agreed or were intimidated by him or he bought their votes outright, they granted his appeal."

"For what?"

Billi aimed the spork at me with one hand while the other three lifted helplessly, palms turning upward. "You've been declared the head of Emerald Eastern Snowfall."

"That can't happen," said Svetlana. "None of the rist with non-Veng have a formal head."

"This one does. It's what the Elder Glarp wanted."

"But why?" I looked around the room; everyone seemed just as confused. "What's the point? Why make me the head? Why go to all that trouble."

Svetlana gasped and stared at me, her jaw dropping. "Oh my god!"

"What? What?"

Billi sighed. "Yeah. As the head of your rist, you and the Elder Glarp are kinda sorta equals. He wants to kill you with his own hands. A blood feud let's him."

"But we're leaving, right? We're not going to give him the chance. Let's go!" I looked around for my carpetbag. Time was wasting.

"Conroy, you need to chill. Why do you think he explained all this and then let bee go. He *wants* you to rabbit. If you bolt, it's easier for him to snatch you up."

"And if I stay, how long do you think it will take for him to find me? He's got to know I'm still in the Pyramidal."

"Yeah, and his people searched this dressing room first thing, just like I thought they would. That's why we came back here after smokey-eyes knocked you out to lunch. You're safe here, for a little while."

Svetlana shook her head. "What happens when that time is up? The Elder Glarp practically owns this city. He has every advantage and we have none. It's like playing in a card game where they deal from the bottom of the deck with marked cards."

I laughed. "Exactly!"

"It's not funny," she said.

"No, but it reminded me of a friend of mine, a professional gambler. He'd love being in that kind of a game."

"Why?"

"Because when the other side is so sure they've got every angle covered, they stop trying to imagine what someone truly desperate might come up with." I wiped the smile from my face. "I think I qualify as truly desperate."

Elroy pushed off from the wall. <<And have you imagined an unanticipated angle?>>

"Maybe. It's a variation on an idea Billi had. I'll need to contact the *Shpeshnoltoc* though."

"The Cliveden ship we were on? Why?" Svetlana moved to stand next to the Celestial.

"I think I can persuade them to come here and lean on the Elder Glarp."

Billi punched me in the thigh. Again. "How? You said it yourself, the Glarp's got buckets of power. How can Telfano put any pressure on him."

"The Elder Glarp's power comes from his ability to export drift juice to other worlds. The Cliveden control what leaves this planet."

"What's drift juice?" asked Svetlana.

Billi skittered across the room and punched her thigh. "Later."

"Ow!"

"The Cliveden are a hateful people," said Relliope. "Why would they come to your aid?"

"Captain Telfano and I have an . . . arrangement. She doesn't have to actually blockade the Elder Glarp, only threaten to."

"Yeah the Glarp's a businessman before all else. Just the threat to his power base should be enough to bake him back off." Billi clasped all four of his hands together. "Brilliant!"

"It's only brilliant if I can get word to the *Shpeshnoltoc*."

"You can't," said Relliope. "Not from here. The Cliveden don't allow others to speak to their ships. The Veng have no equipment to even make the attempt. You'd have to travel to the floating island to do it."

I squatted until I was eye to eye with Billi. "You said you had a plan for getting into the Cliveden lounge. Is it still viable?"

"Partly. I have a guy on the inside, he works an information desk on the primary concourse. He's from a rist that hates the Glarp and would love to screw him over. The problem is still getting up there.

<<What is to prevent the use of public transportation?>>

Billi snorted. "You can leave at any time. They won't stop tall and green, but I'm stuck on account they'll assume I'm trying something. Which I would, if I could. Every cabbie, courier, and cartmonger in the city is on alert for a human of Conroy's description, with orders to transport him directly to the Glarp, or else. And I don't have to tell ya how persuasive his *or else* is, right?" He waved a hand at me and another at Svetlana. "Most Veng can probably tell she's female, but since the two of you are the only humans on Bisto, she'll probably be taken away on general principle. And while a big enough bribe will get a dead body into a cab, you're not gonna find a Veng that will take a rendering for a fare."

Relliope took one of Billi's hands in both of hers. "This is no barrier. Mr. Conroy is a great suggestionater. He can convince the driver that he is the Celestial's twin. He can make them think we all are."

"All?" Billi snatched his hand away.

"You have to take me with you. Please, I cannot stay here."

"Relliope, the Veng are very suggestible, but I can't hypnotize someone that fast, especially not when the instant they see me they're in fear for their lives if they don't hand me in. It's not exactly an ideal stage setting."

Relliope drooped as my words sank in. "Oh. I thought you could cloud their minds."

"Maybe. Maybe I still can. I think you had the right idea, but not Celestial, Sasnakian."

The wrestler jerked his head up. "What was that, Amazing One?"

"Cyrano, I'm going to need your, uh, thong."

"You have a plan, Amazing One?"

"I do indeed. Billi, does the Elder Glarp know that Relliope is with us?"

"I don't think so. The Celestial, sure. And Svetlana. But that's all."

"Great. I want you to sneak her out of here. Relliope, you have access to wherever they store bar supplies, right?"

"Yes, but—"

"Perfect. I want you and Billi to go and bring back all the poki fruit you can."

"Poki fruit? Why?"

"You'll see. But hurry."

Billi dropped to all sixes and opened the grate over the maintenance tunnel. "What are you going to be doing?"

I went to my makeup table and took up the tube of depilatory cream I used before every show. "Me? I'm going to be shaving my head."

The Celestial had put Lew's corpse in the shower alcove while I'd been unconscious. Rigor mortis differs among aliens; the limp body I had hauled off stage had stiffened and now leaned against one wall, much like Elroy had been leaning against the door. He didn't look the least bit peaceful. Lew's ghost had dimmed a bit more. It hovered over the body, nearly as immobile, but jerked its head up as I stepped into the alcove.

"I know you. You're the Entertainer!"

"Hi, Bathatar. Can you make a little room for me?" I reached down and shifted Lew as far out of the way as I could and stripped off my toga.

"What are you doing? Put your clothes back on. Just because I'm a rendering, don't think I'll let you defile the dead."

I held up the bottle of depilatory. "Relax. I'm here for the shower, not for Lew." I gave the bottle a squeeze and filled my hands with a generous dollop of goo.

"How am I to know what you aliens do or don't do? I'm an actuarial forecaster. I make estimates of the likelihood of people dying, not what happens to them after that."

"Do you still remember anything after waking up on stage with me?" I rubbed the depilatory into my scalp, working up a lather. Filling my hands with more goo, I slathered it along my arms and legs, over my chest, and elsewhere. It foamed and started tingling in a not altogether pleasant way as it opened my pores and burned up any and all hair follicles.

The ghost shook its head and gestured at the body of the Younger Glarp. "No, nothing before or after. A fellow from Scintillating Oblong Veracity killed me, claiming blood feud, but it doesn't make any sense. None of this does. Why would I have a deadman vessel? Entertainer, I'm a nobody. I have no business possessing a rendering. Why would someone seek my death in the first place?"

Once again the ghost had forgotten everything. I could answer its questions, explain about my act, but that wouldn't stick either. And I wasn't any closer to figuring out if any of Lew's original memories were still somewhere in the rendering. One problem at a time though. The tingling sensation had progressed to painful stinging. I motioned the ghost back and activated the controls. Pulses from the shower bombarded me, vibrating and whooshing away foam and hair and quite possibly a chunk or two of epidermis.

"Is this something your kind of alien does routinely? Or is it a mourning ritual? I feel like I know you, but I can't remember how or why."

"Neither. It's part of a disguise. I—"

"Mr. Conroy? We're back with the poki." Relliope came around the corner, a large sack in either hand. Blue vapor fluttered into the shower's alcove as her head bobbled up and down, taking in the ghost and my nakedness. "Oh. Your pardon."

I snatched the sacks and positioned them for maximum modesty. "Um . . . Thank you."

"More aliens?" said the ghost, edging closer to where its corpse leaned.

"A friend," I said, though from what I could tell of her lingering stare it was going beyond friendly.

"Not amazing, but certainly respectable, Mr. Conroy." Relliope giggled, turned in place, and marched out as Billi pushed past her, swiping at the fog in the air with a pair of hands.

"I grok what you have in mind, pal, but do you really think it will work?" He opened the pair of sacks he carried in two other hands and began smashing fistfuls of poki berries against my thigh, staining it a deep purple. I flinched. Maybe it was a sensitivity caused by the depilatory, or maybe poki juice was just naturally caustic, but the stuff burned as it dyed my skin.

"Another friend." Bathatar recoiled still further.

"I know you don't remember, but you've met both of them before." I batted Billi's assistance away. "I can do this myself, thanks."

"I was just trying to help. Six hands are better than two, right?"

"You want to help? Mash the poki in the sacks. I'll handle the application myself."

"Whatever." Billi contrived to roll his protruding eyes like a martyr. "The problem with this disguise is, even if visually convincing, it won't pass a scan. It's only skin deep."

"I don't have to pass through any scanners until I try to board a ship. This is just to get me into a cab and safely to the floating island. Then your man on the inside will pass me through to the Clivedon lounge and out of the jurisdiction of the Veng and the reach of the Elder Glarp."

"Oh," said Billi, brightening as it sank in, only to frown a moment later. "But how will you make contact? The guy's gonna be looking for a Pelk or a Human, not a lone Sasnakian."

I kept smearing myself with mashed poki, spreading the juicy pulp all over my body. I didn't want to think how difficult it might be to remove the stain; it was enough to expect that I might have the leisure to do it down the road.

"I'll take Elroy with me."

"Which changes you from a lone Sasnakian to a Sasnakian with a walking vegetable. Still not what the guy is looking for."

"But he'll be looking, right?" I reached into one of Billi's sacks and filled both hands with more dripping fruit.

"Oh yeah. He'll have his eyes open as soon as word of the Glarp's blood feud reaches the floating island."

"Great. Let's hope he's bright enough to recognize a fake Pelk when it's not safe for a real one to show up."

Billi punched me in the thigh. "What the heck does that bean?"

I glanced at the spot he'd struck. The skin was happily purple and hadn't smeared. "See if Relliope can take you and Svetlana to the prop room. They have all sorts of acts here, you should be able to find something that you can fashion into a pair of arms."

"Arms?" He punched me again.

I punched back, which startled him. "Yes, arms. Big, green arms. We're going to put them on Elroy so he'll have an extra set."

"That's stupid. He'll look like a carnival show. It'll draw all kinds of attention."

"Right. And if they're looking at him, they won't be looking at me. Which leaves me free to spot your inside man. Got it?"

"Yeah . . . You want I should hook up your Celestial with some stuffed arms. I'm back to being a taxidermist."

"That's show biz." I shoved him out of the shower alcove. He went, calling for Relliope and Svetlana.

"This is nothing like actuarial forecasting," said the ghost from its spot alongside Lew's corpse.

"I'm glad. I'd hate to know the odds of it working."

I left Bathatar in the shower with Lew's corpse. It seemed less anxious there. Out in the dressing room, the Celestial still leaned on the wall next to the door. Cyrano had moved from his spot on the floor to perch on the edge of my makeup table. He wore a generic toga that was embarrassingly too small for him. I wore his thong and tried not to think much about it. The poki fruit had done a remarkable job staining my skin to a shade of purple only slightly darker than the Sasnakian. My skin tone lacked the deep blue highlights that the wrestler had, but my goal wasn't to pass for a Sasnakian, only to not be seen as a Human.

Reggie had been sitting under my makeup table. He trotted over, whether to inspect me as well or simply drawn by a faint, sweet scent of poki I couldn't tell. He whuffled once, turned, and went back to his spot under the table, returning to his nap. One critic down, two to go.

"What do you think?"

Cyrano frowned. "You look . . . sickly."

"Sickly?"

"Like you have a disease. A contagious disease."

I frowned and turned to Elroy. "What do *you* think?"

<<My perception does not function as yours. I would know you anywhere by the patterns of your fields.>>

"Neither of you are very helpful."

After that we waited in silence until Relliope returned with Billi, Svetlana, and a pair of green foam arms.

"Mr. Conroy, is that you?" Relliope's blue vapor poured from her eyes in the heaviest release yet.

"Baldness becomes you, Conroy," said Svetlana. Her eyes ran up and down my body, as if seeing me for the first time. "Purple does too."

Billi came out of the maintenance tunnel last, dragging the foam limbs. He took one look at me and started laughing.

"What, it's not that bad!"

"Yeah, right. Don't quit your day job, Conroy. Cuz I sure won't be able to book you as a solo-wrestling act. Ever. Anywhere."

"Laugh later. You got the prop arms?"

"Oh yeah. Here. I see how this works. You want the Celestial to look even sillier than you. Good plan."

Elroy took the arms from him. They'd been cobbled together with a belt that went around the Celestial's waist, and a series of fine threads that tied the wrist and elbow of each arm to the corresponding spot on the actual limb above it, allowing both to move in unison. Hokey didn't begin to describe it.

<<I am ready to accompany you. How long will we be away? Surely you do not intend to abandon the Younger Glarp's rendering.>>

"If this goes as I think it will, Captain Telfano will send us back here with both a Cliveden escort and an ultimatum for the Elder Glarp. Once I'm no longer on the defensive and running for my life, I hope to come up with some way to fix Lew's ghost up right. It won't bring him back, but at least it will allow things to proceed the way they're supposed to in this society."

"Yeah, well, just don't dawdle. Your buddy's corpse is gonna start getting real ripe real soon."

I retrieved Reggie from his spot under the makeup table and placed him in Relliope's arms. "Would you take charge of him until I get back?"

Blue mist fluttered at me as she bobbed her head. "It would be my pleasure, Mr. Conroy."

"Thanks." I turned to Svetlana. "I'm sorry that you're stuck here just because we share the same species. Can I ask you to keep an eye on Lew's ghost? It doesn't seem to be able to hold onto any new memories, but it always does remember me. Maybe another human will help keep it calm. I don't know what else to do for it."

“Don’t worry, I’ll handle it. Go talk to the Cliveden, and be sure to keep the Celestial safe.”

<<My safety is not in question. Though I confess, I am looking forward to this experience.>>

“Oh? Why’s that?” I said.

<<It occurs to me that I have some new topics of conversation I wish to discuss with you. And possibly, I can at last answer some of your questions.>>

Elroy and I followed Billi into the maintenance tunnels once more. I did my best not to be sick as we passed through multiple encounters with vermin fields along the way. My agent wound through the tunnels like a well-educated laboratory rat that has memorized all possible routes to some promised, cheddary reward.

“Keep up, and stop complaining. I don’t like feeling like I’m gonna puke either. And after I put you in a taxi, I still have to retrace the route back to your dressing room.”

<<I expressed no displeasure.>>

“Maybe bot out loud, but I can tell you’re thinking it. You and Conroy both.”

<<Curious. Your do not appear to possess the patterns I usually perceive among receptive telepaths.>>

“Because he’s not.” I brought up the rear, dragging the Celestial’s faux arms behind me. “Billi, not a complaint but a question: How much further?”

Billi’s reply came as a sudden familiar crackling, followed by the sounds of traffic. I had to pass through one more round of gut-grinding nausea and then we emerged onto a small ledge outside an employees’ entrance to the Pyramidal’s main kitchen. Several Veng—dishwashers judging by the colors and dampness of their togas and sashes—had formed a queue, and stood waiting for the ubiquitous cabs that accounted for most transportation throughout Bisto’s underground cities.

Billi grabbed the prop from me and shoved it at the Celestial. “Put your arms on. I’ll get you a cab.”

<<There is a line.>>

“So?” Billi pushed his way through the Veng until he reached the front of the queue. “Hey! You see that guy? He’s one of the sex wrestlers performing here. Recognize him?”

Several of the dishwashers nodded, including the one at the head.

"Great. Great. Well, see, he and the others were practicing a fresh bit to add to their show and they underestimated the erotic quotient. I'm sure I don't need to tell you how explosive that can be. This guy took the worst of it, but we're talking almost total orgasmic backlash, right? Fried his brain. He ran right into the first tunnel he could find and we've been chasing him since. He's in a real bad way, so we've got to commandeer your taxi. Thanks for understanding."

This was met with muttering from the dishwashers further down the line but the Veng at the head shrugged. "Oh. Uh. Sure." He stepped back, as a cab arrived, the bubble of its door popping open. Billi positioned himself in the opening, two arms coincidentally blocking the Veng in case he changed his mind and waved us forward with a third. We hustled in, the Celestial mimicking the blocking move with a real arm and the prop arm slaved to it.

"Thanks. I always say you can judge the caliber of a place by the character of its kitchen workers. You're a prince. Top botch all the way. Driver, take my friends to the floating island, and don't spare the horses." He pulled a handful of currency from one of his toga's pockets and thrust it through the slot in the wall and into the operator's compartment. Without so much as a goodbye he dropped back, slammed the door shut, and vanished back amongst the Veng.

CHAPTER SEVENTEEN

Learning with Lounge Lizards

OUR CAB was much like the other pods I'd used since arriving on Bisto, a four-meter long egg partitioned such that the front quarter held the drive, the middle two-thirds served as passenger compartment with a ceramo bench overlaid with a synthetic upholstery fabric, and the remaining portion of the vehicle given over for the propulsion mechanics in the rear. No sooner had we climbed in than the cab shot off through the underground highways, bobbing and weaving through traffic at sufficient acceleration to shove us against our seat backs. Only then did I notice the foul odor coming from the upholstery, as if a dozen infants in advanced need of diaper changing were arrayed around us.

"Ugh. Be glad you don't have a sense of smell." I cupped my hands over my mouth and nose and gained some small relief from the poki berry fragrance that clung to my skin.

The Celestial held out its thumb to me. <<If you will allow, I could sample the experience from you olfactory memory.>>

"Maybe another time. Have you been taking a lot of samples since you've been here?"

<<Very many. I only wish I had realized the importance of doing so much sooner. It has changed everything for me.>>

"How so?"

It lowered its arm and leaned forward, staring silently down at its thumb a long while. It folded the thumb back in line with its other digits and leaned back against the foul upholstery with a outrush of air that served it as a sigh. <<You are not at all as I anticipated you would be when I began this venture.>>

"Me specifically, or flesh and blood sapients at this scale?"

<<The latter. When I began, I would not have imagined having this conversation, but now it is important to me that you understand. I expected your kind to be no more challenging than the complexity of planetary biospheres, every outcome predicated upon the interaction of observable systems and forces. The summation of physics vectors and chemical reactions.>>

I bit my lip. Calling the Celestial *Elroy* had allowed me to think of him in more human—or at least, humanoid—terms, and forget that the body in the cab with me was little more than a walking comm-patch for a much vaster creature. “And?”

<<I was in error. Nor is it solely a matter of scale. My kind are solitary. By comparison, even the most isolated at your level are wildly gregarious. Taken in groups, your actions do indeed fall within predictable parameters, but as individuals . . . you are exactly that, individual. Chaotic. Not truly random, but prone to bursts of behavior that defy control or anticipation.>>

“It’s not so bad once you get used to it.”

<<On this we must agree to disagree. The more I observe you, the more I realize how mistaken I have been, even more than when I first encountered you without the benefit of an anchor.>>

“You’re talking about when you used a starship as your host. The one that exploded above Hesnarj.”

<<I selected you then, much as I selected Svetlana, for your ability to serve as an anchor. I mistook you for a tool, something I could shape to my need. But the very qualities that drew me to you make you the least adaptable to my will.>>

“Good you realized that. Most of the people I know tend to dislike being used like objects.”

<<Yes. Which is why I am pleased we have this opportunity to converse in private. I feel the need to apologize for the situation you are in.>>

“What, you mean with the Elder Glarp? Don’t worry, I have enough leverage with Captain Trelfano to make that Veng see reason. Besides, it’s hardly your fault.”

<<Actually, it is. All of it.>>

“What? How?”

<<I set it in motion. As a test.>>

“What exactly did you set in motion?”

<<Everything. I have kept track of you since our first meeting, years and years to you, little more than an eyeblink to me. From time to time I have

caused various people to cross your path to observe your reactions and study the pattern of your growth. Most recently, I was the mysterious benefactor to the Traken who performed your play.>>

"Excuse me?"

<<My intention was to draw you closer, to allow greater refinement of the tool I was designing you to be. I created a situation to serve as a proving ground; a test. Ironic that my success in manipulating your fate provided the proximity to realize that you and the others around us are individuals, with will and choice and chaos inherent in their systems and fields.>>

"In other words, *not* tools."

<<Thus my need to apologize. In my ignorance, in my need, I have interfered with your life. If it is any consolation, you have exceeded all my expectations that I was testing you for.>>

"Uh, no. Sorry. I can't speak for any one else you've manipulated, but I don't like being used."

The Celestial leaned forward, a movement which could just as easily have been intended as a bow as a shrug. <<I will not presume to suggest how I might atone, but if something presents itself to you, you have only to ask.>>

I worked my shoulders, lifting each one in turn, maybe just because Elroy's husk didn't have the articulation to do so. "Maybe. You'll understand if I'm a little preoccupied with current events. How about we talk more after seeing if this plan works out and I can get the Elder Glarp to call off his blood feud, okay?"

<<Satisfactory. Indeed, the need that prompted my actions is still in place. I hope we can discuss your involvement, not as a tool but as an active participant. Perhaps you might come to think of me as a patron?>>

"Doubtful, but it's a far better choice than puppet master."

The Celestial didn't speak again for the rest of the ride.

The arrival platform of Bisto's floating island mirrored the departure area. Transit pods and smaller taxis landed, disgorged cargo and passengers, and vanished to the opposite side in search of fares to start the process over again. Elroy followed me into the main concourse. Identical Veng scurried past us with never a glance our way. We weren't their rist, so we weren't their business. I studied the projected signage overhead but my limited command of the writing system didn't reveal anything that could direct me toward an information desk.

"Can you read Veng polyglyphs?"

<<Under the proper circumstances.>>

"Meaning what?"

<<I comprehend the correspondence between symbol and referent, but only if I can perceive the sign. The visual system of this husk doesn't function as yours does. I can tell that there are light projections around us, but not discern their content.>>

"So . . . No."

<<Not in this instance.>>

"Me neither. I've learned a few—I could get us to a restaurant or a rest room—but that's no help. So much for the subtle approach." Without warning I thrust an arm into the path of one of the Veng flowing past, stopping him and grabbing his elbow as he tried to slip past.

"Hey! Unhand me, lout. Pfeh! You smell like a brewery." The Veng squirmed and waved his other hand but refrained from actually touching me, all the while muttering about slinko.

"I beg your pardon, friend. My companion and I have lost our way. We would consider it a great kindness if you could direct us to the information desk."

The rest of the Veng traffic continued to pass us, either ignoring or oblivious to our new threesome.

"How dare you! I am of the Sapphire Bell's Meeting. We do not consort with entertainers and such low rist."

"You are of Sapphire Bell's Meeting? What an extraordinary coincidence. We were just dining with Kelbo Fagonst of the Pentahedral Diamond, and he was praising the generosity and helpfulness of your rist to us while we enjoyed crelteckle at the Hidden Wind."

"The Hidden Wind? And Pentahedral Diamond said such about my rist?"

"Truly. I could not imagine greater fortune for my companion and myself than to meet you."

"Yes, of course, we are famed for our benevolence to the lesser rist. The datakeeping staff you seek are up that way, just past from where the concourse curves to the right. You will know them by their blue and violet sashes." He pointed back the way he had come.

"The blessings of all Sasnak go with you, kind sir." I let go of his arm and made a show of kissing each fingertip that had touched him. He blinked up at me, paused only a moment longer, and then thrust himself into the current of Veng once more. Following his example, I put my hand in the middle of Elroy's back and pushed it in our direction up the concourse.

Quite a few desks and kiosks and booths awaited us around that bend, offering everything from fast food to tour guides to tickets for spectator events. The Veng at each of these wore sashes that duplicated the colors of their merchandise and stands, bunting, and displays, or maybe it was the other way around. The information desk stood out among them by the lack of anything for sale and a minimum of decoration save for four Veng in blue and violet sashes over their beige togas sitting on stools behind information plaques.

"Greetings, friends. My companion is the galaxy's largest Pelk. He and I have a wager that could only be resolved by the adjudication of a lounging Cliveden. Can you tell us where we might find one?"

The datakeepers stared at me, at one another, and then at the Celestial. One rubbed his eyes, looked again, and said, "You're a Pelk?"

<<What else could I possibly be?>> Elroy swung his arms about.

Another of the Veng nudged the one who'd spoken. "I'll take this one, Clef. I was just about to go on break any way." He slid off his stool and came around the desk. "Come with me, sirs. The Cliveden don't tend to speak to other races, but I can take you where you might catch a glimpse of one coming or going. Will that serve?"

"Baby it will, and baby it won't," I said, earning another stare from the Veng still behind the desk and a slow nod from our new companion. He led us further up the concourse through the unending pedestrian traffic and down a side corridor that was refreshingly empty in contrast.

"My name's Doyle, and it's a good thing you're not really a Pelk."

<<Why is that?>>

"Because I'm really starting to hate Pelk. Things are never the way they lead you to believe they are."

"I know what you mean, but believe me, they grow on you after a while."

He sneered. "Not if I can help it." We continued down the vacant corridor to where it ended at a large, well-lit gate.

<<That is an airlock.>>

Doyle nodded and began tapping a sequence into a small wall plaque. "The Cliveden are fastidious about their privacy. I know the codes to open this lock, and I know all the guards that work the post on the other side. This sequence will let them know to let you in."

<<Why should they do this for you?>>

"Elroy! We don't need to know that."

"Doesn't matter. We have an understanding. I get them things we have here that they want but aren't allowed to leave to collect for themselves. And vice versa. Every now and then that includes sneaking someone into their lounge. I don't ask questions, and neither will they."

"I'm gaining new insight into Billi every day," I said.

The Veng shrugged. "Stations like this, there's always someone like me. I guess he's just got the knack of figuring out who's who. But listen, once they let you in, go about your business and be quick. Your average Cliveden won't do anything because they won't want to interact with you; they'll barely acknowledge your existence. Eventually someone whose job requires contact with aliens will show up and escort you out at the end of a stun baton. It could happen sooner, could happen later. My advice, don't dawdle."

The wall plaque glowed with a faint green outline and our side of the lock receded into its housing.

"A pleasure doing business with you and your Pelk." Doyle turned and walked away without lingering to see that we got in without any problem. Elroy and I stepped into the lock's middle chamber. The outer door closed again, and we waited for the inner side to open.

Stepping from the lock we were greeted by a rippling chorus of indrawn breath that sounded remarkably like hissing. I knew from my time aboard the *Shpeshnoltoc* that every station receiving Cliveden vessels had a lounge to accommodate crew wishing to sample the wares and flavors of a new world without having to meet any of their actual inhabitants. The lounge gave the appearance of a vast open-air bazaar, with micro dunes of vermillion gravel underfoot and a viridian sky above. A hundred or more booths or stands or tables displayed curios and geegaws obtainable in any of Bisto's underground cities. Tiny signs scrawled with incomprehensible symbols likely described what each object was for, how it was used, or what it cost. Cliveden ranged on all sides of the merchandise, had stopped their browsing and selling, their bargaining and dealing, and turned their pale purple lizards heads to stare at us. Their attention was not due to any sense of awe at having a Celestial in their midst, assuming they even recognized Elroy's husk for what it was.

"Sasnakians are not welcome here. Nor their vat-grown toys." A particularly surly Cliveden dressed in black shorts and painfully pink, fingerless gloves set aside whatever geegaw she'd been examining at one of the stalls and positioned herself in front of us. She was a head shorter than me, shorter than any Cliveden I'd ever seen, and made no attempt to raise her eyes above my collarbone. "I am Throsco, custodian of this facility. By my authority, I instruct you to leave here. Now."

<<Interesting. This one's fields are tighter than any of the others?>>

I glanced back at Elroy. "Meaning what?"

<<Either she is hardened against mental attacks, or exceptionally focused, or both.>>

Neither bode well for trying my first attempt at hypnotic suggestion on a Cliveden. I switched gears and went from subtle to simple and put on my best performer's smile. Cliveden like seeing teeth. "Good custodian, thank you for coming to greet us. It's my understanding that you have the means to contact the ships of your families. Could you kindly lend us assistance? I need to open a communication channel to the *Shpeshnoltoc*."

"Are you stupider than you appear? I said you're not welcome."

"I appreciate that," I said. "Which is why I will keep my exchange with the *Shpeshnoltoc* as brief as possible."

The Cliveden custodian pressed her palms together and her gloves began to pulse. "The facilities here are for the exclusive use of the families; this includes our communication equipment. They will not reach anyone on the *Shpeshnoltoc* who would care to talk to you, just as no one here wishes to talk to you. Including me."

"Telfano sa Rens is an exception. She is the captain of the *Shpeshnoltoc* and will want to speak with me."

Throsco's right hand darted out, lizard quick, and where her gloved hand grazed my upper arm I lost all sensation. I yelped, and stumbled backwards into the Celestial.

<<She has disrupted the flow of a portion of your fields.>>

"I can tell."

<<It appears to be a temporary phenomenon.>>

"Your talking vegetable is perceptive," said the Cliveden. "A light exposure causes no lasting harm. Neural disruption does possess a cumulative effect though, and the results can be permanent. I have observed the mandates of the Veng with two verbal warnings and one nonlethal and short-lived intervention. I am required to state a third time before I am empowered to cripple or kill. Leave now."

A painful tingling had begun in my arm, proof that the paralysis was already wearing off. Muscles twitched as the nerves there remembered how they worked. "Look, there's no need for this. Captain Trelfano will probably reward you for putting my message through—"

Throsco lunged forward. I couldn't back up any further so I simply dropped to the gravel and her palms passed over me and landed flat against the Celestial's chest. It sizzled. As I rolled aside and regained my feet I saw the custodian pull back, brushing her hands against one another to wipe away bits of blackened vegetable matter.

"Are you all right?"

<<Oh yes. This form does not have a nervous system per se, so it cannot be disrupted. The scoring to my surface is cosmetic, but it will not regenerate.>>

The Cliveden reached for me again. "I no longer want you to leave, mammal. I won't let you. Now I get to hurt you."

"That's insane! I just want to place a call."

She chuckled as I ducked behind Elroy. "Bringing a vegetable shield is innovative, but you move awkwardly for a sex wrestler." The pink pulse of her gloves brightened.

"I'm not really a Sasnakian." I lunged left as she lunged right, keeping the Celestial's husk between us.

"I don't care." She reached for me under Elroy's arm but her hand passed through empty air and slapped against his back. It sizzled.

"Elroy, you remember the synthesis of pain you created?" I ducked again, smelling burnt squash.

<<I do.>>

"Share it with Throsco!"

<<I cannot. Even if her fields were not hardened against such a thing, I can only transfer knowledge to beings I am anchored to.>>

The Cliveden feinted left, feinted right, and then dove between the Celestial's legs and rolled to her feet behind. The light from her gloves illuminated her wild grin as she reached for me again. Elroy obligingly bent his knees backwards and hinged forward, and I scrambled over and in front of him then dashed into the bazaar. The other Cliveden who had been content to watch in silence erupted in hisses and fled deeper into the lounge. They whispered to one another in a cacophony of sibilants which turned into a rawkish cheers every time Throsco's glowing gloves came near me.

"Think of something else then!"

<<I am open to your suggestions.>>

I knocked over tables and flung them into Throsco's path. She followed after, still laughing, gathering up merchandise and tiny signs in her glowing hands and tossing them at me. Inspiration!

As I fled down a tiny alley made by several tightly clustered booths, I called out to Elroy. "The other Cliveden here with us, they're not speaking Traveler. Are they using one of the other trade tongues? Shpoto or . . . Um, any of the others?"

<<They are not.>>

The custodian's fingers grazed my wrist as she shoved aside the booth I was hiding behind. I recoiled, backing away, desperate to avoid the pink pulses of her palms.

"Scan those minds, compile the memories of that language. Can you do that? Quickly?"

<<I can. It is nearly done. But to what purpose?>>

I rounded a corner, breaking free. I'd gotten turned all around. The airlock we'd entered from was directly in front of me, Elroy behind me but lumbering in my direction. I started for the lock. Sprinting in from further up the Cliveden custodian arrived there first. She positioned herself with her back to the lock and her arms out in front of her, palms outward. The pulsing had quickened.

"Give it to me," I shouted back at the Celestial.

"That is certainly my intention." She ran toward me.

From behind, Elroy knocked me down and barreled into the Cliveden. The collision drove them both down into the gravel. Throsco flailed her limbs, but couldn't dislodge the Celestial's massive husk. It waved one leg in my direction. I tried to duck, but it kicked me in the head any way, one green toe grazing my forehead.

Concepts that had no frame of reference poured through my brain, found no place to take root, and poured out again. Grammar and speech sounds fared slightly better, twisted but analogous to bits and pieces I already possessed, just enough to cling.

"Stop!" I said. "Just stop." Except I didn't. The words meant something more like *the cessation of actions tolerated in juveniles by overindulgent revered elders secure in the knowledge that they may depart to their own shelters and leave the rabble youth to upset their immediate family instead.* Kind of like grandparents dropping by in, giving the kids sugar, and leaving just when it kicks in and they begin bouncing off the walls.

I'd spoken Thishfiff, a native language of the Cliveden.

Throsco froze. All sound in the lounge had stopped.

"What. Did. You. Say?" The custodian's words were in Traveler. Each syllable clearly enunciated.

I understood her, but for the life of me I couldn't figure out how to answer in kind. My reply came out in Thishfiff. "I am in the employ of Captain Trelfano of the *Shpeshnoltoc*. She promised to send assistance. I am in dire need of that help. Now."

"How did a Sasnakian learn our speech?"

"I told you, I'm not Sansnakian."

"Nor are you Cliveden, but you speak as one of the family. That riddle prevents me from killing you."

"Great. I'm all for that. Now would you open that damn channel for me?"

The custodian's gloves had stopped glowing. She squirmed and got both hands and feet positioned under the Celestial and with all limbs working together managed to push it off of her. She stood and glowered at me. "I will open the lock for you, and allow you and your shield to leave."

"Hello? I still need to talk to Captain Telfano."

"Captain Telfano is doomed."

"What? Why?"

"Linguistic heresy. She has brought the families' words to a lowly mammal. There will be an inquest, but likely she has lost her ship, and all in her egg line will share her dishonor."

"Wait. Okay? Just wait. She didn't teach me Thishfiff. It did." I pointed to the Celestial who had risen as well.

"How would a vegetable learn this?"

<<From you. From all of you.>>

Throsco knelt upon the gravel and covered her eyes with both hands. "Lies. Stories. Leave now. Your very presence pollutes my soul."

"But I still need—"

"Begone!"

Elroy looked at me like he was ready to shrug if he'd only had a neck. We stepped into the lock and activated the cycle. The inner door began to close and the custodian felt the need for a parting remark though she still refused to look at us.

"Mark me! If you speak our language to anyone else not of the families, you will be marked for the skinless death that we reserve for our greatest criminals. You have never imagined such agony.

"Don't bet on it," I said. The door closed, taking with it any chance for contacting the *Shpeshnoltoc*.

* * *

It was all I could to stagger my way back to the departure platform and stumble into a waiting cab. The Celestial climbed in more slowly. It instructed the driver to take us to the Pyramidal and settled in alongside me, turning halfway on the upholstered bench we shared to regard me with white eyes.

The taxi fell away from the docking port and I sighed. My head throbbed. Images and concepts that had no business in a human mind continued to muscle their way into mine, taking up position next to familiar ideas and making them strange by proximity.

<<The Cliveden are not accompanying us. We have obtained neither the economic leverage nor the protection allies you anticipated. This venture appears to have failed. And yet, we are returning.>>

English. Hearing its vowels, the sound of stops and flaps instead of eighteen different kinds of sibilants, hit me like the linguistic equivalent of cutting a hole into lake ice and diving in in the altogether. Elroy's *gift* fled before the onslaught of consonants it could not accommodate and my head became a lot less crowded. "I have to go back. If I don't, the Elder Glarp will take his revenge on the others. Besides, I still need to figure out how to unhypnotize Lew's ghost."

The Celestial remained silent as our cab skirted the edge of a massive electrical storm and then plunged rapidly through the clouds. The air below was thick with lightning that our driver somehow dodged for several minutes. The chaos of Bisto's atmosphere made an apt metaphor of my brain at the moment. More of what it meant to be Cliveden than just one of their languages had been poured into my head, but as easily as I might have made a hypnotic volunteer forget his own name it had all slipped away. All I had left was the memory of having had the experience.

Our driver found a hole in the storm and we dropped with a speed that made it clear Veng aren't prone to motion sickness. The lack of vomit bags in the cab supported that conclusion. The cab leveled off and careened along for several more minutes, the storm now above and behind us, before slipping into one of the underground travel tubes. Next stop: the Pyramidal.

<<Your fields are displaying an unusual configuration.>>

"I'm not surprised. As soon as we step out of this cab, we're going to be running on Plan B."

<<What is Plan B?>>

"I've almost got that worked out."

CHAPTER EIGHTEEN

The Last Word In A New Language

WE EXITED THE CAB at the ledge the Pyramidal's kitchen workers used and once inside the building we crawled back into the janitorial automatas' tunnel, our need for secret access still outweighing my desire for an unsettled stomach. The Celestial climbed in first and began retracing our outward-bound route without hesitation. Perhaps it was following some minute trace of poki pigment left by my knees from our earlier trip, assuming the local inhabitants hadn't been busy cleaning up their own domain after we'd passed through. Or maybe it just remembered it, learning the route from a single run through like a particularly gifted rat in a maze. I followed more slowly and didn't ask. After several minutes Elroy paused to allow a squad of the tiny cleaning bots to roll past at one of the many intersecting passages. I didn't mind the break; the intersection included another vermin field.

"I've covered more distance in these tunnels than in my regular roaming throughout the Pyramidal."

<<Perhaps you need to reconsider your habits with regards to exercise? Walking is a natural exploratory method for your species, and benefits both the body and mind.>>

Once the last of the automata passed, the Celestial began moving again, taking the occasional turn at intersections, selecting among options when our path branched. I followed. One tunnel looked much the same as any other to me, much like the Veng themselves. Eventually Elroy reached our destination and deactivated the holographic cover into my dressing room. It clambered out. I crawled after. Reggie met me, face first, and naturally went all out licking my face.

"Huh." Billi dropped to all sixes next to me, shoving his ugly mug almost as close to mine as Reggie was. "I expected you both to come in through the front door with a team of heavily armed Cliveden. Couldn't you get into the lounge?"

Reggie allowed me to pick him up and cradle him against my chest as I stood, though he continued licking. Much as with the makeup trick I'd taught him, he was restoring my face to its natural coloring.

"We got in all right. But things went pear-shaped after that."

"What? You're saying Telfano didn't send any reinforcement? She isn't giving us any help at all?"

"I didn't get to speak with Captain Telfano."

<<The Cliveden attempted to do us serious bodily harm after requesting communication with the *Shpeshnoltoc*. We were only permitted to leave after Mr. Conroy spoke to them in their native language.>>

"He did what?" Svetlana had been sitting against the wall by the door with Cyrano, but now rushed up and joined us by the hatch.

"Yeah. I remembered what you said about how they never let outsiders hear them speaking. It got the attention of the Cliveden trying to kill me. And if I read things right, she'll make trouble for Captain Telfano because of it."

"Trouble? You don't know the half of it," said Svetlana. "A Veng blood feud is nothing compared to how outraged the Cliveden are going to be. What, did you secretly record some of them talking to one another and play it back at them?"

"No, Elroy put the language in my head. For a while any way."

She whirled on the Celestial, her usual deference forgotten and replaced with indignation. "You *put* it in his head? I asked you for one of the Cliveden private languages ages ago and you refused."

<<I had not yet mastered the technique of synthesizing the schemata from multiple active sources when you made your request. But you are welcome to it now.>> The Celestial grazed Svetlana's forehead with the tip of a thumb.

She gasped, eyes widening and jaw dropping. She staggered backwards, one jerky step at a time. When she struck the wall her legs tried to keep walking for several paces. She rasped and hissed several syllables that felt like I should have understood them but couldn't. Then she shook her head and squeezed her eyes tightly shut.

"What just happened?" said Billi.

"What happened to who—" Relliope came around the bend from the shower alcove, Lew's ghost floating behind her. The green glow of its ectoplasm had faded still more. "Oh! You're back. How did it go?" Reggie jerked in my arms and barked at the rendering.

"It's ergative," said Svetlana, and because I didn't know the word it took me a moment to realize she was speaking English. She opened her eyes. "Their intransitive subjects are marked the same as their direct objects, but not in any way I've ever seen before. Shoshlee zhavro ghifler." She beamed with a childlike innocence.

"I couldn't do that," I said.

Svetlana blinked and noticed the rest of us staring at her. "Do what?"

"Talk. I mean, I could talk, but only in Cliveden."

"Thishfiff."

"Right. I . . . I knew that. Once. How can you switch back and forth?"

"I don't know. Maybe because I don't just speak it, but I can break apart and understand the language too. Wow. This is . . . Thank you!"

<<I am pleased you are pleased.>>

"Oh sure, we all are. Hooray, the girl has got herself a fresh brain toy." Billi hauled back and punched me in the thigh. "Will you people focus? Help isn't coming. We're back to being screwed."

"Maybe not. I have an idea. Relliope, I think you're the answer to all our problems."

"Me? How can that be, Mr. Conroy?"

"Your talent, what the Celestial called your ability to generate and direct, uh, chaos fields. I need you to do that to Bathatar here."

The rendering jerked back. "You want to do what?"

"I don't think I can do that, Mr. Conroy. It's not really a person. Not a living being at all. It's just so much ectoplasm."

"Exactly. And that ectoplasm contains the Younger Glarp's memories. Except they're blocked, buried beneath the false memory that was put on top before he was killed. Kind of like when I was speaking Fishthiff—"

"Thishfiff," Svetlana corrected.

"Right. When I had that language in my head. I couldn't get to Traveler or anything else. Then, it vanished, and everything else was back."

"But I can only wipe away the last few seconds of someone's memory. Ideas and thoughts that haven't been worked into the brain."

<<Her chaos field disrupts new memory during the brief span before it has consolidated. She does not possess the finesse to excise more entrenched recollections.>>

Relliope nodded.

"That doesn't matter. Bathatar's memory isn't like that. It didn't acquire its identity through experience over time. I put it there all at once. The rendering hasn't been able to hold on to anything new since then. It's running on a repeating loop, the same thing I told it just before Lew was murdered. Relliope, you have to try!"

She bit her lip. "I'll try." She took a deep breath and tossed her head, causing her long black hair to fall down her back. She brought both hands up in front of her face and beckoned the rendering closer. "You understood what Mr. Conroy was saying? What I'm going to do?"

I stepped back and half turned, blocking Reggie's view as Lew's ghost floated over and stopped centimeters from her hands. "Will it hurt?"

"You shouldn't feel a thing."

"Will it hurt you?" asked the Sasnakian.

Relliope lowered her hands and cocked her head toward Cyrano, her eyes still obscured by the wisps of blue fog emanating from them. "No. But thank you for asking."

Bathatar took a deep and physically unnecessary breath. "Go ahead. This has all been so strange, I think I'd be happier if I could remember who I'm supposed to be. I'm not good with aliens. No offense."

The fog around Relliope's eyes dissipated without replacement. Within their sockets her eyes shone azure, lit by some inner glow.

"Is it happening? Am I forgetting?"

Her eyes burned brighter. Her fingers curled as if grasping something, flailed uselessly, then curled again.

"That's creepy," said Billi. "Am I the only one who thinks so? It's that blank stare, worse than taxidermy."

"Shut up," I said, slipping into English. "She's nervous enough."

"I'm sorry, I can't do it. There's a memory there but it's too diffuse. I can't get hold of it all."

"Are you sure?" Svetlana put her arm around the other woman. "Maybe if you took a break and tried again?"

Relliope shook her head, wisps of blue mist began to flow again.

<<The disruptive field attenuates as she attempts to spread it around the energy loops you perceive as the rendering. Her conscious control is insufficient, though the ability is present.>>

"It's all right," I said. "There might be another way. Relliope, would you allow me to hypnotize you?"

"Of course, but why?"

"If the Celestial's right, you can actually do this, even if you don't think so. Maybe with a helpful hypnotic suggestion or two you'll believe you can do it. You'll know you can. That might be enough."

"I'm willing to try. I want to help."

Throughout all of this Lew's ghost had spun slowly in place, staring at everyone there and stopping only when it got to me. "I know you. I was on the stage with you. How did I get here? And who are all these aliens?"

"Oh great, all she did was hit its reset switch."

"Not. Helping. Billi." I handed Reggie to Relliope, as much to distract her from the failed attempt as to allow me guide Lew's ghost back around the corner of the shower alcove where its corpse still stood propped against the wall. In the time I'd been to the floating island and back the body had acquired a distinct aroma that reminded me of Lebanon bologna left out in an afternoon sun during mid-August. I held my nose and for the fourth or fifth time since this had all started, I explained again to the rendering what it was and who Lew had been and why it was here and why it needed to wait right where it was until I called for it and everything could be straightened out. The rendering nodded and took up position by Lew's body.

I slumped against the opposite wall of the shower, running in my mind several possible inductions that I might use to put Relliope into trance, build up her self-confidence and generate the ability to tap what Elroy saw in her. With a little luck Bathatar would be gone in just a few minutes.

"Conroy! Would you bind coming out here? Please?"

Had Billi just said *please*? Maybe the fumes from Lew's corpse were getting to me. I stepped back into the dressing room and fresher air despite the small crowd.

That crowd had grown by two. Selstrin, the Pyramidal's manager, stood against the door, one hand on the knob. That hand trembled. Beads of sweat clung to his forehead and earflaps, his chin and the tip of his nose. His eyes flicked to me only long enough to recognize me, and then jerked back to the other newcomer. The Elder Glarp stood next to my makeup table and locked his eyes on me. His right hand gripped a squiggly knife, much like the one Petara of the Vitreous Lozenge had used to murder a Veng named Keleph. He had one edge of that knife pressed against Billi's throat.

"The last time we met, you intimated I would have your undying gratitude."

"Thank you for joining us, Entertainer. I trust you can appreciate that circumstances have changed."

"You manipulated the governing council to raise me to the head of my rist."

"A necessary prerequisite to declaring blood feud on Emerald Eastern Snowfall so I could claim vengeance and kill you."

"As your equal?"

The Elder Glarp spat, something I'd never seen a Veng do. "Hardly. The highest of your rist is still below the lowest of mine. But tradition required you to have rank before I could touch you."

"Which corner of the rist triangle is that then, Privilege? Prerogative?"

"Power, Entertainer. I will take your life because I have the power to do so."

"I didn't kill Lewilocus. You have to know that."

"Your hand did not hold the blade. No, far worse. You denied him his rightful revenge. How dare you come to our world and trample our most precious traditions, and in the name of entertainment? You disgust me."

"So you won't be inviting me to dinner again?"

Selstrin gasped at that remark. Relliope flinched. Svetlana smiled for a moment.

Billi waved a lower arm as if he wanted to punch my leg again while another pointed at his throat. "Hey, how about you wait until he doesn't have a dagger right here before you piss him off further, okay?"

The Elder Glarp ignored all of them. His stare never wavered. I was his world. "I confess, out of your specialized toga and dipped in deep purple, I could have passed you in any corridor of the Pyramidal and not have recognized you. But your voice betrays your identity. I'll remember your voice till I speak my own last word. It's your voice that is your power. Your voice that killed and shamed my idiot grandson."

He swung the knife away from Billi and pushed the Pelk out of the way then plunged his free hand into his toga and pulled a vial from some hidden pocket. He threw it at me but I easily ducked. Less than three meters separated us. It passed over my shoulder and smashed against the wall.

"This is stupid," I said. "I didn't trample any Veng traditions. What happened to Lew was an accident. You started the blood feud, you can stop it. End this."

His voice came from behind me. "I will end it. Entertainer Conroy of Emerald Eastern Snowfall, I am for you!"

I spun around. A rendering floated there, blocking my retreat to the shower alcove. "Bathatar, get back—" But it wasn't Lew's ghost. It glowed with an emerald brilliance that Lew's had lost. This rendering belonged to the Elder Glarp. It had spoken but couldn't harm me in any physical way. Only distract.

"Conroy, look out!"

If Svetlana's warning had come a second later, it would have been too late. I managed to continue my turn in time to see the real Glarp leaping at me. He'd have stabbed me in the back, but looked just as happy to be aiming for my chest. Instead the tip of the blade cut a gash along my arm from elbow to wrist. I stumbled back. Blood ran from the wound, but he'd failed to cut deep. Somewhere in the room I heard Reggie barking.

The Elder Glarp had dropped back into a fighting stance. He was old, even for a Veng, and that one attack had taken a lot out of him. He panted and the hand holding the knife wavered.

"Kneel before me, and I will make it a quick death."

"Excuse me?"

He lunged for me, but this time I saw him coming. I had a good thirty centimeters on him in height, with a corresponding advantage in reach. It wasn't a fair contest, but I didn't care. As he came at me I stepped to the side. I grabbed his arm with both of mine and threw my greater weight behind us as I smashed his hand against the wall. He dropped the knife and I let go of him. He scuttled away, stopping only when he backed into the wall by the door. Cyrano and Relliope hurried further away.

I picked up the knife and pointed at my arm. "First blood. Are you satisfied?"

"I'd hoped to kill you according to ritual, my father's sacred blade buried in your heart." The Elder Glarp paused, gasping for breath, still glaring at me. "But in the end, dead is dead, as long as it is by my hand I'll be satisfied." He reached into his toga again and this time came out with a small air pistol.

And nearly shot Selstrin as he was flung forward by the dressing room's door crashing open. Throsco, the short custodian from the Cliveden lounge at the floating island, stood in the open door taking in the scene. She nodded as her eyes moved from person to person, pausing as she regarded the Celestial and jerking to a halt when she saw me. She stepped into the crowded room and tossed a hover-cam toward the ceiling.

"Begin recording. That's him. The purple one with the pink face. It wasn't pink before, but that's him. I know his scent. He is the recipient of the linguistic heresy. Do you deny knowing him?"

A second Cliveden entered smoothly behind her. Taller, more assured. Captain Telfano sa Rens.

"I know several aliens by sight and scent. Producing one of them is hardly evidence that I had means, motive, or time to provide language instruction—"

"So you *do* know him!" Throsco nodded smugly to the camera.

"Yes, of course. This person was indeed once in my employ—"

"Once?" I said.

"—as a performer on the primary stage. But he disembarked at Bisto during our last stopover, having found other employment." Telfano paused and gestured at the Elder Glarp. "With this individual, I believe. It does not appear to have gone well."

The Glarp didn't aim his pistol at Captain Telfano, though he did wave it in her direction. "You've intruded into a private matter, Cliveden. Leave now."

"That's what I'd told those two," said Throsco.

"W-wa-wait!" Selstrin scurried out of the line of fire, hauling up next to the only other Pyramidal employee in the room, Relliope. She edged away, closer to the Sasnakian.

The Captain nodded. "Custodian, I don't like having weapons pointed at me. Disarm the fellow if you please."

Throsco clapped her hands together. The palms of her fingerless gloves blazed pink. Lizard-quick she slapped at the Elder Glarp as he raised the air pistol in a two-handed grip. His fingers spasmed, went numb, and the gun tumbled uselessly to the floor. Billi scrambled to snatch it up but Throsco kicked it to toward the door and Captain Telfano stooped and picked it up.

Billi scowled, shrugged off the failure and dusted himself off. "Hooray for the cavalry. Better late than too late."

The Elder Glarp arms hung by his side. "You're interfering in a rist blood feud. That's a dire violation of our contract with the families." His rendering fled through the wall; reinforcements would be on the way soon.

"As is calling blood feud on a member of a protected rist," replied Telfano. "Spare me your righteous mewlings."

My arm was still bleeding, and while I didn't feel light-headed yet, the adrenaline from being attacked wasn't going to last forever. Time to get out of Dodge. "Thank you for your timely intervention, Captain. We're obviously not welcome here any longer. I wonder if you could extend your generosity to provide transportation for my companions and me?"

"This was not the plan, Mr. Conroy. I thought we had an understanding." Her eyes held mine, flicked briefly down to the Elder

Glarp, then back to me. Right. She wanted to keep things oblique. I could do oblique.

"We did. You had leverage over me, used it to achieve your goals without regard to my own desires. That situation has changed."

"Indeed. You have the most powerful citizen of the second largest city of an alien world calling for your head, and what do you do? You smuggle yourself into a Cliveden lounge and make a nuisance of yourself."

"I thought you were in favor of my being a smuggler."

"Do not be droll, Mr. Conroy. And do exercise caution; it is not as if we are among friends here."

"Fine, I'll be succinct instead. I have what you want. You were coming to collect it any way before events here got out of hand. Are you telling me you no longer want it?"

"What I want is no longer the most important factor. The custodian here reports she heard you speaking a language you have no business knowing. There is no greater offense an outsider can commit against our families."

"Pass judgment and kill him. It is your right as ship captain. Only when he is dead will the shame of hearing him speak fade away."

"That only applies when you're on your ship and outside the range of a gravity well," said the Elder Glarp. "We're on Bisto, and rist takes precedent."

"Everyone just calm down," said Billi. "Bun of this is Conroy's fault. Your grandson only got himself killed because you insisted the idiot follow Conroy around. And he only crashed your precious lounge because he knew you'd come running to secure your drift juice."

"Drift juice? What does he mean you secured drift juice? Thief!" Sensation must have been returning to the Elder Glarp as he feebly waved his arms at the Cliveden.

"The only idiot here is the Pelk," said Telfano. "Your man there had the sense not to speak. He has to die for his affront to the families. But if word has spread of our arrangement then the simplest course to ensure this goes no further is to kill all of you."

"No! You can't!" Lew's ghost flew in from the shower alcove to position itself protectively and uselessly in front of me. "I don't understand any of this, but this alien is the one person who might be able to help me. I can't let you harm him."

Reggie howled and began barking at the rendering. He squirmed in Relliope's arm, desperate to get free.

"I don't know how you tolerate that noise," said Telfano, taking aim at the buffalo dog and the Bluie holding him.

Relliope screamed. A wall of thick blue fog radiated from her and passed through everyone in the room. An all too familiar mental poker shoved itself through the base of my brain again and I found myself on my knees. Everything slowed down so I had more subjective time to experience the pain in my head. Across the room, I could see Svetlana lying in a heap, moaning. Relliope had also fallen, the buffalo dog tumbling from her arms in the process. She lay clutching her head and sobbing. Reggie raced to me in slow motion, whining fearfully, more that I'd been injured than from any hurt of his own. I sat up, reeling, the sum of every hangover I'd ever survived gathering in my skull for a reunion, and the temporal flow returned to normal. A few meters away Cyrano was cradling Relliope, gazing down at her bare face.

The Cliveden stared at one another and then at the rest of us. "What has happened? How did we arrive here?"

The Elder Glarp staggered towards me, fingers flexing weakly as he reached for my neck. "Entertainer Conroy of Emerald Eastern Snowfall, I am for you!"

"Sir! The creetlebaum!" Selstrin cried a warning just as Reggie leaped to my defense, higher than he should have been able. He landed on top of the Elder Glarp, kicking repeatedly, his tiny hooves dancing impossibly upon the Veng's head.

The Celestial's husk had fallen and gone rigid. Svetlana had managed to rise to all fours and crawl to it. She rolled it over on to its back, thumping it here and there as if to wake it.

And in the middle of the room, Lew's ghost glowed a bright and brilliant green.

"In life I was Glarp Lewilocus, known far and wide as the Younger Glarp. I served as Presence to the Pentahedral Diamond."

Reggie gave off his attack on the Elder Glarp and switched his attention to the Younger. He leapt from the head of the former and sailed through the ectoplasmic form of the latter, landing in a surprised heap on the other side.

"Yes!" The Elder Glarp reached out a hand to his grandson, but the rendering waved it away.

"You sought to kill the very man who restored my right to avenge my murder and restore our rist's honor. I wish I'd had the courage to say this in life, grandfather. You sicken me."

"I did it for you!"

"No, only Friend Conroy can say that. I dedicate my revenge to him." Lew's ghost bowed to me, then sped through the wall in pursuit of its much-delayed revenge. Somewhere, sometime soon, his murderer was in for a surprise.

"Did I do that?" Relliope still clung to Cyrano, but she had recovered enough to glance around. Wisps of blue mist streamed from her eyes again.

"To everyone here except Svetlana and me," I said.

"Svetlana? Oh. Of course. Double the backlash because you've both been touched by your Celestial. Is it okay? I didn't sclajj a thing from it. How is that even possible?"

"It's left the husk," said Svetlana. She rubbed her head. "If it got hit with anything like I did I'm not surprised. Don't worry, that's part of why it needed anchors. It will climb back in when it's ready."

"That was a Celestial?" Throsco knelt alongside the husk. "I laid hands upon a Celestial? My life is over."

"Byah," said Billi. "I kick it all the time. It doesn't feel a thing."

"Pain is not the point. I attempted to harm it. I am not fit to live!" The squiggly knife the Elder Glarp had tried to kill me with lay nearby. I must have dropped it when Relliope blasted my brain. Throsco snatched it up and aimed it at her own chest. Before she could do herself in, Cyrano was on her, bending the small Cliveden's arms back with a wrestling hold that in other contexts might have had an audience gasping with arousal.

The custodian sobbed, tears streaming down her face.

"What is it with you people, always needing someone to die? Do you believe me now about how I got your language? The Celestial gave it to me."

Throsco stared at me, its long jaw dropping. "You travel with a Celestial. It . . . it came to your defense. I can have no claim against you. Forgive me."

"Uh . . . Sure. No problem." Reggie had made his way back to me. I picked him up and managed to stand with a little help from an adjacent wall.

"I ask forgiveness as well, Entertainer." The Elder Glarp rubbed his bald pate. The orange skin already showed a collection of umber bruises with distinct hoof shapes. I'm . . . feeling a bit light-headed. Perhaps from all the excitement. My rendering was leading a security team here but neither of us recalls why. They have been sent away and will spread the word."

"The word?"

"I renounce my blood feud against you and your rist."

"He doesn't remember about the smuggled—"

"The smug remark I made," I interrupted Svetlana and she shut up.

"What remark?" Just that quickly the Elder Glarp went from contrite to haughty.

"It was before you surprised us here to claim my life. I said something foolish and immature, and I regret it now. I'm relieved it never reached your ears."

"Yes, well, we have all been under some stress. Perhaps best for all if we just move on."

"I couldn't agree more."

The Veng gestured and headed to the door. He paused to regard Captain Telfano. "What . . . why are you here?"

"I'm wondering that myself. Good day to you, Elder Glarp. May your rist prosper and know only glory."

"Thank you, Captain. My regards to your family." He left.

Selstrin followed, pausing in the doorway to glance back at the tableau of a bleeding Human, the head of a Cliveden family, a second Cliveden pinned down by a Sasnakian, a lifeless husk being tended to by another Human, a Bluie whispering soothingly to a creetlebaum, and a smug-looking Pelk. He took a step back into the room and addressed Billi. "Article seventy-six, section twelve of the Entertainment Guild constitution concerns allocating sufficient release time for observance of religious holidays, *not* workplace safety. I am not intimidated by glib agents. Your client is fired. With extreme prejudice."

"Yeah? So's your fledge!"

"Remove yourselves from the premises of the Pyramidal before the end of the current shift, or I will instruct security to do so." Selstrin executed a crisp turn and headed out.

"See you, Mr. Loompa," I said.

"Excelsior!" Selstrin clapped twice, and left.

Telfano closed the door behind the departing Veng then approached Cyrano and nudged him with one foot. She aimed the Elder Glarp's pistol down at him. "Release her at once."

The Sasnakian scrambled back with a fluid move that could have been part of his stage performance, joining Relliope near the entrance to the shower alcove.

Throsco looked up. "I am sorry, Captain."

"Am I to understand that, given the circumstances, your claim of heresy is voided?"

"He is the tool of a blessed Celestial. There can be no heresy."

Captain Telfano raised her hand and fired at the hover-cam. A bb struck it and burst, splashing the camera with a shimmering liquid. It crumpled in upon itself, crushed as its weight increased a thousand-fold.

"The inquest's recording—"

Telfano waved the custodian to silence. "It no longer has any relevance. We will both be better served by minimizing any record of your unfortunate allegation. Go now. There's paperwork that needs doing if you are to clean up this mess. And when you are done with that, I've no doubt you have children to dazzle with the tale of how you met a Celestial."

Throsco didn't linger for further discussion, or even bother to close the door after her. Captain Telfano tended to that task again, and then gave me her full attention, waving the air pistol in my direction.

"I have a similar weapon that I use to stun vermin onboard the *Shpeshnoltoc*, though mine fires only simple pellets. Gravity ammunition never leaves Veng worlds. A pity. The effect is spectacular. So tell me why I shouldn't introduce you to it firsthand, Mr. Conroy? You've become quite a nuisance to me."

"Don't be stupid. If you eliminate me you have nothing to show for the effort. It's in your own best interest to endure a little inconvenience."

"You have this all figured out, do you?"

I smiled at the lizard captain and thought of my Aunt Fiona as I chose my words carefully. "You're the one who told me we all act according to our nature. I'm just counting on you being true to yours."

"Oh? And what do you discern that nature to be?"

"Greed. I still have what you want, what no one else can give you."

Cyrano turned to Relliope. "What is the Amazing one talking about?"

"I don't know. Svetlana?"

"No idea."

"Quiet." Billi punched Cyrano in the leg. "Just zip it."

Telfano gestured with the air pistol. "For the continued well being of your friends here, let us continue to speak obliquely."

"As you did when you instructed Thindar to come and collect me?"

"Precisely. So you were successful then?"

"I think you'd consider a liter successful."

Can a lizard drool? Telfano sa Rens lowered her pistol. "I appear to have underestimated you. And yet, a greater problem still remains. While I knew Throsco's specific claim against me was false as to the source of your knowledge, its underlying substance remains. Witnesses at the lounge heard you speak Thishfiff."

"Yes, but I can't speak it any more. My brain couldn't hold on to it."

"That doesn't matter. You spoke Thishfiff!"

"But it's just a cultural taboo. The fact that it exists is proof that it's been violated before. Your civilization won't crumble because I said a few words in your language. Think of what you could do with a liter of, um, the stuff!"

"I am tempted, I admit it. But what you call a taboo I see as a defining precept of the families. Unlike Throsco, I am of high birth and education. I cannot be swayed by the Celestial mythology. Though it pains me to let your success slip away, my own avarice must give way before my culture."

"Meaning what, exactly."

She raised the pistol again. "Meaning, I have to kill you."

Svetlana whistled shrilly, causing the Captain to stare at her and interrupting my death sentence.

"You can't kill him."

"I assure you, I can. This weapon is more than up to the task.

"No, what I mean is, the same culture that makes it blasphemous for outsiders to speak Thishfiff also insists that you let him live."

"What do you know of Cliveden culture?"

"Much more than Conroy does. Language and culture can't be readily separated. When the Celestial gave him Thishfiff, it did so by pulling the knowledge from the other Cliveden in the lounge. He couldn't hold on to any of it, but for a while he had more than just Thishfiff. He had large chunks of history and philosophy and canon law."

"Do you have a point?"

"One of the reasons Cliveden don't like other races is because you doubt their true sapience, which you define as speaking one or more of the families' languages. You see them as a smarter class of animals, with languages all their own, but still not worthy of your regard."

Telfano shrugged but her pistol didn't waver. "This is true. Talking animals may be superior to non-talking animals, but you're all still animals. And the Cliveden culture has no prohibition against the slaughter of animals."

"Unless another sapient requests you not to. That's one of your oldest stories."

"You were on my ship. I had reports on you, always asking the other aliens to tell you tales. Did one of them tell you this story?"

"It doesn't matter how I know. I'm asking you not to kill Conroy. You have to honor the request."

The captain shook her head. "Actually, I don't. You're an animal too."

Svetlana stepped in front of the Cliveden. "*Vrish gharth dhelf Conroy.*" She pushed the pistol aside.

Captain Telfano stared in horror. "How? How is this possible?"

"The Celestial gave me what it gave Conroy. Conroy's a suggestionater, he doesn't understand language. It passed through him like water through a sieve. If I can push the analogy a bit further, it left him damp enough to get out of the lounge, but then even that bit dried up."

"And you?"

Svetlana smiled like a cat with a mouse in its mouth, or maybe a lizard. "Think of me as a bucket. Language and culture is what I do. So, I've formally requested you spare the animal you had claimed a need to slaughter. Cliveden law is served."

The captain let the pistol slip from her hand. It clattered on the floor. "I'm sure there are clerics and magistrates wiser than me who might argue your point, but as they would also quickly point out that I am a simple ship's captain, I can accept your argument well enough and pursue my original profit."

Billi chimed in. "Hey, who doesn't like greed?" He dropped to all sixes and dashed over to reclaim the pistol, slipping it in one of his pockets.

"Just so. Conroy, I will have the *stuff* you have procured for me, and we will continue our arrangement."

"I don't think so. I'm changing our deal."

"You're in no position to make any changes."

I waved Billi over and held out my hand. He pulled the perfume bottle from a pocket. I held it up for Telfano to see. "A liter of this stuff as well as your nature says I am. Fortunately for you, I'm *not* motivated by greed. You can easily give me what I want."

"State your terms."

I waved my arm to include everyone else in the room. "Passage for all of us off Bisto and out beyond the system of Veng worlds. I don't know precisely where the others wish to go, but your ship also stops at planets served by vessels other than the Cliveden. I'm sure one of them will be fine."

Telfano shook her head and pointed at Svetlana and me. "The others can travel on the *Shpeshnoltoc*, but neither of you can ever set foot upon a Cliveden vessel. I am not comfortable with the grey area of talking animals who know Thishfiff. Before my ship leaves orbit I will spread word to all the other ships of the families to prevent you from taking passage."

"No deal. Your people have a monopoly on transit vessels visiting Bisto. How are we to leave?"

"Easy peasy," said Billi. "Captain Telfano is going to give us her yacht!"

She laughed. "Are you mad? Can you even begin to estimate the value of that craft? Impossible."

"Baby it is and baby it isn't. Put it in perspective. Think of all the thousands of yachts you could buy with the dri—stuff."

Captain Telfano sa Rens nodded to the Pelk. "A fair point. Done. The Veng can transport me back to the floating island, and the *Shpeshnoltoc* can certainly send a shuttle for me from there."

"Hold up, hold up. I'm just getting started. This is why I handle Conroy's deals. He isn't savvy like we are. We get the yacht and you get *half* the stuff. After all, it looks like Conroy's getting stiffed for his performances here on Bisto, and we've got expenses to consider."

"Unacceptable. What do I care for his lost wages, I want—"

"You can have it all," I said. "I'm happy with just the yacht. Here you go." I tossed the perfume bottle to Telfano. It soared as if under its own power and she had to snatch it out of the air.

She opened it and peered inside. She smiled. Satisfied, she sealed the bottle and passed several encrypted ceramo chits to Billi. "These are captain's keys, any one of them provides the bearer full access and control of my yacht."

"Handy things," said Billi as he tucked each away in a different pocket. "I don't suppose you're walking around with the pink slip?"

"I don't understand what you want in pink. But you have my word that the craft is yours, and that is enough to transfer ownership. Its onboard systems are coded to allow you free passage through any Cliveden controlled transit portals. Assuming you have someone who can pilot it for you."

"Don't worry about that. I've yet to beat a ship I can't fly."

"If you want to gamble with your lives, the ship is yours. It's well-stocked, but the provisions run toward my people's needs and preferences, and you'll doubtless want to make some changes to the larder. Beyond that though, you're on your own."

"As long as they don't ask for a pilot's license we'll be fine. Where'd you leave it?"

"You'll find it docked outside the Pyramidal. As I understand it, the local authority wants you gone from here in the near future, and I think it best that I follow that same example, though it appears I'll have to find alternate transportation. It has been a remarkable pleasure, Mr. Conroy. Given that I rarely leave my ship and you are never to venture unto it again, I doubt our future paths will ever cross. Farewell."

Clutching the bottle of drift juice to her chest, she opened the door at her back and left.

Billi slammed it shut and whirled around shouting. "I have an idiot for a client! You just gave away our fortune. A fortune of fortune. What is wrong with you?"

I shrugged. "I didn't give away anything. Besides, it wasn't mine to give. But we can discuss all of that once we're in transit. I want to get to the floating island and be on our way out of the system before Captain Telfano gets there."

Billi scowled. "Why?"

"Because I was feeding her suggestions, focusing her attention on getting what she wanted. Think of it as reinforcing the path of least mental resistance. By appealing to her greed I distracted her attention from why she sent me here in the first place."

"What are you talking about?"

I looked under the makeup table where my carpetbag had sat unmolested all this time. I grabbed it, and then took Reggie back from Relliope. He wagged is tail as I scritched him under his beard. I opened the carpetbag and he climbed right in, just like always. Time to go.

I cocked my head toward Billi and asked, "Just what do you suppose is going to happen when Captain Telfano tries to go through customs with a liter bottle of . . . stuff?"

EPILOGUE

Full Circle

AT FIRST PASS the yacht formerly belonging to Captain Telfano appeared as austere as the crew corridors aboard the *Shpeshnoltoc*. Dim red light reflected off walls of burnished metals. A good ten centimeters of vermillion gravel covered the floors and kicked up low clouds of dust at any movement faster than a creep. I'd boarded first with Svetlana, the two of us carrying the still unoccupied husk of the Celestial. We'd made it halfway down a corridor toward what I'd hoped was a cabin when the airlock cycled again and admitted Billi. Relliope came after carrying my buffalo dog. Once inside, Reggie leaped from her arms and raced pell mell to catch up to me, raising a storm of dark red particles that hid everything behind him. Before she disappeared from view Relliope had covered her face with both hands. Billi, lower to the ground began coughing and swearing.

"What's wrong with you, Conroy? Are you bad? Why didn't get rid of this?"

"Get rid of what?"

"All this Cliveden crap."

"We'll shovel it out later when we have time. As soon as the dust settles, get up front to the command console and see if you really can pilot this thing."

"Like I'm gonna wait for that. Ship, reset!"

The dust vanished from the air. So did the gravel, the dim lighting, and the burnished walls. The inside of the ship was now beige ceramo. Light poured from the walls and floor and ceiling.

"Oh. Smart walls."

Billi trundled past. "Duh. It's a yacht. You think they custom-build them with gravel just for Cliveden? That's the kind of thinking that would have bee propped up on phonebooks when I sit in the pilot's chair. Please! Hey, Ship! Show and unlock all interior doors." Oblongs appeared at intervals along the walls. Billi strode to the end of the corridor and shoved against one. It slid soundlessly into a pocket in the wall and he stepped within.

"I could learn to hate him," said Svetlana. We opened the nearest door, conjured up a bed, and set down the husk.

I called for an information panel just like I had in my stateroom back on the *Shpeshnoltoc* and requested a diagram of the yacht. In addition to the control room, it had four cabins on this level, two larger cabins and a mess on the level below, and several storage bays below that. Svetlana began exploring the one with the Celestial so I appointed Relliope to the cabin across from it. Reggie and I laid claim to the one beyond Svetlana's and closer to the control room and went to figure out how the shower worked so I could finally get out of Cyrano's thong and scrub the rest of the poki dye from my skin.

The shower was heavenly. The dye came off but left me rubbed raw. I emerged from the shower pink and hairless as a newborn babe and liberated my work clothes from my carpetbag. I felt and looked more like myself again, though I wished I'd owned a hat.

True to his word, Billi had had no trouble piloting the yacht. He'd gotten us out of the underground and up to the floating island while I'd been going from purple to pink, and a trio of Veng custom agents armed with high-powered sensors were already crawling through the ship. They confiscated the gravitic ammo in the air pistol Billi had pilfered but otherwise found nothing untoward and pronounced us free to leave once I initialed a few documents. I left Billi consulting the onboard systems and plotting a course for the quickest route out of the Cliveden circuit of transit portals and went to join the others in the mess while the Veng finished the search.

Someone, presumably Svetlana, had convinced the smart walls to decorate the room to resemble a posh Parisian restaurant with a view overlooking the Seine, complete with candlelight, fine linen, and scrolled, high-back chairs. A pair of double doors at the far end presumably opened onto the galley. Relliope stood by the illusory window, gazing out across the water. I joined her.

"I think you'd enjoy France," I said. "Would you like to travel to Earth?"

"I don't know. I haven't really thought about it. I'm just so happy to be leaving Bisto. And to not have to travel with the Cliveden again. I was thinking I might make my way to Sasnak."

"Really? Why there?"

She shrugged. Wisps of vapor flowed from her eyes and dissipated into the air around us. "I don't know. Cyrano seemed so kind, and Svetlana says the whole troupe was nice. We talked a bit, while you and the Celestial were away. He told me all about his world. I guess I got curious. And I have to go somewhere, so . . . why not?"

"As good a reason as any. I'll check with Billi and ask him to keep Sasnak in mind as he plots our route."

"You'd do that for me?"

"Like you said, why not? We have to go somewhere too. It's the least I can do. You saved us all back on Bisto. And you restored Lew's memories to his ghost."

"I just got scared and panicked."

"Maybe. But your panic attack was what we needed when we needed it. So thank you."

She brought a hand up and touched my cheek. "Cyrano was right about you."

"Oh?"

"You are the Amazing One."

The doors from the galley crashed open. The Celestial came through bearing a large tray. Svetlana followed carrying a tureen. Relliope's hand fell away.

"Hot stuff, coming through! We've got soup! Hot soup. And sandwiches."

"Elroy, you're back!"

<<I am. Svetlana has instructed me in the creation of something called *comfort food*. She assures me it is necessary to restoring equilibrium after our recent ordeals.>>

"It's almost tomato," said Svetlana. "And the sandwiches are the Cliveden equivalent of peanut butter on garlic rye. Don't give me that look, it actually tastes pretty good."

I nodded, remembering other sandwiches and other ordeals. "Cervantes had it right. 'Hunger is the best sauce.'"

<<Cervantes?>>

"A writer from Earth's past. Wrote about a fellow who fought windmills."

"Why would anyone fight windmills?" asked Relliope, taking a bite out of an offered sandwich.

"He mistook them for evil giants."

The Celestial set the tray down and stepped aside as Reggie dashed toward it. Relliope followed, restraining him to some degree and sampling the fare herself. Elroy joined me at the window and offered me a sandwich. Svetlana was many things, but a gourmand was not one of them. Garlic and peanut butter do not mix.

<<May we speak of evil giants?>>

"It's a metaphor."

<<Mine are not. There are . . . Powers. Beings who have chosen to take it upon themselves to manipulate the course of events in our galaxy.>>

I paused mid-chew. "Are you talking about your kind, or someone else?"

Can a vat-grown husk flinch? Elroy tried to.

<<Despite my own actions, my kind would see the galaxy continue on its own course, guided by fate and not any deliberate hand.>>

I gestured with my sandwich around us. "And you set all of this in motion because you thought I could contribute to your plans somehow?"

<<Essentially, but I have reconsidered.>>

"Good, because I don't like fighting giants. Or being played by them. I'm not a tool. I'm just hypnotist."

<<You are not a tool. But you are more than just a hypnotist. I believe your assistance in this endeavor could serve your needs as well as my own. Would you consider, perhaps, becoming my partner?>>

"I'll need to hear more about what you have in mind. We have a long trip ahead of us; plenty of time for you to convince me." I smiled. A Celestial was asking for my help. Closure, indeed.

About the Author

Photo: Nathan Lilly

Lawrence M. Schoen holds a Ph.D. in cognitive psychology, spent ten years as a college professor, and when not writing currently works as the chief compliance officer for a series of mental health and addiction treatment facilities. He's also one of the world's foremost authorities on the Klingon language, as well as the publisher behind Paper Golem, a new speculative fiction small press. His first novel *Buffalito Destiny* was released in 2009 to critical acclaim and in 2010, his short story "The Moment" was nominated for a Hugo award. He and his wife, Valerie, live in Pennsylvania. They have a puppy named Gej.

CPSIA information can be obtained at www.ICGtesting.com
Printed in the USA
[illegible]7696BV00003B/55/P